MW01614458

## PRAISE FOR TAHC

"ONE OF HIS
— Sunny Solomon, The Pioneer

## PRAISE FOR TAHOE FLIGHT

"WHAT A WILD RIDE! Teeth-clenching nightmare... Heart-stopping moments" — Gloria Sinibaldi, Tahoe Mountain News

"A BARN BURNER" — Cathy Cole, Kittling: Books
Borg's Tahoe Mystery series chosen by Kittling: Books as ONE OF THE TEN BEST MYSTERY SERIES

## PRAISE FOR TAHOE MOON

"ANOTHER AMAZING READ" "BRILLIANT" – Silver's Reviews
"HOURS OF SHEER READING PLEASURE" – Cathy Cole, Kittling: Books
"McKENNA IS BACK, BIG TIME" – Sunny Solomon, Bookin' With Sunny

## PRAISE FOR TAHOE JADE

"THRILLS AND DANGER" – Kirkus Reviews
"A WHITE-KNUCKLE CHASE THROUGH THE MOUNTAINS"
— Cathy Cole, Kittling: Books
"WILL HAVE YOU ON THE EDGE OF YOUR SEAT" – Silver's Reviews

## PRAISE FOR TAHOE HIT

"I'M ADDICTED TODD BORG'S INTRICATE, FAST-PACED MYSTERIES..." – Cathy Cole, Kittling: Books

"ANOTHER TENSION-FILLED SIGNATURE BOOK, with twists, turns, and surprises by master storyteller TODD BORG - Silver's Reviews

## PRAISE FOR TAHOE DEEP

"A SMART, INTRIGUING MYSTERY...A SUPERIOR ENTRY"
- Kirkus Reviews
"JAW-DROPPING INVESTIGATIVE SKILLS... DEEP, THOUGHTFUL AND COMPLEX" – Gloria Sinibaldi, Tahoe Mountain News

## PRAISE FOR TAHOE SKYDROP

"ANOTHER IMPRESSIVE CASE FEATURING A DETECTIVE WHO REMAINS NOT ONLY DOGGED, BUT ALSO REFLECTIVE."
- Kirkus Reviews

"A SURPRISE TWIST WILL GIVE YOU AN EXTRA JOLT...a great addition to the Owen McKenna series." – Gloria Sinibaldi, Tahoe Mountain News

## PRAISE FOR TAHOE PAYBACK
"AN ENGROSSING WHODUNIT" — *Kirkus Reviews*

"FAST PACED, ABSORBING, MEMORABLE" — *Kittling: Books*
Borg's Tahoe Mystery series chosen by *Kittling: Books* as ONE OF THE TEN BEST MYSTERY SERIES

## PRAISE FOR TAHOE DARK
"ONCE AGAIN, BORG HITS ALL THE RIGHT NOTES FOR FANS OF CLASSIC DETECTIVE FICTION in the mold of Dashiell Hammett, Raymond Chandler, Ross Macdonald, and Robert B. Parker."
- *Kirkus Reviews*

"TAHOE DARK IS PACKED WITH ACTION AND TWISTS. THE SURPRISES JUST KEEP ON COMING...THE FINAL SCENE IS ANOTHER TODD BORG MASTERPIECE." - *Silver's Reviews*

## PRAISE FOR TAHOE BLUE FIRE

"A GRIPPING NARRATIVE...A HERO WHO WALKS CONFIDENTLY IN THE FOOTSTEPS OF SAM SPADE, PHILIP MARLOWE, AND LEW ARCHER" - *Kirkus Reviews*

"A THRILLING MYSTERY THAT IS DIFFICULT TO PUT DOWN ...EDGE OF YOUR SEAT ACTION" – *Silver's Reviews*

## PRAISE FOR TAHOE GHOST BOAT

"THE OLD PULP SAVVY OF (ROSS) MACDONALD...REAL SURPRISE AT THE END" – *Kirkus Reviews*

"NAIL-BITING THRILLER...BOILING POT OF DRAMA"
- *Gloria Sinibaldi, Tahoe Daily Tribune*

"ACTION-PACKED IS PUTTING IT MILDLY. PREPARE FOR FIRE-WORKS" – *Sunny Solomon, Bookin' With Sunny*

"I LOVED EVERY ROLLER COASTER RIDE IN THIS THRILLER 5+ OUT OF 5" – *Harvee Lau, Book Dilettante*

## PRAISE FOR TAHOE CHASE

"EXCITING, EXPLOSIVE, THOUGHTFUL, SOMETIMES FUNNY"

*– Ann Ronald, Bookin' With Sunny*

"OWEN McKENNA HAS HIS HANDS FULL IN ANOTHER THRILL-
ING ADVENTURE"  *– Harvee Lau, Book Dilettante*

## PRAISE FOR TAHOE TRAP

"AN OPEN-THROTTLE RIDE"

*- Wendy Schultz, Placerville Mountain Democrat*

"THE PLOTS ARE HIGH OCTANE AND THE ACTION IS FASTER
THAN A CHEETAH ON SPEED"  *– Cathy Cole, Kittling: Books*

## PRAISE FOR TAHOE HIJACK

"BEGINNING TO READ TAHOE HIJACK IS LIKE FLOOR-
BOARDING A RACE CAR... RATING: A+"

*- Cathy Cole, Kittling: Books*

"A THRILLING READ... any reader will find the pages of his thrillers
impossible to stop turning"

*- Caleb Cage, The Nevada Review*

"THE BOOK CLIMAXES WITH A TWIST THE READER DOESN'T
SEE COMING, WORTHY OF MICHAEL CONNELLY"

*- Heather Gould, Tahoe Mountain News*

"I HAD TO HOLD MY BREATH DURING THE LAST PART OF THIS
FAST-PACED THRILLER"  *- Harvee Lau, Book Dilettante*

## PRAISE FOR TAHOE HEAT

"IN TAHOE HEAT, BORG MASTERFULLY WRITES A SEQUENCE
OF EVENTS SO INTENSE THAT IT BELONGS IN AN EARLY TOM
CLANCY NOVEL"

*- Caleb Cage, Nevada Review*

"TAHOE HEAT IS A RIVETING THRILLER"

*- John Burroughs, Midwest Book Review*

"WILL KEEP READERS TURNING THE PAGES AS OWEN RACES
TO CATCH A VICIOUS KILLER"

*- Barbara Bibel, Booklist*

"THE READER CAN'T HELP BUT ROOT FOR McKENNA AS THE BIG, GENEROUS, IRISH-BLOODED, STREET-WISE-YET-BOOK-SMART FORMER COP" *- Taylor Flynn, Tahoe Mountain News*

## PRAISE FOR TAHOE NIGHT

"BORG HAS WRITTEN ANOTHER WHITE-KNUCKLE THRILLER... A sure bet for mystery buffs waiting for the next Robert B. Parker and Lee Child novels"
*- Jo Ann Vicarel, Library Journal*

"AN ACTION-PACKED THRILLER WITH A NICE-GUY HERO, AN EVEN NICER DOG..." *– Kirkus Reviews*

"A FASCINATING STORY OF FORGERY, MURDER..."
*- Nancy Hayden, Tahoe Daily Tribune*

## PRAISE FOR TAHOE AVALANCHE
ONE OF THE TOP 5 MYSTERIES OF THE YEAR!
*- Gayle Wedgwood, Mystery News*

"BORG IS A SUPERB STORYTELLER...A MASTER OF THE GENRE"
*- Midwest Book Review*

"EXPLODES INTO A COMPLEX PLOT THAT LEADS TO MURDER AND INTRIGUE"
*- Nancy Hayden, Tahoe Daily Tribune*

## PRAISE FOR TAHOE SILENCE
WINNER, BEN FRANKLIN AWARD, BEST MYSTERY OF THE YEAR!

"A HEART-WRENCHING MYSTERY THAT IS ALSO ONE OF THE BEST NOVELS WRITTEN ABOUT AUTISM"
*STARRED REVIEW – Jo Ann Vicarel, Library Journal*

CHOSEN BY LIBRARY JOURNAL AS ONE OF THE FIVE BEST MYSTERIES OF THE YEAR

"THIS IS ONE ENGROSSING NOVEL...IT IS SUPERB"
*– Gayle Wedgwood, Mystery News*

"ANOTHER EXCITING ENTRY INTO THIS TOO-LITTLE-KNOWN SERIES" *- Mary Frances Wilkens, Booklist*

## PRAISE FOR TAHOE KILLSHOT

"BORG BELONGS ON THE BESTSELLER LISTS with Parker, Paretsky and Coben" – *Merry Cutler, Annie's Book Stop, Sharon, Massachusetts*

"A GREAT READ!" *-Shelley Glodowski, Midwest Book Review*

"A WONDERFUL BOOK" – *Gayle Wedgwood, Mystery News*

## PRAISE FOR TAHOE ICE GRAVE

"BAFFLING CLUES...CONSISTENTLY ENTERTAINS"
*- Kirkus Reviews*

"A CLEVER PLOT... RECOMMEND THIS MYSTERY"
*- John Rowen, Booklist*

"A BIG THUMBS UP... MR. BORG'S PLOTS ARE SUPER-TWISTERS"
*- Shelley Glodowski, Midwest Book Review*

"GREAT CHARACTERS, LOTS OF ACTION, AND SOME CLEVER PLOT TWISTS...Readers have to figure they are in for a good ride, and Todd Borg does not disappoint."
*- John Orr, San Jose Mercury News*

## PRAISE FOR TAHOE BLOWUP

"A COMPELLING TALE OF ARSON ON THE MOUNTAIN"
*- Barbara Peters, The Poisoned Pen Bookstore*

"RIVETING... A MUST READ FOR MYSTERY FANS!"
*- Karen Dini, Addison Public Library, Addison, Illinois*

WINNER! BEST MYSTERY OF THE YEAR
*- Bay Area Independent Publishers Association*

## PRAISE FOR TAHOE DEATHFALL

"THRILLING, EXTENDED RESCUE/CHASE" – *Kirkus Reviews*

"A TREMENDOUS READ FROM A GREAT WRITER"
*- Shelley Glodowski, Midwest Book Review*

WINNER! BEST THRILLER OF THE YEAR
*- Bay Area Independent Publishers Association*

"A TAUT MYSTERY... A SCREECHING CLIMAX"
*- Karen Dini, Addison Public Library, Addison, Illinois*

# Titles by Todd Borg

## TAHOE MYSTERY SERIES

TAHOE DEATHFALL
TAHOE BLOWUP
TAHOE ICE GRAVE
TAHOE KILLSHOT
TAHOE SILENCE
TAHOE AVALANCHE
TAHOE NIGHT
TAHOE HEAT
TAHOE HIJACK
TAHOE TRAP
TAHOE CHASE
TAHOE GHOST BOAT
TAHOE BLUE FIRE
TAHOE DARK
TAHOE PAYBACK
TAHOE SKYDROP
TAHOE DEEP
TAHOE HIT
TAHOE JADE
TAHOE MOON
TAHOE FLIGHT
TAHOE RESCUE
TAHOE SPEED

## DARK ROAD SUSPENSE SERIES

WILDERNESS VACATION
WILDERNESS JUSTICE
WILDERNESS PUNISHMENT
WILDERNESS THREAT

# TAHOE SPEED

by

Todd Borg

THRILLER PRESS

Thriller Press First Edition, August 2025

TAHOE SPEED
Copyright © 2025 by Todd Borg

All rights reserved under International and Pan-American Copyright Conventions. Published in the United States by Thriller Press, a division of WRST, Inc.

This novel is a work of fiction. Any references to real locales, establishments, organizations, or events are intended only to give the fiction a sense of verisimilitude. All other names, places, characters and incidents portrayed in this book are the product of the author's imagination.

No part of this book may be used or reproduced in any manner whatsoever without written permission from Thriller Press, P.O. Box 551110, South Lake Tahoe, CA 96155.

Library of Congress Control Number: 2025936046

ISBN: 978-1-931296-33-5

Cover design and map by Keith Carlson

Manufactured in the United States of America

For Kit

# ACKNOWLEDGMENTS

I am indebted to two Tahoe skiers. In the 1970s, Steve McKinney was the first person to ski 125 miles per hour. This is the same speed a falling skydiver achieves in the belly-down position, otherwise known, in some circles, as terminal velocity. Steve's record ushered in the modern era of speed skiing.

In the 1990s, Jeff Hamilton became the first person to break 150 mph, becoming by a significant margin the fastest non-motorized human in history.

Since McKinney and Hamilton put speed skiing and Tahoe on the world map, the speed skiing records have continued to fall.

An additional delight is that both McKinney and Hamilton loved and wrote poetry.

Imagine chasing race car speeds with no power beyond gravity, doing it with no protective cage around them, and then describing the experience with eloquent words. Clearly, this is no ordinary sport, and its practitioners are no ordinary athletes.

As for the mechanics of writing and storytelling, no writing works well that hasn't been examined, helped, cajoled, hinted at, and fixed by editors.

Liz Johnston, Eric Berglund, Christel Hall, and my wife Kit worked countless hours to shape this heap of words into something readable.

And no book looks good without a great cover. Keith Carlson is the greatest of cover designers. Pure artistic alchemy.

Thanks to all more than I can say.

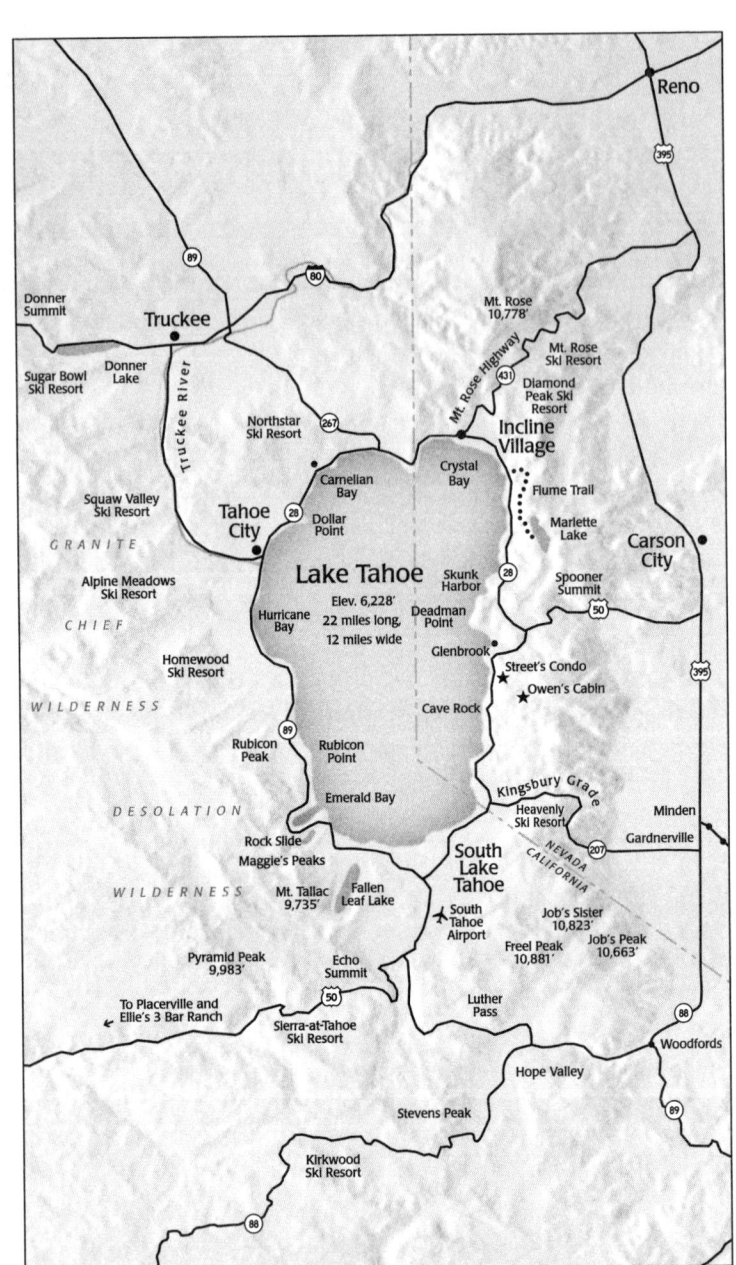

# PROLOGUE

Lake Tahoe skier Colin Burns stood at the top of the speed-skiing course in Vars, France, a ski resort south of Mont Blanc, Europe's tallest mountain. A panoramic view of the snow-covered Alps stretched in all directions.

Below him, the Chabrières couloir at Vars was so steep that it looked, from the top, like a giant, smooth, snow-covered ribbon tipped nearly vertical. It was scary but utterly compelling, a glazed white pathway that led down to possible fame.

But potential fame came accompanied by the ever-present possibility of a body-crushing fall. Which, Colin knew, could mean death.

He didn't mind the risk. He had been waiting for three years. What he was about to do would, in many ways, be a sweet victory, regardless of how fast he skied.

Colin stood sideways to the course, which stretched down to his right. While his right leg was extended nearly straight, the mountain slope was so steep that his left boot and ski were planted on the snow much higher. It was like standing sideways on a very steep stairway, his feet separated by four steps.

There was another racer in front of him. It would be a moment before Colin jumped onto the track. He started his deep breathing. Slow inhalations, followed by even slower exhalations. His eyes were closed, his muscles relaxed.

He thought about Geneviève Laurent, the woman whose love and comfort helped him relax even as his heart sped when she was near. She was his red, red rose, as in the poem by his namesake Scottish poet Robert Burns.

From the time Colin first met Geneviève, she seemed to be especially elegant and wise. Was it because, at 33, she was nine years older than he was? Was he thinking of her now because he was in her country of birth? Was it her smile, which was as mysterious as the human genetics she had studied at the Sorbonne? Or was it because of her physical magnetism?

Maybe it was simply that she understood his obsession with speed. Colin had tried to explain the pull that speed had on him, a pull that refused to let go.

"I suppose it is a kind of addiction, Colin," Geneviève had said in her delicious French accent just the week before at the little six-table French restaurant she'd started in Truckee, California, the town just north of Lake Tahoe. A restaurant named GENEVIÈVE. "Risk takers are attractive, Colin," she said.

Colin could visualize how Geneviève squinted her eyes. And how, when she smiled, her nose wrinkled.

"Now you're trying to become the fastest non-motorized person in human history," she said. "You told me that, just a few decades ago, people said it wasn't possible to ski faster than a skydiver falling through the air. It's called terminal velocity, oui? It was that Tahoe skier, Steve McKinney, who first broke that speed barrier back in the seventies. One hundred twenty five miles per hour. And that other Tahoe skier, Jeff Hamilton, who, years later, was the first man to ski one hundred fifty miles per hour.

"You said people never imagined that someone could crouch down in such an aerodynamic way that he would slip through the air faster than someone falling from a plane. Now you and your buddies in the Tahoe Terminals Club are all going fast like that. Whether you succeed or not, it's a big risk. Of course, some people say that risk is foolish. But I find it..." Geneviève paused, a dreamy look in her eyes. She squeezed Colin's hands and raised up on tiptoes to kiss him. "I find it very captivating. It makes me..." She stopped talking and looked into his eyes as if searching for the words. Then she turned her head sideways against his chest and hugged him, pressing her willowy form against him.

Colin heard the loudspeaker crackle. The announcer spoke in French, and the next skier did a jump turn into the track, his skis rotating 90 degrees in the air so that when he landed, he was pointing down the impossibly steep mountain. Gravity pulled on the man the way an elastic band pulls on a stone in a slingshot. The man rocketed down the mountain, his blue rubberized suit showing off his perfect skier's tuck.

The Vars course was widely regarded as the fastest speed-skiing course in the world. The current world speed record had been set there. Over 158 miles per hour.

Colin watched the man in the skin-tight suit. The skier was very fast, a blue blur. But Colin believed that he would be even faster.

Like most speed skiers, Colin knew the sport was essentially crazy, chasing race car speeds without the protective cage of the vehicle. And yet, the rush of adrenaline and endorphins was more addictive than any opiate. To achieve it with nothing but athletic focus is what made the experience so astonishing.

Steve McKinney had tried to put it in words.

Like all other speed skiers around the world, Colin thought about those words. McKinney said he pursued 'a stillness within speed, a calmness within fear.'

Colin knew that stillness, that calm. Both were keys to greater speed.

Speed skiing was the bad boy of ski competition. Many top athletes considered the standard racing disciplines of Slalom, Giant Slalom, Super G, and Downhill to be the best sports for demonstrating technical skiing mastery.

Of those disciplines, the Downhill race was the fastest, with racers regularly hitting 75 miles per hour as they rocketed down a steep course with a minimum number of curves.

Speed skiers, by contrast, just went straight. All of their focus was on speed. A speed course had no curves, no rises that sent skiers into the air, no technical impediments at all. The only obstacle in speed skiing was the simple death-defying limit of the maximum speed a human could coax from gravity's attraction.

In fact, speed skiers didn't just go substantially faster than the skiers competing in Downhill races. Speed skiers obliterated those speeds. While Downhill racers sometimes hit 80 miles per hour, speeds that some thought risky in a car on the freeway, speed skiers went twice as fast.

One of the journalists writing about speed skiing pointed out that while free-falling skydivers in a belly-down position hit a terminal velocity of 125 mph, a champion speed skier, barely connected to terra firma, would blow past skydivers with the same relative rush as a race horse galloping past a Sunday picnic in a park.

Colin had flown with the other American competitors to Vars. Five of them were from Lake Tahoe, all members of the Tahoe Terminals Club.

The weather on the morning of race day was good. The previous day's sun had softened the snow crystals, and when they refroze at night, it made the track especially fast. The tournament progressed without incident. When it was Colin's turn to race, he paused at the top of the launch slope. He inhaled a deep breath of cold alpine air, held it for several seconds, then let it out slowly. He shut his eyes and concentrated on the task before him. Colin had studied the course. With his eyes closed, he could visualize the steep slope with great accuracy.

Colin repeated the slow breathing. It was a meditation, shutting out all inputs, narrowing his world down to the speed trial.

He was considered one of the few elite skiers. Colin's goal was 160 miles per hour. If he could punch through that speed barrier, he'd take the title of the fastest non-motorized human in all of history.

The countdown began. As the digital readout hit zero, Colin did the rotating jump turn and pushed with his poles. His skis briefly lost contact with the snow as he rocketed down the launch portion of the slope.

Colin felt that his form was perfect. His tuck was low, his skis spread wide, his red polyurethane-coated skin-tight suit as slippery in the air as possible. He had chosen the color for Geneviève Laurent, his red, red rose. Colin's aerodynamic helmet had the unusual bulge that filled in the void at the back of his neck, giving the airflow less to grab, making his path through the air as slick as possible. The fairings behind Colin's calves made the wind pull a little less.

As Colin Burns rocketed toward the timing zone, he accelerated faster than a race car. Zero to 150 in seconds. His legs heated up from muscle tension. His vision vibrated. But he maintained perfect form as he entered the timing stretch. Pushing the limits of human stamina, his thighs burned as if on fire. His back quivered as he absorbed a dozen shocks a second.

At 190 pounds, six feet of height, and nearly zero body fat, he was strong as a rock. And while journalists, in their fatuous focus on looks, commented on how Colin looked nothing like the public's idea of a glamorous, handsome ski racer, even those writers recognized that Colin had something much more important than looks. For Colin was imbued with a desire that was so strong that all other speed skiers noticed. He was relatively new to the sport, but he was talked about more than any speed skiers since Steve McKinney and Jeff Hamilton.

Colin was attempting an astonishing feat, to go almost 40 miles per hour faster than a free-falling body. Skiing that fast required perfect aerodynamic form, slipping through the air like a diving falcon, and with no power beyond the pull of gravity.

Colin held his form without wavering. He visualized his motive and his goal.

As he entered the timing zone, he could tell he was going faster than ever before. And he was still accelerating.

He shot through the zone as if out of a cannon. His form was still perfect, his speed faster than ever. When he came into the runout, he believed he'd broken the world record. He could feel it. Sense it. He had the champion's awareness of a flawless run.

Colin followed braking protocol and raised up an inch, then two, allowing the air to grab at his suit and begin to slow him down. It takes time to brake from 160 mph. He followed the deceleration pattern he'd used countless times before. Everything was perfect.

Far off to one side of the course was a small cheering crowd, held back by black rope looped through the top of orange stanchions.

Colin felt a brief sting on the side of his left thigh, like the sting of a wasp. He thought it was the pinched-nerve problem he'd experienced in the past, nothing serious. He'd had little stinging sensations before. But this sting distracted him from his focus.

His right ski wavered and caught a little bump. The air got under that ski. The sudden wind pressure slapped the bottom of his ski. The impact flipped Colin up into the air. His body turned in a rolling motion.

Colin knew the routine for a fall. Try to stay on the ground. Try to slide to a stop. Avoid windmilling at all costs.

But his speed was too great, and the air pressure was too intense.

The crowd gave a collective gasp as Colin went airborne.

He flew dozens of yards through the air. He was sideways to the ground when he landed. His knee gouged into the snow, flipping him over and then bouncing him back into the air.

Colin Burns windmilled for 300 yards before his limp body, flailing like a rag doll, came to a stop.

Some of the first people to reach him were his fellow Tahoe racers, Danny, Jackson, and Tamir, charging across the steep slope. All were members of the Tahoe Terminals Club, having broken through the terminal velocity speed. All knew the risks of falling.

As they approached Colin's broken form, they could see there was no hope. Colin Burns looked like he'd been crushed by a bulldozer.

Colin's shiny red uniform had been mostly torn from his body. A large piece of red fabric was still attached to his neck and hung down his back like the red, superhero cape he had played with as a child. His left arm was twisted behind him where an arm shouldn't be. His right knee bent in the wrong direction. His helmet visor was broken with one unseeing eye visible and staring at the sky.

Colin achieved the greatest success in his pursuit of speed, yet gave up his life in the process.

# ONE

Spot and I were sitting at an outdoor table with Sergeants Diamond Martinez and Jack Santiago at a brew pub at Palisades Tahoe Resort in Olympic Valley, there to check out the food festival. We'd ordered vegetarian Hungarian Goulash from one of the vendors who came by with her rolling cart. The goulash produced robust clouds of steam as she dished it up.

We were in the pedestrian walkway of the village, which is surrounded by buildings. The buildings provided little shelter from the breeze of early December. The brew pub, which sits in front of the Hungarian Restaurant, had shifted their outdoor tables over to a corner where the low-angle sunshine could reach in and make like it was bringing warmth, even if it was only pretend.

I was at noon on the table position. Spot sat like a gentleman to my right at nine o'clock. Because Great Danes are very tall, his head projected over the table, and he watched each of us very carefully as we ate and drank.

The morning sun caught his faux diamond ear stud. It shimmered as though he smelled filet mignon.

"It's just veggies, Largeness," I said. "No beef to get excited about."

Spot's enthusiasm was undiminished.

Diamond was across from me at six o'clock, and Santiago at three. Diamond kept his left hand on Spot's head and neck, whether from companionship or to reign him in should his goulash enthusiasm get out of control.

"I can't even feel the sun," Santiago said, "that winter wind is so cold."

Santiago was in his dress greens, with the star badge used by the Placer County Sheriff's office. Near the badge were some ribbons and other chest candy. Because he was on duty, he ordered coffee when the waiter with the beverage cart came by.

"Thou winter wind art not so unkind as man's ingratitude," Diamond said, "although thy breath be rude." Diamond, who wasn't on duty, was wearing torn jeans and an old gray sweatshirt with paint on it, and over that a sheepskin suede ranch coat. Like me, he ordered a beer, a microbrew that, when the waiter poured slowly into a tall glass, produced two inches of deep amber and an eight-inch head of foam.

Jack Santiago was a heavy-set man about five-ten. The heavy was all muscle. He radiated competence and professionalism. Yet he always seemed a touch intimidated by Diamond, a man who was a bit shorter and of slighter build and, despite being a Mexican immigrant from Mexico City, had a vast command of English, his second language.

Santiago didn't ask what Diamond was quoting. Instead he said, "What's that called, that big word for people who've read too many smart books?"

Diamond made a hint of a grin. He was used to having people react to his knowledge. "People with erudition?" he said.

Santiago nodded. "That'll do. It's not like I'm trapped in the world of comic books. I read a novel just last month."

Diamond's beer head had only shrunk by a quarter inch. Maybe they put some kind of foaming agent in it. He dipped his finger into the foam and lifted it up. The foam quivered but stood strong, like birthday cake frosting. He sucked the foam off and then slurped some head from the glass.

I was putting chunks of cheese on pieces of Hungarian fried flat bread. I handed one to Spot. He grabbed it so fast, his teeth clicked. I jerked my hand back.

Santiago ate the last of the Hungarian cheese spread. He looked at his watch. "I'm off my shift in five minutes. Another day of brilliant crime fighting in the mountains of Placer County. No one got even a scratch." He sipped more coffee. "At least, not that I know of."

Diamond gestured toward Santiago's coffee. "You could change into your civvies, switch to an adult beverage, and we could talk comics."

"My clothing bag is in the patrol unit, and it's parked way out in the lot. It's a good hike. But thanks for the invitation."

"Officer's prerogative is usually to park on the curb," I said.

"Actually, we've had some smash-and-grabs out in that lot. So my empty ride is doing deterrent duty. By the time I hike out there, I'll be thinking about going home to dinner. My wife gets tired of architecting all day, so she relaxes by cooking. She said she's making a low-sugar, non-fat gelato for dessert. Which one could describe with more of those big words…" He looked at Diamond.

"Low sugar and dessert being mutually exclusive concepts?" Diamond said.

Santiago nodded as he pushed his chair back and stood up. "But even an oxymoron can taste good." Santiago tossed some ones on the table, made a little salute, winked, and grinned like the Cheshire Cat as he walked away.

"He got you there," I said.

"No kidding," Diamond said. "I lost the word battle and the war."

# TWO

As Santiago walked away from us, the sun made a sudden brilliant reflective flash off the aerial tram as it rose behind Santiago on its way up toward High Camp, two thousand feet up the cliff. Both Diamond and I looked up at the tram rising above the little village.

"Easiest way to climb the mountains and avoid fording the streams," Diamond said. "Tahoe mountains ain't fancy like those Austrian hills Julie Andrews sang about. But then Austria ain't got a lake like ours, either." Diamond turned to look at Spot. Spot was looking at something else down at our level. We followed his eyes.

A hundred feet away, in the dark shade of a nearby building, was a medium-sized dog sitting alone in the cold, its leash looped around one of the table legs.

"That dog's been waiting for its owner the entire time we've been out here," I said.

Diamond nodded. "There's laws that say you can't leave a dog in a hot car. There should be laws for the reverse."

"Hopefully, he's got enough fur that he's not shivering."

I touched Spot's nose. "Largeness, you stay here with Diamond." I stood up.

Diamond still had his hand resting on Spot's big neck. Diamond slid fingers under Spot's collar just to be sure Spot stayed put.

I walked over to the other dog. It glanced at me as I approached, then refocused its attention toward the brew pub, although the entrance appeared to be out of the dog's sight line.

The dog had one floppy ear and one upright. Its coloring had broad areas of black and white, its fur long and silky. There was a white stripe running from the top of its head down its nose. Its right front leg was white, as was its chest. Its nose was black. The only other color was the brown of its cheeks. A classic Border Collie.

"Hey, pal," I said as I squatted down next to its side. I faced the same way it faced. Casual. Non-confrontational. The dog continued to stare toward the brew pub. It seemed likely that his owner had gone into the pub or at least walked that way before he left the dog's sight.

I slowly reached my hand out so he could sniff me. He ignored the movement.

I looked at his leash. The way it was looped around the table leg made it clear that it didn't just get caught on the table leg. The dog's owner/walker had purposely tied it there to keep the dog in place until he came back.

"I'm just gonna check your dog tag."

I slowly reached over. A metallic tag hung from his black collar. I turned the tag so it caught the light. It said, 'Lazlo.' As I touched the dog tag, I realized the dog was shaking. Not with nerves. Shivering with cold.

"Been a long wait, huh, Lazlo? Maybe I'll go ask inside, see what's taking your mate so long."

I stood up. Diamond and Spot were both watching me. I pointed to my chest, then pointed to the brew pub entrance. Diamond nodded.

I walked over and pulled open a red door.

The inside was decorated in a Tudor theme. White plaster walls with exposed dark-brown beams. The ceiling was similar but with the beams lowered eight inches below the plaster. The bar and bar stools were dark brown. Around the perimeter of the space were tables with four chairs each. Same dark brown but with cream-colored linen tablecloths. An upscale place compared to most brew pubs and bars. But this was the Palisades Tahoe Resort where everything from skis to steaks was expensive.

There were multiple people in the house. I spoke loudly. "Hey, everybody. Outside is a Border Collie tied to a table. The tag says Lazlo. Does it belong to anyone here?"

There were some head shakes.

I walked over to the bar. A man in his 30s with long messy hair was using a white cloth to dry beer glasses and then set them on a shelf with a hundred other glasses.

The man turned, wiped his hands on his white apron, then looked up at me.

"Any idea who the dog's owner is?" I asked.

The man shook his head. "Slow day. I woulda noticed if someone came in with a dog."

"The dog is tied to one of your outdoor tables. It looks like someone left the dog there before coming into your bar. The dog is looking toward the door to this pub. He's been there awhile. Did you notice anyone come in some time ago? Someone who looked like a dog owner?"

The man gave me a weary grin of tolerance. "What does a dog owner look like?"

"Someone who isn't dressed for the opera. A clue would be outdoor clothes. Jeans or the equivalent, warm shirt and jacket. Probably a warm hat of some kind. Maybe the end of a plastic clean-up bag protruding from a pocket."

The man shook his head again. "There were two guys a coupla hours ago. One had on warm clothes. They each had a beer and drank them while standing over at one of those pub tables." He gestured toward a group of small narrow tables the same height as the bar.

"Can you recall anything about them? They say anything that might connect to a dog?"

The bartender shrugged, then shook his head.

"All I know is one was younger, about my age. No jacket. A big guy. Serious muscles. The other guy was older, and he spoke, like, something foreign and some English, too. He was dressed for the weather. So maybe he had a dog."

"Ever seen them before?"

He shook his head, picked up another glass from the washer rack. "Nope." He began buffing the glass. "But I'm new. This is only my fourth day."

"Any idea what they talked about?"

He looked toward the wall, his eyes unfocused. "No idea. But it seemed the young guy was trying to convince the older guy about something. I heard words like, 'Trust me, you'll think it was worth it.'"

I said, "Like the younger guy was trying to sell something?"

"Maybe. I don't know why I think that. Body language or tone of voice, or something."

"One more question. Did they give you any idea that they would be back in the future?"

The man frowned. "What would make me think that?"

I wanted to grab him and give him a shake. "If one of them said something like, 'I'll let you know tomorrow.' Or 'Let's meet here next Tuesday.'"

"Oh, you mean something obvious." The man shook his head. "No, I was working. But I would've remembered if they'd said anything like that. But they weren't talking loud. So I only heard a few things."

"The foreign language… Any idea what that was?"

"No. I speak a little español. So I know it wasn't Spanish."

He dried another glass.

He said, "But if they left a dog outside, it would be real cold by now. It's been hours."

"The dog's shivering. Okay if I bring him in here? Let him warm up. Maybe give him some food?"

"Sure. I'm not much of a dog person. But if you think that's the thing to do, then yes, bring him in."

"I'll be back."

I went back out and joined Spot and Diamond at the table. The Border Collie was still watching the brew pub door.

I explained what I learned. "He's a Border Collie named Lazlo. The bartender says there were a couple of men in there talking, and one of them might have been Lazlo's owner."

"No info about the owner?" Diamond said.

"Only that the owner might an older man who speaks a foreign language."

Diamond made a single nod.

"I told the bartender that the poor dog is shivering and I was going to bring Lazlo inside his bar to warm up. He was fine with that. But he's not expecting Spot."

"I'll hang onto His Largeness," Diamond said. "We should introduce the dogs, right? Keep Lazlo from getting uptight about a guy this size. And speaking of Border Collies, aren't they supposed to be very smart?"

"Smartest of all the breeds," I said. "Border Collies can learn hundreds of words. One they tested knew over a thousand."

Diamond tugged on Spot's collar. "Listen up, Largeness. You're about to meet a doggie Einstein. So pay attention."

"But," I added, "from my attempt at talking to the dog, it doesn't seem like it knows any words at all."

"Maybe he's a foreigner and doesn't speak English."

"There's a thought I hadn't considered. Tahoe's got people from all over the world. We can't assume their dogs speak the local lingo. I'll bring Lazlo to Spot so Lazlo doesn't feel cornered."

"Good idea," Diamond said. "We can't expect Spot to digest differential equations if his math teacher is feeling stressed."

I walked over, disconnected Lazlo's leash from the table, and walked him toward our table where Diamond and Spot waited.

Spot, of course, was pulling against Diamond's hold on his collar. He was wagging and eager to meet a new friend.

Lazlo was probably 35 pounds, smaller than my girlfriend Street's Yellow Lab Blondie. Lazlo naturally acted a little tentative around a 170-pound Great Dane. But beyond that, he didn't pay Spot much attention. Dogs have a unique quality of accepting all other dogs as equals, regardless of size difference. Unlike mountain lions and house cats, where one views the other as lunch, large and small dogs know they are all the same, even though small dogs quickly learn to play carefully around a dog that could cause injury through a misstep. Unless a big dog is very ornery and poorly socialized, he would never hurt a small dog, although he might scare the small dog if the small dog was poaching his food.

Lazlo glanced at Spot, then looked again over toward the pub door.

Spot strained to sniff Lazlo. Lazlo almost didn't notice, so focused was he on the place where he'd last seen his owner.

Diamond moved with Spot so the dogs could make their olfactory inspections. Then we walked to the brew pub. I opened the door and let Lazlo walk in first.

He held his nose high as if to get general confirmation that his owner had been in the pub. Then he lowered his nose to the floor and pulled. I let him walk around. He paused to carefully scrutinize one of the tall narrow tables.

The bartender was changing out a draft beer keg. He leaned over the bar and looked down at Lazlo. He said, "That table he's sniffing is where the two men were talking."

Diamond came in with Spot and kept him off to the side but near the front door. The bartender looked at Spot and raised his eyebrows. "No one would mistake that guy going missing."

"No, they wouldn't." I didn't volunteer that he was my dog. "He's with my friend. We have to sort out what to do with Lazlo."

"How're you gonna do that?"

"First, he is cold. He could use some food."

"We don't stock dog food."

"But you have appetizers, right?"

The man glanced toward the rear door. "We have an arrangement with the cafe next door. Maybe you could take the dog there."

"But Lazlo smells his owner's presence here. He'll be more likely to eat here."

The bartender pulled out a menu and set it on the bar. I scanned down it for dog-friendly fare. "Let's do four cheeseburgers and two baskets of fries."

The bartender raised his eyebrows and tapped on his computer screen. "It takes about ten minutes."

"In the meantime, two beers, please. And a bowl of water."

"A bowl of water," he said. He looked down toward Lazlo, then over toward Spot. "For the dogs?"

"Yes."

# THREE

After we ate, Diamond had to leave, so I was walking with Lazlo and Spot down the pedestrian street at the Palisades Tahoe Resort. I had a vague hope that someone might recognize Lazlo. My phone rang. Street's adopted daughter Camille had changed my ring tone to the song 'Can't take my eyes off of you.'

I'd learned that even though Camille couldn't hear, she appreciated the vibrations of music, absorbing it into her body directly.

But how a nine-year-old deaf girl can even find and appreciate classic pop songs was beyond me. Never mind whatever iPhone alchemy was necessary to make it your ring tone.

I switched Lazlo's leash to the hand that held Spot's collar and clicked the button, as Frankie Valli crooned that I'd be heaven to touch…

"Owen McKenna," I said.

"Bonjour, Mr. McKenna," said a woman with a pronounced French accent. "My name is Geneviève Laurent, and I own a restaurant in Truckee, California. "

Unlike most locals, she said the word *Truckee* with a slight emphasis on the second syllable.

She continued, "I am in need of some help, and a customer at my restaurant told me you are an investigator and you could possibly help me. I would like to ask if you are available for this help?"

"Maybe. What do you need?"

"Last spring, my boyfriend Colin Burns died in a skiing accident, and my boyfriend's attorney contacted me to say that Colin had a life insurance policy that is to pay out to me. I'm the—I'm not good with this word—beneficiary." She said it slowly but with perfect pronunciation. "But I have not received this insurance. The insurance company is resisting. The attorney called it stonewalling. I am asking if you can help me even though I am not able to pay you much money. At least not at first. However, if I get the insurance, then I can pay whatever it is you charge."

I normally didn't do insurance work or divorce work, nor anything involving excessive paperwork. As a former homicide inspector on the San Francisco PD, my skills were oriented toward crimes of violence.

But Geneviève Laurent had a voice so smooth she could draw the most taciturn introvert into conversation.

"I'm happy to talk," I said. "And I'm sorry about your boyfriend dying."

"Merci. How is it we do this?" she said. "Do I tell you my details now on this phone? Or do I have to sign a contract first?"

"I don't use contracts. If I'm not comfortable working for you, I will decline your invitation."

"I always thought it was the way Americans do business. You have an agreement on paper."

I remembered something Diamond once said, and I repeated it. "A friend of mine says that paperwork is no balm for the wounds of misunderstanding."

"Oh. Your friend is a poet. A romantic."

"Oui, and he does business on a handshake."

"You speak French?" Her serious albeit-delectable voice, suddenly sounded joyful.

"I only know one word. Oui."

"Oh," she said. "You are a funny man."

"We should meet," I said. "You can tell me about your situation over coffee."

"I would like that. Do I drive to your office? I saw on the computer that you are in Stateline, on the South Shore. I am in Truckee. It will be sometime after tomorrow before I can meet. Perhaps next Monday when I am closed. But I am very interested in talking."

"I'm currently at the Palisades Tahoe Resort. Close to Truckee. I could come to you."

"Oh, that is much better. I have to be open for business in three hours. But if you come see me now, we could talk before I open. I will have coffee for you."

A woman walking a long-haired Chihuahua approached. The Chihuahua strained at its leash, pulling toward Spot and Lazlo. The dog barked incessantly.

"I hear your dog," the woman on the phone said. "Bring him or her along. I have a front patio where dogs are quite comfortable."

"I'm currently in charge of two dogs, but not the dog you hear."

"It is no problem. There is room."

"Where should I go?"

"My restaurant is called GENEVIÈVE, just off the main street in Truckee. I would be happy if you come here." She gave me the address.

"I'll be there in less than an hour." I clicked off. I turned down a side street and took the dogs out to the parking lot.

I opened the door into the back seat of my old Jeep. Spot jumped in. Lazlo seemed suspicious. He looked back toward the village. People told kids not to take rides from strangers. If Border Collies were as smart as kids, maybe he was under the same instruction. I gave him a tug. "Don't worry, boy."

He climbed into the Jeep, slowly, no enthusiasm. Spot, the world's most secure dog, didn't mind sharing with Lazlo. But Lazlo immediately figured out that sharing the back seat with Spot could result in injury should Spot not be careful when he shifted position. So Lazlo jumped into the front seat.

Lazlo still hadn't responded to anything I said. But he knew cars. He bumped the passenger window with his nose, turned and looked at me, then bumped the window again.

I hit the buttons to roll down Spot's rear window and the front window. Both dogs stuck their heads out into the fresh air as if they'd spent the last week imprisoned in a dank, musty cellar.

I drove out Olympic Valley to Highway 89, turned north, and was in Truckee twenty minutes later. I drove along the main thoroughfare, found the cross street, and turned up the steep slope that cradles downtown Truckee from the north.

The restaurant was a small white house that jutted out from the slope. It had an attractive sign made of gold metallic script set against a black background. There was no parking. Diners were expected to get dropped off or arrive on foot. Or perhaps the restaurant offered valet parking.

I went back down to the main street and headed to the new

parking lots on the east side of downtown.

It was a reasonable walk back. Both dogs held their heads high, taking in the sights and smells. We went past restaurants and gift shops and the Word After Word bookstore, which Street and I had visited in the past. People stopped and wanted to pet Spot. Or take selfies with him. As always, he loved the attention. Lazlo didn't seem to mind that he was upstaged.

The restaurant's steep cross street was the next block. We headed up and were at the GENEVIÈVE restaurant in a few minutes.

The building was no doubt built as a house, and it had a broad gable roof with dark gray composition shingles. Projecting from the center of the roof was a red brick chimney.

The former house had Dutch lap siding that had recently been painted a soft gray with white trim around the windows and doors.

The patio Geneviève Laurent had mentioned was off to the side of the restaurant entrance. It was enclosed by a short fence topped with acrylic window panels to keep out the winter wind. There were tall propane heaters that radiated down to several tables. The side of the house adjacent to the patio had been retrofitted with large windows and a wide door so that one could go directly from patio to interior, avoiding the main entrance. Both the main entrance door and patio door had oval windows with bevel-cut glass. Like the siding, the doors were painted gray. The door hardware was shiny brass handles with thumb buttons. The brass look went with the gold script on the sign. The look was elegant without being fussy, like an upscale Cape Cod restaurant transplanted from New England to the Sierra.

Still holding Spot's collar and Lazlo's leash, I walked onto the patio and knocked on the closest window.

Although I couldn't see clearly through the window reflections, it appeared that the house had been remodeled to create a single dining room, with two doors on the back wall that probably led to the kitchen and restrooms.

I could see several dinner tables covered with white linen tablecloths and set with elegant silverware. To one side on each table was a silver goblet that appeared to be an oil lamp with a wick that was covered by a flip-down lid when it wasn't burning. Each place setting had two wine glasses, one large, one medium. The glasses had been turned upside down before the restaurant opened for dinner.

On one edge of each table was a wide satin ribbon, bright red, stretched tight over the linen tablecloth. Next to the oil lamp was a large, red metallic Christmas ball sitting on a small glass saucer. It was an elegant, non-fussy bit of decoration for the upcoming holiday. It made the restaurant look very classy.

In the middle of each table was a narrow vase that held a red rose.

At the center of the room was a two-sided brick fireplace, retrofitted to burn gas. Both sides had been enclosed with glass. The dining tables were positioned such that most diners could see the fire as they ate.

I hadn't heard about the quality of their menu, but if the food was prepared with the same loving detail applied to the physical setting, the meals would likely be excellent.

After a moment I sensed movement from inside.

The patio door opened, and a woman came out.

"Hello," she said with a slight smile. "You must be Monsieur McKenna. I'm Geneviève Laurent. It pleases me to meet you."

# FOUR

She reached out to shake my free hand but kept her eyes on where I held Spot's collar with my left hand, as if she were concerned at being close to a dog that was much bigger than she was.

She looked at the dogs. "And you have brought your—how do you say—charges."

"This big one is Spot. He belongs to me. Or I belong to him. This other one is Lazlo, and he is on temporary loan to me. He's not very responsive."

The woman carefully patted Spot on the head, then looked toward Lazlo.

"Lazlo looks familiar to me. I think I've seen him in the past."

"If you can think of where, that would help. He was lost or abandoned when I found him this morning over in Olympic Village. I'm trying to reconnect him to his owner."

"I can't remember. But I'll let you know, if I do." She stepped away from Spot and leaned over toward Lazlo.

"Bonjour, Lazlo. Tu aimes être prêté à cet homme."

Lazlo made a tentative wag.

"It appears he is okay with being on loan to you," she said.

"He hasn't wagged before. He must like you."

"Well it seems he understands some French. Maybe he'd like a cookie." She turned back to Lazlo. "Voudriez-vous un biscuit?"

Lazlo's wag got vigorous. Spot, confusion on his face, looked at Lazlo but didn't wag.

"He does understand French!" Geneviève said.

Spot was watching Lazlo, his brow furrowed with question.

"And Spot obviously doesn't," I said.

Geneviève Laurent went into the restaurant. She came back out with two dog cookies that looked like custom-shaped graham crackers. She held one out to Lazlo. He took it and chewed it delicately.

Spot immediately started drooling.

Geneviève looked concerned as she held one out to Spot. She was ready to pull her hand back in a hurry if necessary.

He took it carefully, barely touching her fingers, chomped once, and swallowed. Lazlo was still chewing.

Geneviève, who looked to be in her early thirties, had intense pale blue eyes and wavy, shoulder-length brown hair that was as thick and lustrous as that in a magazine ad. Her closed-mouth smile was restrained.

Despite the cold weather, she had on a loose short-sleeved work shirt that a house cleaner might choose for unrestricted movement.

She wasn't as thin as my girlfriend Street Casey, and she didn't telegraph the same athletic demeanor, but she was similar in many ways. Strong, handsome countenance, if not pretty, and she radiated an obvious charm and a personality that was friendly and had none of the brusqueness that some people associate with French people.

"Thank you for coming so quickly," she said.

"Oui," I said, grinning.

"Shall we talk inside where it is warm? Or would the dogs not like being out here alone?"

"I think they'll be fine."

She nodded. "I'll light one of the heaters." She reached up to turn a knob. With her arm raised, her short sleeve dropped back revealing a significant bruise that seemed to wrap around her upper arm just above her elbow. I immediately wondered about someone gripping her very hard. Thinking of domestic abuse, I looked at her left hand but saw no ring. But the close-trimmed nails with no polish suggested she worked hard with her hands. She may have taken off any ring before doing cleaning work in a restaurant kitchen.

The gas lit, and a blue flame grew within the heater. I could feel the radiant warmth immediately. Geneviève turned to the door.

I wrapped Lazlo's leash around the patio post and told Spot to be good. I was confident—but not certain—that he wouldn't wander off as long as he could see me through the windows.

Geneviève directed me to a corner table. "What type of coffee do you prefer? I can do many of the barista specialties."

"Just regular coffee, please. Black."

She made a single nod, gave me another slight, closed-mouth smile, and went through the kitchen door.

She came back out very soon, carrying a tray with two steaming cups on saucers and a plate with mini-croissants.

"That was fast." I took a sip. "Delicious."

"I hope you like plain butter croissants."

I nodded as I took a bite. "Excellent. You are a chef by training?"

"No. I am a geneticist. But I grew up in a family of cooks. I came to America after getting my Ph.D. in Molecular Biology and genetics. I taught for a few years at Stanford. But I found it..." she paused. "Difficult. I'd always had a nagging desire to start a restaurant. And I also wanted to spend more time skiing. So I moved to Tahoe and began working on a restaurant business plan." She paused. "Of course, the irony is that when one starts a restaurant, there is no more time for skiing or most anything else."

"Teaching at Stanford and then running a restaurant in the space of a few years is quite the resumé."

Geneviève's eyes suddenly watered. She reached up with her index fingers and dabbed tears. "I'm sorry for having an emotional reaction. This happens often since my boyfriend died. Anyway, my father didn't think I had the chutzpah to teach at a university. He may have been right, because my dean basically forced me out of Stanford. He didn't think women could be serious scientists. Then my mother didn't think I was ambitious enough to own a business. I've been trying to prove my parents wrong ever since."

"Looks like you succeeded."

"It looks like it, oui. But they'll never know. My mother died of a brain tumor three years ago at the age of sixty-two. My father died of a heart attack a year later. I think one caused the other."

"I'm sorry."

"But Colin came along and said he believed I could do anything I wanted to. He was my light. My raison d'être."

"And then he died," I said. "I'm sorry about that."

She wiped away more tears. A strand of her hair caught in one of her earrings. She pulled the hair free and then fingered the earring as if to make sure it hadn't fallen off.

They were small gold earrings from which hung pale blue

stones.

"Nice gemstones," I said. "Like diamonds only blue."

"Merci. Colin gave them to me. He said they went with my eyes."

"They do."

"They're called Benitoite. It's California's state gem. They come from San Benito County, which is just inland from Monterey Bay and Carmel. The mineral has been found in just a few places around the world, but San Benito County is the only place in the world where the gems are found." She took a long, deep breath.

"Coming from France, you must have skied in the Alps?" I said.

"Yes, when I was young, before I went to the Sorbonne. After the university, there was very little time to ski. As you probably know, Tahoe doesn't have big mountains like the Alps. But the climate is much better, and the lake is like nowhere else in the world. But I have skied and gone paddleboarding a few times. I met Colin that way, so I'm very glad for that.

"Anyway, I found this little building to rent, used all my savings to fix it up, and started the restaurant a year ago. I had no chef training. I simply cook my mother's specialties. It hasn't been easy, but I've done okay for a new restaurant. As with most young businesses, there is little money left over for me. But if I can continue to build up my off-season clientele, I should be able to start making more money. I have two part-time wait staff now." She looked up as one of the rear doors opened and a skinny young man came out carrying a tray of glasses. Geneviève and he nodded at each other.

"That's Jimmy Baker," she said. "He is one of my helpers. He sublets the room beneath my apartment." She pointed out the window toward the small building adjacent to the restaurant. "Maybe someday I can even hire a sous chef. It helps that the little building attached to the rear corner is a studio apartment that is also owned by my restaurant landlord. The restaurant rent is pricey, but the apartment rent is inexpensive." She gestured toward the back of the restaurant. "So I live there upstairs. Jimmy lives in the room below."

I said, "I always thought restaurants seemed like a difficult business. So many rules, long hours, and health inspectors showing up at bad times."

Geneviève looked out the window for a moment. "It's also quite challenging for immigrants because the work visa rules are very strict and some contradict others. But I'm happy to have inspectors."

I was still thinking about the woman's bruise. "You met Colin here? Or at Stanford?"

"Here. At Sand Harbor. Then again skiing at Sugar Bowl."

"And he died last ski season?" I said, thinking that her arm bruise obviously didn't come from him.

She nodded. "Last spring. Colin was a speed skier."

"You mean the type where they ski as fast as race cars?"

She nodded, frowned, and shut her eyes.

"I remember reading about him. He set some kind of speed record, right?"

She still had her eyes shut. "Yes. The world record. Just shy of two hundred fifty-seven K per hour. Which I've learned is one hundred sixty miles per hour."

"I can't imagine skiing that fast."

She opened her eyes and looked out the window toward Northstar Ski Resort. We could see the snow-covered runs from where we sat.

"He and his friends had a club of sorts. They called it the Tahoe Terminals Club, and it included the people from Tahoe who have ever skied over two hundred K per hour, which is terminal velocity for sky divers falling from a plane." She paused. "Colin explained to me that there aren't places where you can ski that fast near Tahoe. But they had practice tracks. One was off the edge of the Palisades Tahoe Resort. The other was in the back country near the South Shore. When the conditions were right, they went to Vars, France, which has the fastest course in the world."

"I wonder about the nature of a person who can ski that fast."

Geneviève seemed to look inward. "Colin said it mostly requires that one is tough as rocks and has a heart like a rose."

"Colin certainly thought like a poet."

Geneviève went silent, thinking, turning inward toward her thoughts.

Her helper, Jimmy Baker, finished distributing the glasses. He walked over. He was still holding the tray in one hand and some folded linens in the other. "Just checking, ma'am. You said I should start on the mopping before I wash the next load of dishes?" he asked Geneviève.

"Oui, merci. Jimmy, this is Owen McKenna."

Jimmy looked to be in his mid-twenties, with a flattop of red hair, a thousand freckles, and some acne. He gave me a little wave with the tray.

"Getting into the food business?" I said.

He nodded. "I'm learning from the best. My goal is to own a restaurant someday, just like Ms. Laurent. She's my role model. I took a year of chef classes. Of course, running a restaurant business is a long way from just cooking. So now I'm trying to learn the business from the ground up." He lifted up his armload of linens. "For example, we never learned about laundry services in chef school!"

His words sounded like flattery, but his tone was all earnestness.

"Smart," I said.

Jimmy headed for the kitchen.

Geneviève said, "That boy tries so hard, he's like a dream. I think he has a bad family situation, and this job is a way for him to escape it."

"He'll probably do exactly as he says and have his own restaurant some day."

Geneviève nodded.

"On the phone, you mentioned that Colin had life insurance," I said.

"Oui. Colin and I were very close. Without telling me, he took out a ten-year term life insurance policy, naming me as his beneficiary."

"Just to be sure I understand, the policy is supposed to pay out if the owner of the policy dies within ten years."

"Oui. The policy had some qualifiers, mostly because he was involved in such a risky sport. The main one was that he couldn't compete in speed skiing for the first three years the policy was in force."

"The contestability period," I said.

"You know about it."

"A little. Had the three-year period passed at the time he died?"

She nodded.

"And how did Colin die?"

More of the darkness in her face. "On that world record run. Just after he went through the timing zone, he fell and died."

"And this was in Vars, France?"

She nodded.

To change the subject, I said, "What was Colin like?"

"He was charming, and very smart, and quite the romantic. He could always quote something from a poem for special occasions. Robert Burns was his favorite poet. I think because the poet was from Scotland, and Colin was of Scottish heritage." She paused. "Colin was also kind of a maniac for speed. He even went wing suit flying."

"Where they put on something like a Batman suit and fly through the air without a parachute."

"Oui. They jump out of airplanes or off the tops of mountains. They rocket across the sky and fly down through vertical canyons in mountains all over the world, just inches from the rock, going very fast before they pull the cord to open their chute so they can land."

"I've seen it on YouTube videos," I said. "The speed seems insane."

Geneviève gave me a somber look. "But Colin always pointed out the irony that was so obvious to him."

"What was that?"

"That everyone thinks wing suit flying, shooting across the sky, involves crazy speed." She paused. "But it's not as fast as speed skiing."

The statement was almost shocking.

After a moment, I asked, "Who is the attorney who contacted you about the insurance?"

"Madison Rappaport. She is in Reno. She handled Colin's will. She contacted me after he died. I went to her office. She explained that Colin had named me in his will as his sole beneficiary. He only had a few personal effects and just a little money and the life insurance policy."

"How much is it for?"

"Two million dollars."

# FIVE

"On the phone you said the insurance company hasn't paid. What is their reason?"

"They claim he had a pre-existing condition that wasn't disclosed. They say that Colin had Huntington's Disease, and that allows them to deny the claim because he didn't state it on his application."

"I don't know about Huntington's Disease."

"It is a genetic disease that is inherited. If you get the problem gene, you eventually develop physical and mental problems. The onset of symptoms can happen at any age. But once the symptoms start, you usually die from it in ten or twenty years."

"How did the company learn that Colin had Huntington's?"

"I don't know. But they apparently ordered a genetic test."

"You can do such tests after a person dies?"

"Oui. Much DNA can still be analyzed."

"Did Colin know he had Huntington's Disease?"

Geneviève took a deep breath. "I don't think so. But I've wondered if he suspected it. If so, that might explain his insurance policy. I don't think most unmarried men his age have life insurance."

"Did he have symptoms?"

She shook her head. "Nothing that I was aware of."

"Suggesting something internal?"

"Again, nothing I could sense. He spoke normally, acted normally. And, of course, he was an amazing athlete."

"Is it possible he had symptoms before he applied for insurance and he didn't tell the insurance company?"

"Like I said, not that I saw. But since I got that news from the insurance company, I've wondered if his mother could have the disease. Her movement is a bit awkward. And she's forgetful. She hasn't been tested to my knowledge. His mother's parents could have had it as well. But I don't think they were ever tested, either. There was no evidence that anyone in his background had HD, as it is sometimes referred to. From what Colin told me, his grandparents died from natural causes. His father died in a work accident when Colin was very young. Two or three, I think."

As an investigator, I always wanted to know the details. "May I ask about that accident?"

"Monsieur Burns was a construction foreman. He was on a construction site, and a cable snapped and killed him."

"What is the name of the insurance company that had Colin's policy?"

"It's a long name. Franklin Assurance Holdings International."

"I haven't heard of them."

Geneviève shrugged. "I hadn't as well. The attorney said that the company was connected with Lloyds of London."

"I associate that name with high-risk insurance."

"Oui, I think many people do. I looked it up. It turns out that Lloyds isn't actually an insurance company. They are a kind of marketplace where insurance companies come to do business."

"Like a shopping mall for insurance?" I said.

She nodded.

"Do you have contact info for Colin's mother?"

"Yes, I have it in my phone." She stood, walked over to the hosting podium, and came back with her phone. "I'll email it to you." She gave me a questioning look.

I gave her my email address. She tapped. My phone beeped in my pocket.

I asked. "Did Colin have siblings?"

"No. He was an only child, doted on by his mother."

"What about Colin's friends?"

She nodded. "I don't have those in my phone. But I know several of their names. I can email them to you as well. They were a close bunch. Several of the Tahoe Terminal skiers room together in a townhouse in Incline Village."

"Where do they practice speed skiing?"

"Sometimes they practice in the backcountry near Palisades Tahoe Resort. But they also set up their own practice speed-skiing course in the wilderness off the top of Kingsbury Grade on the South Shore. It's near where Colin's mother lives. Their course goes down one of the valleys toward Carson Valley. They can access it from the highway and use a car to shuttle skiers from the bottom of the course up to the top."

I gestured at her phone. "You were going to write down Colin's other friends?"

"I'm curious about your questions," she said. "How is it that knowing of Colin's friends could have anything to do with Colin's insurance company not paying the policy?"

"I have no idea. I've never investigated a situation like this. So I fall back on the basics. Learn everything I can about all people close to Colin Burns. Then I'll be better prepared when I try to pry into the insurance company and their reasons for denying the policy."

She seemed to think about it, then began tapping out names from memory, using her thumbs, speaking as she wrote.

"Colin's best friend from his childhood and the person who knew him best was Daniel Moretti. He's originally from Turin, Italy. Colin said he came over as a young boy and grew up in the Sierra foothills not too far from Colin. He still speaks some Italian from his boyhood in Turin."

"I've heard of Turin."

"It's where the Winter Olympics were held in two thousand six. It's a big city, close to the Alps. Danny was the person who first told the Tahoe locals about speed skiing in Vars, France. When they would travel to Vars, they'd often fly into the Turin airport. Daniel is a photographer and a very fast skier. He's also very kind. But…" she hesitated. "He's not very interesting." Then she seemed embarrassed. "Why am I telling you this? It is not important." She looked at her phone. "I've written down his name and phone number."

She continued to tap on her phone. "Another prominent person in Colin's world was Jackson Trane. He was the one who did much of the organizing. His mother had some kind of travel agency, so she could get them good tickets when the club members flew to Vars for competitions. Colin said that Jackson is a really good skier. He's gone almost two twenty-five K per hour, which is one hundred forty miles per hour." She continued tapping on her phone. "Nathan Menley teaches English to immigrants. He's the serious one. Focused on doing everything right, down to the smallest detail."

She seemed to think. "Oh, there's also Mo Beane. He's a

professional ski racer. None of these guys are slackers, as Americans call it. Mo Beane's specialty is the Super G race. He competed in the last Olympics. He didn't make the podium, but he was close."

"Can you tell me about speed skiing? I know nothing about it."

Geneviève took a deep breath and let it out slowly. "I only know what Colin talked about. The roots of the sport go back to an American named Steve McKinney. McKinney grew up skiing in Tahoe. He was apparently a bit crazy but also brilliant. He was the first man to break terminal velocity on skis when he went two hundred K per hour in Portillo, Chile. Sorry, I should always convert. That's one hundred twenty-five miles per hour."

"What made him a bit crazy?"

She shrugged. "Colin said McKinney was the first person to climb Mount Everest while carrying a hang glider. Then he used it to fly off the mountain. He set many world speed records, going faster every time. Colin said all speed skiers around the world revere the Tahoe skier Steve McKinney and the more recent skier, Jeff Hamilton."

A roar like a sports car revving came from outside. I turned and saw a dark metallic silver blue BMW racing up the steep street. It made a sudden turn and disappeared behind the restaurant.

Geneviève stood up. "Sorry, I need to deal with this."

She walked back through the kitchen door.

I wasn't sure, but I got the sense that she'd been expecting the blue BMW.

I heard noises, another door opening and shutting, and voices. A man spoke, but his words were not clear. A woman's voice, which sounded like Geneviève, was also unclear.

Then the man's voice raised in volume. "Where is it? You knew…" The rest of the words were garbled.

Geneviève's voice spoke, also louder, but I couldn't make out the words. Then two words were clear, "another week."

"I already gave you a week." The man was shouting.

I heard a loud metallic bang like someone slamming a pot down on a counter or maybe someone slapping a metal cabinet.

"Don't do that!" Geneviève said.

Then the voices grew softer. I couldn't hear the words, but the tone sounded threatening.

Then the man's voice was loud once again. "Okay, I'm coming back tomorrow. I expect to get paid what you owe."

I thought of going back into the kitchen to see if I could be of help. But it seemed things hadn't escalated to that point. Not yet, anyway. If Geneviève was in trouble, she knew I was right there. She could call out.

I went out of the door to the patio, touched Spot on his head as I walked past him toward the rear of the restaurant. The BMW's rear corner was facing me. The engine was running. Why? To keep someone else warm? Someone I couldn't see behind the smoked windows? Or was the man in her restaurant one of those blowhards who leaves his car running as a way to be more noticeable and take up more space?

I heard the sound of an unseen door near the car. A man who was thick with muscles appeared. He got into the driver's seat, slammed his door shut, and sped away before I could get the license plate.

I trotted back into the restaurant. I was back to the corner table when Geneviève came out of the kitchen. "Sorry for the delay."

"Everything okay?" I said.

"Yes. You probably heard me talking to a man. It is… very embarrassing. I owe him money. I was supposed to pay him today, but I'm…" She looked out toward Spot and Lazlo. "I had some other expenses so I won't have his money for another week or so. He's coming back tomorrow. Maybe I will have good business tonight and can get enough money to pay him tomorrow."

"I assume restaurant finances are tricky," I said.

She nodded. "My number one specialty is King Salmon, which I serve on a bed of sauteed greens with garlic mashed potatoes. It's very popular. My seafood distributor is obviously critical. But he has his own financial problems. Now he only sells COD. I have to prioritize his expenses over all others. Without him, I wouldn't be able to pay any of my other bills. Q always warned me…"

"Wait," I interrupted. "Q is…"

"Oh, sorry. After I got to know Colin a little, he said I could call him Q. It would be my private name for him. Anyway, Q worked at a restaurant, and he said he learned that the most important bills to pay were the ones that were from the critical suppliers."

"Q is an interesting nickname. Any idea where it comes from?"

"He said the Q was for quasi-normal."

I said, "Meaning he was partly normal?"

"Right."

"Why would he think he was partly normal?"

"I asked him that. He said he wasn't like most guys. He read books instead of watching TV. He liked poetry instead of sports. And that from a speed skier! Things like that." She stopped.

"You were going to say something else."

"This is embarrassing. He said he felt like a plain man next to me. Which doesn't make sense because, as you can see, I'm not a gorgeous woman. But he had a birthmark on his face. One of those purple colors that went from his right cheek bone up around his right eye. Most of the time he didn't act self-conscious about it. But I think he thought of it because, at the time, we were taking the first baby steps toward getting to know each other in a way that might lead to going out on a date. He probably wondered if I would mind spending time with a man who had a birthmark in a noticeable place. Anyway, maybe he thought that also made him quasi-normal."

"Did you mind his birthmark?"

"God, no. To me it was just part of how he looked. I cared about how he acted. What he thought about. Let's say I had a noticeable birthmark. Would that affect how you thought about me?"

"I don't think so. If it were significant, I might feel bad for you. But if anything, it might make me have more empathy for you. I might care more about you as a result."

"Well, that's the way I felt. Anyway, I called him Q from that point on. But Q was a private name that only we knew about. I felt privileged to have a personal name for him. Q was my dream boat. But I should call him Colin when I'm talking to you."

She seemed nervous, distracted by what had happened. It would be a good time to leave and let her get back to focusing on work.

"I have enough information to make some inquiries," I said. "I'll let you know what I find out."

She nodded absently, her mind on other things.

"Thanks for stopping by," she said. "I'll get my act together, as you Americans say, and I'll be better able to answer questions later."

I nodded, went back out to the patio, gathered the dogs, and left.

# SIX

The next morning, I took the dogs and headed to Truckee again. I was at Geneviève's restaurant around noon. Because her restaurant only served dinner, it was a good time to interrupt her work before the pressure of the dinner hour approached.

We spoke on the patio. Although the air was chilly, the sun was bright and hot. Geneviève again lit one of the propane heaters that was above a shaded area.

"Your dogs are beginning to feel at home here," she said.

"Yes."

"You have more questions? We can sit over here in the sun."

We sat. Spot moved next to Geneviève, his body touching her. She rubbed his neck. He gradually leaned on her, his shoulder against her shoulder. She had to shift position to brace herself.

Lazlo kept his distance from all of us and looked out at the street that led down to Truckee's main street. We could see one end of the train station. The Amtrak California Zephyr was parked just behind it. The train made very loud horn blasts and then slowly started to pull out toward the east on its way to Chicago. Lazlo stared at it with furrowed brow as if wondering if his master had escaped to another city by train.

I said, "You said Colin's father died. What can you tell me about Colin's mother?" I asked.

Geneviève looked at me suspiciously. "You are wondering about the Huntington's disease."

"To some degree, yes. But more important to me is getting a sense of Colin."

"Why would you want a sense of Q? I suppose I should call him Colin?"

"Because he is central to your world. And he is central to why you called me. Your trouble with the insurance company. We don't know if a crime has been committed. But if it has, standard procedure is to learn everything possible about the parties involved."

Geneviève was shaking her head as if very disappointed in me. "When you say that, I think you don't believe the insurance company has done anything wrong. It seems like you think Colin is the one who committed a crime."

"I don't know that anyone has committed a crime. But my experience with insurance companies makes me suspicious of them in principle. They employ adjusters, whose purpose is to whittle down any payout. Many policy holders, when confronted with a loss, simply want a fair payout. However, there are some policy holders who try to get more than they likely deserve. People with insurance go both ways. But while some people try to work the system to their advantage, all insurance companies try to reduce their payouts. An insurance adjuster's very existence proves conflict of interest between the companies and the policy holders. That's not to say that all insurance companies are unfair in how they handle policy holders' losses. But while policy holders sometimes push the boundary of what's fair, insurance companies always push back against those boundaries."

Although I thought my statement would make Geneviève feel relieved, she seemed to steel herself for bad news. "You think there's a possibility that Q... that Colin didn't tell the full truth on his insurance application."

"I have no knowledge about his application. But I allow for the possibility that Colin knew of his Huntington's disease and didn't disclose it. I will talk to Colin's friends and roommates."

"Back to your question. Colin was an only child, and he adored his mother. She worked as a nurse and raised him alone. When he was young, they lived in the foothills near Auburn."

"Her name?"

"Stacy Bell Burns. She goes by BB. Even Colin called her BB."

"I believe you said she lives near Kingsbury Grade?"

Geneviève nodded, picked up her phone, scrolled, tapped with both thumbs. "I have sent BB's information to your email."

My phone beeped as the text came in. I looked at it. "This street seems familiar, but I can't place it."

"It's off Kingsbury Grade. Way up high. I know how to get to her condominium, but I don't remember all the street names. The closest street is called tram something."

"Oh, sure, Tramway Dr. It's just three miles up from my office."

"I've been there a few times," she said. "Her condo is on a ridge with amazing views. You can see the lake one way. The other way, you look down at Carson Valley."

"Do you know BB well?" I asked.

She shook her head. "But we get along well. I was happy to see her now and then. But I didn't want to make her a big part of my life. That would mean losing something."

"I'm not sure I understand."

"Colin and I were very close. And part of that closeness is having privacy. A world just for us. I'm not sure how to explain it." She paused. "If two people make every aspect of their relationship public, telling others their inner thoughts, posting all their pictures on Facebook, there is less intensity between them. They are spread more thinly. But if their personal world is more private, a greater part of their lives is just about the two of them, then their relationship is more intense." She frowned, thinking. "Maybe that is a bad thing for some people. But it was good for Colin and me. If I shared everything about Colin's and my world with others—including with BB—it would dilute it. Does that make sense?"

I nodded. "Yes." I thought that perspective applied to Street and me as well. I glanced at BB's address on my phone. "What can you tell me about BB?"

"BB had Colin in her middle forties. Now she's about seventy. She's a retired nurse. Colin's father never earned much money. And the construction business is a boom-or-bust business. Not reliable. BB was the main income earner."

"Where did she work?"

"Most recently, at the hospital on the South Shore. When Colin was young, she worked at a hospital in Sacramento."

"She lives alone?"

"Yes. But she has good friends, one of whom is Marilyn, a neighbor who lives down the street. They're both big hikers. They hike together on the TRT during the summer."

"The Tahoe Rim Trail," I said. "It goes through their neighborhood."

Geneviève nodded. "And in the winter, they drive down the

mountain. You can usually find snow-free hiking in Carson Valley. Sometimes, the valley gets snow. Then they walk in the towns. Minden and Gardnerville."

"I'm familiar with that. My cop buddy Diamond Martinez lives in Minden. Could you call BB and ask about me visiting her?"

"Oui. Of course. When would you like to go?"

"Any time. Today, if possible."

Geneviève dialed her phone and spoke for a time. She paused, then said, "Thanks, BB," and hung up.

"BB was hiking. She said she'll be home in an hour. I think it takes more than that to get there from here? Is that correct?"

"Yes."

"So I said you'd come by this afternoon. Maybe two hours. Will that work for you?"

"Perfect."

I told Geneviève I'd be in touch tomorrow, and we said goodbye.

The dogs and I drove down the East Shore and turned up Kingsbury Grade.

In the rear view mirror, I saw Spot turn his head as we drove past my office. He knew this was a break from pattern. I turned right off the Grade at the top of Daggett Pass.

BB's street was steep and crowded with vehicles. I parked a block below her building, cracked the windows for the dogs, and walked up.

BB's building was long and narrow and designed so the condominiums had views in both directions, lake to the west, valley to the east. The condos had garage spaces below. Pedestrian access was by stairway. I found the number, hiked the stairs, rang the bell, and waited.

After a minute, the door opened. The woman standing there had brown eyes and short, curly brown hair. She exuded hiker. She wore a long-sleeved red flannel shirt, and long, khaki shorts with multiple cargo pockets and loops for attaching gear. The skin of her muscular calves was tan and had the fine crinkle texture one gets from years of sunshine. She wore thick white socks and white running shoes that were too bright to be anything but indoor shoes.

"Hi, my name is Owen McKenna. Geneviève Laurent called you about me stopping by."

"What?" The woman looked confused. "Oh, yes. Geneviève. How is she? We haven't spoken for... some time. Then she called."

"She's fine," I said. "I was hoping to ask you some questions about Colin. Could we talk?"

She frowned and looked out past me toward Lake Tahoe, a brilliant blue slash set off by the white, snow-caked backdrop of Mt. Tallac and the Sierra Crest.

"Yes. Yes, of course. Come in."

She turned and walked into a small foyer and headed up a staircase.

I shut the door behind me, then followed her. I stepped over two pairs of dusty hiking boots on a "Welcome" mat at the base of the stairs.

The stairs led to a living room with views that created a sense of being at the top of the world.

She walked to the middle of the room. "Do you want to talk here?"

Her demeanor was imbued with a sense of confusion. I immediately wondered if she had Huntington's Disease. After meeting Geneviève, I'd gone home and read about the confusion and other symptoms. She was older than the age when most Huntington's patients show symptoms.

"Yes, here would be good," I said.

She sat on a couch. I took a chair to one side.

I said, "Geneviève hired me to look into the insurance policy that Colin had, a policy that named her as the beneficiary."

"Yes. Of course. Insurance is a good thing," she said, general statements that didn't reveal anything.

"The company hasn't paid her because they say that Colin had Huntington's Disease."

"Right. She told me."

"To your knowledge," I said, "did Colin have Huntington's Disease?"

"Well, I don't know. Anything's possible, right?"

"I understand that Huntington's Disease is genetically linked, passed on from parents to children. Do you know if you carry the gene for Huntington's Disease?"

She frowned. "Well, I like to hike. And Colin likes to ski. So we have that physical connection. I'm no athlete. But I understand his desire to ski."

It was a nonsensical answer. And I noticed that she spoke of her dead son in the present tense. Habit? Or brain fog caused by Huntington's?

"It's wonderful that you had that connection," I said. "Did Colin ever ask you about Huntington's Disease?"

"No. He has asked me about my job. He wondered if it was stressful. Because speed skiing is stressful, I suppose. He also asked what I wanted for Christmas. But I'm retired. I don't need anything." She looked down and used her palms to smooth the fabric of her shorts. "He gave me these hiking shorts last Christmas. He couldn't be here. He was in France doing his speed racing. I haven't seen him for a long time." She made an exaggerated shake of her head.

I realized that I wasn't going to get any useful information from her. We spoke some more, and then I excused myself, thanked her for her time, and left.

# SEVEN

I drove north up the East Shore. Back and forth around the lake, giving my old Jeep lots of exercise.

The air was mostly clear, and I could see across the lake to Tahoe City. But the atmosphere had a sheen of sparkle in it. The sky seemed filled with micro ice crystals.

Just north of the picture-perfect arc of Sand Harbor Beach is Incline Village, Tahoe's second largest community after South Lake Tahoe. Of all the towns that ring the lake, Incline is the one with the tallest mountain backdrop. Relay Peak, Mt. Houghton, and Mt. Rose form a 10,000-foot wall that is close to the water.

I cruised past the turnoff to Lakeshore Blvd., known by locals as Billionaire's Row for the famous businessmen who have dramatic lodgings on the water. I turned right at the main supermarket and drove up the mountain a few blocks, turned twice more, and pulled into a cluster of townhouses.

Incline doesn't have much in the way of traditional box apartment buildings. If you are young and not wealthy, your main option for lodging is to rent a small townhouse and cram several friends in it to help pay the rent. Two people per bedroom is the norm. Three per room is not uncommon.

Geneviève had said that Colin Burns lived with four roommates in a two-bedroom townhouse. She'd given me the address. Although Colin had died the previous spring, she thought that two or three of the remaining four still lived in the same unit. Geneviève also said that two of them had worked at the local ski resorts, one at Diamond Peak and the other up the highway at the Mt. Rose ski area.

Because it was Thursday, I hoped that chairlift attendants were less likely to head to bars after work. I timed my visit to arrive at 5 p.m., when the ski resort workers would be likely to get home.

The parking area was designed like three irregular polygons arranged around five buildings that were attached to one another at the corners.

I found the townhouse number and parked where the door was visible. I left the dogs in the Jeep and walked up the entrance stairs, which were made of heavy lumber two sizes larger than necessary for the snow load. The big, thick steps could handle decades of wear from skiers kicking snow and ice off hard ski boots. The heavy construction also created an attractive rustic mountain look.

I stood under an equally over-built overhang and knocked.

After a minute, I pressed the doorbell. From outside, I could hear the bell ringing, so I knew that anyone at home would be aware.

When there was no response, I went back to the car and waited. Both dogs reached their heads forward from the back seat, sniffing my shoulders and neck as if to discover secret scents that had hitchhiked on me during the short walk back to the Jeep.

Fifteen minutes later, a small Nissan pickup that rode high on a jacked-up suspension came into the lot and parked in front of the townhouse. Its oversized tires seemed to go with the oversized lumber of the steps. Two young men got out. They both wore one-piece snow suits that looked like resort worker uniforms. One was navy with a red logo. That man carried a red backpack. The other wore a gray suit with white shoulder patches. Despite the bulky warm clothes, both men moved like athletes, the one in navy running up the steps two at a time.

After they unlocked the door and went inside, I waited a couple of minutes to give them time to change clothes or use the bathroom. Then I made a second trip to their door.

The door was opened soon after I pressed the bell. The man standing there was still in his navy suit. He'd taken off his knit hat. His mop of curly brown hair was substantial, seeming to add two inches to his height. He held a can of Coors Light in fingers that were noticeable for how thin they were.

He said, "Yeah?" A question.

"My name is Owen McKenna. I'm a private investigator looking into issues with Colin Burns. I was told that Colin Burns used to live here."

"Yeah." A statement.

"I was hoping to get some information."

He nodded and drank some beer.

"Would it be okay if I came in and asked some questions?"

Another nod. He turned and walked inside to a small living room with a large TV screen. It looked like an ominous black rectangular hole in the wall.

The man sat down on an orange couch. He seemed to sprawl back on one corner, his posture slouched, his legs spread wide. He drank more beer. I sat in a chair to the side.

"Colin Burns had a life insurance policy."

The man nodded.

"The insurance company is denying payment because they say Colin didn't disclose that he had Huntington's Disease. Do you know anything about that?"

The man made a thoughtful shake of his head. He didn't seem shy, but I'd never met someone who'd said so little. Since he opened the door, he'd said the word yeah twice and nothing else.

"You didn't know if he had Huntington's Disease?"

Another head shake.

"Did you know Colin had a life insurance policy?"

Another slight turn of his head to the left and then back.

There was a noise from the side. The other man appeared. He'd changed to blue jeans and a T-shirt. He had a towel draped around his neck. His black hair looked wet.

"Oh, hey," he said when he saw me. I raised my hand and was about to speak when the man turned away and went into the small kitchen that was open to the living room. He ran water into a mug, put in a tea bag, set it in the microwave, and hit buttons.

The man on the couch picked up a remote and turned on the TV. The screen lit up with a basketball game.

The microwave beeped. The other man brought his mug of tea and an open bag of corn chips out and sat on the chair opposite mine, near his roommate.

"I'm Owen McKenna, here to ask about Colin Burns."

"Jackson Trane," he said, raising his mug in a greeting. He glanced at his roommate. "The talkative one is Tamir."

I repeated what I'd said about investigating insurance.

"I think I heard that once. Makes you wonder. What company would insure a speed skier? I can just see the application process. At some point the skier would have to 'fess up, right? 'Oh, by the way, mister insurance agent, in my spare time I like to go a hundred fifty miles an hour on skis. No protection. No body armor, no air bags. Just me and the icy track and the rocks and trees next to the track.'" Jackson Trane shook his head. I couldn't tell if his disbelief was about the sport or the idea that an insurance company would write such a policy.

"Did you know Colin's girlfriend Geneviève?" I asked.

"Sort of. We met once or twice. Nice lady. Smart. Some kind of scientist, if I remember what Colin said."

"Were you and Tamir close to Colin?"

"Not really. We all skied. We bunked together. Tamir and I are both terminals, so we had that connection to Colin."

"Terminal..." I said. I remembered Geneviève mentioning the word, but I wanted to revisit the concept.

"The Tahoe Terminals," Jackson said. "All the guys who broke the speed barrier."

"Oh, right, the terminal velocity of a skydiver."

He nodded. "It's crazy when you think of it." He glanced up at the basketball game, then looked over at Tamir. "But while I'm a pretty good speed skier, Tamir is more like Colin. Bat-shit crazy. They'd rather die in pursuit of speed than be sensible. Of course, as a result, I'll never break their records." Jackson Trane seemed to have no awareness that he'd made a crack about Colin and Tamir being willing to risk death while speed skiing, and then Colin had done just that. He died less than a year before.

Jackson looked over at his roommate. "Tamir, you punched through, what, one hundred forty-eight or something."

"Forty-seven. But Colin hit one sixty on his death run. I'm slow compared to that."

The front door opened, and a third man came in. He was wearing dark brown dungarees spotted with stains.

Jackson Trane glanced at him. "Hey, Bob. Still kicking butt on those Subarus?"

The man named Bob nodded. He was a big guy in all ways except height. He didn't look athletic like Jackson and Tamir. He glanced at me, then walked down the short hall to one of the bedrooms.

"Bob is the non-skier in the family," Jackson said. "Helping us pay the rent."

"Do you know the other… Tahoe Terminals?" I directed the question to Jackson Trane, but would have been happy if anyone had answered.

"All of them. Bill Andreeson. He manages a fitness center and has a side gig as a personal trainer. Used to live with us. Then he got a boyfriend. So he moved in with him."

"Did he know Colin?"

"Sure. We Terminals are a close bunch. Not chummy close. Activity close. We've flown to the Alps together multiple times."

"On Colin's last trip to the Alps, when he died, did any of you go with him?"

Jackson looked at Tamir, then looked back at the basketball game. "I think most of us went. Right, Tamir? It's like a tribal thing. We share this primal pursuit. Fastest humans on the planet and all that. It's kinda like a religion. Kneel before the McKinney god and then go break his record."

"Is it really like that, a focus on Steve McKinney?"

"Absolutely. He pretty much created the sport. In its present form, anyway. And he still dominates all these years after he died."

"How did Colin fit into that?"

"He was at the top. Best of the best. Although there was a question about his last run."

"When he died," I said.

"Right. Some thought the fine-print rules meant your run wasn't official if you crashed. But the crash came after the timing zone, so they eventually awarded him the speed record. What's that called? Posthumously. Anyway, skiers still think Colin is the new McKinney. Talk about insane speeds. Danny got pics."

"Who?" I thought Geneviève had mentioned the name, but I wasn't certain.

"Danny Moretti. One of us Terminals. But Danny fell some time back and decided he wanted to live. So now he just goes to competitions as a photographer. Nate Menley replaced him, so we're back to six of us."

I didn't remember Geneviève mentioning Nate.

"Do Danny and Nate live here with all of you?" I asked.

"No. Nate is down in Reno. Works as an ESL teacher with immigrants."

"English as a Second Language?"

"Right. Danny lives up here, but not with us. He does athlete photography. Makes them look fantastic. He sells direct to athletes and also to big media companies, and he's got some books out. Like art photography but featuring sports stars. He makes big bucks. Bought his own house just past Kings Beach here on the North Shore. He's only three blocks from the lake, and his house came with some kind of dock and beach rights. It's a sweet deal. Now when you call his house, usually a girl answers the phone. And it's not always the same girl. If you stop by and he's out at the beach, he's always got some babe in a bikini with him. Sometimes, two girls."

"That's the life of a photographer?" I said.

"Ha!" he scoffed. "The groupies don't care about the photography, or skiing, either. Maybe not even about Danny. The attraction is just a homeowner with beach rights. But I shouldn't make fun of Danny. He's a real nice guy. And he's enjoying the fruits of his niceness."

"How many Tahoe Terminals are there?"

"Let me think. After Colin died and Danny quit, we were down to just four of us. Now, after Nate punched through terminal velocity and Mo moved here from Aspen, we're back to six."

"What's Mo's last name?"

"Mo Beane."

"How do you spell Beane's name?"

Jackson spelled it. "Mo started out as a Downhill racer. Went all the way to the Olympics. Then he discovered real speed and quit that pokey Downhill discipline." Trane made a little grin. "He calls himself Marvelous Mo on account of he's the only other Tahoe Terminal besides Colin to break one hundred fifty miles per hour."

"What does Mo stand for?"

"Got me. I think it's just Mo."

"His job?" I said.

"Waiter in a restaurant. Kind of like Colin. Only the restaurant Mo works in is stuffed-shirt fancy. Whereas Colin's is more basic Hungarian." Jackson Trane glanced at the TV. Giant men who made my six-six stature look short were stuffing balls through the hoops and they barely had to jump.

Trane continued, "Mo is our last Terminal. He used to bunk in Colin's room, but he fell in love with an Olympic snowboarder in

South Lake Tahoe and moved there to be with her. He even got a job in another fancy restaurant on the South Shore." Trane looked out the window. "It's amazing when you think about it," Jackson said. "There's only a few people in the whole world who can ski that fast. And a half dozen of them are right here in Tahoe."

"Do you practice speed skiing here, in Tahoe, or do you have to go elsewhere?"

Again, he looked at Tamir, who remained silent. "No place is like Vars, France, 'cause they have the perfect speed course. But you can work on technique anywhere. There's a ski run behind Palisades. One of the groomers helps out by running his snow cat down an area that's on the side of the regular run. Then he swoops around and makes a path back to the base of the chairlift. The Terminals go down to where the run turns. Then we hand-groom a path that continues straight down below the regular run. The extended run is pretty good for practicing speed runs."

"What do you mean when you say hand grooming?"

"Just old fashioned footwork. We sidestep our skis out of bounds from the official resort area and into the back country. Three or four guys making a thousand steps each creates a good run. Of course, after we ski it, we have to hike out and back up to the chairlift. But it's good for practice."

"Do the Palisades ski patrol know about this?"

"Yeah. But there's an underground buzz in the speed community. When the ski patrol finds out we're on their mountain and they pay more attention, we go to our own course off Kingsbury Grade."

"I've heard about that. But where exactly is it?" I asked as Subaru Bob came back out. He had cleaned up and changed clothes and was holding a Budweiser. He sat down on the opposite end of the couch from Tamir and looked up at the TV.

"You go up to the top of Kingsbury and turn on Tramway Drive. There's a condo strip up there, and the back side faces Carson Valley. Three thousand-some vertical. There's a scree slide in there that's free of trees. Nice and straight. Hidden from most angles. In the winter it makes a pretty decent speed run. And because it's on Forest Service land, no property owners hassle us. Not even the Forest Service rangers. Technically, we're just backcountry skiers, out for fun."

"At terminal velocity," I said.

"Right. Anyway, Colin's mother lives in one of those condos. So her place is kind of our base camp. We can park there and she'll feed us peanut butter sandwiches before our workouts and beer after. She's great."

"I met her. Nice lady," I said. "But she didn't have much info about Colin and his insurance."

Jackson Trane raised one eyebrow. "BB is a little spacey. She doesn't have all her thoughts lined up in a linear fashion. So it's hard to really find out what she knows about anything. Anyway, we created a course down below her place that is all hand-groomed. Fifteen hundred feet of vertical drop, just like Vars, France. Only the gradient is not so perfect."

"You sidestep the entire course to groom it?"

"Yeah. It's actually good conditioning exercise. Although sometimes we get this guy, who goes by Ref, to help groom it. He's got a long-track sled. It doesn't help with fresh pow, because the snow just blows away. But after we sidestep the run and compact the snow some, Ref can come down from above. He makes five or six runs side-by-side, always heading down because the slope is so steep that if he tries to go up, the sled track spins and shoots the snow out into a big mess. After Ref does his thing, the course is packed pretty sweet."

"When you say 'sled,' you mean a snowmobile?"

"Right. A Ski-Doo."

"Ref's name is…"

"Got me. He coaches and referees kids in the Carson Valley leagues. Baseball, basketball, football. Everything but ski racing. He doesn't even ski for fun. But something about speed skiing gets his blood going, so he likes to help out."

"There's no chairlift ride back up from this backcountry course," I said.

"Right. But the Kingsbury Grade highway goes directly below the bottom of our course about four hundred feet down in sagebrush territory. So we take turns driving shuttle, carrying each other back up after we run the course. The biggest problem is there's no good runout for braking. The course goes down and then gets less steep, but the transition isn't enough. It slows us down a little. But even after we've burned off our major speed, we're still running maybe eighty miles per hour. Normally, we would begin a skid until we slowed down enough to stop. But there's no place to do that on our Kingsbury course. So we have to carve our way into a serious turn, which takes us onto a path that eventually levels out and starts going uphill. If we make the turn, and if we don't fall or hit a tree, we come to a stop not too far from where the shuttle driver is waiting."

"It sounds really dangerous," I said.

Jackson held out his hands and turned them palms up. "Hey, it's speed skiing. Practically the whole point is flirting with deadly danger."

I asked, "Can you please give me the last names of all the Tahoe Terminals?"

"I think so."

I got out my notebook and a pen.

"There was Colin Burns, of course," Jackson said.

"His occupation was a waiter?"

"Technically, Colin was the sommelier at The Hungarian Restaurant in Olympic Valley. In case you don't know, a sommelier is the in-house wine expert. Teaches diners about wine and pushes them into buying expensive bottles. But Colin got fired just before he died. I actually think getting fired helped him break the speed record. It fired up his drive and motivation."

"Do you know why he was fired?"

Jackson shook his head. "No idea."

Jackson paused. "Let's see. You wanted to know the other Terminals. There's me, of course, Jackson Trane. I work up at Diamond Peak. And Tamir's last name is Horowitz." Jackson didn't sound awkward at all as he spoke as if Tamir wasn't sitting a foot away. "Tamir works at Mt. Rose ski area. I already mentioned Bill Andreeson, the personal trainer. You want me to spell that name?"

"Yes, please."

He spelled, and I wrote.

"Then we've got Nathan Menley, the ESL teach. And Tommy."

"Tommy's last name?"

"It's a strange one." He paused. "Ready?"

"Yeah."

"Woolgar." He spelled it. I wrote.

"Does Tommy live here?"

"Yeah. He and Tamir bunk in the same room. Tommy's day job is at a ski shop, fitting boots and tuning skis." Trane looked off, thinking.

"Then there was Danny Moretti, the photographer. I think his official name is Daniel."

I wanted to bring the subject back to Colin.

"Back to Colin's insurance," I said. "I already asked Tamir about it. Did you know that Colin had Huntington's Disease?" I asked.

"No. What's that?"

"A genetic disease where people have normal lives for a few decades and then they start to have problems with their brains. It affects their movements and thinking, too."

"Oh, that sounds bad," Jackson said.

I nodded. "It is. So I'm wondering if Colin ever mentioned anything about that?"

"No."

"Did he ever mention his life insurance?"

"No."

"It's possible that someone sabotaged Colin's life insurance by telling the insurance company about his Huntington's Disease. Do you know anyone who might do that?"

Jackson Trane made the briefest glance at Tamir. "No. No idea."

"Can any of you think of anyone who didn't like Colin? Anyone who might wish Colin harm?"

Jackson and Subaru Bob shook their heads. Tamir just watched the basketball game.

"The thing about Colin," Jackson said, "is that everyone was rooting for him. He sort of put the rest of us on the map just by our association with him."

I pulled out two cards and handed one each to Tamir and Jackson.

"If you think of anything that might connect to Colin's insurance troubles, please give me a call."

I thanked them for their time and left. They nodded and all stayed focused on the basketball game.

# EIGHT

Geneviève had given me the phone number of Daniel Moretti, one of the Tahoe Terminals. Jackson had said Daniel had given up speed racing for photography. I called and asked if I could meet with him and ask some questions about an insurance policy Colin Burns had.

"What kind of insurance would that be? I know nothing about insurance."

"It was a life insurance policy."

"Oh. That's certainly interesting. But, of course, I'm happy to have you ask questions. I'm working at home today. Why don't you stop by? Anytime in the next two hours would be good."

I found his house near the little town of Kings Beach.

The driveway was narrow and sloped up. It looked like it would be hard to back down and out from the house. I parked on the street near the driveway. The snow had been cleared, but the driveway was covered with ice. My pull-on ice cleats were under the driver's seat. I stretched them over my hiking boots and left the dogs in the Jeep, cracking the windows before I left.

The house was a large three-story box with a shed roof that sloped down to the north and angled up toward the south to let the sunshine into the house's windows. Projecting from the house were multiple decks facing multiple directions. Each deck had one or two sliding glass doors. The house siding was painted tan. The windows had dark brown trim making a strong design statement of brown rectangles on a big tan box. The end result was a modern cube with a lot of glass.

The lower level was part garage with windows along the top edge of the door. I was tall enough that I could see through the windows when I raised up on tiptoes. Inside the garage was a low-slung silver sports car, a model I didn't recognize. Next to it was a shiny black

Range Rover SUV. Summer car and winter car.

To the side of the garage was the front door entry.

I walked up to a large frosted glass door with narrower frosted-glass panels on each side. I pressed the doorbell button, then reached down and took off my ice cleats.

Muted footsteps pounded down an unseen stairway. The door opened.

The man standing there looked to be in his mid-to-late twenties. He wore tan Allbirds beneath black denim pants. His sweater was the same tan as the shoes. Visible above his sweater was a black turtleneck. Color coordinated.

"You must be Owen McKenna," he said. He reached out and shook my hand. "I'm Danny Moretti."

Moretti looked like the athlete I expected after Geneviève had explained that he was one of the skiers who'd broken terminal velocity. Moretti was 6-2 or more, about 200 pounds. His abdomen was flat, probably hard as a plank. His shoulders bulged, not with steroid show muscles, but the old-fashioned kind gained with nothing but exercise. He was clean-shaven with thick black hair that stood up in a wave above black arched eyebrows. He radiated outdoorsy health and fitness.

"C'mon in," he said. "We can talk upstairs."

He went up the stairs two steps at a time. I shut the door behind me and followed him at a brisk trot. At the top, I was huffing, he was not. I could pretend that it was because I was twenty years older, but I knew the reason was simply that he put more effort into being in shape than I did.

At the top of the stairway was a landing where the stairs doubled back and went up to the third floor.

Moretti walked into a large two-story, glass-enclosed living room that had so much light it was like being outdoors. I stood and looked up. The few areas of wall space between the windows were mostly covered with large, unframed sports photos, dramatic closeup images of athletes in action, some of whom were famous stars that I recognized. There was a baseball player caught at the moment his bat hit the ball, droplets of sweat flying off his face. A figure skater's ponytail swung straight out as she spun in a blur. A basketball player was nearly above the hoop as he dunked the ball. A tennis player's serve was photographed so perfectly that you could see the ball stretching the racquet strings back. A football player was in mid-air leaping over massed bodies, the ball held tightly in his arm, the grimace of intense focus on his face visible inside his helmet.

One of the largest images was also the most dramatic. A red-suited speed skier in a low tuck, heading down a run that seemed nearly vertical. Although the skier was in sharp focus, the background landscape was so blurred there was a powerful sensation of speed. The photo made me feel light-headed, so fast did the skier appear to be going.

"Coffee, beer, water?" Moretti said.

"None for me, thanks."

He nodded. He walked into the kitchen area, pulled a can of seltzer water out of the fridge, and returned to sit on a big overstuffed chair.

I made a sweeping gesture toward the photos spread across the walls.

"I take it these are yours?"

He made a modest grin and nodded.

"Very impressive," I said. "How did you get into photography?"

"When I was young, I was captivated by the work of a guy named Muybridge."

"That name sounds familiar."

"His first name was Eadweard with an unusual spelling." Moretti spelled it.

"He's the guy who did the motion studies, right? Forerunner of movies?"

"Oh, you know. That's cool. Most people don't. But I wasn't so interested in the movie connection as I was in the stop-motion photos. The first time I saw the racehorse studies that showed a horse's movement broken down the way a strobe breaks up movement, I was fascinated. From the time I was a kid, I wanted to try doing that with a camera. Taking sports photos was a natural extension of that interest."

He popped open his can and sipped. "How can I help?"

I sat on one end of a couch. "I'm here to learn more about Colin Burns. I believe you know Colin's girlfriend, Geneviève Laurent."

"Yes, of course, She's a sweet lady. Very serious, but sweet."

"She said you were very kind as well." I remembered that her comment was largely focused on Daniel Moretti being boring. Better to focus on the kind.

"Really? How nice," he said.

"She also said you knew Colin as well as anyone."

"That's probably true. We were best buds always. Although I was two years older, we grew up together near Auburn in the foothills. Went to school together, played sports together."

"Including skiing," I said.

"Yes. My parents started me skiing at the age of six. Colin was four, and his mom was too busy with her work to get him into skiing. His dad had already died at that point. Colin heard about skiing from me. So I eventually convinced my parents to let Colin come with us when we drove from Auburn up to the mountains to ski. I was nine, and he was seven when he started. He took to the sport with the same intensity he brought to everything he did. Of course, it takes some time to get good at skiing, and age helps. I was an accomplished skier as a kid. But even though Colin was younger, he very quickly got as good as me. Like a lot of kids, my main thing was speed. Why turn when you can go straight and fast? That got us in trouble with the ski patrols at every resort we went to. But Colin came with me all the way."

Moretti set his can of seltzer on an end table, leaned back in his chair, and laced his fingers behind his head.

"When I was very young, I'd heard about Steve McKinney and Jeff Hamilton and how their speed records had made the world aware of Tahoe. So I had to try speed skiing myself. I'd also heard about a speed-skiing camp some Tahoe guys were running, and I really wanted to go. But my parents wouldn't allow me to attend because they believed it was too dangerous. Of course, from the perspective of a parent, it was too dangerous. Extreme speeds but with no protection. But when I turned eighteen and was able to legally do what I wanted, I signed up. The camp was run by two guys who'd raced in Vars, France. You've probably never heard of Vars. But it has the fastest speed-skiing course in the world. One of our Tahoe camp leaders had skied with McKinney and had gone one hundred twenty. Not enough to win the top prize. After all, the record at that time was one thirty-five. But our camp leader was fast enough to get noticed. So the camp had street cred in the speed world."

Moretti sipped water.

"Of course, when I went to the camp, Colin wanted to go as well. Colin's mother was a little tentative about him going before he turned eighteen. And she didn't have the money for the camp fees or the specialty equipment or the plane fare to France anyway. She was emotionally supportive, but the speed-skiing expense was large, and a single mother couldn't afford it. Meanwhile, Colin had gotten a dishwashing job at The Hungarian at the Palisades Resort, and he'd saved all his money. He came along with the speed camp group and paid his own plane fare. He watched from the sidelines and cheered me on."

Moretti scooted forward on his seat so that he was leaning forward, elbows on his knees. A posture of excitement.

"I repeated that camp the next two years. Just before my third year at the speed camp, Colin turned eighteen so he was able to sign the form, and he'd saved enough money to join me and the other guys.

"There were five of us from Tahoe. We all made practice runs and got a feel for the place. On race day, I drew the toss and went first. I'd never done especially well in Vars. But with Colin watching and giving me support, I uncorked my best run ever and hit that magical one hundred twenty-five miles-per-hour mark. It was a great experience, let me tell you. I was so excited because I equaled Steve McKinney's first big record, or what our local group now calls terminal velocity because it is as fast as a skydiver falls. Of course, I had better equipment than McKinney had in his days, and I also benefited from the knowledge that it could even be done. Of course, McKinney went on to set many faster records. But mostly, I was relieved I hadn't crashed."

I asked, "Were you worried about doing well?"

"Not especially. But when I got up that morning to race, I felt that something had slipped in my resolve. It was a mental issue, not physical. I had no concern about the course or the weather. And everything else was perfect. But I suddenly no longer had that unshakable drive to be the best. And, to some extent, I felt fear creeping in." Moretti looked up at the photo of the speed skier hanging above our heads.

"In a sport like speed skiing," Moretti said, "there is no room for doubt or hesitation. And, especially, there is no room for fear."

He paused and leaned back in his chair.

"But then Colin raced. It was his first time down the course as an official race participant, and he blew us all away. He went one hundred thirty-one miles per hour! We knew he'd practiced hard on our Tahoe courses. But they're slower courses than Vars. For him to go that much faster than terminal velocity on his first race at Vars... It was amazing. The only skier who went faster than Colin that day was a Frenchman with years of experience." Moretti seemed to think back on the event. "I suppose it was Colin's immediate success that increased my thinking that I didn't have the focus of a champion. And that, plus losing my unshakable drive led me to thinking of another career." He paused and looked out one of the big windows. "I wasn't the only one affected. I believe every other racer in Vars sensed Colin's drive. And I've no doubt that some of those racers were like me in recognizing they would never have his intense focus."

I pointed up at the photo of the speed skier. "Who was that skier?"

"That was Colin a few years later, the day he broke one hundred fifty-two miles per hour. It was another astonishing achievement. Yet he kept breaking his own records. I had been to most of his races and documented them with photos. Right up until the end when he touched one hundred sixty. The rest of us were in awe. Actually, we're all still in awe. The whole world is in awe."

"Any chance you were in France last season when he set the world record?"

"Yes. I took photos of his record run. But I haven't done enlargements of them because they didn't have that spark that makes them special like the one up above us." He gestured toward the spectacular photo above my head.

"Any chance I could see the photos of his record run?"

"Sure. I keep them in a binder." He got up and walked over to a bookcase that was filled with three-ring binders. He ran his fingertip along them, pulled one out, and brought it over to me.

"Check them out. They're still exciting even if they don't sing like the one from a few years ago."

I flipped through the pages. What he said was easy to see. The lighting wasn't as good. The sky was kind of white with mist. The course didn't stand out as crisply. Anyone who wanted a truly remarkable speed-skier portrait would prefer the one that was on the wall above me.

Ironically, the photos in the binder that were most interesting to me were the ones without the telephoto quality. Those showed Colin Burns more like a red dot moving against a huge white slope. There was no sense of speed, no drama. The red dot showed just how alone the racer was. The only people in the frame were very far away.

"These really reveal how critical your telephoto lenses are."

Moretti nodded. "I'm always using a telephoto lens. But I gave a friend another camera with a normal lens as a documentary camera, to show the scene in wide angle."

I closed the binder and set it on the table near my chair.

I said, "You say one twenty-five is terminal velocity. How can a skier go much faster?"

"It all gets down to aerodynamics. A speed skier adopts a form that has very little resistance to the air. I suppose you could say that a speed skier is slipperier than a falling sky diver. The rubberized suit and the fairings on the legs help, of course. But it's the way a skier molds his body into a perfect tuck to slip through the air that makes the difference. If you watch a diving falcon, you see that the bird takes on a shape that is much different than its shape during normal flying. Same for a speed skier."

"What do you think was Colin's...you know, the thing that drove him to greatness?"

"His secret sauce? I know exactly what it was. It was fire."

# NINE

"Just to be sure I understand," I said, "when you say Colin's secret sauce was fire, you mean his internal drive?"

"Yeah. His motivation. I'm not the only one who will tell you that Colin did not have perfect technique. He didn't have the perfect athletic body. He didn't have the charisma that some champions seem to exude, something that some observers think helps an athlete perform at an extra level of greatness. But Colin had a fire unlike any athlete I've ever known or photographed. His determination was amazing. Like his favorite role model, the racehorse Secretariat, Colin was unstoppable. We all sensed it."

I asked, "Is there money in speed skiing?"

"Not in the sense of prize money. The only real money comes from endorsement contracts. Colin had some sponsors, a ski company, a goggle brand, two clothing deals. If he'd lived, he might have grown that into a good income. But dying as young as he did, he never got to that point."

I looked around at the nice house. "It seems that you've done well."

Moretti looked a little embarrassed.

"Yes, I have. It's all from photography. In the beginning I got good fees from media companies. But the real money came after I'd gotten good press for photographing some stars. Those guys spread the word that the right photo from me could go a long way toward building a sports brand. So I segued from traditional sports photography into the specialty of sports portraiture."

"Sports stars hire you to make portraits?"

"Yes." He pointed at the range of photographs above our heads. "Two or three of these photos resulted from companies like Nike hiring me to provide a certain look. But most of these came from the stars hiring me directly."

"I imagine the fees you charge are substantial."

"I guess you could say that. In addition to the photos, I sell athletes the copyright so that they can use them to build their brand."

He grinned. "In several cases, the reputations of sports stars have become inextricably linked to the photos I took. Those people get paid millions. They don't seem to mind paying me to make them look like gods."

"Do you still race?"

"No. I go to the races with my camera."

I pointed at the photo of Colin racing. "How do you get a photo like that? Do they let you get close to the course?"

"No. That was taken from a long distance with a long lens."

"Were you there when Colin had his fatal fall?"

He made a solemn nod. "Yes. It was horrible."

"Considering you knew Colin well, I would have thought he'd mention his life insurance policy?"

He frowned. "Yeah, you'd think so. Maybe he just wanted to keep it private. The policy surprises me, though. Not just that Colin didn't mention it. But I wouldn't think a speed skier could even get such a policy."

"I don't know the details of how they issued the policy," I said. "But the insurance company refuses to pay the beneficiary."

"Oh? I wonder why. I suppose there was some kind of clause that said the policy wouldn't pay if he died in a speed-skiing accident."

"Actually, no. They claim Colin had Huntington's Disease and didn't disclose it when he filled out the insurance application."

"What's that?"

"It's a genetic disease that I don't know much about. It takes a long time to manifest, but it is eventually fatal."

Moretti was shaking his head in confusion. "Oh, wow. More surprises. The man I thought I knew..." He frowned. "Anyway, Colin died in a ski accident, not because of Huntington's Disease, right?"

"Right. Furthermore, the policy had a ten-year term. Even if they'd known of the disease, the policy would have expired long before Colin would likely have had symptoms."

"But they're still being buttheads," Moretti said. "Colin's mom must be so sad about it." Then Moretti gave a little start. "But I shouldn't assume she's the beneficiary."

"Actually, she's not."

"Oh? That's interesting. The beneficiary must be devastated."

"Yeah. Insurance companies seem not to realize that their decisions can destroy lives."

I glanced again at the photos overhead. "I'm curious how you get such large photos printed."

"I print them myself. Follow me, I'll show you." He stood and headed down toward the front door. At the bottom, he about-faced and headed toward the back of the house. He flipped a light switch as he walked by, and a work space became ablaze with bright white overhead lighting. It was another large space, set up in two formats. Half the space was used as a gallery. It was carpeted and had a row of photos that stretched around the outer walls. The photos were more action shots featuring every kind of sport. The athletes were pictured in ways that made them look both accomplished and glamorous. In the center of the space were four upholstered chairs arranged around a conference table. On the table were loose leaf binders. I could imagine that an image-conscious athlete would walk around and gaze at the photos on the walls, then sit at the table, leaf through the notebooks, and find images that appealed.

The other half of Moretti's big workspace was set off from the gallery by having a white-tiled floor, two large, tall work tables on which photos could be spread out, and three over-sized ink jet printers that each had large spindles that could handle various rolls of photo-printing paper or canvas. Connected to the printers were two computer stations. On one wall were large flat files and vertical bins that held large cardboard tubes. Leaning against another wall was a stack of large sheets of white substrate, something like foam core on which photos could be mounted.

"This is where I print my work," Moretti said. He walked through the space, gesturing. "Computers, printers, mounting board." He pointed to a large machine that had big metal rollers. "This is my laminator. I can coat photos with glossy or matte finishes."

"You have a real pro setup," I said.

He shrugged and made a shy smile. "If you're an athlete and you want to look like hot stuff, I'm your guy."

Past Moretti were two cork boards, anachronisms in a modern

photo workshop.

"Mind if I look?" I said as I gestured toward the boards.

"No, not at all."

I walked over toward two bulletin boards, side-by-side. On the left one was a sepia-toned poster that showed a sequence of photos of a man on a galloping horse.

"This is Eadweard Muybridge's work, right?" I said.

"Yes. That's a horse named Sallie Gardner. She was one of several horses owned by Governor Leland Stanford. Stanford wondered whether horses ever had all their feet in the air, or did they always have at least one foot on the ground. Stanford thought horses are periodically completely airborne. He had heard about the photographer named Muybridge doing stop-motion studies. That was back when photography was still a new art. So Stanford tracked down Muybridge and hired him to study horses."

Moretti had appeared at my side. He pointed at the photos.

"Muybridge developed a way to take high-speed, sequential photos and proved that horses do, in fact, often have all their hooves in the air."

"You've probably studied the photos in terms of techniques you can use on your sports photos."

Moretti turned and grinned at me. "And then there was this other achievement in that his work made possible the development of motion pictures."

"Yeah, no small thing, that." I turned to the right cork panel.

It had many photos, cards, and notes push-pinned to the cork.

I recognized none of the people. But many of the pictures were of one young man. In some, he held a pair of very long skis, wore a red, skin-tight suit, and held a strangely-shaped helmet under his arm. In others, he was wearing jeans and held trophies. One of the photos showed him in a race, bent down in a low tuck, the background blurred similar to the large photo hanging upstairs. Beneath the group of photos was a printed piece of red card stock, trimmed to an inch high by a three inches wide. The letters said:

Colin Burns, Tahoe Speed Maestro, RIP

I leaned in to look more closely.

One of the photos showed Colin next to Daniel Moretti. Colin was smaller and shorter than Moretti. He didn't have Moretti's handsome looks or bright smile. Colin had a dark purple birthmark around one eye, and he was balding. He didn't telegraph the charismatic engagement that was so obvious with Moretti.

But even in a simple photo, I believed I could see that Colin had fire.

"One more question, if I may," I said.

Moretti looked at me.

"You knew most of Colin's friends. I'm wondering if he got along well with them? Was there any tension among them?"

Moretti shook his head. "No. Colin was a master of finding that balance between being the best skier but not having it get in the way of his friendships. Why?"

"As an investigator and former cop, I'm trained to look for discord."

"That's curious. Is there some way discord could affect his insurance?"

"Probably not. But I still ask."

I thanked Moretti for his information, said goodbye, and left.

# TEN

I called ahead and got Street Casey on the phone.
"I'm heading home after a day of swashbuckling, and I could regale you and Camille and Blondie with exciting tales were you to invite me, Spot, and Lazlo to dinner.

"Lazlo?" she said.

"A Border Collie I found abandoned in Olympic Village. I am temporarily his captain until I find his owner."

"Two dogs plus you. It would be like having The Three Musketeers for dinner," she said.

"Closer to The Three Stooges, but yeah."

"Presumably this rescue dog has good social skills, if you're willing to bring him into my living room."

"He seems polite. But I don't yet know if his chess game is up to speed."

"That's right. Border Collies are the ones who are smart as seven-year-old kids. Okay, bring him by."

Right after I clicked off, Frankie Valli started singing again.

I felt like the switchboard operator in a stage play.

"Hola," I said.

"Bonjour, Monsieur McKenna." It was Geneviève. "You speak español, if not Francais."

"Only hola."

"I'm calling because I remembered where I've seen the dog Lazlo."

"Ah, good."

"I was at the Modern Chef conference in Reno a few weeks ago, talking to the chef from The Hungarian Restaurant in Olympic Valley. The Hungarian is where Colin Burns worked before he got fired. The man had Lazlo with him. At least, I think the dog was Lazlo. He was wearing one of those Service Dog vests. I noticed because the chef wasn't blind, and he could walk okay. But maybe the dog provides a different kind of service."

"Do you know the man's name?"

"No. But I'm sure you could find out by asking at the restaurant. In fact, I think he's the owner of The Hungarian."

"Good to know, thanks. I'll be in touch." We said goodbye.

I realized that we'd found Lazlo quite close to The Hungarian. If only we'd canvassed the businesses in that direction. I could go back there tomorrow.

# ELEVEN

When I arrived at Street's, she let Blondie out, and the three dogs raced around the forest outside of Street's condo. Lazlo was reserved but he seemed more comfortable around Blondie than around Spot because, I think, she was closer to his size. I hugged Street. A shiver of attraction went through me, and I realized that we hadn't had much affection since Camille had come on the scene. There was no problem with that and no fault of any kind. But I missed private closeness with Street.

Camille came outside. I picked her up and turned in a circle. When the dogs were tired of running, I introduced Camille and Street to Lazlo. Lazlo kept his distance although he allowed Camille to pet him.

Street and Camille went inside.

Diamond pulled up in his antique, rolling rust machine that approximated a truck. He got out carrying a bottle of wine.

"Called your phone, got no answer," he said.

"Cell phone shadow," I said.

"Next best way to find you is to check Street's. Saw your Jeep and a whole lotta hound dogs running around. Suggested you might be around. I thought this might be an opportunity to see if a Windwalker Malbec would open doors. An ironic thank you from a lawyer in our cell for a DUI."

I leaned in through the door and called out, "Street, a grape-juice drifter is begging entry and trying to bribe me with wine. Probably a box wine he decanted into an upscale bottle."

"What's the bottle say?"

"Windwalker Malbec."

"Let him in. On the off chance it's real, it could be the start of his re-entry to the upper levels of society."

Street had been showing Camille how to set a somewhat elaborate table, possibly using more dishes and silverware than she ever did when she and Camille ate alone.

I walked over and smelled the beautiful flowers in a vase on the table. "Nice aroma," I said, although the smell was faint.

"Amaryllis," Street said. "My favorite winter flower."

"They're poisonous to dogs," Camille said. "So they go on top of the fridge when we leave the room."

"Smart."

Camille turned and saw Diamond coming in the front door. "Diamond," she said with delight in her voice. She ran over to him.

"Hello, Camille." Diamond was wearing his civvies, meaning he was off duty. "How is my favorite skateboarder doing today?" He did a bit of signing as he spoke, but stalled on the word skateboarder. He eventually mimed it by putting his feet in a skateboarding position, holding his arms out front and back, and doing a hula hoop sway as if he were about to lose his balance and crash.

Camille giggled. "I could ride my board while I help with dinner, but I don't think Street would like it." Camille took the wine that Diamond held.

Diamond walked over and gave Street a hug.

I looked at Street. "Perchance there are dinner tasks appropriate for a cop and a lonely private investigator?" I asked.

Street glanced at the wine that Camille held, then at Diamond and me.

"Yes. You can teach Camille how to open a bottle of wine."

I raised my eyebrows.

"Street Casey's finishing school for girls is thorough," Diamond said.

Street said, "Some day, it might be assumed she has these skills in her repertoire. So we may as well start instilling them now."

"Does she have a college picked out?" I asked.

Street shrugged. "No idea yet. Based on her current interests, it could be that she will want to do physical work as a forester or a home builder or maybe a racehorse trainer. She's reading those Dick Francis novels."

"Ah," Diamond said. "No kid books for the kid."

"She loves reading about the horses." Street opened a cupboard and set out three wine glasses.

"Okay, Camille," I said, turning so she could read my lips. "Time for wine skills."

Street said, "Diamond, are you okay having fancy wine with vegetarian tacos?"

"It'll be perfect," he said.

I wondered about vegetarian tacos. Tacos seemed to me to be a delivery device for beef or chicken or fish. Maybe wine would make them more enticing.

While Street finished dinner preparations, I showed Camille how to work the corkscrew and open the bottle. When the cork came out, Diamond spoke to Camille in a solemn voice that she couldn't hear but could probably sense as she watched him speak. He said, "If you take a long smell of the cork aroma and then make a serious nod of approval, people will think you're very sophisticated."

Camille widened her eyes with pleasure at learning the inside scoop. She picked up the cork, sniffed it, wrinkled her nose, and made a soft harumph of displeasure.

I explained how to hold a napkin at the rim and rotate the bottle after each pour in order to keep it from dripping. I demonstrated and promptly dribbled wine on Street's table. The volume was at least equal to the volume I'd managed to dribble into the glass.

Diamond flashed his toothy grin, which always looked dramatic on his dark face. Camille started giggling.

"Glad it was you, not me," Diamond said.

Camille looked at Street and said, "Can I taste it?"

"Yes, but I don't think you'll like it," Street said.

Camille picked up the glass with the splash of wine, carefully got three drops on her tongue, screwed up her face, and said, "Yuck!"

Street made a knowing nod. "Camille, would you please call in the dogs? We're almost ready to eat."

Camille nodded, walked over, and opened the front door. She put her fingers in her mouth and made a very loud wolf whistle. It was another one of those sounds that she must have learned by the feel of the vibrations.

The dogs showed up in a minute. Camille pointed to the dog cushion in front of the fireplace. She got all of them to lie down near each other. Blondie took a proprietary interest in her cushion and lay down on it before the other dogs could usurp her position. Spot and Lazlo seemed fine on the carpet. Spot made a big sigh, rolled over onto his side, and almost immediately shut his eyes.

"Tacos," Street announced as she served dinner. We all dug in. Then to me, Street said, "This is where you would explain to Camille when to pour the wine."

"Ah, of course." I picked up the bottle. "Typically, Camille, one would pour the wine a little before the food is served. I think." I handed the bottle to Diamond. "The honor goes to the gentleman with a surfeit of sophistication."

Diamond demonstrated, pouring a little for Street first. He didn't spill a drop.

Street took her glass, swirled the wine, smelled it, then sipped it, and pronounced it to be good.

"Why do you make a circle with the glass?" Camille asked.

"Because swirling the wine helps bring out the bouquet," Street said. "The aroma," she added.

I said, "Once she says the wine is acceptable, then it is okay to pour some more in her glass and pour the other glasses."

"Is that important?" Camille asked. "Saying the wine is acceptable? Or is it for show?"

I looked at Diamond.

"Mostly," he said, "wine protocol is about show." He poured Street's glass, then mine, and then his.

"It seems very fussy," Camille said.

"Fussiness is what ritual is all about," Diamond said. "Society often invests more in the ritual than in the underlying subject."

"What do you mean?"

"By several metrics, people care more about weddings than about marriages, more about the style of a car than the function of a car, more about clothes that look fashionable than clothes that keep a person warm and dry, more about whether a person is rich and famous than whether a person is good, more about whether a funeral casket is fancy than whether the deceased is well remembered, and, especially, more about whether a person is good looking than whether a person is kind, honest, and sensible."

"More about how to serve wine than if the wine is tasty," Camille said.

"Sí," Diamond said.

"Diamond's essential guidebook for life values," I said.

# TWELVE

The tacos were fantastic. Beans and veggies in spicy taco sauce, with brown rice, wild rice, shredded cheese, cut cherry tomatoes, and spinach on the side.

Street had cooked most of the moisture out of the mix so that the toasted taco shells stayed crispy.

The chili peppers and other flavorings were so well chosen, I didn't miss meat at all.

In time, I told them about Geneviève and the insurance company denying the payout from her dead boyfriend's policy. I made sure that I was facing Camille as I spoke, so she could read my lips. She was just a kid, but Street insisted that she always be included in adult conversations, and if she got bored, she could focus on something else. But she never did.

When I told them that Geneviève was French, Camille said, "Grandpa Charlie told me my name is French. How do you spell Geneviève's name?"

I spelled it, speaking the letters while also using the basic sign language letters that Camille and Street had taught me.

Camille nodded, then said the unfamiliar name with good pronunciation except for a hard G.

Street spoke and signed at the same time. She was getting very good with American Sign Language. "The G is soft, hon. Like the letter J."

"Does Geneviève speak French to you?" Camille asked, this time speaking with a soft G.

"No. She's aware that the only French I know is the word Oui."

"That means yes, right?"

"Oui," I said, grinning. Camille's knowledge was impressive for any kid, never mind a 9-year-old.

"While I don't understand French," I said, "Lazlo understands some."

Camille got an excited look on her face. She turned to Street. "I should say something to him in French! What would be good?"

"I don't know. You could look up something in Google Translate."

After Camille finished eating, she asked to be excused to look up French. Camille went over to the edge of the counter, pulled out a laptop, and started typing. She paused, looked out the window as if thinking, then typed some more. I saw her mouthing some words, using exaggerated lip movements as if memorizing foreign words.

She shut the computer and said, "I figured out how to tell if the dog understands French. And I studied the pronunciation guide. I won't say his name, and I won't look at him. I'll just speak French, and you will watch and see if he reacts."

"Okay," I said.

She turned toward the center of the room and spoke loudly in French. "Tu veux faire un tour?"

Lazlo swung his head toward Camille, his ears perked up. Blondie also looked at Camille but showed no excitement. Spot was asleep.

Camille made a shriek. "I think he understands!" Camille was bouncing on her feet. "I asked him if he wanted to go for a ride!" She ran over to Lazlo and rubbed the top of his head. "Good boy!" she said. "I'm sorry I can't take you for a ride." She turned to me. "Did Geneviève speak French to him?"

"Yes, that's how I knew he understands French. She asked, in French, if he wanted a cookie. Lazlo seemed to understand. Spot also heard her, but, of course, he didn't react."

Camille's interest in foreign languages was remarkable. The fact that she was deaf made it astonishing. Then she doubled the shock.

"If Geneviève speaks English but grew up speaking French, her English would have a French accent. What does a French accent sound like?"

I was dumbfounded. How would a deaf child even think of such a question? I turned to Street. "You can probably answer that question better than I can."

Street made a slight smile and shook her head. "I think you will do just fine."

So I turned back to Camille and struggled. "A French accent sounds like..." I trailed off, trying to think of how to describe an accent. I started again. "It's a very smooth and pleasant kind of speech. I think it is the most attractive of accents."

Camille looked frustrated. "But what does it sound like?"

I looked at Street. "What do you think, hon?"

Her smile widened into a mischievous grin. "I think you're doing very well."

Camille was waiting.

Diamond looked at the vase of flowers in the center of the table. "If accents were like flowers," he said, "a French accent would be like those Amaryllis flowers. Very distinct. Beautiful and elegant."

Camille partially stood up, leaned forward, put her nose to the flowers, closed her eyes, and took a deep sniff. She held her breath, savoring.

I looked at Diamond and spoke in a low voice. "You're good."

We all ate heartily and then mixed some taco filling with dry dog food and gave some to all three dogs, the portion sizes adjusted to each dog's size but kept small so they could run without stress. Spot used his "overnight" bowl, which we kept in Street's closet for just such occasions.

Because the wine was special, we saved half the bottle, recorked it, and put it in Street's fridge.

Then we took all three dogs for a walk in the forest behind Street's condo.

It seemed that we might be keeping Camille up past the time when Street would want her to move toward bed. So Diamond and I said goodnight, and Diamond followed me in his ancient pickup truck up the mountain to my cabin. I parked close to the camper pickup that Camille had lived in before Street adopted her. The pickup belonged to Camille ever since Grandpa Charlie died. With my Jeep tucked in close to the truck, there was room for Diamond to pull off the road and park near my front door.

Once inside, I lit a fire in the wood stove, and Spot and Lazlo immediately went to sleep. I opened Sierra Nevada Pale Ales. I took the rocker and Diamond the upholstered chair, and we sat in front of the flickering light and talked about Geneviève's dilemma.

Diamond said, "Learning that her deceased boyfriend had left her a large insurance policy would be a huge surprise that would possibly help in adjusting to his absence. But having the insurance company deny a two million-dollar payout would be as upsetting as an assault."

"Yes, it would," I said. But what stuck in my mind was a different kind of assault, the bruise on her arm and the man who raised his voice behind her restaurant. I told Diamond about it.

"You think the man caused the bruise," he said.

"Logical inference suggests that the bruise and man might be connected. But there is nothing to connect that to the insurance problem."

Diamond said, "Despite no logical link between the man and the insurance issue, the crime business has taught both of us not to abide coincidences. If we have a client with two separate problems, we have to consider every possible connection between those problems. To do that, you need to talk to Geneviève again."

"I'll do that tomorrow morning. On the way to Truckee, I'll also pull into Olympic Valley and stop at The Hungarian Restaurant and see if any of the employees know Lazlo."

We finished our beer, said goodnight, and Diamond headed down the mountain toward his tidy house in Minden, Nevada, a house which, although small, was more than twice the size of my 500-square-foot log cabin.

# THIRTEEN

The next morning, I let Spot and Lazlo into the Jeep, and we drove back north around the lake, headed up 89, and once again turned into Olympic Valley. We'd gotten three inches of snow overnight, which isn't enough for locals to even notice. But tourist skiers chasing snow always pay attention, so the giant parking lot was more crowded than normal. I parked out near the edge, and we made the long walk to Olympic Village. Once we were on the pedestrian street, we turned the opposite direction from the brew pub and came to The Hungarian Restaurant a minute later. It was late morning. I didn't know if they would be open. The pedestrian street was mostly empty. Lazlo pulled us forward as we approached.

Unlike the Tudor style of the brew pub I'd visited the day before, The Hungarian's facade was made of faux stone blocks as if it were a medieval castle. There was a large arched door made of heavy wooden planks. The door was five feet wide and looked like something you'd come to after crossing an arched bridge over a moat.

I pulled on the door. It was unlocked and swung wide open. I walked in holding Spot's collar and Lazlo's leash in one hand. The leash was taut with Lazlo's tug. He was eager to go inside.

There were no diners in The Hungarian. Apparently, they hadn't yet opened.

The restaurant walls were covered in heavy blood-red fabric. The floor was made of dark brown stone. There were just a few small windows that let in light from outside. The light filtered through small panes of colored glass, giving a soft glow to a huge arched ceiling made of countless red and brown bricks coated with dark heavy varnish. The ceiling was only eight feet high at the walls but rose to twelve or fifteen feet in the center. The restaurant looked as if we'd gone back in time several hundred years.

The tables were built of planks like well-built picnic tables. In the center of the big room, the tables were long enough to accommodate eight diners each. Around the sides of the room were smaller tables for two or four people. On the red fabric walls were several large oil portraits showing men on horseback. The men wore dramatic uniforms as if they were famous warriors from centuries before. Some of the warriors wore medieval armor. The paintings had thick, ornate, gold frames and were lit from the bottom by dim picture lights, which made the paintings seem very serious.

It felt as if the restaurant was an homage to a serious past when Hungarians were preoccupied with tumultuous wars, a time when there was little or no frivolity. A time when food was hearty and nutritious, with large portions that were filling but not fancy. I recalled the Hungarian food cart from the previous day. They'd served us what Americans call comfort food. Delicious stew that harkened back to favorite dishes from childhood.

I imagined that the focus of The Hungarian was the opposite of what Geneviève served at her restaurant, French food with delicate flavors and light portions.

Lazlo pulled toward the hosting station. We stood and waited. A minute later, a young man in his mid twenties came out of a back room. He wore a black bow tie on a wing-collar white shirt. I recognized him as the man who pushed the beverage cart and served us coffee and beer the day before. Today, he carried a tray with a dozen large glass beer mugs etched with THE HUNGARIAN.

He stopped mid-stride and stared at Spot. Then he saw Lazlo.

"Lazlo! Lazlo baby! Where have you been?"

He set the tray of mugs on a table, then came forward. He carefully stepped past Spot as if he was worried about Spot's reaction, then bent down to Lazlo, petting him and rubbing him.

Lazlo spun around, wagging with joy.

"Where did you go!"

Lazlo slapped his paws against the man's pant legs, spun again.

The man hugged the dog, lifting him off the floor.

Spot wagged as if waiting for his turn to get a hug.

The man stood up. "Where did you find Lazlo? Do you know where János is?" He pronounced the name Yahnoosh.

"We found Lazlo yesterday. He was shivering in the cold, leashed to a table outside the Brew Pub a block to the west. We were outside near the brew pub and got our beers from your rolling cart. Lazlo had been there for hours. He was probably there when you came by. Although he was around the corner."

"Oh, Lazlo," the man said, bending down and petting the dog again. "I'm so sorry." He turned to me. "We've been so worried about them. János left with Lazlo yesterday morning, and we haven't seen them since. I'm so glad you found Lazlo. But now I fear something bad must have happened to János." He paused. He tentatively reached out his arm and gave Spot a pat on the top of his head. "You know of János, right?" he said.

"No. The name János sounds Hungarian. He must work here?"

"Yes. He's the owner and head chef."

"His last name?"

"Szabó."

"Have you reported him missing?" I asked.

"Yes. Both him and Lazlo. I called the sheriff's office yesterday evening. They said to wait twenty-four hours because people who seem to be missing often return within twenty-four hours. I was about to call again now."

"That would be smart. Are you in charge when János is gone?"

"Yes, mostly. I'm Kyle Kramer, the manager. Julian is really in charge when János is gone. He's János's partner. Maybe part owner as well. I'm not sure. But he's out of town on a ski trek in the Cascades. He told us he'd be out of cell coverage. János said Julian wouldn't be checking in for another few days." Kyle glanced down at Lazlo. "So when János and Lazlo went out yesterday and didn't come back, I didn't know what to do." Kyle acted awkward. "You knew Lazlo's name. Did you know him before?"

"No. I just found his name on his collar tag."

"Oh, right. And he was leashed to a table? That's terrible."

"Right."

"Do you know János? Or Julian?"

"No. I'm a private investigator. I only learned of The Hungarian Restaurant yesterday."

Kyle looked down at Lazlo. "Did you give Lazlo some food? I'm not actually a dog person, so I don't really know how long he can go between meals. But we all love Lazlo."

"Yes, Lazlo's had food and sleep and exercise. Have you tried calling János? He's probably not out of cell coverage."

"Yes, I've left him a bunch of messages. William, our sous-chef, is good at running the show when it's slower. But last night was really busy, and it's too much for one chef. Of course, János can do everything by himself. Cooking, waiting tables, everything."

"Can you give me János's number?"

"Sure. Our contact info is on our business card." Kyle reached behind the hosting table and pulled out a card. "I'll add János's personal number. Mine, too." He wrote and then handed me the card. I handed him my card.

I asked, "Is it okay if I leave Lazlo with you?"

Kyle looked alarmed. "Oh, I don't think so. There's just me and Tammy and Alissa. None of us could take on Lazlo. Don't get me wrong. He's a good dog. Very smart. But we don't have the... You know, the space and such."

"How about William, the sous chef?"

"No. You don't want to go there."

"Why is that? Is he mean to Lazlo?"

"No. He's just... Trust me, you don't want to mix Lazlo and William. William can deal with people. More or less. But he's bad juju, if you know what I mean."

"No, I don't know."

"William has rough friends. I've heard some things... I'd hate to think of Lazlo depending on William and his buddies."

"Speaking of rough friends, have you been approached by any man who claims to protect restaurants from crime? Someone who charges cash to guard a restaurant?"

"No. That sounds like it might be scammy. Like in the movies."

"It is. I know of at least one other restaurant that's been targeted. If you are approached by a so-called guard, I'd appreciate it if you would let me know."

"Will do. Come to think of it, János said he'd heard about restaurants being burglarized, and he was concerned about security. Maybe that would motivate him to hire a guard?"

"Maybe. Did he mention any name?"

"No. I thought it was just a casual comment, not like he was making a plan."

A corpulent man came out of the back of the restaurant. He was in his late twenties and had a bland, round head with buzz-cut blond hair. He had a short black toothbrush mustache. Considering the blond hair, it seemed that his mustache must have been dyed black. Or, judging by the dark hair on his arms, maybe it was the blond hair that was dyed.

The man wore faded, torn blue jeans and a snug black T-shirt with a large motorcycle emblem on it. The shirt was tight enough that it seemed to cup and emphasize his breasts. His huge bare arms were covered in tattoos. At the neck opening of the T-shirt were tattoos that suggested his entire body save his head was tattooed.

"Oh, William," Kyle Kramer said, "this man found Lazlo!"

William made a single nod. He scowled at me and gave me the singular impression that his essence was about being mean. He didn't look in Lazlo's direction.

"I'm looking for the floor mop. It's not in the mop closet." His voice was high-pitched but rough with phlegm.

"I left it and the mop bucket out the back door to drain."

Another nod. The man turned and left.

"He's the sous chef?" I said.

Kyle nodded and looked embarrassed. "He's not the most personable, but he gets the job done."

I now understood that William wouldn't be a good host for Lazlo. He never even glanced at the dog.

"Let me know first thing if you hear of János's whereabouts."

"I will. We badly need him back running his restaurant. I don't know how long we can keep the place open with him gone."

I turned to go and was walking to the door with Spot and Lazlo when I had a thought. I turned.

"Kyle, were you here when Colin Burns worked here?"

"The speed skier? No. But I've heard of him. He was… I think I was hired to replace him."

"Do you know why he quit?"

"Um, maybe I shouldn't say, but William said Colin was fired."

"Did William say why?"

Kyle looked very uncomfortable. "William thought that Colin didn't like upselling customers. János has this thing where every time a customer chooses an item, we're supposed to suggest a more expensive choice, or an additional side dish, or, if they choose a wine, we're supposed to push them into a better bottle of the same type.

He always says that if you can increase each tab by ten percent, it makes a huge difference at the end of the year."

"And Colin didn't like to upsell the patrons?"

"That's what I heard. So János let him go."

"Oh. One more thing. Do you know where János lives?"

"No. He never talked about that. Let me ask in back." Kyle went into the kitchen and came back out a minute later. "Sorry, none of us know."

"No problem. It won't be hard for me to find out."

I turned and went out with the dogs.

I put in a quick call to Sergeant Jack Santiago.

"McKenna," he answered.

"I found out about the owner of Lazlo, the Border Collie we found at Olympic Village."

"Oh?"

"His name is János Szabó. He owns The Hungarian Restaurant."

"Where the food cart came from," Santiago said.

"Right. According to Kyle Kramer, the manager of the restaurant, János and his dog Lazlo left the restaurant the morning we were at the pedestrian street, and they didn't come back. Kramer has left messages for János but hasn't heard back."

"He file a missing persons report?"

"He tried," I said, "but he was told to wait a bit."

"Twenty-four hours."

"The time is now up. He will, no doubt, try again."

"Got it. I'll pay attention. Meantime, I'll see if we've got any reports of unidentified bodies, harsh as that sounds. Let me know if you hear anything else."

"Will do. Oh, I got János Szabó's phone number. Let me read it off to you."

"Ready," Santiago said. After he took the number he said, "Do you have a home address?"

"No. The business card only has the restaurant."

"Okay. Thanks."

We clicked off.

I immediately dialed János's number. I got his voicemail. I left my number and asked him to call.

# FOURTEEN

I knew that small restaurant owners worked all hours. Even in the winter when there were no farmer's markets to shop at for fresh produce, restaurateurs were at work in the morning receiving deliveries from suppliers, cleaning the kitchen and bathrooms, checking inventories, filling salt and pepper shakers and liquid candle lamps, posting specials on social media, arranging work schedules for wait staff and other employees. Even though Geneviève's restaurant was probably open until 10 o'clock in the evening, she would probably be there early most days.

It was mid-morning when I dialed the restaurant.

"Hello?"

One word. Same delicious accent. Elegant. Like Amaryllis flowers, as Diamond had suggested.

"Good morning, Geneviève. This is Owen McKenna calling. I'm sorry to interrupt your schedule."

"It is not a problem. I want to hear from you. You have something to report?"

"No. It has only been one day. I'm following up on our meeting."

"Okay."

"I have a question about the man who talked to you at the back door of your restaurant. He said he was coming back the next day, which would be this afternoon. After he left, you didn't want to tell me about him. But I'm thinking he may have something to do with the insurance company declining your insurance claim."

"But that is not possible. He did not know Colin or have anything to do with his death. It makes no sense. And he certainly can't be connected to the insurance company, which is in some other state. I forget where."

"Part of my business is to explore possible connections between problems. You have a problem with the insurance company. You also have a problem with the man who visited you. As you say, there may be no connection. But I need to be sure. I heard him raise his voice at you. I heard you say something about paying him later. I would like you to tell me the nature of your business with him, please."

There was silence on the phone.

I waited.

After a long period of silence, she said, "He is like a guard. I pay him to watch over my restaurant."

"Did you approach him?"

"How do you mean?"

"Did you look up restaurant security, get a referral, and then call him up and ask for his services?"

More silence. Eventually, she said, "No. I had a burglar two months ago. Someone had broken one of my door windows, reached in, and unlocked the door. The burglar came in and took the money in the cash drawer. I keep very little money at the restaurant. But it made me very nervous. The next day when the glass company came to fix the door, two men were walking by. One pointed to the repairmen and asked me if I'd had a break-in. I said yes. He said he owned a business down a few blocks and he'd also had a break in. He said he was organizing a neighborhood watch group. He said that in the meantime, he had hired a guard, who was the man he was walking with. He was showing the guard the neighborhood so the man could make plans.

"I talked to both men, and then I hired the guard to watch my business, too. This guard is big and strong and convincing, too. I've felt much better since I hired him."

"How much does he charge?"

Another pause. "Do you really think you need to pry into my business like this?"

"If you want my help, yes. I need to consider all aspects of your situation."

I could've made a slow count to ten before she answered. I was wondering if we'd been disconnected when she said, "He charges five hundred dollars a week. At first, I thought it was a great deal of money. But I haven't had any break-ins since hiring him."

"How do you pay him? Does he give you an invoice and you write him a check?"

"No. He likes cash. He says it saves everyone time and expense not to have to generate paperwork. It is like the neighborhood where I used to live in Paris. We had a neighborhood group. The group would send a man around to patrol. It was more effective than hoping the police would deter criminals. The businesses in the neighborhood would pay the man."

"How often does this man in Truckee come to collect?"

"It is usually twice a week. On Thursday I pay him two hundred, and on Sunday I pay him three hundred. When you were here yesterday, I could not pay him because the restaurant was so slow at the beginning of the week. That's why he was upset. I owe him money."

"Think back to the two men who were walking together and stopped to talk to you. Did the one who had a business that had been broken into, did he say the name of his business?"

She paused. "I'm not sure, but I don't think so."

"Geneviève, I don't want you to feel bad, but I'm quite certain these men are criminals. They're running what we call a protection racket. These people ask for cash, and they charge high fees. The chances are very high that they are the ones who broke into your restaurant. If you go down the street looking for the other man who said he had a business, you won't find him. The two men were working together. It was a setup."

I heard Geneviève gasp over the phone. "What? This is ridiculous. How could you know? You haven't talked to him, have you?"

"No. But this is what I do. I was a cop for twenty years. I know how criminals set up their scams."

"I cannot believe this." Her stress made her voice ragged.

"It's a common crime. Extortionists prey on people who are afraid to resist."

"If I stop paying him, he might break in again?" It sounded like she might start crying.

"Maybe. He might want to punish you for stopping. But if you hire a legitimate guard and have video cameras and motion lights installed, you may be able to convince him that there are easier targets to find."

"A legitimate guard, as you call it, and the lights and cameras, won't they be more expensive than this man's five hundred dollars per week?"

"Initially, yes. And you will have to do the work of finding such a person. But you can't believe people who come to you. You usually can believe people if you research them first, get referrals, and then you go to them. If we can persuade this man to go elsewhere, you could eventually stop hiring a guard, and that would be less expensive in the long run."

"It would be easier to just keep paying him," she said. She sounded very weary.

"True. But it's wrong. And as your restaurant gets more successful, he will raise his price."

"How would I stop paying him?"

"Just tell him you can't afford to pay him anymore. Don't threaten. Don't accuse. Just tell him you don't have the money."

"I... I worry he will find ways to cause trouble."

"Is there any way he can easily do that? Threaten you? Does he know where you live?"

"I don't think so. But I have a risk with my papers. My work permit expired. I'm embarrassed to say that I haven't followed all the rules. If the man found out about my permit, he could tell the government. I would have to go back to France."

"What about where you live? Are you vulnerable there? You said you live alone in an apartment next to the restaurant."

"Yes, I'm in the upstairs apartment, and my employee Jimmy Baker is in the downstairs room."

"Okay. I want you to be very careful. Try not to be alone. Don't go out at night."

"But when I close up the restaurant, it is dark. I am always alone, even if it's only to walk across to my apartment. Jimmy and I don't always finish our work at the same time."

"Do it at different hours each night. Carry a spray can of mace. Stay where there are lights. Don't be predictable. I'm going to show up at your restaurant today. I'll just sit out on your deck during the afternoon. If the guard man shows up, I will observe. I won't let him know that you and I have spoken." I paused, thinking about one more thing.

"There is another question I need to ask you," I said.

I heard Geneviève take a deep breath over the phone. "Okay, if you must." Her exasperation with me was obvious.

"When I was at your restaurant before, you had a bruise on your upper arm. I'm wondering if that came from the man. Did he grab your arm?"

This time she waited even longer before answering.

"Oui. It was from a week ago. Another time when I didn't have the money. He grabbed my arm because he was frustrated. Of course, you are going to say he is not allowed to do that."

"Correct," I said. "Any unwanted physical contact is what we call battery. It is a crime. You can show the police, describe how it happened, and he will be arrested."

"I… I'm not prepared to do that."

"Because you are afraid. That's another crime. Making someone afraid is technically assault. The two together are called assault and battery. He could be sent to jail."

I didn't want her to feel more anxiety, so I said goodbye and we hung up.

# FIFTEEN

An hour later, I was at the Truckee Police Department, which was out at the airport southeast of town.

I parked near the station house, left Spot and Lazlo in the Jeep, and walked in to tell the police my plans.

To one side of the front room was the entrance to a small jail. To the other side was a high counter, and behind it were two desks. One was occupied by a young man in a blue uniform. His name badge said Robert Emerson. He radiated newbie yet looked focused and serious about his desk work.

He looked up at me. "Help you?"

"Yes, please. My name's Owen McKenna. I'm a private investigator on the East Shore. I'm licensed in both Nevada and California." I held up my license. He couldn't read it from his distance, but he could probably see that it looked of a size and shape and style that made it likely legitimate. "I'm going to be doing some work in Truckee, and I wanted to inform you of my presence in town."

He frowned, thinking. "What kind of work?"

"I'll be on a stakeout at a local restaurant watching for an extortionist enforcer. If I find him, I may interview him. If he is resistant, I may try to persuade him to talk to me."

I held out my card. The man stood and took it from me. He appeared to study it carefully.

"I, um, should check with the lieutenant. Would it be okay if you wait a minute?"

"Yes, please."

The man went back through a door, was gone a minute, then came back.

"Lieutenant Oberman would like to see you."

I walked around the counter and followed the officer through the door. There was a short hallway. At the end was a glass-walled conference room where personnel would go over each shift's plan.

The other rooms would be used as offices.

The newbie officer made a diffident tap tap on one of the doors and opened it. He held it for me as I walked in and then shut it behind me.

There was a small window across from me and a desk on a side wall. Behind the desk was a thick man with buzz-cut gray hair short enough to show skin on his temples. He also wore a uniform, but this one had more chest candy than the officer who'd first greeted me. Ribbons, badges, embroidered emblems.

"I've heard of you, Owen McKenna," the man said, standing up. He reached out and shook my hand. "Ken Oberman," he said. His hand was huge and had as much meat on it as a catcher's mitt. His stubby fingers were so thick, he probably couldn't bend them all the way. But if the man put some effort into a squeeze, the result might be closer to a bear trap than a major league catcher plucking a ball out of the strike zone.

Oberman sat back down on his desk chair. I sat in one of two chairs in front of his desk. "It was Jack Santiago in the Placer County Sheriff's Office who told me about you. You used to be SFPD, right? Sometimes Jack has business in Truckee, what with Placer County rubbing elbows with Nevada County. So I sometimes hear of his cases." Oberman tipped his head toward the wall that backed up to the PD front room. "Officer Emerson says you're working an extortion case? We don't hear that too much in our friendly little town."

So I told Oberman about what I'd learned from Geneviève Laurent.

When I was done, he said, "It definitely sounds like a scam. You think the extortionist and his shill are just a two-man operation?"

"I don't know. The man's Beamer is a pricey ride, and his threats sounded practiced. So it could be he's part of a group. Resources, other bruisers, four-oh-one K plan. Although he collects in cash, so maybe his pension plan is in a mattress."

Oberman said, "Santiago said you're a funny guy." His voice was dry.

"Either way," I said, "I'm pretty sure I'll know the shape of his gig as soon as I talk to him. And I'll check him for swag that suggests he's not a one-man show."

"You mean ballpoint pens with their protection racket logo?" Now Oberman made a hint of a grin.

"Yeah."

Oberman regarded me as if he were trying to come to a decision.

"You know the routine on bracing suspects," he said.

"Everything needs to be admissible in court," I said. Not exactly the first principle I'd followed regarding what I'd done in the past and might do in the future.

Oberman nodded. "From what Santiago says, you sometimes get a little rough."

"I've never had any problem."

Oberman looked disbelieving. "I heard you were involved in an incident on the East Shore where a guy was—how do I describe it—vivisected. Normal lingo would say something more like he was smooshed between a truck and a tree and smashed flat. And you sort of helped him along on his journey. That true?"

"Yeah. Bad guy, bad situation. I tried to get him out of his truck. But I couldn't save him." More partial truth.

"And you've been sorry ever since." Oberman's words sounded sarcastic, but his eyes didn't waver.

I shrugged. "Not too much. But I'm still sorry the girl he kidnapped had to be there when it happened."

"I didn't know there was a kid there. How old was she?"

"Nine." My turn to give Oberman the steady eye.

"I've got a little girl who's ten," Oberman said at last. "That's a terrible age for a kid to be exposed to that kind of violence." His voice no longer sounded sarcastic. "If she were kidnapped, I'd hope you could be there to smoosh the perpetrator."

"Me too. Anyway, all I'm gonna do at Geneviève's restaurant is see if this brute shows up. If he does, maybe I'll talk to him. Nothing physical unless he gets mean and starts something." I didn't think it appropriate to explain that I went to meet Geneviève about the canceled insurance policy payment. Best not to change the focus of the situation.

Oberman said, "When do you expect this guy to show up?"

"Geneviève said he usually comes late afternoon on Thursday and Sunday. Two visits per week. I happened to be there when he came by yesterday, and she told him she didn't have the money. He started yelling and making banging noises in the kitchen. He said he'd come back today. I figure it's likely he'll come at the same time. So I'll be there to observe."

"She say how much the premium is?"

"Five hundred a week. She pays him his so-called protection fee in cash."

Oberman looked out the window. "Over two K per month." He looked back at me. "He chose to sell her his protection scam why?"

"I don't know. It might have something to do with her being French. Could be there's leverage there in her not feeling confident about restaurant owners' rights in America."

Lieutenant Oberman made a knowing nod. "Here's what I'd like to do," he said. "We've got two rookies in the department. You've already spoken with Emerson. He doesn't have a lot of initiative, but I think he's going to be a good cop. We've got another rookie we've just started training. She's even newer than Emerson. But she's got major potential if we can keep her around. I'd like her to go with you on your stakeout."

"You know that's a PI's last wish."

Oberman didn't react.

"Does she have cop training?" I asked.

"Nothing except book study. But she passed the tests. High score on the physical. Perfect score on the written."

"How do you know about her potential?"

"You'll know when you meet her. She's big and strong and smart."

"Why'd she want to be a cop?"

Oberman made another shrug. "As far as I understand, she went to UC San Diego and studied math. Then she worked for NASA, of all places. From what she said, the math nerds at NASA are as sexist as you can get. They're not accommodating to women, especially not to a large woman who looks and sounds commanding."

"So she ditched the NASA job to go in a direction where she might be more appreciated?" I said.

"Something like that."

"Can she go in plainclothes?"

"She needs to learn that her uniform, like her radio, is her most powerful weapon," he said, shaking his head.

"You want me to go on a stakeout with a mathematician in a uniform. That'll double the chance I get made. Quadruple the chance things go sour."

He nodded again.

"I much prefer to do stakeouts by myself."

"I'm sure you do," Oberman said. "But you're working in our village, and our rule book has a whole chapter about private cops needing to fit into our way of doing things."

I made a slow head shake. "So I take her off your hands and save you the trouble of training her."

"We're the ones paying her salary."

"What's her name?"

"Hattie. It stands for something else, but I can't remember what. Hattie Foster. When does your stakeout start?"

I glanced at the wall clock. "This afternoon. I'll plan to park down the road from Geneviève's at three-thirty and watch until six when the dining schedule gets busy. If the man doesn't come around today, maybe I'll be back on Sunday."

Oberman said, "Swing by the station at three and pick up Hattie."

"She won't want to be in my Jeep with my dogs. One is very large."

"She loves dogs," Oberman said.

"You're just saying that."

Oberman made a slight forced grin. "I can tell. She's got an outgoing personality. You know how dogs love outgoing people."

I gave up and left. I headed to a fast-food restaurant, bought five cheeseburgers, one for Lazlo, and two each for Spot and me. After we ate, I found a hose out back so Spot and Lazlo could drink a quart of water and rinse off their teeth.

I was back at the Truckee PD at three p.m.

# SIXTEEN

I once again parked in the far corner of the lot to minimize interaction between people and my dog cargo. I got out and was heading for the door when it opened and out walked an officer. She wore the blue uniform. She was a very large Black woman, over six feet and hefty enough that she probably had 25 pounds on my 215. She looked very strong.

"Are you Owen McKenna?" she asked in a big voice.

"Yes." I reached out my hand to shake hers.

"My name is Hattie Foster."

We shook hands. She gave me a powerful squeeze.

"Good to meet you, Hattie." We turned and walked toward my Jeep.

"Lieutenant Oberman said you're staking out a protection racket extortionist."

"Indeed." I looked at her as we walked. "Hattie is an unusual name."

"Yeah. Long, boring story."

"Like what we tell at stakeouts."

"Understood," she said. "The short version is my parents wanted to inspire me. My mother was a high school math teacher, and my dad taught Greek history at USC. So they named me Hypatia after a celebrated Greek mathematician who was born in Alexandria, Egypt in the early middle ages." She pronounced the name Eepahtia.

"For centuries, Hypatia has been a model for what women can achieve. She might have been the first feminist. But when I was a toddler, my parents learned that Hypatia had been murdered by an ignorant mob that hated intellectuals. How my parents missed that earlier is a case study in why parents should do some research before they dive into the baby business. So they started calling me Hattie instead."

"Yet, the lieutenant said you went on to study mathematics

anyway. Just like Hypatia."

"Funny how things work out, right? The thing is, I was a large baby and grew to become a very large woman. The list of careers that aren't good matches for a woman my size is as large as me. Add in my rebellious instinct, and I decided to pursue the career that got my namesake murdered."

"Has the Greek Hypatia always been a presence in your life?"

"Somewhat. It was another aspect of how I didn't fit in. My parents wanted a small, delicate, feminine beauty. They were hoping for contrast with my three older brothers who are all huge and two of whom perform on the professional wrestling circuit. Not only am I not delicate, I spent a measurable part of my childhood with my brothers teaching me how to do body slams, power bombs, and jackhammers."

"Did you try professional wrestling?"

"No. I drew the line when I realized that, even though wrestlers are actors, they still have to do piledrivers. The idea of possibly breaking someone's neck didn't appeal. Besides, I sensed a trend in the fighting world toward little women. The number of small cheerleader types in wrestling, boxing, and mixed martial arts is surprising. Viewers obviously like five feet tall, one hundred pounds, and beautiful if possible."

"Little women do piledrivers?"

"Sure. What could be more exciting than watching tiny pixies wearing almost nothing throw each other head first down onto the floor?"

"A world I've never considered," I said. "But then I don't watch male wrestlers, either."

"Oh." That seemed to surprise her. "Don't tell me you're one of those men who read books instead of watching televised sports." She paused to gauge my reaction. "Even if they're super entertaining theatrical sports?"

I shrugged.

"And now you're a private detective. Like the fictional detectives in books."

"But my life isn't that exciting."

She gave me a skeptical look as if reconsidering what she might have been told about me. "I'm new to the cop world, so this will be a learning experience. Do we drive in your vehicle?"

I nodded and pointed. "The old Jeep with the very large dog, whose head is out the window."

She looked where I was pointing. "Oh, a Great Dane! How fun. Doesn't he get cold in the winter with so little fur? But then, bodies stay warm as a function of body mass per unit of surface area. He has a lot of mass. His fur is short, but it's probably like wearing total-body long underwear. So maybe he stays warm like me."

"Good scientific description."

"Look, there's another dog." She sounded excited.

"That's Lazlo. A recently-homeless Border Collie."

"You adopted him?"

"No, he's lost, and I'm just dog sitting him until I can track down his owner."

We came to the Jeep. Spot had his head three feet out the window. He was wagging. Hattie walked up and, without hesitation, hugged his head. Spot's wag sped up, his tail whacking the inside of the door in one direction and Lazlo in the other. I could see Lazlo trying to duck and get away.

"Meet Spot, AKA His Largeness. And this is Lazlo."

While she hugged Spot, she reached an arm through the window and gave Lazlo a pet.

"Border Collies are the super smart ones, right?"

I nodded. "He can probably do basic math."

"Is His Largeness intimidated hanging around a doggie genius?"

"His Largeness isn't intimidated by anything or anyone."

"What about extortionists?"

"Especially not extortionists."

We got into the Jeep, Hattie being careful to accommodate her police duty belt as she squeezed herself into the passenger seat. I held my arm up to block Spot from reaching forward from the back seat and sniffing her face with his cold wet nose.

I started the Jeep and drove off.

I sensed Hattie turning in her seat and giving me a long look. "He told me I wasn't like any other job applicant he'd ever had. I don't know what that meant. Did he say anything else to you?"

"Just a few comments about your past work," I said.

"Anything you'd be willing to pass on?"

"The main ones were that you went to UC San Diego, you studied math, and you worked for NASA. I think he mentioned that because it's likely that no cop lieutenant has ever seen NASA on a cop employment application and resume."

She nodded. "I would have stayed at San Diego and finished my Ph.D. if I could've been invisible. But there's a lotta sexism among those JPL chalk pushers. Ironic, because JPL was one of the earliest places where women mathematicians were hired."

"JPL is the Jet Propulsion Laboratory?"

"Yeah. NASA took it over from Caltech in the late nineteen fifties. But I ended up in a rough arena where they don't like girls working on their conjectures. Especially girls who outweigh them by a factor of two. Even more especially, they don't like girls who can beat up their favorite superheroes. They made my presence untenable."

"If I may ask a philistine question about chalk pushers, what does a mathematician-turned-cop do with chalk and such?"

"At NASA, I worked in a corner of the three-body-problem world. I was making some progress in Giuseppe Lagrange's back yard."

"I heard about him on one of my cases."

"Back in the eighteenth century, Lagrange figured out how the gravity of the sun, the planets, and moons interacted to create gravity wells in space. They are often called parking places where we can put spacecraft. They're called Lagrangian Points."

"That also rings a very vague bell."

She continued, "Near those points are what's called weak stability boundaries, and they affect spacecraft orbits. This stuff was something that a Princeton University mathematician named Edward Belbruno figured out back in the nineteen eighties. He was working in chaos theory, and his discoveries changed rocketry and orbits."

"One of those super achievers?" I said.

"Maybe not in the beginning. I heard a rumor that he started out at a junior college and then dropped out. Now he's changed the world of space."

She turned and looked at me again. "I can see your eyes glazing over. Anyway, the new orbit stuff is very exciting," she said, her eyes sparkling. "For a mathematician, anyway" she added.

I came to the intersection at the edge of Truckee's downtown. I turned left on Main Street and headed west past the railroad station.

I asked, "What makes this weak stability thing exciting?"

Hattie continued, "It used to be that we burned a lot of rocket fuel to put a spacecraft into orbit. Then, if we wanted, we burned more rocket fuel to send a craft along to the moon or Mars or somewhere else. And, when the craft got there, we had to burn yet more fuel to slow the craft down for landing or whatever else we wanted."

"It's different now?"

"Oh, you wouldn't believe. Based on Belbruno's discoveries, we've developed math that allows us to send spacecraft on these looping orbits that go here and there, careening around Lagrangian points like they're just so many large objects rather than empty space where different gravity sources cancel each other out. Casual observation suggests this stuff is crazy. But it really works."

"Because of weak stability?"

She nodded. "Let's say we're trying to do some lunar exploration. We float a spacecraft into a region where the pull of the Earth, and the moon are equal. The spacecraft can barely sense which way gravity wants to pull it. Then we bump the craft into a lunar orbit. Sometimes it takes no fuel at all. If we wanted, we could bump it into an Earth orbit instead."

"Because the spacecraft has weak stability," I said.

Hattie raised her already loud voice. "See?! You could be a mathematician!"

"Except for the little problem that I don't know how to do math."

"Okay, a conceptual mathematician."

"Never heard of that. So the floaty loopy orbits burn less fuel," I said.

"Yes! Floaty loopy. I'm gonna tell that description to one of my JPL buds." Now Hattie was vibrating with excitement. I could feel the Jeep rocking.

"These paths take longer to get places, but they're hugely more efficient," she said.

"And it's all done with math?" I said.

She nodded, still excited.

"Then why'd you quit the math job?"

"Because I got so much shit. I thought, I can do this work at home. I don't need to rub elbows with the pencil necks who tell jokes about the priest, the mathematician, and the fat woman who go into a bar. I decided to get into a line of work where I can use my size by day and my brain at home by night."

I turned off onto a side street. "Is it working?"

"The benefits of size remain to be seen. From what I've heard, there are girl issues at most police departments. But I like the Truckee PD so far."

I pulled over and parked. In front of us, up a short hill, was the restaurant GENEVIÈVE.

"Saint Geneviève was a consecrated virgin, right?" Hattie said. Her broad knowledge made me think of Diamond.

I shrugged. "One more thing I've never heard of," I said. "I thought your gig was math, not history."

Hattie grinned. "So says the book-reading detective with philistine claims. My dad's history rubbed off on me. I think Saint Geneviève was born in Paris in the four hundreds, about half a century after Hypatia, who, interestingly, was also a virgin. One was a big deal in the church, the other was a celebrity in Alexandria, Egypt."

"And the church lady was canonized, while the math celeb was murdered."

"Life ain't fair, huh?" Hattie said. She looked up and down the street where we were parked. "What do we do now? Just wait?"

"Yeah. But I'm thinking about your uniform."

"I do stand out, don't I? If anyone walks nearby they'll see that I'm a cop and they'll wonder if I'm on some kind of work business. Not exactly incognito."

"Right. Let's instead go up to the restaurant and hang out on their patio. We'll look like Truckee locals who are just hanging out on a lovely winter day."

"And other Truckee locals might not pay any attention to a cop who was in the area and stopped to shoot the weak stability breeze," Hattie said.

# SEVENTEEN

Hattie opened her car door. "Do we bring the canines on this stakeout?"

"I've learned it's always a good idea to bring Spot."

At the sound of his name, he pushed his head forward and planted his nose on the side of my neck. I reached up and wiped nose juice off my neck.

"Is it because he can sniff out bad guys?" Hattie said. She was still sitting in the Jeep, the door standing open.

"Sometimes. Mostly it's because he's my sidearm substitute. I don't carry."

Hattie frowned. "I thought the lieutenant said you were an ex-cop. SFPD."

I nodded. "Twenty years. But I had to use my weapon on a bank robber who turned out to be a boy who wasn't yet a teenager."

"And you decided never to be in that situation again. You're the rare ex-cop with no weapon."

"Yeah. Except for His Largeness."

"Sorry to hear that happened." She sounded genuinely pained. "How does a law enforcement officer cope with gun-toting bad guys when the LEO doesn't carry."

"I have to be creative. Sometimes I resort to trickery and deception, and sometimes I have to duke it out. Once in awhile, I have to MacGyver my way out of situations. And Spot fills in now and then."

"But you wouldn't bring him if the threat level was high."

"You know about dogs," I said.

"Enough to know that having them shot would be like having any family member shot. I grew up with a Labradoodle. He was more loved than I was."

I opened my door. "So I try not to let him get shot."

I got out and let Spot out the rear door. "You can let Lazlo out the other side. His leash is attached. I'd appreciate it if you'd take charge of him."

"Happy to."

A minute later, we were walking up the hill to the restaurant. The sun was close to setting, and twilight was coming soon. Spot stayed at my side, his eyes and ears tuned to the surroundings. He was always alert when daylight faded, automatically aware that darkness presented threats that were non-existent during the day.

Lazlo pulled on the leash that Hattie held. We bypassed the restaurant's front door and went out onto the side patio. Both dogs showed their familiarity with the venue by ignoring the general layout and focused instead on the aromas, or odors, as the case might be, of the patio surfaces. Their noses were active and appeared to miss nothing.

The winter breeze was bracing. I remembered how Geneviève had lit the propane heaters. I found the sparker buttons and got two of them fired up. The patio instantly became a comfortable place. Because of the waning daylight, the yellow circles of the heater flames cast a warm glow.

"I'll talk to the proprietor," I said.

I knocked on the glass door, waited half a minute, then knocked again.

Geneviève came into the main room through the kitchen door and then stepped out onto the patio.

The dogs trotted over to greet her.

"Monsieur McKenna," Geneviève said. Her eye passed over me to take in Hattie.

"Hi, Geneviève. I'd like you to meet Hattie Foster, a new officer at the Truckee Police Department. She is on patrol with me."

Geneviève reached out and gave Hattie a soft fist bump.

"You are going to help on this problem of mine," Geneviève said. "Thank you in advance." She said it with no brightness in her voice. It was clear she wasn't enthusiastic about me showing up.

Hattie smiled. "Happy to help."

"Can I get you tea or coffee?"

Hattie looked at me before turning to Geneviève. "Coffee would be good."

"Same for me," I said.

Geneviève smiled, nodded, and withdrew backward with a little bow, a classic move of deference in restaurant service.

Through the window I saw a younger woman come in the front door and immediately go to work, checking the computer at the front hosting podium. She bent underneath, pulled out menus and counted them.

Then Jimmy Baker came out, spoke to the young woman, then went around and lit the candles on each of the six tables. The candlelit tables looked very festive. Unlike the day before, Jimmy was wearing nice clothes befitting an upscale restaurant.

Geneviève came out carrying a tray with coffee. She set it down on a table, then reached into her pocket, pulled out dog biscuits, and gave one to each dog.

She stopped and looked at me.

"You plan to intercept my business guard when he comes to collect his money."

"I just want to observe, not make trouble."

Geneviève glanced at Hattie. "But you have the police with you. So your assumption must be that the guard man will be a problem."

"Have you had any more contact from him?"

"No. In the past, he hasn't contacted me in advance of his visits." She turned to go. "Let me know if you need anything else."

After Geneviève had gone inside, I spoke in a low voice. "When I was here before, Geneviève had a bruise on her arm that the man gave her by squeezing her very hard. I didn't see him. They were out of sight behind the restaurant. I heard him raise his voice. Then I heard Geneviève say she didn't have the money and she would have to pay him next time. Next, I heard a car door slam, and the car left."

Hattie looked thoughtful. "What do you think might happen if he shows up today?"

"It probably depends on Geneviève. If she pays him as usual, he might just leave. But if she tells him she's not paying him anymore—as I've suggested—then he might get argumentative."

"What do you want me to do?" she asked.

"We will have to see what transpires and play it by feel. Last time, the man drove into the back alley from that direction." I pointed. "He parked behind the restaurant. My desire would be to have you stay out of sight but within hearing distance. It's clearly a manipulative idea, hoping that if he doesn't see us, he will be more aggressive."

"You want to bait him into acting."

"Yes. But he may keep his cool and not overreact. Even if we wait outside of his line of vision, we need to stay close so we can appear quickly."

"And if he acts out?" she asked.

"Lieutenant Oberman said you got a perfect score on your written, so you know the rules for assault and battery. If he gets physical with Geneviève, one possible result would be that you arrest him."

Hattie's face showed worry. "I've never arrested anyone."

"It's not hard. Be polite. Announce your arrest. Read him his rights. I'll be on his other side." I looked at a device on her shoulder. "It's good you have a BWC."

She nodded. "The Truckee PD requires body worn cameras and dash cams in their patrol units. Of course, I'm on foot patrol. So I just have the BWC."

I sat on one of the patio chairs under the propane heaters and sipped coffee. Hattie followed suit. Spot came over and nuzzled Hattie. Lazlo stood off to the side, looking across toward other town buildings.

There was the whine of a vehicle that sounded familiar, an engine revving as a car came up the hill on the other side of the restaurant. The sound grew. The dogs turned their heads. A vehicle was approaching from behind the restaurant, out of our sight. The whine dropped but remained a low hum, a vehicle idling.

A car door shut. There was a rapid thudding, someone knocking on Geneviève's back door. I stood up, took hold of Spot's collar, and moved toward the corner of the patio where I could hear better but still remain out of sight.

Hattie joined me. Lazlo turned his head and ears but didn't move. It was as if he knew exactly what we were doing.

There was the sound of a door opening, then a man's voice.

"You have yesterday's money?"

"Oui," Geneviève said. There was a pause as she apparently paid him.

"This will be my last payment," Geneviève said.

"There is no last payment. Your business still needs protection. You can't quit."

"I must. I cannot afford this expense anymore."

I leaned toward Hattie and whispered. "Get ready to step out where your BWC can point toward the man."

"You have no choice," the man said, his voice raised.

"I'm sorry. I'm broke. There is no more money."

"There is always money to save your business." He was almost shouting.

I tapped on Hattie's shoulder and pointed. She stepped out into the alley, moving slowly. I followed with Spot.

The man was visible at Geneviève's back door. He was facing slightly away from us. He was a big man, thick with muscles. Geneviève was beyond him, blocked from our view by his bulk. If she saw us, she didn't show it. I walked around the rear of the BMW, which was still idling. The car faced away from me. Despite the nearby building lights, the car's interior was hidden behind smoked windows. I pulled Spot with me into the shadows under a fir tree and next to an adjacent building.

I hadn't been able to get the BMW's license plate the last time I'd seen it, so I wasn't going to miss that again.

I looked at the plate, said it to myself three times. I pulled my pen out of my shirt pocket and reached for the notebook I keep in my pants pocket. That pocket was empty, breaking one of the first rules of investigating.

I wrote the license number on my palm.

"The arrangement was clear," the man said, nearly growling through clenched teeth. "I provide protection. You pay the bill."

"No," Geneviève said, pleading. "I won't. I can't." That was a surprise. I hadn't expected her to make that decision nor show such resolve if she did.

The man grabbed her upper arm where I'd previously seen the bruise. "You don't have a choice. It's a man's world, Frenchie. You pay, or you lose protection. And when that happens, you never know what might come next. Your business will be dead."

Hattie had moved up behind the man.

"Please take your hand off the lady's arm, sir." Her voice was clear but not strong like before. She'd said she had never made an arrest. Her fear was obvious.

The man jerked and turned to look at Hattie. He held onto Geneviève.

Hattie repeated herself. "Let go of the woman, sir."

He stared at her as if he couldn't believe a woman was a cop. He still hadn't seen Spot or me on the far side of his car.

He released Geneviève's arm with a jerk as if he were throwing something away. The jerk made Geneviève stumble.

"Sir, I'm Officer Hattie Foster with the Truckee police, and I'm arresting you for assault and battery. Step over and face the building. Put your hands behind your back." Hattie had unclipped her cuffs from her duty belt. She held the cuffs in one hand. Her other hand was touching the butt of her gun.

The man looked at her with wide eyes. Then he bolted. He ran around the front of his car, still not seeing me in the shadows. I didn't understand why he headed for the passenger door of his BMW. Perhaps just to have his car between him and the cop.

As the man ran, he was looking back toward Hattie. I stuck out my foot. The man's foot hit my foot, and he tripped and sprawled onto the alley. I couldn't see clearly, but it looked like his face hit the pavement and maybe slid enough to remove skin. His howl reinforced my perception. He thrashed and writhed and then pushed up onto hands and knees. His eyes showed shock as he saw Spot and me. I expected him to stand and charge. Instead, he reached and opened the passenger door and dove toward the seat.

There must have been another person in the driver's seat all along, because the BMW roared and raced away before the injured man was fully inside. I could have grabbed the man's ankles, but neither Hattie nor I had control. There was too much risk that one of the men might pull out a gun and shoot.

I watched the man pull his dragging feet into the car as it sped away. A moment later, I heard the passenger door shut as the car turned onto a cross street and headed down toward Donner Pass Road, the main street of Truckee. I could tell by the sound that the BMW turned west and sped away.

# EIGHTEEN

I walked toward the women. "You did well," I said to Hattie. I then turned to Geneviève and said, "Are you okay? How does your arm feel?"

"I'm okay. I'm—how do you say—very unnerved. He is a bad man. I think I always knew that, but now I am sure. Do you think he will harm me more? What he said, it was a threat, wasn't it? It makes me very afraid."

There was a ding. Geneviève turned toward the restaurant's back door, which was still open.

"Those are my first dinner guests. A party of four who pre-ordered my salmon specialty."

"Go," I said. "Take care of them. We'll finish up here and leave via the patio. Do you want me to come back when you close and escort you home?"

"No. I'll ask Jimmy to wait for me."

"Okay, I'll call you tomorrow morning."

Geneviève nodded and turned to Hattie. "Thank you for your effort." Geneviève walked back inside, rubbing her arm where the man had bruised her once again. She shut the door, and I was pleased to hear a lock click shut.

Hattie took a deep breath and blew the air out forcefully. "That was tense. A kind of debut for me. My first exposure to violence on the job. The most I've done up to now is write a speeding ticket. I didn't know the right words to say to him. And I didn't know the proper sequence. I felt like a such a rookie." She was breathing hard.

"It was a tough situation, and you handled it well."

"But I should have gotten him cuffed. I should be calling the sergeant for backup and transport as we speak."

"Don't think that. You stayed calm. It didn't escalate. Geneviève is safe. That's all that matters."

Spot walked over and stood next to Hattie, slightly leaning against her thigh. She rubbed the side of his neck.

"He knows I'm stressed, doesn't he?"

"Yes. Dogs empathize with people's emotions. They can tell whether you're happy or sad."

Lazlo had come to the alley, but he stayed back.

She took another breath. "What next?"

"I take you back to the station. You can write up this incident. I'll also give you the license plate number."

"You memorized it in that short period of time?"

I shook my head and held my hand up, palm out, so she could see what I wrote.

She looked as surprised as if I'd carved the number into a stone tablet. She pulled out her phone and took a photo of my hand.

"Lieutenant Oberman can show you how to access the databases and get the name of the car's owner."

"He already did."

"Great. Let me know when you find out."

# NINETEEN

The next morning, I met Geneviève at a cafe a block away from her restaurant.

The sun was shining in through a window next to our table. It highlighted Geneviève's cup and also made a harsh spotlight on the side of her face, showing the deep circles under her eyes. Through the glass, I could see her old Nissan and just past it my Jeep and the dogs with their heads out the windows. Beyond the Jeep and dogs, the road went up the hill to her restaurant.

She seemed to hesitate. "You wanted to talk to me about something."

"I want to get the autopsy report on Colin."

Geneviève frowned. "Why? What could you possibly learn? Colin died falling. A ski accident. It was witnessed by many people. There was no possible connection to Huntington's Disease."

"I suspect you're right. An autopsy is not likely to add any useful information to Colin's death."

"Then why pursue it?"

"Because it might add information. Those of us in law enforcement learn early in our careers that any death that isn't from natural causes deserves an autopsy report. States like California require an autopsy. Colin died in France. France also requires an autopsy in situations where the death is not from natural causes, such as an accident."

Geneviève took a deep breath as if exasperated by my statement. "I understand that you want the autopsy report. But I'd like to know what you might learn that you don't already know. And tell me how that would change the situation."

I thought about it. "Okay. Here's a situation that seems unreasonable but has happened. What if the insurance company conspired to create a situation that makes it so they could deny the payout?"

Geneviève was shaking her head before I finished my sentence.

"But insurance companies are big businesses. They wouldn't do something that is so obviously illegal."

"There are many examples of big businesses engaging in illegal schemes to increase their profits or to hide their problems. Enron, British Petroleum, Lehman Brothers, Volkswagen. All huge companies. There are many situations that motivate executives to pursue illegal, immoral actions. For example, higher profits bump the stock price, and nearly all executives own stock in their companies. An illegal scheme can put millions in executives' pockets."

"Okay, I understand that concept. Some companies do illegal things. But I'm still waiting for a reason why they would interfere with Colin's insurance."

"Denying your two-million-dollar payout makes them two-million-dollars richer. For a small cost, they can make millions."

"Of course I am very upset that they haven't paid me. They imply they think Colin committed fraud on his application. But how could they interfere in his situation to justify that?"

I slurped some coffee. "Let's imagine that Colin had told a journalist that he was so determined to set a new world record that he was willing to die trying. Imagine the insurance company read that. The insurance company might want to make it appear that he took a drug that would help him achieve his aim. A stimulant of some kind. More powerful than caffeine. Knowing he was willing to die, they could have spiked his morning coffee with a drug. Amphetamine or something similar that would suggest he took drugs."

"But that wouldn't disqualify his policy from the payout that was to come to me. The policy had already passed the three-year contestability period."

"Unless," I said, "they could plant information in his apartment or car that would suggest he'd purchased the same drug in the past, back before he applied for the insurance. They could hire a person to put some of the same drug in the glove box of Colin's car. Or in Colin's bathroom cabinet."

"You think insurance companies would go that low? Planting drugs?"

"I doubt it. The idea might not be likely. But it is absolutely possible. It would be nothing compared to what Enron did. They lost seventy or eighty billion dollars and then closed shop because of their illegal scheme."

Geneviève spoke slowly. "The planted drugs would make it seem that Colin wasn't truthful on his application."

"Exactly. The application Colin originally filled out probably has a statement saying that he hadn't ever taken drugs."

Geneviève said, "And if they put the same drug in his coffee—even just the smallest amount—it would be found in his system. The combination would be very convincing. Everyone would think that Colin lied on his application."

Geneviève was silent. She stared down at her coffee. Without lifting her head, she said, "If you knew the autopsy report, that would give you a direction to look."

"Right."

"But simply knowing what is on the autopsy report wouldn't make it so they had to pay on the policy. You'd have to prove that they committed fraud to try to prove that Colin lied on his application."

"True again," I said. "But if the autopsy showed anything unusual, that might give me an idea for how to proceed. Even if I couldn't prove they were illegally obstructing the payout, I might be able to make them sufficiently worried that they would pay you just to make us go away."

"Why even talk to me about this? Why not just go ahead and get the autopsy report?"

"Two reasons," I said. I drank the rest of my coffee and leaned back in my chair. "First, I want you to be comfortable with what I do regarding Colin. I'll be asking questions that could possibly be interpreted as impugning his character."

"What is this word, 'impugning?'"

"Oh, sorry. Impugning means to call into question someone's honesty or their character. To question whether or not they are legitimate."

"Oh. In French, we say impugner."

"My second reason to mention this to you is that I would need help. I don't speak French. It would take me many hours and much effort to figure out who to contact in France, how to get access to an autopsy report. Because you speak French, you could make the process much easier and faster."

"But I know nothing of this world. Why would the French

authorities tell me anything?"

"Because you are French and you are charming, and you would know the questions to ask to get to the right person. I don't even know the calling code to make a phone call to France."

Geneviève seemed to think about it. "I have no credentials in medicine or pathology or law enforcement."

"You could tell them the truth. You are calling as a translator for a law enforcement officer in California where Colin was born and where he lived. You are not an insurance adjuster or an insurance expert. I'll give you a short list of questions to ask."

"And what things do you want to know?"

"Anything unusual or surprising about the autopsy."

"Okay. What are your questions?"

"I'll write them down."

Geneviève went to the counter of the cafe to get some food and more coffee while I wrote in my small notebook. I tore off the little pages and spread them out on the table to make it easier for her to make sense of them. Some of my questions had arrows pointing to the edge of the page and these words, 'If the answer to this is yes, then ask this question,' and another arrow that pointed to the proper piece of paper.

Geneviève came back with two blueberry scones and two more cups of coffee. I said, "There will be international calling charges. You can use my phone." I held it out.

She shook her head. "No, thank you. I call my aunt in Paris every week. I have a good plan for that." Her eyes turned to my little pieces of paper. She read them, then moved them into a new order.

"I didn't bring a pen."

I handed her my pen and my blank pad of paper.

"I think," she said slowly, "that I should first use your computer to find out about Vars, France, where Colin died."

I nodded, opened my laptop, and put in my password. I opened a new tab. The Google page came up. I turned the computer around to face Geneviève.

She started typing. I could imagine what she might be looking for. But I had no idea how to search in French or look for French-specific information.

After a time, she looked at the questions I'd written down. Then she typed some more.

"Oh," she suddenly said, talking to herself. "Of course."

I didn't respond.

She typed some more and then picked up her phone and dialed.

I could hear a man answer in French. She started to speak to him and then realized his voice was a computer.

"Merci for nothing," she said and hung up.

She looked at me. "I always call my mother in the morning because France is nine hours ahead of us. And they have short business hours. It would be best to call when it is mid-morning there. This is when French offices are open but not very busy."

"Ten a.m. French time?" I said.

"Oui. So we need to call at one in the morning Pacific time," she said.

"Can you do that for me? I could pick you up. Or I could come to your place if you want to make calls there."

Geneviève frowned, thinking.

I said, "After you close the restaurant tonight, I could come to your apartment."

She shook her head. "Noise from my apartment is very loud in the room below. It would keep Jimmy from sleeping."

"You could call from my Jeep."

She looked at my notes and questions spread across the table.

"That wouldn't work," she said. "I would need space like this, at a table. And your dogs are in your car. We could go to an all-night place. But Truckee is asleep in the night."

"Some coffee shops in the Reno casinos are always open."

"I hate casinos," she said. "All that cigarette smoke and the endless loud beeping slot machines. You will wonder why we don't use my restaurant. But people leaving the bars walk by late. It is good for them to see the restaurant all dressed with linens and table settings and put to bed. Not like an office with people working on the tables."

"I understand. We could go to my office. But it's an hour or more from Truckee."

"Let's do that. I can sometimes think best when driving at night."

# TWENTY

We agreed to meet at my office. Geneviève would close her restaurant and drive down the East Shore. I checked the weather, and the conditions were supposed to be reasonable. I was at my office with the dogs at midnight. Lazlo was, as always, tentative as he came into the office, another new place for him that he'd never visited. It was as if Lazlo understood that visiting a strange place at a strange hour was suspicious. But when he saw and sniffed Spot's large black-and-white camouflage bed, he seemed to relax a bit. A dog can recognize acceptable conditions on the basis of past olfactory experience. He knew Spot's bed at the cabin, and that assured him that this bed in my office signalled a safe zone. After Lazlo made a tour of my small space, he crouched down on a corner of the camo bed. It was clear he knew he should leave a majority of the bed terrain clear, if for no other reason than to minimize the chance that Spot could hurt him as he lay down. Even a horse knows not to get crushed by an elephant.

After a minute, Spot lay down as well.

Geneviève showed up at 1:00 a.m. As instructed, she called my office number to let me know she was in the parking lot. I left the dogs in the office and trotted down the stairs to let her in the building.

"I hope the roads remained dry and the traffic sparse," I said as we walked up the stairs.

"Oui. I listened to a recording of the Gnossiennes by Erik Satie as I drove. It helps me stay awake and is calming."

Once Geneviève was inside the office, both dogs greeted her, Spot wagging, Lazlo holding back. Careful. Thoughtful. I had the idea that, because his owner had apparently suddenly gone missing, he was not going to trust anything in his life.

Geneviève gave them soft pets, looked around briefly.

"I made some coffee," I said. "I don't know good coffee brands, but it's freshly brewed, so it might not be too objectionable to a gourmet."

She nodded.

I poured two mugs and set one on the desk.

"Merci," she said. She picked up the mug and took a sip.

"I cleared off the desk so you'd have a place to sit and make notes if necessary."

She nodded and sat down in my desk chair.

I had put my notes to one side of the desk. She took her own notes and note pad out of her small briefcase and spread them out on the desk so she wouldn't have to sort them out of a stack. She looked the aggregate of papers over, frowning, and wrote some things on her pad.

She said, "Do you have a way for me to think about this before I start making phone calls?"

"Not much. I'm hoping you can call authorities in Vars, France. Although perhaps you'd call the next higher governmental tier. I forget what it's called. The Haut something."

"When Colin told me about racing in Vars," she said, "I looked it up because I'd never skied there. I remember that Vars is in the Hautes-Alpes department," she said, correcting my bad pronunciation. "There are ninety-six departments in France, which are government administration districts. They are a little like counties in California."

"Ah," I said. "I'm hoping you can find out who is in charge of handling accidental deaths in Vars."

"And thus who would perform autopsies," she said. "Or who is in charge of autopsy records."

"Right. But it won't be easy. I've read that France has a law called the Medical Secrets Act. Autopsy reports are only released to a physician who makes a written request, and the process takes up to nine months."

Geneviève's eyes got wide. "Ah, la bureaucratie française est impossible! How can we get past that?"

"We probably can't. But we can possibly go around it, if that makes any sense. I imagine that if one asks directly for an autopsy report, one is told to go through the standard channels. But if you could speak to the pathologist who performed the autopsy, or better yet, that doctor's assistant, or, perhaps best of all, an office person who doesn't have medical credentials at risk, maybe we can get a simple anecdotal response."

She frowned. "A response to what?"

"To the question, 'Was there anything unusual about the autopsy?'"

"And why would someone tell me that?"

I thought about it. "Let's imagine that I've met Colin Burns's fiancée, and, because you're my translator, I've told you about the woman and how she is distraught."

Geneviève said, "This is a joke?"

"No. Why do you ask?"

"Because I am Colin's fiancée. Was. And I am distraught."

"Oh. I'm sorry. I didn't realize you were going to be married."

"That's okay. I never told you. I'm still trying to come to terms with his death. My life had so much potential before Colin died." Her voice suddenly choked up. "And now he's gone."

She planted her elbows on the desk and leaned her head and face onto her hands. The tears came fast. Her breathing spasmed as her crying grew to full sobs. Tears dripped through her fingers onto my desk. One of the pieces of paper with her notes had a corner that curved up, and when the tears hit the corner the small impact made the paper turn. The blue ink from her pen dissolved into light-blue puddles.

It was as if thinking about Colin's autopsy made his death more painful.

She gasped, tried to breathe deeply, started coughing. As her crying intensified, she made small gasps of distress.

I stood up and walked around the desk. I set my hand on her hunched back and gave her a gentle rub, up and down. Her cries were gut-wrenching.

"I'm sorry, Geneviève," I said.

"No, I'm sorry. I shouldn't come apart in your office. You didn't ask for this. I just never…" her words were loud but nearly unintelligible and then were choked off by her crying.

I continued to rub as she struggled to breathe.

After a minute, in a voice a little less loud, she said, "Do you think I'll ever get over this? What will it take?"

"I think it's the same as what Colin told you about taking deadly risks skiing. You have to be 'tough as rocks, and you need the heart of a rose.'"

Geneviève inhaled again. She breathed heavily for another minute, then calmed a little.

"A month ago," she said, "I heard someone quoting a Robert Burns poem saying, 'But pleasures are like poppies spread, You seize the flower, its bloom is shed,' And I started thinking about how Colin quoted that poem so often. He always said, 'seize the flower,' and then he'd go on about how the seeds from the flower sprout, and the pleasure goes on to multiply. And when I heard it, I burst into tears because all I could think of was Colin's passion. No one I'd ever met had his romance, his sensitivity, his love of poetry."

Her back trembled as I rubbed it. Eventually, she reached into her purse, pulled out a small pack of tissues, and removed several. She blotted her eyes and blew her nose.

"I'm sorry that I am still so upset," she said.

"Anyone would be."

She took several deep breaths.

She said, "I need to work my way back to a situation in life where I'm helping others. I used to have that with the restaurant. Helping, serving, assisting... These are the things that put me on an even keel."

I nodded.

"Are you married?" she asked.

"No. But I have a long-term girlfriend."

"What is her name?"

"Street Casey."

Geneviève made a single nod. Unlike most people, she didn't comment on Street's name.

"Have you thought about getting married?" she asked.

The question was more personal than our short relationship called for. But I realized that Geneviève was just searching for ways to cope.

"I've twice asked Street to marry me," I said. "But she declines. We don't live together, but we're very close."

Geneviève said, "She doesn't want to feel like she is losing her independence and becoming part of a family..."

"I think so, yes. But she is adopting a nine-year-old girl, so now she has a family, anyway."

"Has she introduced you to her new daughter?"

"Yes. Camille and I have become good friends." There was no point in saying that I was the one who found the lost child and introduced her to Street, Diamond, Jack, and others.

Geneviève seemed to steel herself. "It sounds like you are even closer to Street than I was to Colin. If you can imagine losing Street, then you know something of how I feel."

"I think so. Without Street, and now Camille, I would be bereft. Life would have no meaning."

Geneviève nodded. She blotted her eyes again.

She said, "Is Street... I wonder what draws you to each other?"

"It's some of what you said about Colin. She is passionate about many things. She's a romantic who thinks a lot about matters of the heart. Love and idealism and friendship. She reads poetry, which I don't really know much about."

"She has a job?"

"She's a scientist. An entomologist."

"Insects," Geneviève said. Her voice revealed something, but I wasn't sure what.

"Yes. Maybe it seems a surprise, but that is part of her romanticism. She cares a great deal about the lives of all creatures, even the smallest ones. She sees the value in insects."

"Do you mean that they pollinate our plants so we have food?"

"That's good of course, but the values she seems to focus on are their persistence, their determination, and their patience against all odds."

"That does sound a little romantic."

"Street has told me that many insects also give gifts to the objects of their affection. Food is an especially popular gift. Some insects wrap their presents with silk before presenting them to their intended mate."

"Oh! Just like humans. Perhaps we're hard-wired to wrap presents. I may have told you I was trained as a geneticist."

"Yes. A scientist like Street."

Geneviève leaned back, arching as if to stretch her muscles.

"Okay," she said. "I'm going to make phone calls. I'll try to get through to someone who works in the medical examiner's office, someone who knows about Colin's autopsy report. Then I'll try to find out if there was anything unusual about..." She paused and shut her eyes. "About his death."

"Yes. Thank you for your efforts."

"May I use your computer?"

"Of course." I picked it up, opened the lid, typed in the password, and turned it to face her.

She typed a little, then wrote on the pad of paper. She took another deep breath.

"If this makes you feel self-conscious," I said, "I can take the dogs for a walk. I can give you privacy."

She shook her head. "No. When I was at the lycée, I studied theater and was in plays. We learned to not let the audience distract us."

"The lycée?"

"It is like high school in France."

"Ah, I understand."

She bent her head forward and appeared to calm herself. It looked like meditation. Then she picked up her cell phone, looked at the pad where she'd written, and dialed. After a long wait, she spoke in French. In time, she said, "Merci," then hung up and wrote on the pad.

She dialed again, spoke again, then went silent for a long time as if on hold.

I got out my cell phone to check email. There was nothing but some advertisements. I deleted them. I went to a weather website, then a news site. I kept holding my phone up in order to keep Geneviève from feeling like she was under a spotlight.

She started speaking French again, took notes as she spoke. Said, "Merci beaucoup," and then hung up.

I remained quiet.

The pattern continued. On one call, she spoke for a long time. Her voice alternating between cajoling and emphatic. Yet another call seemed to elicit great frustration. She spoke quickly, raised her voice, and then appeared to hang up on someone.

My desk phone rang just after she'd placed another call.

I stood up, reached for the phone, and answered it.

"Hola amigo," Diamond said in my ear. "Estas trabajando hasta tarde. You are working very late. I saw your office light and thought I should check and make sure someone wasn't making off with the McKenna art collection."

I glanced over at where I'd hung Camille's drawing of my Jeep with its smiling grill and cheerful headlight eyes. "Actually, it's Geneviève Laurent who's working. While you are speaking Spanish in my left ear, she's speaking French in my right ear. Maybe Lazlo the dog understands it all, but I'm having a monolingual brain cramp."

Diamond said, "You are at your office with Geneviève in the middle of the night, and she's speaking French, and you call it work. As a cop, I wonder if that's a euphemism."

"You wish. Geneviève is placing multiple calls to France in an effort to shake loose information about her boyfriend's death during the speed skiing contest."

"And you had her do this very late at night. Oh, of course. It's mañana in Francia. I'll let you get back to your inquiries. Adiós."

"Same to you."

Geneviève made another call, got stuck on hold, hung up. There were several calls where she sounded very appreciative, although one of them seemed like play-acting because she spoke with a smile in her voice, but hung up and acted exasperated.

It was an hour and a half and many calls later before she put the phone down. She made some more notes, then sighed, then looked at me.

"Any success?" I asked.

"Maybe. I probably don't need to explain all these calls and everything I learned. But the essence was that no one connected to the medical world would tell me anything."

"As we expected," I said.

"However," she continued, "I spoke to a police woman who said that she didn't really know anything but that she'd heard two other officers talking about Colin's accident and how his body was very damaged from the fall."

I nodded.

"Then one of the two officers said that he expected broken bones and such, but not a cellulose injury."

"Cellulose?" I said, wondering if I had heard that correctly.

"Right. So I asked the police woman about that in several ways, and she kept saying that she didn't know, and that what she'd overheard was unclear. So I practically begged her to give me more information. She again said that she didn't know why they mentioned cellulose. I eventually said that I wouldn't hold her to it and that I didn't even know her name, but that the law enforcement officer I was working for would very much appreciate it if she would just guess at why the other officers mentioned cellulose."

Geneviève paused as if to catch her breath.

"Did she have a response to that?"

"Oui. Her guess was that, when Colin fell, he'd struck a stick of some kind and it punctured his leg, and some woody material was in the wound."

"Woody material being cellulose," I said.

"Right. But the woman said something about it being confusing because the woody material wasn't like little chunks of wood. It was more like sawdust."

"Sawdust in a puncture wound," I said.

She nodded. "It doesn't sound like useful information, does it?" she said.

"On the contrary. That is exactly what investigating is all about. We always look for the kind of information that is not what we expect to find."

"But what possible use would hearing about sawdust be?"

"I have no idea. That's why it is useful knowledge."

Geneviève picked up her coffee mug and looked in it as if to see if there were a few more drops. She set it down.

"Would you like more coffee?" I said.

"No, thank you. I'm awake enough to drive home." She looked at her watch. "Do you think this was worth it? These phone calls?"

"Absolutely. We learned information we didn't expect. And we didn't hear things we might have expected."

"And this is information you were maybe hoping for?"

"Yes."

"What will you do next?" she asked.

"The call that came in while you were talking to France was my friend Diamond Martinez. He's a cop and very smart. He's good for talking over these kinds of questions. I'll see what he thinks."

"Will you call me if you hear anything interesting?"

"Yes."

She stood up and walked around the desk toward the door. I stood as well. She turned to me. Her eyes were still red.

"You really think this was helpful?" She sounded plaintive, which wasn't surprising considering that she had just spent hours talking about her fiancé's autopsy.

"Yes." I touched her shoulder. "I really appreciate your help."

She nodded, turned to the door.

"Are you sure you're okay to drive," I said. "I can follow you if you like."

"I'm okay. Thanks."

# TWENTY-ONE

I got back to my cabin at 3:00 a.m. After firing up the wood stove, the dogs and I got some sleep. We were up a few hours later. The morning had dawned sunny, breezy, and so cold that it reminded me of a time when I was in Fargo, North Dakota during the winter. I put on my big boots and heavy jacket, pulled on gloves, and drank my coffee from an insulated mug while I walked the dogs. We went north along the trail that hugged the west face of Genoa Peak. The trail was a mile down from the summit, so it wound and curved and lurched in and out of the ravines that had been carved out of the mountain by glaciers during the last ice age.

The mountain-hugging trail gradually climbed from 7200 feet up to 7600. When we got to the point where you can look down on Shakespeare Rock a few hundred feet below, we about-faced and headed back toward the cabin.

Back inside, the dogs immediately stepped over to the wood stove, crowding the cast iron. I opened the stove door, put some pieces of kindling on top of the coals that were left over from when I first got out of bed, and crisscrossed two splits on top. I slid the air input all the way open, and shut the door.

In a minute, sparks crackled and popped, making miniature fireworks behind the glass. Then flames grew. I got a second cup of brew, pulled the rocker up close to the stove, and called Diamond on my landline, something that was rapidly going extinct despite the fact that the voice quality was far superior to cell phones.

Because Diamond had called me in the middle of the night when I was at my office with Geneviève, I knew he had worked the graveyard shift. It was now late morning, and he might still have been in bed. If so, he would have his voicemail turned on.

However, he picked up. "Sí, McKenna."

"I thought you might be asleep."

"I'm experimenting with my diurnal sleep cycle, using the two-sleep cycle like so many did in the Middle Ages before electric lights. Sleep for four hours, get up for four hours, then back to bed for my second sleep. I'm about to start my second sleep. I have another night shift tonight."

I was used to Diamond's wide-ranging intellect, which, though interesting, could sometime be tedious.

"Is this going to be a Middle Ages history lesson?"

"A short one, yes. You just completed it. I'm handing out tests tomorrow. You have news?"

"Yes. Last night Geneviève placed calls to France in an effort to learn if there was anything revealing in Colin Burns's autopsy report."

"Was there?"

"Yes. Our information was third hand, from a cop who heard from other cops, who heard from medical personnel. You may recall that Colin broke the world speed record and then died in a fall at one hundred sixty miles per hour. He was seriously broken up. No surprise there. But the surprise was what they found in a puncture wound on his thigh. Despite the course being all smooth snow, it looked like he had hit a stick. And inside the puncture wound was some cellulose."

"From the stick?" Diamond asked.

"That's what one would logically think. But the French police woman Geneviève talked to said it was more like wood pulp. Sawdust."

"Interesting. Hold on a sec, por favor."

I waited.

"Okay, I'm back," he said. "Something's nagging my memory. I want to check on my computer." I heard him slurping coffee. "Sawdust and ice," he said slowly as if typing while he talked.

"We don't know it was a wound from a stick," I said. "It just looked like a wound a stick might cause."

"Right." I heard Diamond typing.

Eventually, I said, "You there?"

"Sí. Just doing some R and R." After a moment, he said, "Research and ruminate."

I waited.

"Ah," he said. "Here's what I remembered reading about. You

know about Pykrete?"

"No. What's Pykrete?"

"Back during World War Two, an inventor figured out that if you mix sawdust into water and freeze it, you get a very tough substance. If you lower the temp down to single digits, it becomes as strong as concrete, pound for pound. It was named Pykrete for Geoffrey Pyke, the guy who promoted it."

"Tougher than regular ice," I said.

"Much. And unlike concrete, it floats The inventor's original concept was to use it during winter to build a floating island on which to land planes. Kind of like an aircraft carrier made of ice."

"How would Pykrete explain cellulose in the skier's puncture wound?" I asked.

"It probably doesn't. But it could if the man was hit by a Pykrete bullet."

I said, "You're thinking that Colin Burns didn't get a puncture wound from a stick."

"Not thinking. Just wondering."

"Your idea implies that someone mixed up water and sawdust and then poured it into a little bullet form. They froze it and then somehow fitted the frozen bullet into a bullet cartridge that was pre loaded with gunpowder. Then they smuggled the gun into France, which has notoriously strict gun laws, loaded it with Pykrete bullets they somehow managed to keep frozen, and then, in full view of spectators, they shot Colin Burns while he was breaking the speed record on skis."

Diamond didn't respond.

I continued, "Even though this Pykrete sounds strong, it's hard to imagine Pykrete standing up to the stresses of explosive gunpowder."

"Yeah, the idea's a bit of a stretch," Diamond said. "I agree that a Pykrete ice bullet would be destroyed by the power and heat of gunpowder. But it's worth thinking about. Maybe someone threw a Pykrete spear at the skier as he flew by. Actually, don't even respond to that. Bad idea."

I said, "Valuable inventions sometimes come from ludicrous ideas, right?"

"Sure. I remember reading that the British dude who invented the modern umbrella was relentlessly ridiculed until people got over being called sissies for using them. Then the umbrella market exploded. Could be sawdust ice is waiting for an explosion in its demand."

"Back to your thought about Pykrete bullets, I stopped by Colin Burns's oldest friend, a guy named Daniel Moretti. He used to be a Tahoe Terminal speed racer but gave it up. Now he's a photographer of athletes, and he was in France taking telephoto pictures during Colin's world record run. He showed me the photos. Some of them were taken with a normal lens. They show the large distance between Colin and the spectators."

"Meaning," Diamond said, "that it would be unlikely anyone could have shot him in any manner, Pykrete bullet or lead-core bullet."

"Right. And with Colin going one hundred sixty miles an hour, the most accurate distance sniper would find it virtually impossible to hit him."

Diamond mumbled understanding. Then, "You got a plan?"

"Turn over rocks, see what crawls out. Good luck with your second sleep. And thanks for the ludicrous idea."

We hung up.

# TWENTY-TWO

A fter the wood stove was hot, the dogs arranged themselves on Spot's big mattress. Lazlo seemed more comfortable than the previous evening. He still wasn't friendly or affectionate, but he seemed resigned to his current situation. For several reasons, not the least of which was my tiny cabin didn't have much space for two dogs, I was determined not to take ownership of a second dog. But I nevertheless wanted to give him a good stay at the Owen-and-Spot Lodge and Spa. The most important thing for him was to track down his owner if at all possible.

Kyle Kramer at The Hungarian told me Lazlo's owner's name was János Szabó. I looked him up online. There was very little information, but I eventually found his address in Tahoe City.

Before we headed that direction, I called Street Casey.

"Checking in to see how you and Camille are doing on a cold morning," I said after she answered.

"We're well. How did it go at the French restaurant yesterday?"

"Not so well. I went there with a Truckee cop. The extortionist showed up and threatened the restaurant owner."

"That's a crime, right?"

"Very much so. The cop attempted an arrest, but the man escaped. So he's been warned off, but I don't anticipate it being effective. My hunch is that this turmoil in Geneviève's life might be connected to the insurance policy that the company refuses to pay. I have no idea why, but that's the way hunches work. So I wanted Geneviève to make calls to France and learn about the autopsy report on Colin Burns." I explained what Geneviève had found out, and then I changed the subject.

"How is Camille?"

"Camille appears to be teaching Blondie poker."

"The kind of poker one plays with cards?"

"As far as I can tell, yes."

"Is Blondie is a good student?"

"Camille acts as if she is. I think it's mostly like playing with dolls. However, I know Blondie understands some things. Camille taught her to recognize Aces. Whenever Blondie spots an Ace, she grabs it and chews on it. Three of the aces are now destroyed. But all the other cards are fine."

"Blondie has an ace up her sleeve."

"Diamond says you're funny. Or was it Sergeant Santiago?"

It was the second time I'd heard it in the last day or two. Which meant I wasn't funny at all.

"Lazlo probably already knows how to play poker. And read sign language. Is he getting along with Spot?"

"He keeps his distance, mostly just to avoid physical injury. But he's courteous, not condescending at all."

"They keep learning more about canine intelligence," Street said. "A new study says wolves are smarter than dogs when it comes to solving puzzles, but they can't touch dogs' emotional intelligence." Street went on to give me some details about what she'd read.

As Street was talking about intelligence, I thought about the sudden surfeit of intelligence in Spot's and my life. In addition to Lazlo, I'd just met Geneviève with her Ph.D. in molecular biology—or was it genetics—and now Hattie, who was close to a Ph.D. in mathematics. Add to that Street, whose Ph.D. was in entomology. The females in my local group were all highly educated, a trend that was growing in American society.

Meanwhile, I had a certificate that indicated that I'd put in time at cop school, and Spot nearly flunked out of the dog academy. Luckily, we had Diamond and Lazlo to hold up our end of the gender intelligence teeter totter. Besides, Spot and I relied on street smarts, but it wasn't clear how much we had of that.

When there was a break in the conversation, I said, "Would you and Camille like breakfast companions tomorrow?"

"Yes, that would be fun. But I should remind you that, other than eggs and milk, we don't have much animal protein."

"How does Camille feel about no bacon or sausage?"

"She can quote statistics on how much land and water and grain it takes to raise a pound of beef or pork. So she's onboard with plant-based diets. But don't ask her to give up sugar."

"I remember her strong thoughts about Honey Nut Cheerios."

"Right," Street said. "When does passionate desire morph into addiction? We'll find out in the morning. Love you."

"And you."

I finished my coffee, got into the Jeep with the dogs, and drove to Tahoe City.

I found János Szabó's house on a hill just northeast of town. It was a nice-but-unremarkable two-floor design painted a gray green with dark green trim.

I parked and let the dogs out. Lazlo raced to the door, then disappeared as he ran around the house. Spot followed him.

I knocked but got no answer. I went back to the Jeep for my gaiters and put them on to keep snow out of my boots. Then I walked around the house through two feet of snow. I peered in windows. Lazlo reappeared and disappeared again.

Because he was eager and excited but not distressed, I knew that János was merely absent, not lying dead inside.

Lazlo eventually stopped at the front door, pawing the outside edge, which showed a thousand scratches, obviously his way to signal the desire to come inside.

"Sorry, Lazlo. János is gone." I tried the door. It was locked. I made another trek through the snow and checked the back door. It was also locked. I thought of breaking in, but I didn't see the point. So I coaxed the dogs back into the Jeep, and we headed home.

Because of my sleep deficit from the late night with Geneviève calling France from my office, I went to bed very early. How she could be running a restaurant while I slept was beyond my comprehension. The fact that she had done that international calling because I had the whim that autopsy information might help with the insurance debacle was a little embarrassing for me and likely very stressful for her. There was no concrete gain, but there was a definite loss of both her time and her comfort. When she finally got to bed, she would be thinking about sawdust in her fiancé's leg wound.

The next morning, I drove down the mountain to Street's and Camille's, and we all went for a brisk winter morning walk.

"Where are you on the home-school plan for Camille?" I asked.

"Moving forward. I asked her again, and she definitely wants to continue what she was doing with Grandpa Charlie before he died. She told me she likes other kids, but she doesn't want to be held back by them. Just to be sure I was getting as much information as possible, I asked one of the teachers at our local school if it would make sense to just put Camille ahead a grade or two, and that woman said she'd recommend home schooling if I had the time for it. Then I asked Camille if she'd be willing to come with me to work, and she said she loved the lab and thought she could do useful entomology projects like studying pheromones."

"She knows about pheromones?"

"Yes. She says that not having hearing made it so she has always used alternative communication. She thinks that makes her suited to studying how insects use more than just their basic senses."

"Sounds brilliant to me," I said.

Street nodded.

After our walk, we crowded around Street's gas fireplace. Lazlo was alert, focusing on the door as if still waiting for his owner to suddenly walk back into his life. Blondie was not so alert, but awake and very aware of her surroundings. Spot was sleeping as if under general anesthesia.

After we warmed up, Street, Camille, and I ate oatmeal, and scrambled eggs, and whole wheat toast, and a fruit salad of oranges, apples, bananas, and berries imported from somewhere south of the equator.

Camille turned to me and said, "Street said you would miss having bacon with your eggs." Despite being deaf, her pronunciation was astonishingly good.

I nodded.

"Me too," she said. "Grandpa Charlie always cooked bacon or sausage." She took a bite. "And you're not eating toast."

"Yes, I am. Just slowly and without enthusiasm."

She leaned in close to me and spoke softly. "Dry toast is too dry. You can have some of my jam." She reached into one of her sweatshirt pockets and pulled out a restaurant-style packet of raspberry jam. She glanced at Street, saw that Street was focused on eating, and handed the jam to me under the table.

Moving my lips but trying not to make a sound, I silently said,

"At home I only have jam in jars. Where do you get these packets?"

"Street found them at Costco. She only lets me have one packet per day. That way, she can keep track of how much evil sugar I eat."

I continued with my silent speech. "Does she monitor how much sweet cereal you eat?"

Camille gave me a serious look. "One cup a day, maximum. Street says health depends on what we eat. But I think happiness is another kind of health. And sugar makes me happy."

I continued my lip movement. "I'm with you."

Even if Street couldn't hear me, she could hear Camille, thus our secret communication was not secret at all. No doubt, Street wanted to get Camille and me off our surreptitious subject. "You said a Truckee cop was at Geneviève's restaurant?"

"Yes." I told them about meeting rookie Officer Hattie Foster and going with her to the restaurant. I explained about Geneviève's bravery in telling the extortionist she would no longer pay him.

Camille said, "What did the bad man do?"

"He was mean. He grabbed Geneviève's arm."

"What did the police officer do?"

"She went to arrest the bad man for assault and battery, but he ran to his car and drove away."

"So now he's really mad." Camille's eyes were intense.

My cell phone rang.

I pulled it out of my pocket and looked at it. There was no 'Potential spam' message but no caller identification, either, because I had never learned how to enter contacts.

"Excuse me," I said to Street and Camille. I stood up, walked toward the door, and answered the call.

"Hello?"

"Owen?" Geneviève's voice. Very stressed.

"Hi, Geneviève. Are you okay?"

"No. There was a fire at my restaurant last night. It is gone. Burned to the ground."

# TWENTY-THREE

The news of the fire was bracing. "I'm at Street Casey's right now. I'll be there in an hour."

The firemen were doing cleanup when I got there, coiling hoses, stowing tools on the fire trucks, sweeping and hosing off the street so that traffic could eventually resume.

Geneviève's restaurant building had been reduced to a chimney surrounded by piles of ash all hemmed in by short, blackened remnants of walls. There were some twisted metal shelves and blackened sinks in what had been the kitchen area. A large black, metallic box lay like a bent parallelogram, and on it perched two smaller boxes. A microwave on top of an ice maker on top of a refrigerator? They had burned so hot that they sagged into a diorama of a black volcanic mountain range. The grill top was on its edge near a hole that went down into the crawl space. It looked like jail bars at the entrance to a cellar prison.

The four outdoor propane heaters had been melted off their mounts. The support posts lay on the patio floor, curved into a dystopian calligraphy of a post-fire message. They vaguely looked like childhood scribbles followed by the letters O S T. Everything is lost?

Every surface was covered in wet soot. The entire area looked and smelled like wet charcoal, stirred into mud.

Geneviève stood near where the front door had been. She was slouched and bent as if she too had melted, her face covered by one hand, the other arm holding onto what had been the brick wainscoting on the front of the restaurant, bracing herself against hurricane-force psychic winds.

As I walked toward Geneviève, I saw that she was talking to a fireman. I didn't want to intrude, so I thought to wait a few minutes.

Hattie Foster came along with a roll of yellow crime-scene tape. She was finding few places where she could attach the tape. The big woman looked up at me, her eyes wet with tears.

"The man made good on his threat, Owen. He said Geneviève's business would be dead. Then he made it happen. Maybe if I hadn't tried to arrest him…"

I spoke in a voice that was louder than I intended. "Please don't think that. You did the right thing. You were trying to protect Geneviève. You are not responsible." As I said it, I was thinking that I was the one who pushed Geneviève to stop paying the man. If anything, I was more responsible than Hattie for the result.

Hattie wiped her eyes with the back of her hand.

I added, "It may well be that the extortionist set fire to Geneviève's restaurant, but that hasn't been established yet."

"You're right. Sorry about that presumption. But if he did burn down her restaurant…"

Hattie's voice was full of venom.

"Any chance you were able to run the license plate we got the other night?" I asked.

She nodded. "The plate you saw belongs to an eighty-six-year-old woman in San Jose. She has a similar kind of BMW. Even the same blue metallic color. I got her on the phone. She went into her garage and looked at her car. She thought the numbers looked different. I looked it up. The plates that are currently on her car belong to a Ford Escape. She took a picture with her phone and emailed it to me. She has no clear idea when and where her plates were stolen and switched. She thought it might have been when she got groceries at the supermarket last week." Hattie held her phone out so I could see it.

I looked at the photo. It revealed nothing beyond what Hattie had said.

"Do you know where the Ford Escape belongs?"

"Yes. The address attached to that plate number is in Fremont. Not too far from San Jose. I haven't contacted that owner to see what plate is currently on the Ford."

I nodded understanding. "You can put a BOLO on the San Jose plates that are on the bad guy's car. If it shows up on any ALPRS camera, that would be revealing."

Hattie frowned. "I've heard about ALPRS..."

"Automatic license plate readers," I said. "There are quite a few in the Tahoe Truckee area, mostly on utility poles at intersections."

Hattie wrote in her notebook, ever the good student.

"Now that I think of it," I said, "I think the Truckee PD patrol vehicles have them."

"Oh." She looked up at me. "That's where I learned about it. You can be on patrol and you get an alert if the plates on the car in front of you have been linked to a car that was reported stolen. But, if I'm understanding this correctly, if the plates were taken from another car and that owner hasn't noticed, they won't trigger an alert. Of course, the bad guy may have already switched to another set of stolen plates."

"Keep me informed as you learn more?"

"Yes, of course."

I saw that the fireman was finishing with Geneviève.

"I'll go talk to Geneviève," I said.

Hattie nodded.

I walked over and approached slowly.

Geneviève looked up at me. Her eyes showed the fear and terror one would expect of someone who'd just lost everything. She shook with tremors.

"I'm so sorry, Geneviève. So sorry."

She looked like she was about to collapse to the ground. I didn't know what else to say. I finally uttered, "Do they know how your restaurant caught on fire?"

She shook her head. It seemed just the head movement was a crushing effort.

I said, "The restaurant is a total loss. But you are okay. That is the main thing."

She shook her head. "It's not just the restaurant." She pointed toward the brick chimney, the only part of the restaurant left standing. "If you move to the side and look behind the chimney, you'll see the metal dumpster. My apartment was on the other side of the dumpster."

I leaned sideways and looked. It was a pile of burnt rubble. "I'm so sorry," I said again.

"I got out of my apartment in time. But Jimmy Baker suffered smoke inhalation. He's in the hospital. He's in bad shape, Owen, real bad." She could barely breathe.

"Is he conscious?"

She shook her head. "They dragged him out of the fire, put an oxygen mask on him and rushed him away in an ambulance." She held up her purse which was hanging from her shoulder. "I grabbed this when I ran out. It's all I have left."

I reached my arms around her and hugged her. We didn't speak for a long time. Her sobbing spasms jerked hard.

"If Jimmy dies…" she gasped and choked.

"Let's try not to speculate. Let's just stay with what we know."

It took several minutes for her crying to lessen. She said, "Without my car, I'm trapped. I can't…"

"Your car burned."

"Oui."

I said, "I can find a place for you to stay."

She shook her head. "My friend Katherine already told me I can sleep at her place. She will help me." She pointed down the block toward an old Toyota with a woman in the driver's seat. I could see two kids in the back seat.

"Okay." I looked again at the burned rubble.

She nodded once again and looked down at her purse. "Everything left in my life is in this purse. But that loss is nothing compared to Jimmy if he dies. He trusted me to provide a safe place. I was the adult he thought he could trust." Her words were airy with stress and worry.

I couldn't find the words for a proper response.

Eventually, I said, "The fire was in the middle of the night?"

"Oui. Three or three-thirty in the morning. I don't know. It is all a blur. I had had trouble falling asleep. Then the smoke detector started shrieking. They make those things ten times as loud as they should be. They don't just wake you up. They send you into a panic to get away from the noise. I couldn't think to grab anything important. As a result I grabbed nothing."

"You should expect things to be a blur. You've had no sleep. The previous night you didn't get home from my office until the middle of the night. Last night you were awakened by fire. You can't expect anything of yourself."

Two firemen walked up to us. One looked like the fire marshal. "McKenna," one of them said to me as he touched the front of his fire helmet in greeting. I recognized him, but I couldn't remember his name.

I nodded.

"Okay if we talk to Ms. Laurent?" he said. "We have more questions."

I looked at Geneviève. "Are you up to this?"

"Oui. You should go. When I'm through with questions, I will get into my friend's car, and she will take me to her apartment."

"How did your friend hear about the fire?"

"I had my phone in my purse, so I called her. Now my phone is out of charge. I had chargers in both my apartment and my restaurant. I've always thought I should have a backup. But I didn't. Maybe my friend has a charger that will work. If not, that will be one more problem I don't know how to solve. I could order a charger to be shipped from Amazon. But my laptop burned. My password book burned, too. And I no longer have an address. My life is destroyed. If Jimmy dies…" She started crying again, deep, chest-wracking sobs.

I glanced at the firemen, who were waiting. I was thinking of many unanswered questions. I said, "You need sleep. We'll talk later."

She frowned so severely, it was as if she was facing the end of the world. She took several deep breaths, wiped her eyes, and then turned toward the fire marshal.

# TWENTY-FOUR

After witnessing the destruction of Geneviève's restaurant and the destruction of her life as she knew it, I was listless and depressed. I couldn't shake the sense that, no matter how justified I'd felt in trying to shake the extortionist off her back, the result had nevertheless been the fire. Great move, McKenna. Try to fix a little wrong and create an immeasurable disaster.

I tried to think of something productive to do as I wandered aimlessly back to the Jeep.

The only idea that came to me was to check other restaurants and see if they'd been visited by the extortionist. Maybe I could expand on my wrecking-ball track record. Other restaurants would burn just as hot.

Because Geneviève was an immigrant, and because I'd wondered if Geneviève was targeted because the extortionist thought immigrant restaurateurs were more likely to feel intimidated, I considered other immigrant-run restaurants.

I sat in my Jeep and used my phone to make a list of restaurants in the Tahoe Truckee area. I separated them into two groups. One group was franchise restaurants and ones that served typical American-style food. The other group was more of what might be called international cuisine, of which there were dozens. Mexican, Italian, French, and Chinese were the most popular.

I assumed those would be the most likely to suffer at the hands of someone exploiting immigrants.

I started in Truckee near where GENEVIEVE'S had been located.

The process was simple. Walk in, talk to the manager or the host, and ask if they'd been approached by anyone who wanted to sell them protection services.

No one admitted to such activity. One Basque restaurant had a very nice woman named Amaya who was more talkative than most.

She took my card and said the restaurant business was very difficult and that she had no doubt that dangerous men preyed on hard-working people like her. She said she would call if she heard about any... She used a couple of words with very unusual pronunciation. Probably Basque. Her tone was loud and agitated, so I understood that she was describing someone disgusting.

"You know... criminales," she said. "I'll call if I learn anything."

"Thank you. I'd appreciate that."

It took two hours to visit each Truckee restaurant on my list. No one told me about any protection rackets.

I got back in the Jeep and headed down 89 toward Tahoe City.

I turned off at Olympic Valley. I knew there were several restaurants, but I thought I'd start with The Hungarian close to where I'd found Lazlo. During my last visit, the manager Kyle Kramer had told me he wasn't aware of any protection racket man stopping by to sell guard services.

I parked and walked with the dogs to the pedestrian street.

I walked to the tables in the plaza near The Hungarian. I chose one that was farthest away from the other people to minimize the chance that the dogs would bother anyone, and looped both Spot's and Lazlo's leashes around the table legs. I heard the table make a scraping noise as I walked away. I looked back. Spot had turned to watch me, and his leash pulled on the table, rotating it. The leash also pulled against Lazlo, squeezing him against one of the other table legs. Lazlo was trapped.

I reconfigured their leashes in hopes that Lazlo wouldn't be stressed and then headed toward the restaurant door.

A group of six college-aged boys came strolling down the pedestrian street. They each held a beer bottle. One had two and would drink from first one, then the other. Their voices were loud and obnoxious, speaking of women and professors and basketball teams seemingly all at once. They all appeared to be thoroughly intoxicated. They paused here and there with no apparent destination, looking in windows, stopping to point up at the cable car as it climbed up the cliff face above us.

I stepped to the side to let them pass, then turned to see if they would ignore Spot and Lazlo. Fortunately, they were so self-focused, they didn't notice the dogs. After they passed, I went into the restaurant.

Kyle was working like before. I asked him similar questions.

He shook his head. "Nothing new to report," he said. "No protection racket scammers have stopped by or called."

"Are there any other restaurants nearby that are run by immigrants?"

"Sure. Three doors down is Johann's Heidelberg. They are famous for their Schnitzel. Maybe check with them?"

"Will do. Thanks."

I walked down the pedestrian street and went into the Heidelberg.

The host came forward. He was holding several menus. "Table for one?" he said. "Or are you meeting someone?"

"Actually, I have a question for your manager."

"Oh." He looked disappointed and irritated. He sighed as he set down the menus, turned, and walked back toward the kitchen. The kitchen had double swinging doors. I'd seen the arrangement before. Waiters holding trays of food could simply push through. As long as they used the door on their right, there were no collisions, and traffic flowed smoothly.

After a minute, the host came back out, followed by a woman in nice business clothes. Her pants, shirt, and vest were all black and looked to be made of linen. Her pumps stood out because they were shiny black.

"Can I help you?"

Immediately after she spoke, the swing door through which she'd come opened again. A big man came into the room.

"You don't wanna mess with me, lady," he said in a voice I recognized.

He continued, "It's a simple deal we have."

She turned back to look at him. He had his arm out, stabbing with a pointed finger toward the floor, a finger stab with nearly every word.

"My service is reliable. Ironclad. But I gotta be paid. You unnerstand? I gotta be paid."

I remembered the voice. And I recognized the scab on his face.

He was the man who'd been shouting at Geneviève in the back of her restaurant and who'd fallen on his face when I tripped him. The man did not appear to notice me. He turned around and went back into the kitchen, using the wrong door and nearly colliding with a waiter.

The manager turned away from the doors and looked at me again. Her face was pale. "Can I help you?" she said again. This time her words were shaky.

"I think it's that abusive man in your kitchen who can help me."

I walked back toward the kitchen. As I pushed through the door, I heard the manager speaking toward my back.

"Sir? Sir? You shouldn't…"

I pushed through the door into the kitchen. The big man was at the rear of the room. He turned the doorknob on the back door and walked outside.

I followed and found myself in the access drive behind the restaurant. The big man was talking to a tall skinny man. When they saw me, they looked uncomfortable. They turned and walked out toward the main pedestrian street. At the corner, they turned right and went out of sight.

I followed. I didn't want to appear furtive, so I did like they did and kept my normal walking speed. I turned right at the corner, and was hit in the abdomen with a blow that blew the air out of my lungs and doubled me over.

I staggered, stumbling with upset balance, gasping for air. I didn't know what had hit me, but the pain in my gut was overwhelming.

Still bent, I turned my head a little. I saw a vague shape swinging a club of some kind. It looked like a piece of stairway railing. The swing came in low and arced up, hitting me in the soft tissue again. The blow was so hard it lifted me up a little before I collapsed to the brick pavers.

I lost track of what was happening. I lay on my side, curled up in a fetal position gasping for air. One of them said, "This is the guy who tripped me behind Geneviève's restaurant."

Then there were other, younger voices, words about basketball and rap musicians. The two men still leaned over me. They kicked out, one hitting me on my back. The other kicked me in the chest.

The kicks were frightening in their focus and earnestness. These men were going to beat me to death.

A third kick hit me on my left hamstring muscle. It felt like I'd never walk again.

The stairway rail slammed down on my shoulder. I heard a squeak of tearing tissue.

I could barely perceive anything but pain and lack of breath. My vision was dimming. The pain increased, rushing me toward unconsciousness. But some laughter and younger voices came through. "You know, the best women are skiers, right? Because that makes them strong and confident and... Hey what's going on here? Why are you kicking that guy? Hey, Liam, you've got your phone out. Take a picture. Bob, call the police! Tell them there's a guy being assaulted..."

My perception faded to darkness. As I lost consciousness, I realized that the drunk college kids had walked up, and their presence made my attackers flee.

Some minutes later—I had no idea how long—I recovered some consciousness. My perceptions were blurry.

A voice said, "I still think we should call an ambulance."

"But he was clear when he said, 'Don't call nine one one.'"

"He was mumbling. You heard him. He could barely make his mouth work. I think he was talking while he was unconscious."

"Right, but we all heard the words. We should wait a bit. He sounded... I don't know, authoritative."

"This is a crime victim who might be dying from internal injuries, and you think he's authoritative?"

"Yeah. My uncle was a cop. That's the way he sounded when he talked. Even when he was on his deathbed and told us not to call nine one one, just call the doctor, because the ambulance is super expensive and he was dying, and he had a do-not-resuscitate order."

I managed to mumble. "That's right, guys." I said. Even I could tell my words were thick as if the dentist had injected me with novocaine and turned my lips and tongue into blubber.

"I was a cop," I added for credibility. "Twenty years." I was gasping for air, for voice. "I have to check the A,B,Cs before I can call nine one one."

I couldn't tell if they understood, but they didn't immediately make phone calls.

"What's that mean?" one of the kids said, not to me.

Another kid answered. "It means he's, like, totally gomered. Next, he'll be singing the children's alphabet song."

"Airway," I said. "Breathing. Circulation."

"See?!" one of the kids said to the others. "I told you. Like my uncle."

While they jabbered, I slowly rolled myself until I was on my elbows and knees.

"So why does he do the ABC thing? He could be dead before he makes his check."

"It's because of the cop code," the first kid said. "I saw it on TV. When cops call in, they have to give their precinct number and their badge number and something else. I forget what."

I pushed up, straightening my arms until I was on hands and knees. Every part of me screamed pain. But, so far, nothing seemed broken except maybe where I'd been kicked in the ribs.

"I remember," one of the kids said. "They have to give their last name using the phonetic alphabet. Like Jones would be Juliet Oscar November Echo Sierra. My brother learned it in the Army, and he taught it to me."

"I've never heard such shit," the other kid said.

"You mean Sierra Hotel India Tango."

"Oh, you are a regular stand-up comic."

With great effort, I lifted one of my legs and got my foot on the ground.

"Help me stand, please." My brain was starting to clear even though it sounded like I slowly said, 'Helmestanpeez.'

Two kids lifted on my elbows. A third pulled up on my belt.

"You gotta use the belt. That's what my uncle taught me."

They got me upright. I wavered. One kid kept hold of my elbow.

"Did you guys hear those bruisers say anything?" My words were still mumbled.

"No," said one. The others shook their heads.

"Have you seen them before? Out in the parking lot? Maybe getting out of a car?"

"Nuh uh," said another.

"Would one of you please give me your phone number in case I have other questions when I get my thinking back?"

"I could text you," one said. "Then you'd have my number."

"Okay, great."

"But I'd need your number to text you."

"Right. Let me think." The most prominent number in my head was my landline. "The landline doesn't help, does it? I'll remember my cell. Soon. I'll remember it soon."

The kids stared at me. They were in the adult zoo, seeing the range of how adult animals acted. It probably didn't reflect well on my generation. Some numbers came into my head. I mouthed the numbers to myself to see if they seemed familiar. They did. I recited them. One kid thumb-tapped his phone.

I felt my phone vibrate in my pocket as the text came through.

"Thanks, guys. I appreciate your help."

The kid who texted me said, "Aren't you going to tell the cops you got beat up?"

The kid who still held my elbow said, "He is a cop."

"I'll be fine," I said. "I just need to spend a few years in bed. Maybe have some of that Sierra Nevada Pale Ale medicine."

"See?" said one of the kids who hadn't yet talked. "Cops can be cool."

"Kinda."

"Are you okay to walk? If I let go of your elbow?"

"Yeah. Thanks."

He let go, and I felt all their eyes on my back as I walked away.

# TWENTY-FIVE

Moving very slowly, I got to the dogs, then got all of us to the Jeep and drove, impaired by pain and stress, back to my cabin.

I let the dogs run while I went inside. I wasn't up to explanations, so I texted Street.

'Bad problems. Geneviève's restaurant burned. I'm okay. Geneviève is not. I'll be out of communication until tomorrow. XO'

I got some food into both of the dogs and me. I slept for six hours. I realized I would be down for much more time, so I let the dogs out again, let them back in, then went back to sleep for another eight hours.

When I woke, I had two realizations. I probably had no broken bones, and I was going to be very sore for a long time. I looked at the time. Nine in the morning.

It was a monumental task to get out of bed and pull on my jeans and hoodie.

Once that hard physical work was done, it was a serious cognitive task to figure out the coffee maker.

After I'd drunk two cups, I started to sense life coming into my system. I called Geneviève. She said she was okay, though I knew better.

"Any news on your employee Jimmy?"

"No. He's still unconscious. I can't stand it."

"Hang onto your hope," I said. "Did you get some sleep at your friend's apartment?"

"Not much. She has two kids. I slept on the couch. Katherine realizes that this can't continue, so she's going to drive me to a hotel. And she'll give me rides wherever I need to go. She is a dear."

"Did she have a phone charger?"

"Oui, thank God. So at least I have communication."

"Good." I had another call coming in. "If it's okay with you, I'll check in with you later."

She said goodbye, and I answered the incoming call.

"Yeah?" I said into the phone expecting a telemarketer. It was a brusque answer.

"Owen McKenna?" A man's voice.

What was the simplest reply? "Yeah," I said again.

"Roger Anderson, Truckee Fire Marshal."

"Oh, hi, Roger. Thanks for calling."

"You wanted to know when we made a determination on the fire at the Geneviève restaurant."

"Yes, I certainly do."

"It was arson. At approximately two a.m. the night of the fire, someone pried off the vent cover from the kitchen grill exhaust fan. They bent the blades of the fan enough to make a space and pushed in a glass jar filled with gasoline. It broke when it hit the metal grill. The arsonist probably waited a couple of minutes for the gas to drip down around the grill and onto the floor of the kitchen. Then he lit a wooden match and tossed it in. There was enough gas vapor by that time that it caused a powerful explosion that blew out part of the back wall of the restaurant kitchen. If the arsonist didn't dive for cover, he might have been injured. And maybe he was hurt, burned by shooting flames blowing out toward the alley. He might also have ear damage from the boom of the explosion."

"You said, 'he lit a wooden match.'"

"Wow, you're gender aware. But it's good to be thorough. I just said 'he' as a figure of speech. But you and I both know that the vast majority of firestarters are men."

"Right," I said. "Thanks much for the information. If and when I have a sense of who the firestarter is, I'll let you know."

"Same here. Lieutenant Oberman assigned that rookie woman to the case. Hattie something. I spoke to her. Way too green to take on a big arson case, if you ask me. But she's smart. She told me her mission is to chase down leads. Unfortunately, we don't have any leads. Who knows. Maybe she'll find a clue and do fine."

That afternoon, I talked to Geneviève again. She'd checked into a hotel room. Katherine was going to come back with some groceries and other supplies. Geneviève said she was okay and that I didn't need to worry.

But I knew better. I worried a great deal, and I didn't know what to do about it.

I called Street and told her all the details I could remember.

She insisted I come for dinner and that I bring the dogs with me.

We said goodbye, and I went back to bed.

At 7 p.m., I headed down the mountain and turned into her lot.

Street and Camille served a nice dinner, and five minutes afterward, I couldn't remember what I'd eaten. Afterward, the dogs lounged in front of the gas fireplace. Street and I sat on her couch, and Camille sprawled sideways in one of the upholstered chairs, her back against one arm, her knees over the other arm. She was reading another novel about race horses. Blondie was on her cushion next to the chair, her chin down on her front paws, her eyes open and craned up to look at Camille. I think Blondie had learned that because Camille was deaf, communication was more likely to come from Camille's signing than from her words. Thus Blondie couldn't snooze with her eyes shut, or she'd miss whatever action Camille might produce.

There was a general air of discomfort regarding our good fortune compared to what Geneviève was going through.

"Where is Geneviève staying?" Street asked me.

"I spoke to her this morning and also a couple of hours ago. Last night, after the fire took her restaurant and her apartment, she stayed on her friend's couch. But her friend has two kids in a one-bedroom apartment. That was kind of an emergency situation. When I last talked to her, it sounded like she wasn't able to sleep at all. So, today she checked into a hotel in Truckee."

"Did she get your input on how to handle her restaurant burning?"

"Not really. I've never had a client this marooned and isolated, so I have no advice. I'm feeling my way through how to deal with a client facing such a tragic loss. When I talked to her later today, I thought of inviting her to stay at my place. But a little log cabin with four hundred-plus pounds of man and dogs and only one bedroom and no couch doesn't seem appropriate. I don't imagine she'd want to sleep in my bed, especially considering she would be aware that her presence forced me to sleep on the floor in front of the wood stove.

Street made a single nod, frowned, and looked very concerned.

"A hotel in Truckee must be expensive," she said.

"No doubt. There are almost no lodgings in Truckee. I'm sure that makes them exorbitant. She could find cheaper options in Reno, but that's thirty-some miles away, and she has no car. It's hard to deal with business and apartment issues from a long distance, and she still might not have the basics like a kitchen and a work space."

"Did she have business insurance that covers a fire loss?"

"She mentioned her policy and said that she hasn't yet met with her agent. She spoke to the agent on the phone, and the agent said an adjuster would be out. But, as of this afternoon when I spoke to her by phone, Geneviève had yet to see anyone. There's also some kind of complication that I don't understand. She said the apartment where she lived next to her restaurant was not listed on her building lease. She had made a separate side deal with the landlord. I think she paid her apartment rent in cash in return for an extra cheap rental rate and in exchange for being unofficial. Why, I don't know. Maybe the landlord knew the apartment wasn't legal in some manner. The landlord probably had fire insurance on the apartment. But it means that Geneviève has no standing with any insurance company that might cover the apartment. She's stuck waiting for her landlord to make arrangements."

"In other words, she'll be homeless for some time," Street said.

"Yes. But unlike many homeless, Geneviève has lost all of her possessions. She doesn't have a shopping cart full of personal stuff. No clothes, no personal effects, no computer. She woke up in the middle of the night when the smoke alarm went off. She grabbed her purse and ran outside. So she has nothing except her phone. Even her lease, her passport, and other papers burned up."

"Does her current hotel room have a kitchen?"

"I don't think so. And all of her thoughts are focused on the young man who lived below her apartment."

"Who's still in the hospital with smoke-burned lungs." Street shook her head.

"I can't imagine her stress."

"Do you think Geneviève has any money?" Street asked. "Any savings to help her get through this situation?"

"We haven't talked about it in any specific way. I got the idea that she had some debt after going to graduate school. After getting her Ph.D., Geneviève needed money, and she was hired to teach genetics at Stanford. So she came to America on some kind of specialty visa. She spoke about saving for four years before she started the restaurant. I have no idea how much money is involved in starting a restaurant. And I don't know how well Stanford pays their teachers. But I imagine that equation didn't leave much of anything."

Street shrugged. "Teacher pay varies widely. Stanford pays better than many schools. But most adjunct professors only earn enough to share a small apartment in the Bay Area."

"She also made it sound like she spent all of her savings on leasehold improvements on the restaurant."

"Fixing up the building." Street was gazing out the window, her focus on something she couldn't see. "So Geneviève is probably broke or close to it."

My cell phone vibrated in my pocket.

"I've got incoming," I said as I pulled out my phone. The readout showed the number. It seemed familiar.

"Hello?"

The caller didn't immediately answer. "M... Monsieur McKenna?" Geneviève's voice was extremely shaky. She could barely get the words out.

"Hi Geneviève. This is Owen. What's wrong?" I felt Street tense beside me. Camille looked up from her chair. She must have sensed my movement as I pulled my phone out of my pocket.

"I..." Geneviève started, then stopped. "My phone rang," she said. "It was..." she inhaled sharply, like a frightened gasp. "It was scary. I'm in trouble," she said in a tremulous, airy whisper.

"Geneviève, where are you?"

"My..."

"Are you at your hotel?"

"Oui," she said. It was one simple word, but filled with stress and fear.

"Did you call nine one one?"

"No. I would have nothing to tell them."

"Are you in your room?"

"Oui."

"Are you alone with your door locked?"

"Oui."

"Did you get a threatening phone call?"

I heard sudden sobbing over the phone.

"Geneviève, focus, please. I need you to answer my questions. Did you get a threatening phone call?"

A big inhalation as if she were suffocating. "Oui."

"You checked into the West Mountain Village Inn, correct?"

"Oui." Her crying garbled her single-word answer.

"I will come to your hotel. What is your room number?"

I waited. I heard some sounds. She was probably looking for her key card sleeve, on which they would have written her room number.

"Three four one."

"Three forty-one," I said. I worried that her teary, blurred vision might cause her to read it wrong. "That is correct, right? Three four one."

"That is correct," she said.

"Okay, I will leave now and come to room three forty-one. It will take me about an hour. Do not open your door for anyone else. No matter what someone says. I will identify myself as Owen McKenna Security."

She didn't respond.

"Repeat my words, Geneviève, so I know you hear me."

"Owen McKenna Security," she said.

"One hour," I said. I hung up.

"I could hear her in your phone," Street said. "She's in rough shape."

I nodded. "She said she got a phone call. Something frightening from her reaction. Geneviève probably realized that her restaurant burning wasn't an accident. She would have to face the fact that a predator has taken everything from her. To have that stalker/hunter continue to pursue her, it would push her—anyone—over the edge."

I stood up, my body screaming with aches.

Street stood up as well, reached her arms up, and held the sides of my neck.

Spot got to his feet and pushed between us.

"Why do you think this is happening to Geneviève?" Street asked. "Why would someone target her like this?"

"I don't know. But when I find him... I may not think he's innocent until proven guilty."

"That's scary, Owen. Both what it implies about her predator and what you might do." She turned just a bit to glance at Camille as if to make sure Camille couldn't read her lips. Street said, "You make it sound like you might kill him before you call the cops."

There was no right answer to that. I touched Street's face, kissed her, then waved goodbye at Camille.

"C'mon, Spot, Lazlo," I said.

We walked to the door. Lazlo followed Spot.

"Owen," Street said as I opened the door.

I turned and looked at her.

"You can bring Geneviève back here, so she's not alone with her thoughts in a hotel room. She could sleep on the couch. Or we can put the camping cushions on the floor in Camille's room, and she could sleep there. I think it would be better for her to be around supportive people. A person can't put their life back together in a hotel room. If she came here, she could use my little desk, or she could spread out on the dining table. If she needs a copy machine or other office stuff, she can use my desk at my lab." She paused. "Oh, and having a kitchen is critical to having a normal life."

"Thanks, Street. You keep saving people. Years ago, after I shot the bank robber, you saved me. Recently, you saved Blondie and now Camille."

"It's only right."

I blew her a kiss and left.

# TWENTY-SIX

There was a frosty mist in the air that produced a faint sparkle in my headlights. The highway was mottled with white areas that were slick with frost and dark areas where there was just enough ground warmth to slow the formation of icy slicks.

An hour later, I parked in the lot at the West Mountain Village Inn. I left Spot and Lazlo in the Jeep, went in, took the stairs to the third floor, and knocked on room 341.

I heard sounds, then silence. Maybe she was looking through the peephole.

"Who is it?"

"Owen McKenna Security."

The door opened an inch, then shut. I heard the safety latch squeak as she pulled it away. Then the door opened fully.

I walked in, shut the door behind me, turned the bolt and swung the safety latch.

I turned back and looked at Geneviève. The attractive, lithe woman I'd originally met was a frumpy mess, ungroomed, with worried, fearful, red eyes. She was permeated with a deep sadness and terror. Both of her hands had a tremor as if she was receiving electric shocks.

"I don't... I thought..." she said. "Thank you for coming. I didn't know what to do. I sort of fell apart. I haven't really slept since I woke up to the smoke alarm. I'm kind of in pieces. Sorry about that."

"Nothing to be sorry about."

I gestured toward the single, upholstered chair. "Let's sit and talk a bit."

She sat on the foot of the bed, and I took the chair. She sat with one leg bent up underneath her. Her mouth twitched, the left side of her lips jerking back. She was wearing a gray sweatshirt, heavy socks under her gray sweatpants, the same clothes she'd been wearing when she escaped her burning apartment. The socks had a pattern I'd seen on Norwegian sweaters, white and gray and blue, a blue that brought out the unusual blue in Geneviève's eyes.

"Tell me about the phone call," I said.

"There isn't much to tell. I was standing by the window, looking out, when my phone rang. I was surprised because I get no reception elsewhere in the hotel room. But there is one bar of reception next to the window. So I answered. I heard breathing. I said, 'Who's calling?' There was no answer. The breathing was heavy. I could tell it was a man."

"How do you know that?"

"I can tell. I don't know how. Something about the way air moves in a big chest. It sounds different than a small person."

"What did he say?"

"Nothing. So I hung up. A short time later, he called again. I thought about not answering. But I thought the second call could be my friend where I stayed last night. I don't have her number in my phone, so it didn't give me caller ID. So, I answered, and it was the same heavy breathing. That told me that he meant to call me on purpose. That he probably knew me. That maybe he was the arsonist and he wanted something else. I don't know what."

"So it wasn't someone you know. Unless, I suppose, the man used a burner phone."

"I don't know what that means."

"There are apps for disguising your phone. And there are prepaid phones that you can buy. You don't need a service plan. They all give you a number that doesn't identify the caller."

"Why would someone do that?" she asked. "Burn up my restaurant, my apartment, my world? And then he calls me. Why? To… What is the word? Gloat?"

"I don't know, Geneviève. Psychologists have their theories. Some arsonists simply seek thrills. Some are trying to collect on insurance. Others set revenge fires for perceived wrongs."

"This guy wants to torment me because I stopped paying him blackmail money?" Her voice was tiny.

"It could be. Of if someone else thinks you harmed him, that could be motivation."

"But I haven't harmed anyone. I'm nice to everyone."

I shrugged. "You can do everything perfectly and still anger someone who envies your success."

"But I have no success to speak of! I'm a broke chef who is struggling at every aspect of life. My restaurant was barely paying the bills. My boyfriend died. Before my parents died, they thought I was a failure. I have almost no friends. My apartment is ashes. I'm homeless and staying in a hotel I can't afford. And I have no money for clothes or anything else. And some evil guy is breathing over my phone." She looked over at the wall. The room light reflected off her eyes, which were brimming with tears. "And I'm so afraid. I don't know what to do. And Jimmy Baker is lying on a hospital bed in Intensive Care with his lungs filling with liquid from a reaction to smoke inhalation."

"I'm sorry," I said. "Can you think of anyone who might have wanted something you have?"

"What could that possibly be?"

"Think of your teaching job at Stanford. Was there anyone else who wanted that job?"

Geneviève frowned. "There would be no way for me to know that."

"So there's a possibility. What about when you rented your restaurant building. Did someone else want to put a restaurant there, only you got to it first?"

"Not that I know of."

We sat in silence for a minute. I could see the fatigue on Geneviève's face. The smudges under her eyes seemed even darker than when I'd first come into her room.

"What do you think I should do?" she asked. "Do I just sit in this hotel room? I feel trapped. I can't even make a phone call from the desk. I have to stand next to the window glass. I can't solve business insurance problems. I can't cook a meal. And one more night here will use up the rest of my credit card limit."

"When you called, I was talking to my girlfriend at her condominium. She offered to let you stay with her."

Geneviève turned and looked at me, surprise on her face.

"She is the person named Street Casey you talked about?"

"Yes."

"Do you live with her? I think you told me, but I don't remember."

"No. My dog and I live in a log cabin not far away."

"She lives alone?"

"No. She has a nine-year-old, recently-adopted daughter named Camille Dexter." As soon as I said it, I realized I needed to stop referring to Camille as adopted. The qualifier was part of my adjustment to the major change in Street's and my life.

"They also have a Yellow Lab named Blondie."

"Why would Street want to let someone she doesn't know into her house?"

"I told Street about you. She is worried about you staying in a hotel and not having a normal place where you can figure out how to put your life back together."

"When we talked before, you said Street is a scientist."

"Yes. Entomologist."

"Is her condominium large? Or would I cause much impact?"

I shook my head. "No, it's not large. It's just two bedrooms with a small kitchen. But it's nice. I think you would like Street. And I can guarantee you'll like Camille and Blondie."

"You say she has two bedrooms, but there are two people. Where would I sleep?"

"First, she said you can sleep on her couch. Then she thought she could make a camping bed for you in Camille's room."

"I would be disrupting their world. I would be bringing my problems into their house. It would be a huge... the French word is imposition."

"We use the same word in English. But it is something refugees deal with all over the world, right? Instead of being a political refugee or a flood or forest fire victim, you are a crime victim refugee. It is reasonable for Street to want to help. It wouldn't be forever. Just until you get back on your feet."

Geneviève looked around at her hotel room as if seeing it anew. "Street's offer is so kind. I don't know how I could accept it."

"This is part of your burden, Geneviève. You are dealing with a huge loss. You also have to deal with other peoples' generosity. It would make Street and Camille feel good to help you."

"How would this happen? When would I do this?"

"You would come with me now. I would drive to her place. You will have a hot meal and be ready to sleep in a few hours."

I saw again the deep fatigue in Geneviève's face. And maybe a bit of hope as well.

"But this is not what you planned in your life. This interruption."

"Remember what I said? You have to accommodate other peoples' generosity."

"Oui. It is part of my burden." Geneviève made a tiny smile. "But you are too kind."

"No. I'm just doing what's reasonable. But first I have to call Street. It won't take me long."

I walked over next to the window in hopes my phone would work.

"Hi honey, I'm at Geneviève's hotel room," I said when Street answered.

"Is she okay?"

"Yes. A bit fractured and stressed. But okay. I told her about your offer to let her stay at your condo. She's going to take you up on it."

"When do you think you'll be here?"

"The roads are a bit icy, so I'll drive slowly. An hour or more."

"We'll watch for you."

From behind me, I heard Geneviève raise her voice. "Tell Street and Camille they are très gentil to help me."

I repeated that to Street. Then I heard her turn and say it to Camille.

"It's no problem. Camille is next to me signing that she's excited because now she'll be able to learn more French."

"Thanks. Talk to you soon."

I hung up and turned toward Geneviève.

"Street said Camille was already signing that now she can learn more French."

"Signing?" Geneviève said.

"American Sign Language. Camille is deaf."

"A nine-year-old deaf girl is learning French?"

"Oui," I said with a smile.

"That is so sweet."

# TWENTY-SEVEN

Geneviève went into the bathroom and came out after a few minutes.

"I have turned into a dragon lady. I should take a shower. But I have no clean clothes."

"You look fine. Street is about your size. She will have some clothes you can wear."

"But I don't want either of you to see me like this."

"Don't worry. Neither Street nor I would ever look at a dragon lady. They put people under dragon spells."

I walked past her and over to the door.

"Ready?" I said.

"Oui."

I opened the door and stepped out into the hallway.

I turned back. "Do you have everything?"

She held up her purse.

"Do I need to go to the hotel desk to check out?"

"No. Just leave your key card on the table."

"But I told them I would be here for a few days."

"Then use the phone and tell them you have a change of plans and are leaving."

She did as suggested, and we headed out to the parking lot.

I opened the door of the Jeep, and Spot jumped out. Lazlo looked out to be sure there was room, then jumped out as well.

Both dogs greeted Geneviève as if she were an old friend. I think it lightened her mood a little.

I got in and started the engine.

Soon, the Jeep was warm, and we drove off.

"Are you still certain it is okay that I stay at Street's home?"

"Yes. Street is not given to impulsive decisions. She thinks things through. Once she makes a decision, you can count on it."

Geneviève nodded. "It is so very nice of her."

# TWENTY-EIGHT

I realized that Geneviève was probably very cold with nothing but a thin jacket over her sweats. So I kept the heat up high. In addition, she was likely uncomfortable about going to stay with strangers she'd never even met. Add to that the ongoing stress of her employee Jimmy Baker being in the hospital, loosing everything but her life in the fire, and then the fear from the stalker breathing over the phone, and she was in a very difficult situation.

Our drive was uneventful. I went extra slowly through the areas where the road was icy.

We pulled into Street's condo parking lot a little more than an hour later.

I let the dogs out.

Street's door opened a little, and Blondie ran out. All three dogs headed into the woods.

Geneviève walked beside me.

"I'm afraid," she said. Her voice was shaky.

"It's okay," I said. I touched her arm.

Camille stood in the open door, grinning.

"Bonjour," Camille said. "You must be Geneviève, oui? I'm Camille." Then she looked worried. "Is it okay if I call you Geneviève? Or should I call you Ms. Laurent? I'm working on... What did Street call it? My social graces."

Geneviève turned to me and gave me a smile that was mostly delight but contained a little bit of surprise and alarm.

She looked back at Camille. "My dear Camille, your social graces are superb."

Camille reached out, and she and Geneviève shook hands. Camille ushered us inside.

Street came forward. She also reached to shake hands, but Geneviève put her hands on Street's shoulders and gave her air kisses on both sides.

"I'm so glad you could come and stay with us," Street said. "You must be freezing in those sweat pants." Street stepped back and seemed to gauge Geneviève in a quantitative way. "You're skinny like me. I'm sure I have clothes that will fit you. But first, come sit by the fire and warm up. Would you like tea or coffee?"

"I would love coffee. Decaf, if you have it."

Camille went to the other side of the counter. "Cream or sugar?" she called out as Geneviève sat in one of the chairs.

"Black is fine, thanks."

I realized that Camille couldn't see Geneviève's face.

I said, "Because Camille is deaf, she needs to see your face to read your lips."

"Oh! I'm sorry." She turned to face Camille in the kitchen. "I like my coffee black, please."

"Arrive bientôt," Camille said.

"Your French is très bien!"

Camille grinned.

Street sat on the couch and spoke to Geneviève, "Ever since Owen called and said you would come stay with us, Camille has been practicing. She thinks of a phrase that she might say to you, then plugs it into Google Translate to find out how to say it in French."

"But how does she know the pronunciation so well?"

"She studies the International Phonetic Alphabet and then watches one of the Youtube translators say it and reads their lips. The combination gives her a pretty good idea."

"But...pardon me, with her being deaf, how can she ever know how to say anything? It would be so difficult to make sounds you can't hear."

Street smiled. "I agree. It is amazing. But to her, it's just like another part of growing up. Instead of getting their inputs from hearing, the deaf person learns by watching people speak. Deaf people also feel sounds in their body."

Geneviève frowned, thinking. "Like when we feel the rumble of a truck coming down the road outside our houses?"

"Yes, exactly. Deaf children also put their fingertips on a speaker's throat, feeling the vibrations. Then they feel their own throat vibrations as they experiment with making sounds. They watch the mouth and tongue movements of people who are speaking.

Then they watch their own mouth movements while they look in a mirror. Many deaf children get speech lessons from a young age. It's remarkable what they can learn."

Geneviève looked away from Camille as if self-conscious of what she was about to say. "Does Camille have hearing aids or those surgical implants?"

"No," Street said, shaking her head. "She was born with a congenital defect. Her brain is missing the auditory cortex, where we process sounds. Without the auditory cortex, there is no sense of sound at all."

"No sound to analyze, no sound to amplify," Geneviève said.

"Oui," Street said, smiling. Street stood up. "I'm thinking you both need a good bedtime snack." She tapped Camille on the shoulder. Camille turned to watch her lips.

"You could show Geneviève where she will sleep," Street said.

Geneviève stood, as well, and said to Camille, "Owen said you and I will share your room."

Camille walked over. "Actually, my room is now yours. We made a camping bed for me in Street's room so you can have mine."

Geneviève protested, "But that's not right for you to leave your own room! You won't have—you know—the space you need."

Camille shook her head. "I grew up in a pickup camper with my grandpa. My space was a little bunk that had only three feet of height. So I'm perfectly comfortable in small spaces. Come, I'll show you where you will be."

They went into Camille's room.

Street got busy in the kitchen.

I walked over behind Street and wrapped my arms around her.

"You are something," I said.

"It's the least I can do. Geneviève has lost everything."

"How can I help?" I said.

"There's a pack of mixed, frozen berries in the freezer. You can start thawing them in the microwave."

I opened the freezer and found the raspberry, blueberry, strawberry, blackberry package.

Street cut up some broccoli and put it in a serving bowl with hummus on the side. Then she made miniature peanut butter sandwiches using whole grain crackers in place of bread. She set out a selection of cheeses, bananas, and a bunch of grapes.

Street pulled some miniature whole grain tortillas out of her fridge and made some wraps with spinach, sun-dried tomato spread, and cranberries.

She also pulled out the Windwalker Malbec that was left over from when Diamond came by.

It was not the kind of feast a beer-and-cheeseburger guy like me would normally be attracted to. But when Geneviève and Camille reappeared, they ate a bit of everything, I joined in, and it turned into a small feast.

Geneviève exclaimed, clearly touched by the effort.

"And you have this great wine," she said. "I sell this in my restaurant!" I saw Geneviève smile for the first time, but then she made a look of deep sadness. "I used to sell this."

Street looked at me, her face showing worry. I shrugged.

The conversation was lively considering that Geneviève was barely a shell of a person, and it seemed that Geneviève and Street and Camille were already finding a good connection and communication. There were a few moments when I believed that Geneviève was not aware of her loss. It would continue to haunt her for years. But a break from the stress was nice for all.

When we were done eating, I went outside with the dogs. They disappeared for some time.

After a minute, they appeared. I opened Street's door, let Blondie in, and said, "If you three are okay, I'll take Spot and Lazlo up to my cabin, and we can all get some sleep."

Geneviève nodded. "I need to take a shower and do that, too."

I walked over, hugged Camille and kissed Street.

"Monsieur Owen," Geneviève said, standing up from her chair. "I owe you a big merci." Her eyes teared.

I took her hands in mine.

"I'm happy to help. Get some sleep. We'll talk later."

I said goodbye and left. Spot and Lazlo jumped into the Jeep, Lazlo claiming the front as before, and we drove up the mountain.

I got a small fire going in the wood stove. As soon as it was warm, Spot spread out on his bed, and Lazlo claimed a small corner.

I turned down the draft on the stove and went to bed.

# TWENTY-NINE

My cell phone rang and woke me at eight the next morning. I didn't recognize the number.

"Owen McKenna," I answered.

"Hola, my name is Amaya from the Ruiz Restaurant in Truckee," a woman said with a pronounced accent. "You are the police detective."

I had told her I was a private investigator, but it probably wasn't a critical distinction for this phone call.

"Yes, I remember" I said. "You are from the Basque restaurant." Her restaurant was one of the ones I'd stopped at to ask about the enforcers who'd threatened Geneviève.

Amaya continued, "You asked about a man with the scrape on his face. You made me think he is an evil man."

"Right."

"Such a man and his friend came into my restaurant last night."

"Did you notice what he looked like? I only saw him at night."

"I didn't notice to describe. He was unusual. Like he has a Chinese mamá and Latino papá. Medium height. Large. Big muscles. His friend was more tall but more skinny."

"Did you learn their names?"

"No."

"Did he order food?"

"Bai. I mean, yes. They bought two pinchos. Like tapas if you don't know. One for each man. No man that big eats just one pinchos. It made me think he was not there to eat."

"What do you think his purpose was?"

"I do not have this knowledge. Maybe to meet someone. But no one else came. The two men talked and ate and left."

"Did they pay with a credit card?"

"No. They paid with cash. Tiny tip. They looked at my restaurant and said some strange things."

"Can you remember any of what they said?"

"Sí. I was writing my paperwork at the counter. They sat in the nearby chairs. I could hear them talk. When I was to understand the strange talk, I wrote it down. Should I tell you?"

"Yes, please."

"One said, 'Basque food is like eating on a desert.' The other said, 'I like Korean food. Definitely Korean.'"

"Hold on a minute," I said. "I'm going to write it down, as well." I had a pad of paper on my kitchen counter. I wrote.

I spoke to Amaya. "Did they say anything else?"

"Yes. The first said, 'I like Korean food, too. When should we eat?' That was my first time to think it was strange. They were already eating at my restaurant. So why would they make that question?"

The woman continued. "The skinny man said, 'I work the late shift, so I eat very late, after I get home. Midnight or one. Want to eat with me tonight?' Then the big man said, 'I'll pick you up after your shift. We can eat Korean and be fed and happy by bedtime.'"

I wrote the words.

"Then they were in the big hurry," the woman said. "They left the few coins and went away."

"Did you see what kind of car they drove?"

"Yes. They parked it in front of my restaurant. Some people, they want you to see their car. It is the symbol of status. The skinny man was the driver. The car was the BMW with the blue paint. It made more noise than most cars. Like the truck."

"Can you remember anything else about them? Clothes? Jewelry?"

"Oh, yes. The big man had the gold ring on his pointing finger."

"Right hand or left hand?"

"Let me remember." She spoke several words that sounded like none I'd ever heard before, talking to herself in Basque, probably. I heard movement. Maybe she was gesturing to herself. "Left," she said.

"Okay, great. Thank you, Amaya. I appreciate your help."

"And you will remember my restaurant? We have beer and food you will like."

"Yes, of course."

I said goodbye and hung up.

I put the coffee on, got the wood stove fired up, poured a mug, and called Street.

"Did your night go okay?" I asked.

"Yes. I think Geneviève got some sleep." Street was talking softly, probably from her bedroom so as not to be easily heard. "I couldn't say she is rested. But any sleep is good at this point. And Camille is especially good for keeping Geneviève from being too dark."

"Do you think it's appropriate for me to stop by and check in?"

"Yes. We could all go for a short walk in the forest. Let's plan for the late afternoon. Four?"

"Sounds good. I'll see you then."

I hung up and my cell phone immediately rang. Frankie Valli still singing that I was too good to be true. The readout said 'Diamond.'

"Hola," I said. "I've got information for you."

"My shift ends at three. Meet for a brew this afternoon and tell me about it?"

"If you come to Street's. I'm heading there today at four. I want to check in on Geneviève. We moved her to Street's last night."

"You think it's okay if I stop by?"

"You'll be a good distraction for all."

At some point, I had told Diamond about Geneviève's fire. But so much had happened in the last day or so, I couldn't keep track.

"Geneviève okay?" he asked.

"No. But she's trying hard. A lot depends on the fate of her employee in the hospital."

"I'll be thoughtful with what I say. See you at four."

An hour later I was at the Incline Village townhouse that was shared by Colin's former roommates. Because it was the middle of the day, I thought it likely that no one would be home. I knocked on the door, and it was opened by Subaru Bob. He was dressed in greasy overalls, home from the shop for a lunch break. He held a peanut butter sandwich in one hand. His mouth was full as he chewed.

"Hi Bob, I'm Owen McKenna. We met the other day."

"Yeah, right. You were Colin's friend."

"Not really a friend. But I'm helping to settle up his affairs. I wonder if any of your roommates are around?"

He shook his head. "They're all at work. Tamir and Jackson, anyway. Tommy has unusual hours at the ski shop. They seem to change every day. So maybe he's at work. But we got a nice snowfall last night up at higher elevations. He's probably cutting fresh tracks up at Mt. Rose. Tamir gets him the latest deals. Two-fer Tuesdays. Fab Fridays."

"I guess I could ask you my questions."

"Sure. Gimme a try." Bob turned and looked at the clock readout on the lower corner of the giant TV. "I can hang here for about six more minutes before I have to head back to the garage."

"I'm just looking for sources of tension in the ski race world."

"I don't get it," Bob said.

"From what I've heard, Colin Burns was a super confident speed skier. It would seem that something must have really shook him up to have him fall so badly. I'm wondering if something bothered him enough that it would destroy his concentration on the speed course?"

Subaru Bob lifted his shoulders and then let them drop.

"No idea, man. I always thought Colin had his act together."

"Did he ever have any disagreements with the others about speed skiing?"

Bob made a slow head shake.

"What about the non-skiing parts of his life? Anybody he argued with? Did anyone dislike him?"

"No."

"Did he ever get boisterous? Drink too much in bars? Flirt with other mens' girlfriends?"

"Not at all. Colin was kind of like the total good kid. Do his chores. Don't complain. Work very hard. Never goof off."

"Okay, thanks for your help. It sounds like Colin was really well adjusted."

Bob frowned, and looked down the hall towards the bedrooms. "I just remembered, Jackson wanted to give you a box of Colin's stuff. He thought it should go to Colin's girlfriend, but I think he asked her and she said no. All I remember is Jackson said we could maybe give it to you. If you want it, that is."

"I think it sounds like something Geneviève should have. Why don't I take it. I'll be seeing Geneviève again. I'll check and see if she has changed her mind."

Bob turned and walked down the short hallway. "It's here in Jackson's room."

I followed Bob into the room. Bob bent down and picked up a box that was sitting on the floor near one of the twin beds.

I stepped over to a desk to be out of the way. Something on the desk caught my eye. It was a cream-colored business card with elegant black printing and a metallic gold logo. It said Franklin Assurance Holdings International. Next to it was an envelope that was turned over so the address was face down. On the back of the envelope was scrawled the insurance company's name and the mailing address.

I picked them up. "This is unusual," I said. "This is the insurance company that had Colin's life insurance."

"So?" Bob said as he turned. He was holding the box.

"Why would these be here in this room? Was this Colin's room when he lived here?"

"No. He was in the next room down. Where I am now."

"Is there any other stuff in this room that belonged to Colin?"

Bob shook his head. "No, it's all in this box."

"Who sleeps in this room?"

"Jackson and Tamir."

"Did either of them talk about this company? Franklin Assurance Holdings International?"

"Not to my knowledge."

Bob turned and walked out. He was standing by the front door, holding the box.

"I gotta go," he said. "I'm going to be late."

"I'm sorry I kept you overtime."

"No sweat. I'll drive fast."

"Thanks again."

We both left.

# THIRTY

When I got to Street's, the women were playing charades, a game that Camille was astonishingly good at. Maybe being deaf had caused her to fine-tune her other communication skills, such as mime. As she acted, she also signed, so she was an entertaining sign language instructor.

Blondie took to her bed leaving the carpet in front of the gas fireplace to Spot and Lazlo. They lay down. Street and Camille were gesticulating, being emphatic. Geneviève was participating but with no energy. Her face looked drained of joy, which was to be expected. There are times in life when your goal is just to get through the day. Geneviève remained seated on the end of the couch. She had showered, her hair had been brushed, and she wore Street's jeans and shirt and sweater. But she still looked forlorn.

Spot lifted his head off the floor. His eyes stared at nothing. Blondie was already alert, looking toward the door. Spot's ears turned this way and that following sounds I couldn't hear. Lazlo followed suit, watching Spot and Blondie to see what was up. It seemed he was looking at Spot's ears, as he quickly adopted the same demeanor, looking at the walls but listening to what was apparently a symphony of sounds below the threshold of human hearing. Lazlo imitating Spot reminded me of when a dog yawns after seeing another dog yawn.

Spot rose to his feet and walked over to the door. He stood, nose-to-doorknob, his tail wag on medium-low.

Lazlo also stood. He knew that someone was about to arrive. Maybe he already knew the model and year of the visitor's vehicle.

There was a soft knock. I got up and opened the door. Diamond walked in. He gave Spot a rough head rub. Spot's wag moved to the high-speed setting.

Diamond looked over at Lazlo, who appeared interested but was keeping his distance.

"Señor Lazlo is still reserved," Diamond said. "The wise student is careful not to immediately join forces with the popular student?"

"Yeah, probably."

"Diamond!" Camille called out. She'd been standing up playing air violin, which I found interesting considering she'd never been able to hear a violin. Although she had seen them played.

Diamond waved at her. She kept playing. Street was calling out names, facing Camille so the girl could read her lips. Camille shook her head and giggled.

Diamond walked over and gave Street a hug. Then he kissed his fingertip and planted it on Camille's cheek. Camille smiled but kept playing the violin.

Diamond turned to Geneviève. "Bonjour, my name is Diamond. Owen told me on the phone that you are Geneviève. It's a pleasure to meet you."

They gently shook hands. Geneviève remained seated on the couch.

"You have come to visit with Street and Camille?" Diamond said.

Geneviève nodded. "Visit with and temporarily live with. Owen may have told you…" she hesitated.

"I understand you were the victim of a fire," Diamond said. "I'm very sorry about that. If there is any way I can help McKenna with your case, I will. I'm a cop, so I know something of these struggles."

"Merci." Geneviève looked at Diamond's civvies, worn-out brown denim pants, frayed, brown leather bomber jacket, brown hiking boots. With his brown skin, he was invisible at night. Unless he flashed his high-watt smile.

I spoke in a low voice to Diamond. "Camille has engaged Street and Geneviève in a game. Let's go outside and talk."

He followed me out the door.

"This morning, I got an interesting phone call," I said.

We walked over to Diamond's pickup, which was so old, I couldn't figure out its year. And because the logo had come off the hood in the last few years, I wasn't even sure of its make. The closest I could guess was late '40s or early '50s American, probably a Studebaker.

"A woman named Amaya called me," I said. "She works at the

Basque restaurant in Truckee. It felt like she was the owner."

Diamond raised his eyebrows. "I like Basque pie."

"You have a singular focus on your fondness for sweets."

"Like all macho Mexican cops," he said. "We have a dark occupation, so we need sweets to motivate us."

"Donuts mitigate murder?"

Diamond kept a straight face. "Of course."

"Amaya, the restaurant woman, never mentioned their pie. But she did tell me that a muscular man with scabs on his face came in and talked funny to his companion. She wrote down his words."

"The scabs suggesting the man you tripped when he put the squeeze on Geneviève."

"Correct," I said. "The man who beat me to a pulp behind The Heidelberg restaurant at Olympic Valley."

"What were the words these dirtballs spoke?" Diamond looked at me.

I walked over to my Jeep, got my pad of paper, and read what the men had said.

I looked at Diamond. "What do you make of it?"

He shrugged. "Could just be small talk. Guys figuring out where to eat after work."

"Or?" I said.

"It could be a cant."

# THIRTY-ONE

When Diamond said it could be a cant, I said, "Are you saying 'can't' like the contraction for cannot?"

"No. A cant with no apostrophe. A cant is a kind of codespeak. Say one thing but mean another. Developed by Scottish, Gaelic, and French crooks way back in the sixteenth century. They could carry on entire conversations and the coppers had no idea what they were talking about. You likely heard versions of a thieves' cant when you were with the SFPD."

"News to me," I said.

"You still heard it, even if you were oblivious. Teenage boys use cant speak as a way to talk sweet or mean about girls or teachers without the girls or teachers knowing their meaning. Criminals in prison use cants to plan crimes, and the prison guards have no idea what they're saying. Victor Hugo called cants the language of darkness."

"Hugo. I've heard that name."

"French dude who wrote Les Misérables and The Hunchback of Notre-Dame."

"Of course," I said, shaking my head. "The Hunchback and language of darkness. How did I forget?" Jack Santiago would say that Diamond was unnecessarily displaying his erudition. But first he would have to ask Diamond to remind him of that word.

"Give me an example of a thieves' cant?" I said.

"Take what the lady told you. One guy said Basque food was like eating out on the desert, while the other guy said he really liked Korean food. That could mean they think Basque food doesn't generate much cash income, while Korean restaurants are cash cows."

"Thus a good target for robbery," I said.

"Sí. When one asks, 'When should we eat?' he might be really asking, 'When should we hit the place?' The answer, 'midnight or one,' is self-evident."

"Which then suggests a burglary rather than a robbery," I said. "So they're planning to break in to steal the cash after hours."

I imagined that Diamond's nod was one of tolerance for the slow people. But he smiled. He wasn't being condescending. He just couldn't constantly edit out his smarts.

"The cant thing makes sense," I said. "I probably could have figured out most of that all by myself."

"And you always have Lazlo to help you if you get stuck." Diamond grinned. "So do we intercept these guys tonight?" Diamond asked.

"In my world, that makes sense. I don't know anyone on the Truckee PD who would plan a stakeout on my last-minute suggestion. Not even Oberman knows me that well. More reliable to do it myself. But you volunteering your time to help is beyond anything I could ask for."

"My job is fighting crime," he said, "volunteer or not. The state of Nevada or any other."

"Very nice of you. However, considering that you are a peace officer sworn to protect the citizens of Douglas County, Nevada, that would suggest a proscription against going across the state line into a California town where you have no jurisdiction."

"Proscription," Diamond said. "Good word."

"I learned it from Lazlo."

Diamond seemed to think about what I'd said. "Even though California Penal Code says—with muddy language, I might add—that a Nevada peace officer can operate in California within fifty miles of Nevada if helping the CHP on a law enforcement situation, I won't try to operate with that. Best for me to go in as a citizen. If I witness a significant crime, I can make a citizen's arrest, same as you. I'm sure that's your goal, right?" He started to grin, then stopped. "Or we simply detain these guys and hand them over to the local PD?" Diamond said.

"After a fashion, yes."

"There you go using a cant yourself."

I raised my eyebrows.

"'After a fashion' is a copper's cant for slapping them around first as payback for beating on you."

I shrugged. "My abdominal pain is still eight or nine on the pain scale, and my neck grinds like broken glass. Which, from my perspective, makes a little retribution something highly desired. If I'm up to it."

Diamond looked at me. "Most philosophers say that retribution is not a proper way to handle crime."

Maybe I frowned.

Diamond continued, "But some dudes, like the German philosopher Kant, thought retribution was okay and maybe even proper under certain conditions."

"And those conditions?"

"Kant's main concern was whether the punishment was proportional to the crime."

"Meaning, even though the scabby guy seriously beat me up, I shouldn't kill him. I should only beat on him until he pleads 'uncle.'"

Diamond made a little grin. "Killing him would be out of proportion, sí."

"You have your sidearm?" I asked.

"Two, as always. The Glock Nineteen is in my shoulder holster and the P Three sixty-five is in the ankle biter. But considering a mission in California, it's probably best if I leave my metal in my pickup."

I looked at his rundown vehicle. "The door locks on that thing don't appear very robust."

"True. The one on the passenger side doesn't work at all. But under the driver's seat is a cubby I had welded in on the undercarriage. The floor-panel cover has a hidden latch that most people couldn't find in a thirty-minute search even if they knew it existed. Without knowing how to work the latch, you wouldn't be able to get into the cubby without putting the truck up on a lift and firing up a cutting torch."

"Be easier if you did like me," I said, "and just carry a Tee Ball baseball bat. It's short enough that I can slip it into my backpack."

"I'm pretty sure a Tee Ball club is illegal for our purpose." Diamond said. "And it's lethal, too."

"Says the guy packing two semi-automatic pistols. Imagine if I went into your Sheriff's Office and filled out a concealed-carry application for a baseball bat."

"It would make a great story at our local watering holes."

I gestured at Diamond's ankle. "Have you ever even fired one of your guns?"

"Not outside of the range. But as you know, you don't carry a gun so you have the casual opportunity to fire it. You carry it in case you have the serious need to fire it."

"And if you must fire them, your weapons are much more lethal than my little potentially-illegal club for which I couldn't get an official carry permit."

"Actually, if you're close enough to use a club, it can be just as lethal as a gun. And, like a gun, it all depends on where you aim the club."

While Diamond de-armed himself and stashed his weapons in his secret lock box, I walked back to Street's condo and told her and Geneviève that we were heading to Truckee on a tip that might lead to the man who burned down Geneviève's restaurant and apartment. "I'll be back late. Okay if I leave the dogs here? Rather than wake you up to fetch His Largeness when we get back, maybe I could stop by tomorrow morning?"

Street nodded. "Yes, of course, we're happy to be dog sitters." We kissed, I hugged Camille, and I touched Geneviève on the shoulder. I left, but not before I saw a pained look on Geneviève's face.

I locked the door behind me.

"Shall I ride with you?" I asked Diamond.

"Sí. The guys who beat you up may recognize your Jeep. On our way back, I can pull back into Street's condo for you to transfer to your Jeep."

I gazed at his pickup. "You think this crate has enough life left to make it to Truckee?"

He scoffed. "It's your Jeep that's full of bullet holes."

# THIRTY-TWO

"You think we should have our warrior wraps?" Diamond asked.

"Body protection? Not much downside to it," I said. I reached into the hatchback of my Jeep, pulled out my gear bag, and removed my old Kevlar vest. I took off my jacket, put on the vest, and rezipped the jacket over it.

Diamond extracted his vest from behind the passenger seat.

As he pulled it on, I said, "Your ride is a good disguise. No one would expect a cop and an ex-cop to show up in a vehicle that has enough rust that you can't be certain the windshield is held in securely." Diamond made a serious nod.

"You got your baseball bat?"

I held up my daypack. The bat was mostly enclosed with just the end sticking out.

We got in Diamond's truck, and he drove up the East Shore through the growing twilight. North of Street's, Highway 50 turns east, curves around the face of Shakespeare Rock and climbs up toward Spooner Summit. Just down from the crest, Diamond turned left on 28, and we continued north up the curving road, past the turn-off to Skunk Harbor and past the entrance to the Thunderbird Lodge, the summer estate that San Francisco playboy George Whittell built during the Depression on his little 40,000-acre spread along the East Shore of Lake Tahoe.

In the distance to the west across the lake was the Sierra Crest. The orange glow on the snow from the fading sunset reflected in the 12-mile-stretch of water. The orange was gradually shifting to a cold dim white illuminated from a spoon of moon overhead.

Diamond continued on to Sand Harbor, with its picture-perfect curved beach lit by the moon. Behind the beach was the natural amphitheater where the Shakespeare-on-the-Beach company performs in the summer.

North of Sand Harbor was Incline Village, its restaurants full of
après ski diners recounting their thrills of the day on the mountain.
We curved through Crystal Bay and on to Kings Beach with its
boutique stores and art galleries and ice cream parlors and ski boot
shops.

"Hyper cute little hamlet," Diamond said.

"Like Tahoe City," I said.

"Nah, Tahoe City is even hyper cuter."

Diamond turned right on 267, which leads up to Brockway
Summit, the steepest of the passes that come into the Tahoe Basin. I
couldn't see him press the pedal to the metal, but the straining sound
of the old straight-six engine made me think that any greater flow of
gasoline to the carb would cause the engine to blow its head gasket.

We eventually made it to the top, and Diamond switched from
pushing on the accelerator to pushing on the brake. From the way
the pickup pulled to the right, I suspected that only one or two of
the brakes worked, and only on the right side.

Diamond kept it slow until we came down to the Martis Valley
floor. Once we were out of danger of becoming a run-away vehicle,
he sped back up to a stately 35 mph, and we were in Truckee minutes
later.

"You got a parking preference?" he asked as we drove through
downtown and headed out to the shopping area where the Basque
and Korean restaurants were located.

"I think a dark, nondescript place would be good."

Diamond nodded and pulled into an unattractive commercial
center that hosted the Korean restaurant. We found a place far from
any stores or restaurants.

I left my pack and bat in the truck when we got out. We walked
the perimeter of the center, getting a feel for the layout, probably
looking like vagabonds who were interested in the food that
restaurants threw away.

The Basque restaurant was one space in from the end of a row
of stores. The Korean restaurant was several storefronts in from the
other end. As we went by the restaurants, we took surreptitious
photos with our phones.

"You think our phones give away our disguise?" Diamond asked as he made hip shots, never looking to see if his phone's camera lens was properly aimed.

"Even homeless people have phones," I said. "People will still think we're dumpster divers."

We walked around the back of the shops. There was an alley just wide enough to handle delivery trucks. The doors weren't labeled with store names, only suite numbers. But there was a dumpster with food smells, not all pleasant. On the ground was a food-stained to-go box with what might be Korean printing. We stopped and looked at the heavy metal door that was set into a concrete block wall. Next to the door was a wavy-glass window with reinforcement wires in the glass. Up above and over to the side were two small windows. They didn't have security glass, but they looked too small to crawl through. They were probably restroom windows.

"Our most important concern," Diamond said, "is establishing likely ingress and egress points for these dudes. I'm voting they break in someplace that isn't wired with an alarm and go out the same way."

"It probably won't be this door. The front door would be much easier, but that's likely wired, and it doesn't seem a good choice for escape. Too many people could see them."

Diamond looked at me. "We'll have a better idea if we go inside and eat."

We walked back around to the front of the building.

Because it was a week day, we had no trouble getting a table without reservations. We didn't want to be visible from the windows, so we asked the host to put us in a rear corner. He frowned but did as requested. We ate well. Diamond had something I didn't recognize and couldn't pronounce, but it smelled great. I had Korean fried chicken. We drank Korean Pale Ale and followed it up with Korean tea. Which, after a time, gave us each a truthful reason to visit the restroom and peek into the kitchen as we walked by.

The food was inexpensive. But looking at the menu, I figured out that two desserts plus tip would bump the bill to just over $100. My goal was to receive change so I could get a sense of where they kept their cash. The answer might indicate if a thief would choose burglary after hours or robbery while they were open. So we each ate a scoop of green, melon-flavored ice cream. When it came time to pay, I went to the checkout counter and pulled out two Ben Franklins. The waitress took the bills, went to the hosting station, and opened a small metal box. She riffled through the money and then carried my two bills back to the kitchen. In a moment, she was back with change, four twenties, a ten, a five, and some coins. Her speed in getting the change suggested that either there was no safe, or the safe was kept open. It made me think that the thieves might break in at night.

After we left, we once again walked around the shopping center, discussing how things might play out.

"The only alarm wires I saw were on the front door," I said.

"Me too," Diamond said. "The window on the alley side has wire-reinforced glass," Diamond said. "The glass would be hard to break, but I'm guessing the window's not wired to an alarm. The window looks like it's fitted into the cement-block wall with mortar. If someone spent some time working on the mortar with a chisel, the entire window could be released from the wall and lowered down behind the nearby dumpster. They could crawl in through the window, find the money, and come back out the same way. I wonder if they have reason to think there is no safe."

"I just had a thought," I said. "Maybe it doesn't matter if there is a safe. Maybe the enforcers tried to extort this restaurant, and the restaurant said no."

"You're thinking this attack could be like when they burned down Geneviève's digs? Payback for not paying the weekly ransom?"

"Could be," I said.

"If this is just about punishing the restaurant, does that change what we're doing now?"

"I don't think so. We still want to catch them during their burglary or arson attempt, whichever they choose."

Diamond nodded. He looked around and gestured up at the wall. "When you were in the restroom, did you notice this small window?"

"Yeah. Small and up high. I don't think they could climb through it. Especially the big guy."

"So," Diamond said, his voice disappointed. "We don't have a good idea of how they will break in or how they will break out. We don't even know if the restaurant has cash on the premises."

"When I arranged for the woman to get change, she went into the kitchen and came back with change very quickly. Not enough time to enter the combo on a safe."

"But I imagine a lot of businesses leave their safe open during business hours just for the purpose of making change or having petty cash to pay a courier delivery. Then they would lock it at night."

"Sorry to say it, but I hope our thieves don't encounter a safe," I said. "If they show up and break in, and if we catch them, it will work out best for us if they have the restaurant's cash proceeds on them."

Diamond nodded. "A whole lotta greenbacks always look suspicious. You got a plan for a stakeout? We could hang out in the shadows near the back of the building."

"It's possible they will try to go in through the front door. So one of us should have that door in view. If they can crack the lock, the alarm will go off. But if they're very fast, they could be back out with money before the alarm generates a response." I turned and looked around.

"If you hang out by that brown utility box near Donner Pass Road, and if I wait over at the far side of the shopping center parking lot, you could see the back of the restaurant, and I could see the front. At least one of us would be able to see them regardless of where they showed up. Each of us could inform the other on the phone."

"I'm guessing," Diamond said, "that one or both of them will be early compared to their midnight comment in their thieves' cant. I think they'll come after the restaurant's closing time, but before midnight. That way they can watch and judge when the restaurant staff goes home. They'll stay separate at first and communicate by phone."

"Sounds good." I pulled out my phone. "Let's put our phones on vibrate. Probably good to dim the brightness, too. You head to the utility box. With your brown skin, you'll blend right in. Just don't smile. I'll head over to the corner of the parking lot. There's a fir tree I can stand under. I'll be nearly invisible."

"What's the chance the restaurant owner takes his cash receipts home with him?"

I shrugged. "Slim. He or she would be an easy mark. It's dark.

There's almost no one around. I'm guessing the owner leaves the cash in a safe or hides it someplace in the kitchen, then takes it to the bank during daylight the next day."

"What's your ideal as this plays out?"

"We let them break in and wait until they are leaving the restaurant with their loot. We accost them and tie them up, call the local police and report them. The police will come and find them with their loot and gear and whatever else they have, and take it from there."

Diamond said, "Sounds good. But they could shoot us dead and then make their escape."

"True. So we keep our heads down until we see an opportunity to grab them before they can shoot."

"We can still call the Truckee PD," Diamond said.

"True. But I think the chances are unlikely that anything goes down. If I call and I'm really convincing, they'll send an officer out to this restaurant. If nothing happens, they'll move my name from the PI friend column to the quack column."

"And you still want a chance to throttle these guys for beating you up."

"That would be satisfying, yeah."

Diamond looked at his watch. "It's ten forty-five. The restaurant has closed. Our tough guy dirtballs could show up at any time. We should get into position." He used his fist to give me a soft slug on the shoulder. "Good luck," he said, then turned and walked away, slipping off into the shadows and disappearing into the dark.

# THIRTY-THREE

There were ugly-but-effective utility power pole lights in various parts of the parking lot. They put out round spills of light that were blue-white and were so bright they felt like military issue, searing the retinas of anyone who glanced at them. The night-sky movement that allows Tahoe tourists to enjoy the stars had no chance against these lights.

Near one light were three scraggly fir trees casting shadows from the light. I walked out to Diamond's pickup, reached into the cab, and opened my pack. I pulled out my Tee Ball bat and headed down the sidewalk as if I were focused on walking home.

My path took me through the tree shadows. When I was at the deepest part of the shadow, within touching distance of one of the tree trunks, I dropped to a squat. Unless an observer had been watching carefully, their perception would be that I'd dropped out of sight because I made it to my destination, whether a car parked on the next street or one of the paths that angled through the forested lot behind the restaurant.

The night was quiet. Only a few cars were parked in the lot, probably belonging to employees of the liquor on the opposite side of the lot. No doubt the liquor store brought in more cash than the Korean restaurant. But liquor stores are more likely to protect that cash with a locked safe or a gun. Whereas a restaurant is more likely to protect their cash with subterfuge.

An old, small Ford pickup with no muffler pulled into the lot and parked in the middle. The volume was dangerous to unprotected ears, like an Indy 500 racer. The engine turned off. Two men got out. They shut the doors and said a few words to each other, speaking across the car's roof. They walked over to the liquor store and pushed through the swing door. A minute later they came out, one carrying a six pack, the other a brown paper bag the size of a whiskey bottle. One was using his free hand to hold a cigarette pack to his mouth so his teeth could grab at the plastic wrap. He got the wrap off, released it with his teeth, and it fell to the pavement. Still using his teeth, he got a cig out and held it in his lips. I saw a flame flare and heard the click of the lighter shutting. They got in their pickup, started up their noisemaker, and drove away.

In the distance, I could make out the utility box where I assumed Diamond was waiting. He was invisible.

In the distance, a night bird called. It sounded mournful. From farther away, a Harley revved over and over as it shifted gears, making its loud blat blat blat, telling the world, 'I'm here, stop ignoring me, I can make enough noise to force you to pay attention to my insecurities and my doubts about my masculinity.' Or maybe the message was one of confidence. 'I'm strong and hyper-masculine, and this noise can get me a certain kind of girl you could never have, so choke on that, nerds.'

I heard the distant bass rumble of a sports car specifically tuned to make another kind of noise. People love making noise. I turned to see a dark blue BMW pull into the lot. It parked in the center of the asphalt where the Ford pickup had parked. Two men got out. One was thick and strong, and one was tall and skinny.

One of the men opened the BMW's hatchback and pulled out some kind of narrow object. It looked metallic. When they turned, I saw that it was a stepladder, about five feet long. Probably the maximum size object one could fit in a BMW. The men walked over to the Korean restaurant. They put their faces close to the windows and cupped their hands around their faces. In the harsh parking lot lights, I saw that they wore gloves. They said a few words under their breaths, and walked on down the sidewalk. They went around the building and disappeared.

My phone vibrated. I answered in a low voice.

"Hello?"

Diamond said, "The guys just walked around the side of the building. Now they're turning down the back side. Do you think these are your guys?"

"Yeah."

"Okay. I'll come from my end. You go from your end. We'll close in on them."

"Roger that." I clicked off.

I stood up and walked over to the building. I was now in the bright light. I stayed against the building wall and walked around the end of the building.

The back side of the building was in the dark. After the harsh lights in the parking lot, I felt like a night creature, craving the darkness. There was a security light on a neighboring building, but its light was far enough away to leave the building next to me relatively dim. I could sense movement far down the building, but I didn't know what I was seeing.

There was a metallic bang. I saw a flashlight turn on near a dumpster. My sense of distance made me confident the men were at the rear of the restaurant. I watched and waited. There was more movement, but I couldn't tell what it was.

I started moving along the back wall of the building. I kept my back to the wall and moved sideways so that I didn't present an obvious profile.

There was more noise. Soft thumps and metallic sounds. Their flashlight turned off.

There was a rumbling bass note that gave me the idea they were rolling the dumpster.

As I got closer, I tried to stay flattened against the building's back wall. It seemed the men would see me at any moment. After another ten yards, I could make out their movements.

They were up on the dumpster. They had opened the folding stepladder and set it on top of the dumpster lid. The skinny man was just disappearing over the top edge of the building. The thick man was on the ladder, leaning against the wall and taking a careful step onto the top step. He reached up and hooked his arm over the top of the wall. He scrabbled one foot against the wall, found a little bit of purchase, then tried to pull himself up.

As is the case with all animals, the bigger and stronger ones have less strength-to-weight ratio. A monkey can swing through trees. A T-Rex can't do a single pull-up.

The skinny guy reached over and down, grabbed the big guy's arm, and helped pull him up. The two men disappeared over the wall and onto the roof, leaving the stepladder on the top of the dumpster.

Behind the stepladder was the wavy-glass window with wire

reinforcement. Above and to the right were the restroom windows. I saw movement on the other side of the dumpster. Diamond approached. We stood close to each other and pressed against the wall to minimize the chance that the men might look over and down and see us.

Diamond whispered.

"They're going to look for a way into the restaurant from the roof."

"Right," I whispered back.

"When they come back down the ladder, we can topple it at the right moment. Maybe tumble one of the guys to the ground."

"What's your guess as to how long this might take?"

Diamond looked back up at the edge of the roof.

"First they have to establish if there is an access point. Some kind of stairway. Or a big kitchen exhaust fan. Then they have to find what they want to steal. Cash."

"Or, if arson is their goal, they have to set the place on fire."

A light caught my eye. I turned and looked down toward the far corner where I'd just come from. There was a flashlight, going up and down, back and forth.

"Cop," I whispered to Diamond. "On foot patrol."

"You okay with staying here?" he said.

"Yeah. I think we should answer his questions truthfully." I looked at the cop coming closer. "Her questions," I corrected.

"No way," Diamond said. "Look at the size of that guy."

"I've met her. Hattie Foster. She's a rookie on the Truckee PD, and yes, she is large. Her brothers are pro wrestlers."

As she got closer, I leaned my bat against the wall, moved toward her, and spoke quietly.

"Hello, Officer Hattie Foster. Owen McKenna, here. We met at Geneviève Laurent's restaurant."

She approached us very slowly, wary of two guys apparently hanging out in a dark alley. She briefly shined her light on our faces and then let her light linger on our bodies. I held up my empty hands. Diamond saw me and followed suit.

I added. "This is my friend Sergeant Diamond Martinez from the Douglas County Sheriff's office."

Hattie stopped twenty feet away, still being careful. Her free hand rested on the butt of her sidearm.

She spoke. "Can I ask what you are doing here?"

I gave her a quick rundown, beginning with the tip I got from the Basque restaurant woman. I didn't tell her details about the thieves' cant and our interpretation of its meaning. But I did explain that we'd seen the men who had extorted Geneviève arrive in their BMW, which was parked in the lot out front. I told Hattie how we'd watched the two men climb up on the dumpster with a stepladder and then climb it to the roof.

"And you think they broke into the restaurant."

"I can't say I think that they broke in. But I believe that was their intention."

She looked at Diamond, "And you, sergeant, are here with Mr. McKenna in what capacity?"

"McKenna's a friend," Diamond said. "I'm helping as a citizen. No official capacity."

"Because you are out of your county and out of your state, right?"

"Right."

"So you're not carrying?"

"Correct."

Hattie nodded. "Thanks for that. You can probably tell I'm a rookie cop. This is a new situation for me, so I'm feeling my way."

"You're doing fine," Diamond said.

"Lieutenant Oberman is systematically exposing me to new situations. This is my first time doing commercial building checks at night. We're short staff, so I'm doing a solo mission. But I didn't mind because Truckee isn't exactly a dangerous big city. But I certainly never expected to come upon a burglary in progress."

She paused and looked at the building. "What do you expect from this situation?"

I answered. "The two men have been up on the roof for several minutes. They probably found a way inside. So my guess is that they'll be coming out soon. When they come over the edge of the roof…"

There was an explosion of sound as the window behind the dumpster blew out toward us, and the stepladder was propelled from the top of the dumpster to the far side of the alley.

# THIRTY-FOUR

The window broke and folded in the middle as it blew out of the building, but its embedded security wires held the pieces together. Behind the window, coming at high speed, was one of the men, his feet against the glass. He was in a sitting position as he flew through the air. It was as if he'd swung from a ceiling pipe like a circus performer and kicked out the window.

While the broken window shot out across the dumpster and landed on the alley pavement, the man landed in a sitting position on the dumpster, his legs straight in front of him.

Diamond and I were at the side of the dumpster, while Officer Foster was standing in front of it. My impulse was to run to her, but I stopped when I saw the skinny man crawling out of the window. He was holding a small satchel. I was tall enough to reach across the dumpster and grab the man's arm as he came through the opening.

I heard Foster shout.

"Stay right there, sir!"

I turned and saw Hattie Foster fumbling for her weapon. She pulled her stun gun out of her duty belt with one hand and reached her other hand out to grab the thick man sitting on the dumpster. Her movements were awkward, what one would expect from a rookie officer confronting an unusual crisis for the first time.

The thick man scooted forward so his legs could bend at the edge of the dumpster. But instead of trying to kick Hattie out of the way and jump to the ground, he lifted his legs up onto Hattie's shoulders, propping them on either side of Hattie's neck. Then he hooked his knees around the back side of her neck, crossed his ankles, and straightened his legs, putting her head in a crushing leg lock. Diamond came up behind Hattie and tried to separate the man's ankles. He would need more than muscle to do that.

I was pulling the skinny man off the side of the dumpster and didn't dare let go of him because he might pull out a gun.

Although the thick man had his legs locked onto Hattie's neck, he turned his head and looked at me. "Oh, you're the skunk who tripped me and cracked my cheekbone. I'm coming for you when I'm done with this cop."

Hattie was flailing as the thick man's leg lock cut off the blood flow to her brain. The hand with the stun gun was in the air, unfocused.

The man was reaching under his jacket toward his shoulder, as if about to pull his gun. With Hattie and Diamond and me all occupied, we were about to lose control of the situation. The thick man would shoot Hattie, and we'd have an unnecessary tragedy.

Then Hattie Foster did something extraordinary.

She dropped her stun gun to the ground, reached both of her hands forward, and grabbed the thick man's jacket. She must have been about to lose consciousness from the lack of blood to her brain, yet she yanked the man toward her so that his head and chest were bent over her head. While she pulled him down onto her head, she jerked him off the dumpster.

He was now supported by his knees bent over her shoulders, still reaching for his gun. Although he probably weighed well over 200 pounds, Hattie rotated so that she faced away from the dumpster. Diamond stepped back, astonished, not seeming to know what was best to do. But it didn't matter, as it was quickly obvious that, while we didn't know what to do, Hattie Foster did.

She stepped one foot forward and kept the other back for stability. She arched her back for a moment and then did a kind of forward crunch and flung the man off her shoulders and onto his back.

He landed on the pavement. His head bounced off the asphalt as Hattie landed on top of him, his body cushioning her fall.

Then Hattie rolled off of him and lay on the pavement, gasping for air.

In the meantime, I'd pulled the skinny man off of the dumpster, spun him around, his arm in a severe hammerlock, and shoved him hard against the concrete block wall.

He screamed in pain.

I reached out with my free hand and patted him down to his waist. Once I knew he had no easy weapon to grab, I pulled a zip tie out of my jacket pocket and tied his wrists behind him. I turned him away from the wall, used my knee against the backs of his knees, causing them to buckle. I collapsed him to the pavement, face down.

I patted down his legs, found no weapon, no wallet, no ID. Kneeling across the backs of his legs, I zip tied his ankles while he howled in pain. Then I jerked his ankles up and zip tied his ankle tie to his wrist tie so he was hog tied from behind.

I got off of the skinny guy, went over, and kneeled next to Hattie, who was still gasping for air. Diamond had pulled on latex gloves and was removing the big man's weapon from his shoulder holster.

"A glock like mine," Diamond said. With his forefinger against the barrel and away from the trigger, Diamond pressed the magazine release and put the magazine in his left jacket pocket. He pulled the slide back and carefully ejected a round that the man had previously loaded into the chamber. Diamond caught the round. He held the gun up to look through the chamber and make certain the gun was empty. Then he put the round in the same pocket as the magazine and put the gun in his other jacket pocket. The thick man was still unconscious, struggling to breathe. He'd probably had the wind knocked out of him.

Diamond checked the man's other pockets.

"No wallet, no ID," he said.

"Same with the skinny guy."

Diamond squatted down next to Hattie.

"That was amazing," he said to her, awe in his voice.

Hattie just breathed.

"Are you okay?" Diamond asked. "Anything broken?"

"Yeah," Hattie eventually said. Then, "No. Yeah, I'm okay. No, nothing's broken."

"That move was like something in pro wrestling." Diamond was doing a slow head shake. "Only it wasn't for show. You did it for real."

"That was a Power Bomb," Hattie said. "Never thought I'd actually use that move."

"How did you know how to do that?" Diamond asked.

"Childhood training from my brothers," Hattie said. She turned her head toward the man she'd just thrown on the ground. "Is he still breathing?"

"Yeah, I can see his chest going up and down," I said.

"We better get an ambulance," she said, still professional. "His head hit the pavement. He could have traumatic brain injury." She reached for the radio on her belt, her fingers feeling for it but not finding it."

"You want help?" Diamond said.

"Yeah. Can you call it in? I don't remember how to use the radio."

Diamond pulled her radio from its holster, flipped it on, and spoke.

"Douglas County Sergeant Diamond Martinez calling in for Officer Foster. She's seems okay but is quite winded after taking down a burglar at the Korean restaurant. I forget the address. We need Truckee PD backup, a medic box for one of the suspects, and prisoner transport for another suspect. Officer Foster, the suspects, myself, and PI Owen McKenna are in the alley at the rear of the Korean restaurant in the shopping center off Donner Pass Road."

Diamond was starting to put her radio back in its holster when he stopped.

"One more thing," he said to the dispatcher. "Can you connect me to Lieutenant Oberman, please?"

Diamond was quiet for a minute, then came a voice.

"Lieutenant Oberman, here."

Diamond repeated what he'd already said. Then he said, "What I just witnessed was an astonishing display of valor from Officer Foster. I've never seen anything like it. Thought you'd want to know."

"Roger that," came the reply. "Put McKenna on before you go."

I took the radio from Diamond. "Yes, Lieutenant."

"I don't know this Douglas County sergeant. You can verify what he just said?"

"Yes, including what he said about Hattie Foster."

"Do you remember her given name?"

"Yes. Hypatia. Good call for verification technique. No burglar would know that. Officer Foster is a major asset. You'll want to figure out how to prevent her from going back to work at the Jet Propulsion Laboratory."

"Will do. Can you put her on?'"

I handed her the radio and pointed to it. "Push here to talk. Lift up to listen."

She pushed the button. "Officer Foster, here."

"This is Lieutenant Oberman. You alright?"

"Yeah."

"They said you kicked some butt."

"I suppose that's true."

"I hope you didn't take unnecessary risks."

"I don't think so, sir. The man was trying to... I don't know. Kill me, probably."

"Okay. Glad you're okay. Check back when everything is calm. Roger and out."

She held the radio up in the air as if she didn't know what to do with it. Diamond took the radio and replaced it on Foster's belt, then helped her to sit up and lean against the dumpster.

I rolled the thick man over onto his stomach and zip tied his hands behind his back. Because he was big and strong and violent, I used two ties. I shined my flashlight at the back of his head. There was no blood or broken skin. He probably had a concussion, but he'd likely live.

I returned him to his back, then double zip tied his ankles. I noticed he still had a scab across one cheekbone. No doubt it was a daily reminder that I'd tripped him. He probably still regretted that those drunk college kids had interrupted him when he beat me up.

# THIRTY-FIVE

When Hattie Foster got her wind back, she picked up her stun gun off the ground and holstered it. She walked over to the skinny guy, arrested him for burglary and read him his Miranda rights. She then moved over to the unconscious man and did the same thing, even though he didn't respond.

Then she sat back down on the ground and once again leaned against the dumpster.

Diamond, with his unshakable charm, had Hattie talking about orbital mechanics by the time the Truckee patrol SUV arrived with one officer in it.

The man got out. "I'm Officer Chamberlain. Where are we at?" he said toward all of us.

Diamond introduced us and briefly explained what had happened.

"You're just in time to take this suspect," I said. I cut the hogtie zip tie, disconnecting the skinny man's ankles from his wrists. Chamberlain held the rear door of his vehicle while I directed the skinny guy into the back of the patrol unit, which had a heavy-duty wire mesh between the front and back seats.

The ambulance arrived, and the paramedics pulled out a gurney. They lowered it to the ground next to the thick guy, transferred him to it, raised it up so its wheels dropped into place.

"We need to cut these zip ties," one of the paramedics said.

"No, you don't," I said. "This man is murderous and devious. He'll feign unconsciousness and then try to kill you."

"Right," the man said in a mocking tone as if I were an idiot. "Nevertheless, he can't lie on cuffed wrists. I still have to free his arms so I can start an IV."

"We'll first cuff one of his arms to the gurney, then rotate him, then cuff his arms together on his front side," I said.

"The man's out cold," the medic said. "You're overreacting

because of the stress of arresting him."

The medic was frustrating me. "You are, what, twenty-eight or thirty?" I said. "You haven't been around long enough to understand the deviousness of some suspects."

"I took a psychology course in nursing school and learned all about psychological trauma and criminal minds, too. I also know how to tell if someone is feigning unconsciousness. And," he got a condescending tone in his voice, "I don't believe you are part of official Truckee law enforcement. So I out-rank you in the town limits."

"Keep the man cuffed," Hattie called out. "McKenna knows what he's talking about."

"I still have to have the man's arms at his front to start an IV. This man could be dying of a subdural hematoma. We have to be ready to act."

So we rolled the gurney over to the ambulance, leaned the suspect to his side. "You're making a mistake," I said as the paramedic cut the man's wrist cuffs. We rolled the man back onto his back. I was getting another zip tie into place to cuff his hands in front when the suspect leaped to his feet, grabbing the medic. He put a headlock around the medic's neck from behind. Then he bunny-hopped backward on his cuffed ankles, dragging the medic with him.

The medic's face turned a shade of blue from choking. His eyes bulged and his jaw muscles clenched. The Truckee cop who'd come as backup unit pulled his weapon, pointed it at the suspect and medic.

"Freeze," he shouted.

Hattie wisely stayed back and to the side, realizing the situation had escalated far past what her level of experience prepared her for.

I saw Diamond shift so he was standing behind her. He appeared to whisper up toward her ear. She might have made an imperceptible nod.

Diamond was blocked from the suspect's view by Hattie's sizable form. He slowly unsnapped her stun gun and slipped it into his jacket pocket where he'd put the Glock magazine. Then he appeared to whisper something else.

Hattie made another nod. "Hey, McKenna," Hattie shouted. "Didn't you pat the suspect down?"

"Yeah, I did, and you'd be surprised at what I found," I said, making my voice dramatic.

All eyes turned toward me when I spoke.

Diamond chose that moment to move a few feet over into the shade of a tree where the utility lights didn't shine. From there, he moved through more shade until he came up on the side of the ambulance. He was behind the suspect and the medic.

The suspect didn't notice. "Stay back!" the suspect shouted toward me and the cop. "McKenna didn't get my backup gun which is pointed at this medic twerp's back as we speak. If any of you move, I'll put a hole in this jerk's heart from behind."

As the suspect spoke, Diamond moved softly up from behind him. Diamond reached out with the stun gun. A blue arc of electricity lit up the suspect's back. The man jerked and arched his back in a powerful spasm.

Diamond continued to hold the stun gun. There was an electrical crackle. The suspect dropped to the ground. The paramedic fell another direction and crawled off into the dark on hands and knees.

Diamond leaped onto the suspect, who was still having convulsions. He rolled the man onto his stomach and once again zip tied the man's wrists behind him using two ties. Then he turned to me.

"McKenna. Maybe you could help me put this scumbag where he belongs."

I walked over, and the two of us picked up the man, one of us on each of his cuffed arms. We lifted up and dragged him over to the patrol SUV. We laid him face down on the ground next to the vehicle's rear door.

The man started to resist. Diamond put the stun gun on the man's neck and gave a quick pull on the trigger. The man's muscles all seemed to contract at once.

Diamond kneeled on the man's back while I bent his knees and used another tie to attach his ankles to his wrists so that he was again hog tied from behind. Officer Chamberlain once again opened up the rear door.

The skinny man seemed to cower toward the far side of the back seat.

Diamond and I each picked up an arm in one hand and a leg in the other, and lifted the suspect off the ground.

"Ready?" Diamond said.

We swung the man back and forth like a battering ram.

Diamond counted, "One, two, three," and we tossed the man into the rear seat.

Maybe the thump I heard was the man's head hitting the far door. Or maybe it was the skinny guy's knee.

We shut the door.

Chamberlain got on his radio and called in a report to the Lieutenant.

"The paramedic misjudged the situation, sir. He wanted the injured suspect's cuffs off despite Officer Foster's clear warning and the PI's clear warning that he shouldn't do that. Then the suspect grabbed the medic, began choking him, and threatened to kill him."

As he spoke, I saw the medic hanging back in the shadow behind the ambulance.

"Then the off-duty cop from Douglas County managed to hit the suspect with Officer Foster's stun gun. The suspect released the medic. The off-duty cop and the private investigator subdued the suspect and put him in the back of my patrol unit with the other suspect. I'll be bringing them both in. He doesn't deserve a ride in the medic box."

"What about Officer Foster?" Lieutenant Oberman said over the radio. "Is she still okay?"

The cop turned to Hattie.

"Yes, I'm fine," she said. "I'm okay driving myself back."

The cop told the Lieutenant.

"Okay," the lieutenant said. "Is the paramedic still there?"

"I believe so."

"Put him on."

The cop called out to the medic who was still standing in the shadows. "Lieutenant wants to talk to you," he said.

The medic came over and took the radio. "Hello?" His voice was very shaky.

"Are you the medic who authorized taking off the suspect's cuffs despite being warned not to?"

"Yes. I thought that the sus…"

"Never mind what you thought," the lieutenant said in a harsh voice. "What you did was negligence, a flagrant disregard for safety. Officers could have been killed. You could have been killed. I'll be reporting this to the service that employs you. We can no longer have you putting our officers and the public at risk. If I see you around here again, I'll arrest you and charge you with enough broken laws and rules to put you on a long trip through the court system, a trip that will end with you in jail and unable to ever again get a job. Do you understand me?"

The medic didn't respond immediately.

"Do you understand me!"

"Yes," came a feeble reply.

"Give me back to Officer Foster."

The medic handed the radio to Hattie and slinked away.

The Lieutenant said, "I'm double checking to be sure I understand correctly. You caught two burglars coming out of the Korean restaurant."

Hattie looked at the radio as if to remember how to use it.

She pressed the button. "Yes," she answered.

"You arrested both of them and read them their rights."

"Yes."

"The off-duty cop said you exhibited valor. Was that exaggeration?"

"I'm not sure how best to categorize it, sir."

"Well, what did you do to make the off-duty cop say that?"

"When the, um, bad guy blasted out of the restaurant window, breaking it and such, he landed on the dumpster right where I was standing. Before I realized what was happening, he locked his legs around my neck and started to squeeze such that I was going to pass out. So I lifted him up and put a Power Bomb on him, which basically means throwing him onto the ground. That was a pretty hard fall for him and it, um, settled him down quite a bit."

"Is this so-called Power Bomb some kind of move you learned from your wrestler brothers?"

"Yes, sir. They taught it to me when I was a girl."

"When the recipient of this Power Bomb falls, he lands how?"

"On his back, sir."

"And where do you land?"

"On top of him."

"So his body more or less protected you from breaking your own bones."

"Yes, sir."

"Is this the kind of thing you expect to do with future criminals you catch?"

"No, sir. Not unless they put a leg lock on my neck."

There was a pause before Lieutenant Oberman asked, "Are you sure you're okay to drive?"

"Yes, sir. I'm sure. I've been moving around. I'm a little stiff, but nothing is broken."

"When do you expect to get back to the office?"

"Soon. But first I should inspect the restaurant where they broke in, right? And before you ask, yes, Officer Chamberlain has the two suspects in his SUV."

"He should stay with the prisoners," the lieutenant said. "Take McKenna with you into the restaurant."

"Okay. Roger and out. Wait. Is that the right thing to say?"

"Yes, that will work," the lieutenant replied.

Chamberlain had heard the lieutenant. He moved over next to his SUV as if to guard it.

As Hattie put her radio back on her belt, I remembered the duffle the skinny guy had carried when he came out of the broken restaurant window. I walked over and found the duffle bag behind the dumpster, where it had fallen when I grabbed the guy. I lifted it up. It was heavy, maybe twenty pounds. I opened it up and shined my flashlight inside. It was full of cash. Wads of hundreds, fifties, and twenties. No doubt, many thousands of dollars. Either the money was illegally obtained, or the Korean restaurant owner didn't trust banks. I brought it over and showed it to Hattie. I shined my light on the duffle.

Hattie used her phone to take a photo.

I opened the bag and shined my light inside the bag.

She gasped, then took another photo.

# THIRTY-SIX

I handed the bag to her. "Don't let go of this."

I heard a squeak like a rusty hinge. The heavy steel back door of the restaurant opened a crack. It was dark in the narrow opening. I saw someone peek out. I didn't have to interrogate the person to know it was someone innocent who was working late hours at the restaurant.

"It's okay," I said. "I'm Private Investigator Owen McKenna, and these are cops. We caught the thieves. This is Truckee Police Officer Foster and off-duty officer Diamond Martinez from Douglas County. Over there is Truckee Officer Chamberlain."

The door opened farther. An older man of Asian background looked out. He was wearing a cooking apron.

"Are you the manager of the restaurant?" I asked.

"The owner," he said.

"Your name?"

"Joon Kim."

Hattie turned to look at me, hoping, it seemed, that I would continue to take the lead.

I asked, "Did the burglars see you when they came inside?"

"Yes. They busted the lock on the roof door and came down the utility stairs." He had a very slight Asian accent as if he'd lived in America since he was a young adult. "They forced me to open the safe, then took my money and went out through that window." He pointed at the broken window with its embedded security wires.

"How did they carry the money?"

"They took my duffle bag." We followed him as he moved into the restaurant. He pointed at the duffle hanging from Hattie Foster's shoulder. "From when I was in the Army." He opened the door wider and pointed to a series of jacket hooks behind him. "It was hanging on one of these hooks."

"How did they force you to open your safe?"

"They showed me a wire cutter and told me they would cut off my fingers and then cut off my niece Hana's fingers if I didn't obey. She lives in Washington State. But they knew her name. It made me afraid. So I opened the safe."

He stood next to a little desk. On it was a phone, a stack of menus, and a framed photo of a teenage girl. Near the left edge of the photo it said, 'Love you, Uncle Joon, from your favorite niece Hana.' I didn't say anything.

"How much money do you think they took?"

"They took all of it."

"Can you guess the amount?"

"I know the exact amount. One hundred fifty-four thousand, nine hundred thirty."

Hattie looked at me. "I should write that down."

She pulled out her phone and started tapping.

I turned back to Joon Kim. "How do you know the exact amount of money?"

"I have a system. Each night I figure out my daily rent and expenses and taxes, and I put that in my box to deposit in my checking account. Sometimes there's nothing left after those expenses. Other times, I have some after-tax profit left over. I put that profit in cash in my safe. If I only have checks and credit card slips, I write down the profit amount and add it to the safe the next time I have cash. I record my sales in my sales journal and keep a running total of my after-tax profit in my safe ledger."

"Can anyone who sees the safe also see the ledger and tell how much money is in the safe?"

"No. I use a code. Only I know what it means. And I never open the safe when anyone is around." He didn't speak for a moment. "Until tonight." It sounded like he was about to cry.

Hattie was tapping on her phone, taking notes. She shifted the duffle bag to make it easier.

"That is my money," Joon Kim said. "Can I have it back?"

"Eventually, yes," I said, filling in for Hattie because this was all new territory for her. "The money is evidence in the robbery, and it will have to be secured until the legal system determines it's time to give it back."

"It's my life savings," Joon Kim said. He sounded very worried and afraid.

Behind us, the ambulance started up and drove away.

Officer Chamberlain must have seen that the back door to the restaurant was now open. He moved several steps away from the SUV as if to possibly help, then thought better of it and moved back to stand next to his SUV. I had the sense that he didn't have much more experience than Hattie.

Diamond, Hattie, and the other officer didn't speak.

"You don't have a bank?" I asked Kim.

"I have a checking account for business expenses. But I don't trust banks for my savings."

"Bank deposits are insured by the government."

He shook his head. "Don't trust government. My neighbor, Akio Tanaka, owns a Japanese sushi restaurant. His parents were born in America but they were still put in the internment camps during World War Two. The government took everything from them. Confiscated all their property. My other neighbor is Hupa Indian. You know what happened to the Indians."

It was an inarguable point. If you were a member of certain groups, robbers and government seemed the same.

"We will do our best to protect your money," I said.

Diamond said, "Hattie, you should update your report to your lieutenant and ask him to send another backup."

"You mean, radio him now?"

"Yes."

Hattie got back on her radio and explained the situation.

"Okay," Lieutenant Oberman said. He repeated what I'd said. "Don't let go of that duffle. Take McKenna and the Douglas County sergeant with you into the restaurant. Lock the door once you're inside. Consider this a high risk situation until we get that money locked in our evidence room."

"Officer Martinez thinks you should send another backup."

"Unfortunately, Pickett and Narnel are on a domestic. I don't have any other personnel to send your way. Chamberlain, you stay at the back of the restaurant until they come out."

"Roger that," Chamberlain said.

Hattie put the strap of the duffle over her shoulder and hung onto it as Diamond and she and I went inside the restaurant.

Joon Kim locked the door behind us, then slid a bar into brackets to make the door nearly impenetrable.

"Why didn't the robbers come out this door?" I asked.

"I told them I lost the key and had to come and go through the front door. They didn't want to do that."

We walked past the desk into a dimly-lit kitchen. Joon Kim pointed to another door that stood open.

"That's the door to the roof." He stepped past the door and pointed to a set of shelves. "There is my safe."

It was a large safe, three by three by three, much too heavy to haul away by ordinary means, strong enough to protect a lifetime of savings. Unless someone threatened to cut off your fingers.

The door of the safe stood open.

Hattie used her phone to take pictures of everything. She then went through the utility door and climbed steep stairs to the roof. I looked in but didn't go up. I could see where the roof door had been pried open. I saw Hattie's phone flash go off multiple times.

When she came back down, she took general area pictures, the restaurant's front door, the dining room, the kitchen, the restrooms. She never let the duffle strap leave her shoulder.

I thanked Kim as we moved to leave and reassured him again that I believed his money would be safe.

"Do you give me a receipt?" he asked.

"Sure." I pulled out my little notebook, tore off a piece of paper, and wrote. 'Received a duffle bag of uncounted money, which was stolen from Joon Kim, which he says contains...' I stopped writing. "Tell me again how much money you think is in the duffle?"

He repeated what he'd said earlier. "One hundred fifty-four thousand, nine hundred thirty."

I wrote the amount, added the date, signed my name 'Owen McKenna, proxy for the Truckee Police,' and handed it to Hattie. She signed it and handed it to Kim.

"How did you know I was being robbed?" He looked at Hattie then at me. "Is that connected to you being a private investigator?"

"Yes. I was working for another restaurant owner, and I got a tip that some men thought you had a lot of customers who paid in cash. They thought you might keep the cash overnight and deposit it in the morning when going to the bank is safer."

Joon Kim made a troubled frown.

"If I didn't have cash customers, they wouldn't have even tried to rob me?"

"Maybe not."

He looked down at the floor and shook his head.

"Are you going to be okay?" I said. "Do you want to call anyone?"

"No. I don't have people to call. But the robbers did."

"What do you mean?"

He looked up at me. "Before they broke out the window to get away, the big man made a phone call."

"Did you hear what he said?"

Joon Kim nodded. "He said, 'Hey, bud. We scored. We've got some serious bank in a duffle bag. We're leaving the restaurant as planned.'"

"That's all?"

The restaurant man nodded.

"Do you have some other suitcase or box we could put your money in?" I asked.

"Why?" Hattie asked.

"So we can make a decoy. If we put the money in some other container, we could fill the duffle with other material so the duffle just looks like it has the money. The man you power bombed probably saw you with the duffle over your shoulder. Just in case the person he called comes before we leave, I want you to carry a decoy. We'll put the container with money in the trunk of Chamberlain's patrol."

I reached for the duffle and took it off Hattie's shoulder. I turned to Joon Kim.

"Do you have something we can put the money in?"

He frowned and looked around the kitchen. He walked into a small storeroom and came out with a heavy cardboard box.

I held up the duffle and compared it to the box. "Perfect," I said.

We transferred the money from the duffle to the box. Kim carefully stacked all the bundles. I was in a hurry, but I understood his care. He'd spent untold hours earning that money. When we'd transferred all the bills, there was a little room left over. Joon Kim found some packing paper, crumpled it up and fitted it into the extra space, so the money wouldn't shift. Kim taped it shut with packing tape, using extra tape to make the box strong.

"Now we need material for the duffle to make it the same size and weight as it was with the money."

The man nodded, then looked around the restaurant kitchen. He walked over to the little desk that had the telephone. He pulled open two drawers, lifted out old telephone books, and put them in the duffle. Then he went over to some shelves, got some boxes of mailing envelopes, and added them to the duffle. He lifted up the duffle and moved it up and down, judging its weight. He carried the duffle over to some other shelves that were stacked with food supplies. He picked up a partially-used bag of flour and hefted it. He folded over the open top, squeezing out excess air. Clouds of flour puffed out into the air. Joon Kim wrapped packing tape in circles around the flour bag, then put that in the duffle. He hefted it, nodded, and handed it to me.

I turned and handed it to Hattie. She hefted it as well and put the strap back on her shoulder.

We went out the back door, me carrying the box of money, Hattie carrying the decoy duffle. We heard Kim lock it behind us.

Chamberlain was still standing there.

"Did you get photos of the stepladder?" I asked.

Hattie shook her head and used her free hand to take multiple pictures of the stepladder, which was still lying on its side at the far side of the alley.

I was thinking about the phone call that Joon Kim had overheard, and it made me worry.

"Let's put this other evidence in your trunk," I said to Chamberlain in a loud voice in case the prisoners in the back seat could hear me.

He nodded, pulled out his key fob, and pressed the button to open the trunk. I set the box with the money in first, then laid the stepladder on top of it. I went back and picked up the major pieces of broken security glass, set them in on top of the other items, then closed the trunk.

"Your vehicle is around front?" I said to Hattie.

Hattie nodded. She used her radio to once again call Oberman and tell him that we were now leaving the restaurant.

He responded that she should keep the duffle of money with

her.

Oberman added, "McKenna and the Douglas County sergeant should follow you back to the station. That will give you and Chamberlain some security, and we need their statements, anyway."

Chamberlain opened the driver's door on his patrol SUV. Diamond turned to him. Chamberlain looked expectant in the harsh utility light. It seemed they all knew that Diamond and I were the most experienced people on the scene.

"McKenna and I will walk in front," Diamond said. "Behind us will be Officer Foster. Chamberlain, you will follow Foster. Once we're all in our vehicles, you follow us out onto the road. Same order. McKenna and me, then Foster, then Chamberlain. Be aware and be careful," Diamond said. "Don't let any traffic pressure you as you drive."

Diamond and I started walking, Hattie behind us.

We were nearly to Diamond's pickup when a late model Chevy pickup careened around the end of the shopping center building, raced down the alley toward us, then braked to a hard stop just in front of us.

Two men jumped out of the pickup bed and the driver got out as well. They all wore black ski masks that had red Harry Potter lightning bolts above the eye holes. The mask on the man closest to me was torn at the mouth. With his lip exposed, it looked like he was sneering at me.

The two men aimed pistols at Diamond and me.

The driver held a shotgun. Although the only light was from distant utility poles, it looked like an auto-loading model that could fire multiple rounds. I was quite certain it was a 12 gauge, big enough to nearly take a man's head off. That man stepped past us and Hattie, walked over to the driver's door of the patrol SUV and pointed the shotgun at the window, just inches from Chamberlain's face.

"Any of you move, this cop dies."

# THIRTY-SEVEN

The two men with pistols holstered them, then ran to the rear door of Chamberlain's SUV. They opened the door and grabbed the thick man by his arms, dragged him over to their pickup and, with effort, hoisted him up and into the back of the pickup. They repeated it with the skinny guy. Then the man with the shotgun ran over and pointed his shotgun at Hattie's head. The barrel was just 12 inches from her face. One of the other men grabbed her duffle off her shoulders. All the men jumped back into the pickup. With tires spinning and shooting out grit, the truck backed up in a tight curve, braked hard, then shifted forward in another hard turn so that it had reversed direction, and drove away at high speed. The entire process only took about fifteen seconds.

"Hurry," Diamond shouted as we three started running. Chamberlain drove behind as before.

"They've already got our prisoners," Hattie shouted between huffing breaths. She sounded very dejected in addition to quickly getting very winded. Running was obviously not her strong suit.

"They might be back soon," I said.

"Oh, right," Hattie said, realizing that the moment one of them looked in the decoy duffle, they would be back, possibly shooting. Hattie sped up with renewed energy.

We rounded the end of the building. Diamond jumped into his pickup, got it started. Hattie and I stood on the rear bumper and held onto the tailgate as Diamond drove fast to the middle of the parking lot where the BMW had originally been. But it was now gone.

At the far end of the lot, Diamond braked to a fast stop, one or two of his tires making a skidding noise. Chamberlain stopped his patrol next to us.

Hattie jumped off the back bumper of Diamond's pickup, unlocked her patrol car, and started it. I got in the passenger side of

Diamond's pickup. We all drove off as planned, except without our robber/prisoners or the decoy duffle bag.

Diamond led our group. He drove briskly but not recklessly.

As I thought about what had just happened, feeling like an idiot for not remembering to take the robbers' phones, I questioned, for the hundredth time, my decision years ago to not carry a gun. I did it for a good reason. But I wondered about the ultimate price of principle. The world was a dangerous place.

The chance assembly of good people like Street and Camille and now Geneviève was serendipitous. Those three all showed that people could respond to stress with goodness. People could sort through chaos and form safe havens. But those safe zones were always fraught. Despite large groups of good people across society, bad people were always out there, looking for a way to pry open other peoples' lives and scam them, steal from them, prey on them.

And those bad people seemed to always enforce their dark world with guns. For me to voluntarily give up guns in pursuit of the notion of not contributing to the world's violence seemed the height of foolishness. My ideals didn't take a single bad guy off the street, and they didn't serve as a role model for any good guys, either.

Mine was an old-fashioned chivalry, obeying outmoded rules about which weapons were fair and which were not. In our modern era, my choices seemed to have no redeeming qualities at all. For the last several years, my decision had done nothing but make me feel a little better. And now it was making me feel worse.

Lieutenant Oberman had plenty of judgmental looks for all of us when we returned without the robbers. The fact that he didn't eviscerate us with words was a model of restraint.

It made no difference that other law enforcement officers might have experienced the same, or even worse, result. We still allowed many violent men to slip through our grasp.

Oberman showed Hattie the procedure for the evidence room. Then he had Hattie take Diamond's statement and mine. It could be that he thought the repetition would be a good learning experience. More likely, he realized that as Hattie went through the process, step by step, she would realize many ways that we all could have done a better job, never mind her impressive physical performance.

Oberman was especially upset that we hadn't gotten any single bit of evidence that would indicate anyone's identity. No ID, no license number on the Chevy pickup, no comprehensive physical description of any suspect. Everyone had dark clothes, dark hair, and, to the best of our recollections, dark eyes. In addition, three of them had worn black ski masks. I had previously gotten the BMW plate, but that had been stolen from the Bay Area. It seemed the only good thing to come out of the night was that we'd managed to hang onto the restaurateur's money.

It took two hours before Diamond and I had given our statements and answered all questions. We made certain that Oberman was comfortable with us leaving even as we knew how uncomfortable he was with the overall situation.

I told the Lieutenant I would be in touch as I learned anything.

I thanked Chamberlain said goodbye to Hattie.

Diamond and I were quiet as we headed home. He pulled into the parking lot at Street's condo so I could switch to my Jeep. I worried that Spot would sense us just 50 yards away and bark. But I thought it best not to knock and wake everyone up. It was four in the morning. I'd be back come daylight to fetch Spot and Lazlo.

Diamond whispered goodbye, an effort that was probably rendered unnecessary once I started up the Jeep, the sound of which Spot could probably hear. I drove up the mountain to my cabin while Diamond headed back to Kingsbury Grade to head up and over the pass and down to Minden.

I built a small fire in the wood stove, sat in front of the flames, drank two Sierra Nevada Pale Ales, and went over the night's events. My thoughts were mostly self-recrimination about the robbers getting away.

Ever since Geneviève had first called me, I'd done nothing but make matters worse. I convinced her to quit paying the extortionist and as a result her restaurant and apartment had been burned to the ground. I'd been beaten up. The bad guys had made fools of Diamond and me along with the Truckee police. And I'd made no progress on the reason Geneviève had called me in the first place, which was the insurance company that had refused to pay out on Colin's policy.

# THIRTY-EIGHT

I got a few hours of sleep, then drove down the mountain to Street's to pick up the dogs.

I used the key Street had given me to unlock the door. But first, as a proforma move, I gave a slight knock, then slowly opened the door. Street saw me and gave me a slight smile of acknowledgement. Camille was talking to Geneviève, explaining that she was learning how to jump on her skateboard. Geneviève didn't look happy, but neither did she appear as devastated as I'd last seen her.

Camille signed as she talked. At one point she made an interesting sign, and Geneviève asked her to show it to her again.

"Jump is like this." Camille held out her left hand, palm up. She placed the first two fingertips of her right hand on her palm. I immediately understood that her right hand represented someone standing. Then she quickly raised her right hand into the air while bending those fingers. It was uncanny how well the movement represented jumping.

Geneviève and Street both made the movement. They repeated it multiple times while they laughed.

Who knew that American Sign Language was so intuitive and entertaining?

"Jumping is easier in sign language than real life," Geneviève said.

I saw Street make an exaggerated nod. I found my own hands making the movements.

I didn't want to interrupt their conversation, so I waved goodbye, took Spot and Lazlo, and left, locking Street's door behind me. They would eventually want to know how the night had gone for Diamond and me, but that could wait.

# THIRTY-NINE

I drove south to Kingsbury Grade and took it up to the condo owned by Colin's mother, BB Burns. I didn't know how she could help me, but I wanted to ask BB if she'd seen or heard anything that would suggest that anyone had animosity for Colin.

I parked on the street below, rolled down the windows for the dogs, and got out. It had been snowing lightly. The street BB's condo was on had two inches of fresh snow, soft and fluffy.

I went up the staircase and knocked on BB's door. I waited, knocked again. There was no answer.

I was turning around, reassessing, when I saw a doorbell button. I pressed it and heard the dingdong sound from inside.

After another minute, I tried again. No answer.

Maybe she was napping. Or in the bathroom.

As I was heading down the steps, I stopped on the first landing.

Being careless, I hadn't thought to look for any footprints when I'd first arrived, and now I'd trampled the upper level, obscuring any previous footprints. But, at the landing where the staircase about-faced, there were two footprints I hadn't walked on.

They were small sized and facing down the stairs. I peered at the steps up above and saw what looked like portions of other small prints, also facing down the stairs, all prints I'd walked over. As best I could tell, there were no small prints facing up.

When a person leaves home and walks through snow, they leave one set of tracks. When they return home, they leave another set of tracks.

The implication was that two sets of tracks, one going, one coming, suggested the homeowner was at home. Just one set of tracks leaving home suggested the homeowner was gone.

On the lower steps, there were only my footprints coming up the stairs.

It appeared a person with small feet had come out of the condo, gone down the steps, stopped at the landing, and not returned. BB checking on something?

From down on the stairway landing, I turned and looked back up at BB Burns's condo. From this vantage point, I could see that her windows were ablaze with light, and it made me pause.

One of the most natural habits of people is to turn off the lights as they leave home.

When I had last visited BB, she was a little spacey. I remembered that her comments had been disorganized and forgetful. It had made me wonder if she was suffering the symptoms of Huntington's. But when I asked myself if she would leave all the lights on when she left home, it didn't make sense. A person with a foggy brain would probably still turn off the lights as they left the house. Unless they were just checking something and planned to immediately go back inside.

The conclusion was that BB had left her condo and not come back. And she left all the lights on.

Further inspection suggested that she'd only come down to the landing and hadn't continued down to the street.

I looked over the railing.

Below the landing, fifteen feet down, were multiple boulders. The biggest one had less snow on it than the others. I leaned out, hoping the railing was strong. Next to the boulder was the small form of a person.

I ran down the stairs, jumped off the bottom step onto the boulder-strewn slope, and scrambled my way on all fours up the slope. When I got to the person, I saw it was a woman. The snow was accumulating on her face. There was not enough body heat left to melt the falling snow. Just to be sure, I put two fingers against the front side of her neck where the carotid artery normally created a strong pulse. There was nothing to feel.

I leaned in to look closer. It appeared that her head had struck the boulder. Just visible, on the underside of her jaw where no snow had accumulated, was a large, round wound. Blood had flowed, but not a large volume. I thought about the likely sequence. The best explanation was that the wound had happened before her fall. Maybe the wound would have eventually killed her. But it appeared that when she fell, she struck her head hard on the boulder. Traumatic brain injury had killed her faster than the wound would have.

Leaning over her, my body cast a shadow.

I shifted to the side to let light in so I could get a better look.

There was something strange about the blood that had flowed from the wound under her jaw and down her neck, where it dried in an abstract S-shape.

The blood wasn't smooth. It had a texture. I looked even closer, squinting my eyes to try to bring the texture into focus.

I couldn't tell for certain, but it appeared that the blood had material in it. It looked like sawdust.

# FORTY

Diamond and two Douglas County deputies responded to my call. It took two hours for them to process the scene, which, Diamond and I both agreed, looked very much like a crime scene, albeit with a wound that wasn't created by any weapon we'd ever seen.

That night, I slept very poorly. Too many images of BB Burns crowded my head. Too many questions.

The next morning, I took my coffee out on the deck. The winter air was crisp enough that the coffee steamed like a geothermal vent.

I watched the wind patterns on the lake as I sipped. Normally, individual waves from a thousand feet up were invisible, and one could only see the general pattern of squalls. But the north wind was hard enough that the sun glinted off countless rows of white caps. Those waves, large enough to surf on, tracked 22 miles from the North Shore to the beaches of the South Shore, where they crashed on iced sand.

I had to drink my coffee fast.

After Spot and Lazlo had run in the forest, they bounded up the short stairs to the deck. Spot briefly greeted me and then rested his jaw on the deck rail while Lazlo poked his nose between the boards 18 inches lower. It was obvious that I was never the main attraction unless I was bringing food.

For a few moments, the breeze went away and the hot, high-altitude sun was toasty warm, despite the cold winter temperatures. So I brought out my laptop to check email.

The first email stopped me with its subject line. 'I know who yer girlfriend is.'

The message was nearly illiterate.

'You theef you scamd my money from the Korean restront. You been following me to take my biznes. You probly faked out the cops to. If you dont email how to give me my money back Im gonna hurt yer girl then kll you.'

The sender address was a bunch of numbers and letters at one of the major email services.

I immediately forwarded it to Diamond with the comment, 'What do you think?'

Then I called Street.

"Hi hon," I said when she answered. "So sorry to bother you, but I just got a threatening email that mentions you."

"What does it say?"

I read it to her.

"Do you know who it's from?"

"Not his identity. But it's the man who robbed the Korean restaurant two nights ago. The man had five or six friends who were armed with pistols and shotguns, and they broke him and his robber pal out of a police vehicle in Truckee."

"What do you think we should do?" Street's voice was shaky.

"First, check to make sure your 'to go' bag has what you need for a few days. Same for Camille and Geneviève. All of you should leave in your car as soon as I get down the mountain to follow you. Blondie included. We'll all drive to the sheriff's office at Stateline. I've left a message for Diamond. We'll get his input about what hotel would provide the safest cover."

"And you? What will you do?"

"I have a vague plan about how to set a trap. I'll call you back as soon as I hear from Diamond."

"Okay. Thanks. Love you."

She hung up.

My phone rang seconds later.

"Still no idea who this jerk is?" Diamond said.

"No. Of course, I can't even process the problem while I'm worrying about Street and Camille and Geneviève. You got any advice?"

"Yeah. I checked with the sheriff about Douglas County's safe house. He already texted the owner. We'll see if he gets a response."

"I remember now. The Bay Area venture capitalist who wanted to give the sheriff the favor of using his spread up at the top of Kingsbury Grade."

"Sí."

"We used it to house Adam Simms, the pro-footballer with traumatic brain injury. Adam was Blondie's owner before Adam died. So she will recognize the house. She stayed there for some time."

"Yes again."

I asked, "Do you think that businessman is still willing to do this?"

"From what I gather, his house loan is a permanent favor. I'm not sure about the motivation. It was something like our department saved his wife's life. But the house is not available when the VC is using the house himself. Oh, here's the incoming text now. Hold on."

I waited.

Diamond was back in less than a minute. "We're on. The sheriff is going to alert the staff that needs to know. Everyone else will be unaware."

"The owner is okay with dogs, right? Because we've got a large group."

"They are well-behaved, so that shouldn't be a problem."

"I don't remember the address nor the gate code."

"No problem," Diamond said. "I'll come with you."

"You want us to come to your lot?"

"Yeah. We'll caravan from here."

"I'm not sure how long we'll be. Maybe an hour."

"I'll be here either way."

I thanked him and called Street back.

"Sorry again for this disruption in your lives. All of you."

"It's the hazard of loving you," she said. "I understood that years ago. We're all ready."

"Okay, I'll drive down from my cabin and meet you in your condo parking lot."

I hung up and headed down the mountain with Spot and Lazlo. As I pulled into the lot, Street, Camille, Geneviève, and Blondie came out Street's front door.

Spot was wagging hard when he saw them. Lazlo jumped into the front seat, trying to get away from Spot's tail. Spot didn't understand why I wasn't stopping and letting him out.

When the women and Camille and Blondie had all loaded into

Street's VW Bug, we pulled out of the lot, and headed down the East Shore.

Diamond walked out as we pulled into the sheriff's parking area. He waved, then got into a Douglas County SUV. He pulled out, and we followed, Street, then me.

Kingsbury Grade goes up three miles before it reaches Daggett Pass and then pitches down the 3000-foot descent to Carson Valley. Just before the summit, Diamond turned north on North Benjamin and wound his way back and up to a house that was on a ridge, yet was simultaneously nestled in among giant boulders and conifers. The place was fenced and gated with a strong wrought iron fence. Diamond pulled up to the gate, punched in a code, and the gate opened. He drove in, and we followed. There was a turn-around and parking for five or six vehicles. Diamond parked facing out so he could leave when he was done.

We all got out. The dogs ran around exploring. Blondie probably recognized some aspects of the place considering that she had spent time here with Adam Simms before he died of dementia.

The front door had a passcode lock. Diamond entered those numbers, and we all walked into the large, modern living room with astonishing views of the lake in one direction and Carson Valley in the opposite direction, not unlike the views from BB Burns's condo off Tramway Drive a mile to the south.

Street remembered the layout from our previous visit, and she showed Camille and Geneviève around. Camille was quite excited. I remembered that she had grown up living in a pickup camper. Other than being in Jennifer Salazar's house and yacht a couple of weeks ago, she'd maybe never seen such opulence as a house like this. A few minutes later, we all convened back in the living room. There was a wide range of furniture, and we sat here and there. Camille lounged on a broad chair that looked like a double bed mattress upholstered in forest green fabric and curved into a huge, shallow S shape. She spread her arms wide and then shifted left and right like a movie star luxuriating on exotic furniture, exploring the ways one could inhabit a piece of furniture

Spot stood at the windows looking at a view that was like the view from our cabin's deck. Lazlo stayed back and watched Spot and all of us as if trying to understand why he was here.

Only Blondie continued to roam, possibly resurrecting memories of her previous owner, Adam Simms. I could not tell what thoughts she might be processing. But I will never forget the time that she had what seemed like an anxiety attack, which we later found out was her recognizing an oncoming epileptic attack that Adam was about to have. It was one of those moments that show the amazing abilities of dogs, the mysterious sentience of a dog being able to smell some kind of change in a person who is about to have a seizure.

Street said, "I told Geneviève and Camille what you said on the phone, Owen. But maybe you could be more clear about the email and such. You said something about a robber threatening you, and you also said you had a plan to possibly trap this person."

"Yes. I don't actually know this person's identity. But he was the man who targeted Geneviève in an extortion racket and then burned down her building."

Geneviève inhaled in shock.

"He's also the man who, with his partner, beat me up. Last night he robbed the Korean restaurant in Truckee and stole the owner's entire savings, which the man had in a heavy safe. The total was one hundred fifty thousand plus. I got a tip about the theft from another restaurant owner who heard the man and his partner talking about their plan. So Diamond and Truckee Officer Hattie Foster and I managed to be there during the robbery. We foiled him, and the money is now locked in the Truckee PD evidence room. Although this man doesn't know that. As a result, he's determined to get back the money. Because he stole it, in his twisted mind, he now thinks it's his money. And he thinks I stole it from him."

I turned and looked at Diamond, talking to him as much as Street. "My thought is that I can possibly entice him to meet with me under the guise of giving him the stolen money."

"Half the money," Diamond said. "These guys will expect you to bargain hard."

"You said the police came to the restaurant and that you and Diamond put him in the police car," Street said. "So how could he not think the money is in the possession of the police?"

"I have no idea how he imagines I kept the money from the cops."

Diamond said, "It could be he thinks you tricked them the same as you did with him. Gave them a decoy bag or something."

I shrugged. "Either the guy is quite stupid or delusional or both."

"So you would get him to meet you someplace," Street said.

"Right."

"When he found out you didn't have the money, wouldn't that push him over the edge? Wouldn't he be outraged and maybe kill you?"

"Probably, that will be his desire. So I'll have to come up with a plan where I can give him what he thinks is the money and then escape before he realizes it."

Geneviève said, "I don't know about this stuff, so I shouldn't even be talking. But I'm wondering, what's the point of making the guy think you're giving him the money—or part of the money—back? If he's going to eventually find out you're not following through on the plan, won't he still be outraged?"

"Yes. But if I can control the circumstances where we meet, maybe I can stop that and deliver him to law enforcement. Take him off the street."

Everyone was quiet for a moment. Geneviève broke the silence.

"Do you think this guy threatening you could possibly be connected to my insurance situation?"

"On the surface, it doesn't seem possible. Life insurance and protection rackets are completely different worlds." I glanced again at Diamond. "But those of us in law enforcement learn not to abide coincidence even if drawing a connection between events seems an extreme reach. The result is that we'll pay attention to everything. We won't forget the broader picture of your problems."

Diamond nodded, then stood up.

"I need to get going." He looked at Street and Geneviève. "I think there's some basics in the house. Coffee. Frozen pizza. There are clean towels for showers. I don't know about dog food. But Owen can probably come back with supplies in the next day or so. Do you feel okay here? Owen and I are just a phone call away."

"Yes, this feels safe," Street said. "My only concern is how long we'll be here. It's like evacuation during a forest fire. When you're suddenly disrupted with no time to plan or grab clothes, and you're unable to do your work or get food out of your own refrigerator, it's very unsettling."

"I know about that feeling," Geneviève said, "having to suddenly leave without any possessions."

"I'm so sorry," I said.

"Don't worry. Do what you need to do. You and Diamond are just trying to keep us safe."

"Do you want me to stay here with you tonight? If not, I'll leave Spot. He'll be comfortable with all of you."

Camille surprised us all when she answered, another reminder of her ability to read lips. "We've got three dogs to protect us, and one of them is bigger than a mountain lion. I don't think anyone would dare try to come in here."

Diamond grinned.

"Kid's got a point," he said.

I hugged Street and Camille, and I took Geneviève's hand in both of mine. She searched my eyes, but neither of us spoke. I tried to give her a warm smile, but she could probably see my worry and distress.

I gave Spot a rub, but he was more interested in the new environment than me.

Diamond and I were leaving, when Geneviève's phone rang.

She answered it, listened for several seconds, then gasped and started crying.

She sagged down onto the nearest chair, dropped her phone, and made the most heart-wrenching howl.

Camille ran over to her, kneeled down, and leaned on Geneviève's lap.

"What's wrong, Geneviève? What's wrong?"

Geneviève couldn't breathe. Her body seemed to convulse as she choked while trying to get air. Street kneeled next to Geneviève's other side and took one of her hands.

Eventually, her sobs morphed into long howling torment.

"What's wrong, Geneviève?" Camille said again.

"That was the hospital. My employee Jimmy Baker died from his smoke inhalation."

# FORTY-ONE

We all tried to attend to Geneviève. Camille and Street stayed by her side. Diamond and I hovered nearby. But there was nothing to be done. Geneviève's life had been effectively destroyed, her heart ripped out.

All I could think of was catching the man who tormented her, extorted her, battered her on multiple occasions, burned down her restaurant and her apartment, and now murdered her employee, a young, eager man who wanted to be a productive future restaurateur using Geneviève as his role model. The fact that the murderer also stole the life savings from a hard-working restaurant owner just after trying to beat me to death added more fuel to an indescribable hatred. In addition, he put the leg lock on Hattie Foster's neck while reaching for his gun to shoot her. Along with my contempt for the man who perpetrated this horror, was my hunch that he was possibly connected to the murder of Colin Burns and his mother BB. His evil was beyond description.

Many long minutes later, Diamond and I tried to express our sorrow to Geneviève, then excused ourselves and left.

Once outside, Diamond stopped and turned to me. "What's your plan?" His words and tone sounded very bleak.

"I'll email the jerk back and, like you suggested, offer to split the money. I think the important thing is to meet him where I'm in control of the environment."

"And that place would be…"

"I'm thinking about skiing. We meet on the slope. It's easy to come together, transfer a bag, get away. I'm not the world's greatest skier, but I'm likely to be at least as competent as this guy."

"You're assuming he skis," Diamond said.

"Do you know any local who doesn't ski? Nearly all of us moved here, in part, to ski where we live."

Diamond nodded. "Keep me informed," he said.

I didn't give the extortionist a choice in our meeting. I assumed he was well motivated to get back his stolen money.

So I simply emailed him my meeting terms.

In the subject line, I wrote the name of the ski resort and the name of the closest chairlift.

In the email body, I wrote, 'I've got the money, so I'm in charge. Deal with it. I'll give you half if you promise to leave my girl alone. I'll be on skis. Meet me at noon tomorrow halfway down the Majordomo run. There's an overlook near the ski area boundary. To the left is a view of the lake. To the right is the out-of-bounds marker.

P.S. You touch Street or anyone else I care about, I'll cut off your favorite body parts and feed them to my dog.'

I was up on the mountain at 11:30 a.m.

I skied a run, made a chairlift connection to move up and across the mountain and then skied down to a spot where I could observe the meeting point I'd specified.

The ski traffic was moderate because it was December, a week before the holidays, which was still the slow season for skiing, and the weather was brisk. There were thin high clouds that showed the sun but blocked its heat. The breeze was enough to produce a serious windchill.

I stopped at the edge of the ski run where the heavy tree cover blocked some of the wind. I wore a medium-sized backpack about half the size of the duffle bag the robbers had put Joon Kim's money into.

Ten minutes after noon, a thick-set skier in a white ski suit came down the trail. He went past me, then slowed to a stop. He looked around as if to get his bearings, then continued down and over to the meeting point. He stopped again and turned to watch the ski traffic above.

I pushed off, gauged the ski traffic, merged in with other skiers, and came up close to him.

I knew the meeting would be much more dangerous if I stopped where he could grab me or shoot me up close. My goal was to get him agitated. The angrier he was, the more dangerous he was, but also, the more likely he was to make a mistake.

So I cruised by him, edging my skis and doing a skid to control my speed.

"You fell for my email?" I shouted. "I figured you were stupid, but this is far beyond what I expected. Needless to say, you won't be getting any money from me today. C'mon idiot. Give it your best shot."

I sped up, looking behind.

The man pushed off and came toward me, accelerating fast.

"You bastard!" he shouted. "I'm gonna tear you in half!"

I sped up. I turned hard, shot out into the middle of the run. Looking behind, I saw him trying to keep up. He put both his ski poles in one hand and pulled out a gun with the other. I heard a gunshot.

I turned hard again and then took on a slalom pattern, linked turns back and forth, but irregular and hard to anticipate. I heard another gunshot. I kept turning. I varied my rate and made my turns dramatic. Unless he could get right next to me, he wouldn't have much chance of hitting me. Another gunshot.

The third shot seemed to come from a slightly different direction. Turning as I skied, I saw another, thinner man, with blue stretch pants and a blue jacket, the skinny man from the robbery. He was behind me on the other side. He too, had his poles in one hand so that he could fire with the other.

The ski run was a well-groomed corduroy texture. When I edged hard, I flew back and forth across the run. I kept looking back, making sure neither man was close. I also kept track of the lay of the land. I had an idea about how to get the better of my pursuers.

We went faster, then faster still. My speed was nothing to even notice compared to downhill racers. And, of course, not even on the same planet as speed skiers. But I'd probably sped up to 40 miles per hour. Glancing back again, the men with guns were still far back but were also going fast.

I used my ski edges to slow a bit on my turns. The thick man closed the gap. Then I changed my cadence, did a hard turn, flying across the ski run while slowing dramatically.

The man was too slow to recognize that I was stopping.

He shot by me, yelling and cursing.

I pushed off, did a quick tuck, and accelerated behind him. He tried to stop, then realized I was on him. I went by him on the side he'd least expect and then did another hard stop.

Gunshots came from the skinny man on the other side of the trail.

The thick man still had his gun out and was firing as he flew by me. If he had another Glock, like what Diamond had taken off him during the robbery, he probably had at least 15 rounds in the magazine. So far, he'd fired maybe six rounds. He had plenty left to kill me with.

He slowed. This time I passed him on his other side. I was hoping to confuse him, make him exasperated. He was a good skier, but it was clear from his moves that he was no better than I was.

He came after me again.

I sped up and saw that the ski run made a turn to the left 100 yards ahead.

He had his gun vaguely pointed to his left.

I raced by him on his right.

As he turned to the right, I turned to the left then skidded to a hard stop.

Once again, he was unable to anticipate, and he sped by me fast.

I pushed off and tucked, quickly regaining speed. I went by on his right. I pulled in front of him, no more than twenty yards distant. I heard his gun firing. I sped up, then did one more hard left turn just as the ski run was turning left.

I did a hard brake. He passed me. I could easily sense his confusion, his loss of balance, holding both ski poles in one hand and the gun in the other.

I sped up to just over his speed and came up directly behind him.

More gunshots came from across the trail.

At the last moment, before the run turned left, I overtook the thick man on his left. He likely hadn't even registered that I was next to him when I gave him a shoulder hit on his left side.

Sometimes such a hit results in a fall. Other times, it will merely bounce two skiers apart.

As the ski run turned left, I also went to the left. The thick man shooting the gun bounced to the right, off the side of the run, through the ski area boundary.

The skinny man slowed and stopped but was well down the trail below us.

I stopped hard and fast and watched.

The thick man went into the heavy crud, where powder had long since melted and refrozen. The junk snow locked his skis in their current direction making it very difficult for him to turn. The backcountry slope was steep. He seemed to accelerate as he went straight down the mountain. His right shoulder brushed by a tree. He came close to another tree on his left. But he couldn't seem to avoid a larger tree directly in front.

I had to lean to the side to keep him in view, so thick was the forest.

Although he was now far away from me, the impact made an audible thud.

The rule in skiing is to never hit a tree because they always win.

At the speed he was going, the impact might rupture his aorta or, if his head hit the tree, cause deadly blunt force trauma.

All I could tell from my distance was that he stopped, up against the tree, and didn't move. Within seconds, a red stain began to appear on the top of his white ski suit, and it spread down the man's back.

Whatever had happened was a severe injury. The man appeared motionless, and it didn't look like he was going anywhere. I was fairly confident that he'd still be there in an hour, perhaps slumped to the ground, perhaps still alive but maybe not for long.

I pushed off and headed on down the ski run, looking for the skinny man.

# FORTY-TWO

I let gravity pull me to a high speed. I didn't want to be a hazard to other skiers, so I stayed near the edge of the run as I flew down the slope.

The run made a big S-curve, first to the right, then back to the left. I was a quarter mile down when I saw a skier with a blue jacket and blue stretch pants. I was on the right edge of the run. He was to the left. I was skiing straight and fast. He was going at a good speed, but I was gaining on him. He wasn't linking parallel turns. His turns were a type of stepped turn. To change a carving turn from one direction, across the fall line to the other direction, he stepped out with his uphill ski, making a wedge. As that move began a turn in the new direction, he brought his downhill ski parallel to his uphill ski. The momentum of his new turn brought him around in a gradual curve. The wedge turn was a simple but slow way to do linked turns as he went down the slope.

His gun was no longer in view. He'd put it in his pocket and once again had a pole in each hand. His focus was on the hill below. Maybe he'd seen me force his thick companion off the trail. More likely, he had no idea of the fate of his companion. Either way, he was trying to make a getaway.

I came up on his right. I mimicked his moves, staying close, inching closer, crowding him.

"Give it up," I shouted. "Come to a stop, or I'll take you out."

I wanted him to be worried and unnerved, to think I was brash and dangerous.

"Now!" I shouted again.

He hesitated. Made another wedge. Turned away from me, trying to separate us.

I stayed next to him, moving closer still. Just at the point that he was most unbalanced, I body-slammed him, harder than I'd done on the other guy. Practice makes perfect. It bounced him off the left side of the run. His skis hit the ungroomed crud, and he flipped over and down a bank. His head dug into the snow as his skis went through the air.

He came to a stop lying on his back, head down the slope, with one arm behind him. His legs above him were scissored open, his skis spread wide. His face was covered with snow.

On a groomed slope, getting up would be a simple matter of rotating on the snow until your skis were below you. Then you could push up until you were in a sitting position, and then use your poles to help yourself stand up.

But lying upside down in deep crud snow with broken crust, it was a nearly helpless position and would require a lot of writhing and jerking to get to one's feet.

He was well down off the edge of the ski run.

I skied just below him and stopped when my skis were next to, and slightly below, his head. Looking up, I could see that we were enough off the ski run that we were out of sight. I lifted up my upper ski, moved it above his face, and rested it on his chest.

"Don't hurt me," he suddenly pleaded.

"Interesting request from a guy who carries a gun and shoots people when he's not robbing old Korean restaurant owners."

"I was just following orders! I didn't want to hurt anyone. And I was trying to miss you when I fired in your direction. I just did it because Roland was watching."

"Does that kind of blathering actually work on anyone? Do you think I'm that gullible?"

"I'm just a worker bee," he said. "Honest truth."

"Okay, I'll make you a deal. You answer my questions, and I'll let you live. If you don't, or if I'm unhappy with any of your answers, I'll lift this ski off your chest, set it on your neck, and ski away. As you know, the metal edges of skies are very sharp. They won't cut your head clean off, but they will slice deeply into your neck. Windpipe, jugular vein, carotid artery. You'll bleed out in sixty seconds. It'll leave none of my DNA or any other hint who was involved. People will think it was a very unfortunate accident."

"I'll tell you whatever you want to know."

"Your name."

He was silent.

"Wow, that's forthcoming." I did a quick, sideways squat, bending my knee all the way. My weight came down hard, the impact going through my ski. I heard a deep crack come from within his chest. A rib, maybe.

He exhaled in a banshee cry. With my ski pinning his arms in place, he couldn't do much of anything beyond trying to breathe. And he was too weak to attempt to buck me off his body. I took my hand out of my pole grip and patted him down.

"You broke something bad inside," he wheezed. "I can't breathe."

"I gave you the choice to tell me your name. You refused."

I felt a bulge in the side pocket of his ski jacket.

"Ah, let's see what this weapon is," I said as I pulled a gun out of his jacket pocket, holding it with my gloved hand. "A Smith and Wesson MP Shield. Nine millimeter, right? Kills a man with a single round. Good choice! You can really contribute to society with this piece of iron." I made sure the safety was on and pointed the pistol at the man.

He winced.

"Eight rounds in the magazine, right? Which means there's a few left. I could make it look like you got so tired of falling in deep snow, you decided to take your own life. I saw you were right-handed, so I should shoot from over here."

I leaned toward his head.

He winced again, whimpering this time.

I released the magazine and ejected the round from the chamber. I put the gun and magazine and extra round in my jacket pocket.

"Let's try another question. Is Roland your ringleader?"

"Yeah," he wheezed. "But he gets his direction from another guy."

"Who's that?"

"I dunno."

"How does this other guy give him orders? By phone? Email?"

"I dunno. Phone maybe."

"Where does this other guy live?"

"I dunno."

"What were you supposed to do after you and Roland killed me?"

"Roland never said. Probably we'd leave you in the woods."

"Like where you are now?" I said.

I resumed the search. There was a zippered pocket on the inside of his ski jacket. I worked the zipper and pulled out a wallet. The driver's license had his name.

"You are Hud Tenery Wallen. That was so smart for you to refuse to tell me your name, when it's right here in your pocket."

Hud was still wheezing.

He had a Visa debit card in that name and $700 in hundred dollar bills.

In another pocket were keys to a BMW.

In a third pocket was an iPhone. I turned it on. There was no passcode. Another mindless crook who apparently thought that even though he abused, stole from, and probably killed other people, no one would dare take his phone.

His other pockets had nothing but wads of facial tissue, some new, some used.

I took all of his pocket items and put them in my own zippered pocket on the inside of my ski suit.

I had to leave him to get help. But first, I wanted to visit Roland's body, and I didn't want Hud to escape.

It took several zip ties to go around his knees, because the ski boots and skis didn't allow his ankles to get close to each other. I released Hud's ski bindings and took off his skis. Because the ski brakes popped out, I couldn't send his skis on a long ride into the forest. So I took his skis and gave them javelin throws. When they entered the snow, they disappeared beneath the surface. Because they'd left no track, their location was invisible.

When I reached for his ski boots, he started kicking.

I stood on his body, my skis digging into his chest and abdomen.

"You helped Roland rob an old man of his life savings. You helped Roland extort a female restaurant owner and then burn down her restaurant and apartment. Her employee just died, which makes you guilty of manslaughter. Then you helped Roland beat me up. Had those drunken college kids not happened by, you and your buddy would probably have killed me. So I'm looking for ways to return the favor of violence."

I bent down so my mouth was near his ear, and I spoke in a hiss. "In my waist pack, I have a slotted screwdriver which is the most lethal weapon that Californians can legally carry without a permit. This driver has a slender shaft. If you try kicking me one more time, I'm going to see what I can do with that screwdriver. In your ears, up your nose, you get the idea."

He stopped kicking.

I removed the man's ski boots. I took off Hud's gloves and hat and stuffed them into his boots, and threw them into the woods. The boots sunk beneath the snow. They'd be impossible to find, as the snow's surface had been broken all over by falling branches and chunks of snow that had accumulated on branches and then fallen to the ground. A man without boots or skis in ski country, is severely hobbled. A man without hat or gloves is more severely hobbled.

I zip tied his ankles, then rolled him over onto his stomach and zip tied his wrists behind him.

He protested, groaning loudly. I pulled off one of his socks and stuffed it in his mouth. The other sock I punched down into the snow. I leaned down and whispered harshly in his ear.

"You are disgusting. Maybe I come back. Maybe I send the cops and ski patrol to look for you. Maybe not."

"One thing's for certain. If you're not rescued, you won't be alive come morning. Freezing to death is no fun, barefoot or not. It'll be hard for the pathologist or anyone else to understand how you could be so stupid as to get yourself into this situation."

I started side-stepping up the slope to the ski run, paused and said, "It could have been so easy. If you had answered my questions, I would have taken mercy on you, and you would soon be in a warm place with constitutional protections, hot meals, and a reasonable bed. Instead, you want to be a tough guy. Look where that got you."

I took note of the number on the nearest chairlift tower and skied down to the chairlift loading station.

On the ride back up, I watched the chairlift tower numbers, and looked for the hobbled man in the blue suit.

I got a glimpse of him, a snow-dappled blue form well down in the trees. But it was unlikely anyone else would notice him.

At the top of the lift, I skied down the right side of the run, going slowly, trying to remember where Roland went off the run and down into the backcountry.

There it was. Where the ski run turned to the left, tracks went off to the right. The tracks were faint. I stopped and looked down the slope. When viewed in a straight line, his tracks were more clear, as was his unmoving form embracing the tree. But I could only see him when my head was in the exact right position for viewing. Nevertheless, I wanted to obscure the vision of the man splayed against the tree, the large red bouquet of blood obvious against his white ski suit.

The slope he'd skied down before his fatal encounter with the tree was steep, so I didn't want to try it. Nor did I want my tracks to obscure any forensic analysis of where Roland had gone. So, I skied down the main run another fifty yards, then headed off the groomed slope and traversed at a gentle angle through the deeper backcountry snow, back to where Roland was mashed against the tree. I took a course that was close to level but sloped down just enough to bring me directly to him. His face had a dramatic look of surprise and shock. His skis had spread apart from one another as if to slow himself, and it appeared that he tried to cushion his blow with his outstretched arms. But he hadn't counted on a sharp two-inch-diameter branch at neck level, a branch that stuck straight out a foot.

I could imagine his sudden attempt at screaming as the branch went in the front of his neck and out the back. His eyes were open wide in shock.

His body was hanging by that tree branch through his neck.

Near where I'd stopped was a small branch of green fir needles that had blown down from a storm or was maybe chewed off by an industrious squirrel. I picked it up and hung it on the bloody protruding branch. Its needles covered most of the blood-stained white fabric. What was visible of him now blended in with the snowy landscape.

I did with Roland as I'd done with Hud, emptying his pockets. It was an easier job this time because his body was held up by the branch that had impaled his neck, making his pockets accessible.

Unlike during his robbery of the Korean restaurant, he had a wallet and ID on him. His driver's license identified him as Roland

P Dippman. In the wallet was $849 in cash, a debit card like Hud's, and a few scraps of paper.

Roland's gun was in the side pocket of his jacket. I pulled it out with my gloved hand. It was a Glock. Twice the number of rounds as Hud's Smith & Wesson. I released the magazine and emptied the chamber. Because my pockets were now full, I put the components in my waist pack.

I tried Roland's phone. Unlike Hud's, it did have a passcode lock. The little symbol asked for a thumbprint.

Roland had died hugging the tree. I had to lean forward and reach out to remove Roland's closest glove. I pressed his thumb against the screen. Nothing happened. I side-stepped down below the tree and did a kick turn to reverse my direction, then side-stepped back up until I could reach his other glove. I pulled it off and tried that thumb against the screen. It worked.

I knew the phone would time out and go dark, and I wanted continued access to his phone. I figured there was a way to change the passcode requirement, but I wasn't phone fluent. So, I started exploring, pressing the settings button, going down the menu, looking for anything connected to passcodes.

It was an absurd situation, standing in the snow and cold, unable to leave the dead man and his thumb until I'd figured out how to turn off the passcode requirement. I had no luck.

Eventually, I went to the Google page and typed in 'How to turn off thumbprint access' and read the instructions. That worked. I found the switch and toggled it off. I turned off the phone, then turned it back on. No code was needed.

I traversed back to the ski run, skied down the mountain, and hiked out to my Jeep. I switched my ski boots for my walking boots.

# FORTY-THREE

As I headed back to my Jeep, I thought about the cliché that says the death penalty doesn't bring closure for a victim's family and friends. But the death of someone indescribably evil can absolutely bring relief. The idea that all life is sacred is perpetrated by those who haven't known people like Roland P Dippman and haven't seen the pain and fear and misery and damage they create. There was nothing sacred about Dippman's life.

With Roland Dippman dead and Hud Tenery Wallen tied up on the mountain, I still had three more men to find and disable. One was the driver of the pickup truck at the Korean restaurant, and the other two were the gunmen. They'd all threatened Truckee Officers Hattie Foster and Chamberlain with a shotgun and pistols.

Hud Wallen had said that Roland had a boss of sorts. So I assumed there was yet another man who directed their efforts or at least manipulated them into doing his bidding. But that guy was a complete mystery to me.

Now, however, I had access to the gunmen through Hud's and Roland's phones.

I sat in the passenger seat of my Jeep, took out the pad of paper I keep under the seat, and used it to write down the phone numbers listed on Roland's and Hud's recent phone calls.

Next, I made notes of all their recent texts, the phone numbers they were sent to, and the names that were referenced.

After that, I read their emails. Hud's emails and texts were uninteresting, the literary equivalent of grunting. Roland's at least had some revealing content in the sense that he appeared to have been the motivator behind the robbery of the Korean restaurant. I reread the threatening email he'd sent me about hurting my girlfriend.

Then I looked through a smattering of other emails and texts, where he issued orders to his foot soldiers, telling them where and when to show up. There was no record of the outgoing call he'd made that brought the gunmen to the Korean restaurant, men who, on arrival, discovered that Roland and Hud were in police custody, men who used guns to take Roland and Hud from the police vehicle. Nevertheless, I thought I'd figured out the gunmen's names.

Each of Roland's emails revealed how asinine and mindless he was. The spellings, the syntax, and his inability to say something lucid was amazing. I considered that it might be part of a pose, but I couldn't convince myself of it.

Last, I listened to Hud's and Roland's recent voice mails.

There was nothing of note.

Once I'd taken all my notes, I looked for repeated names and numbers and other patterns. I created a list of the other soldiers that Roland ordered around.

Three other men were prominent in his communications. Those were likely his gunmen.

I repeated the process with Hud's phone.

My goal in collecting information was to use it to draw them into a trap.

I didn't know what shape and form that trap would take. But the basic needs were clear.

The men needed to be enticed. How? Money would be the most powerful attractant.

The men needed to show up at the same place and at the same time, preferably from a place where they couldn't rush off in a car.

Once at the meeting place, the men needed to be neutralized or arrested and taken into custody.

Every scenario I could think of had substantial flaws.

You can't arrest men unless you have evidence that they have committed a crime.

You generally can't neutralize them unless they have attacked you and forced you to retaliate.

Because I had both phones that I had taken off Hud and Roland, I could contact their tough-guy pals and draw them into any number of scenarios. But first I had to come up with a workable plan.

I thought about it as I started a grid search of the parking lot. I walked all the way down to the end, moved over two rows, walked back.

I found the BMW on the fourth trip. I hit Hud's key fob. The door unlocked, and the lights flashed. I opened the trunk and put the guns, Hud's phone, the men's wallets, and other pocket detritus from Roland and Hud in the trunk. Then I put the key fob in the glove box.

I sat in the BMW and, using my own phone, I dialed the Placer County Sheriff's Office and asked to be connected to Sergeant Jack Santiago.

"Sergeant Santiago," he said.

"Hey, Sergeant, McKenna here. Got some serious crime to report in your county."

"I talked to Diamond. He said your sweetie and the Truckee woman whose restaurant burned down are hiding in a safe house. What's up? And why call me?"

"Long story. Do you have a minute?"

"Depending on, probably."

"The safe house happened because I got an email from one of the restaurant robbers who escaped police custody. The man threatened to hurt Street. I told Diamond, and he got an okay to use Douglas County's safe house.

"After Street and Camille and Geneviève were in the safe house, I sent an email reply to the man who threatened Street. I implied I had an inside connection at the Truckee Police. I made him think I still had access to the money he stole, which is at the police department. Anyway, this guy and his partner showed up to take the money away from me. He and his partner repeatedly shot at me while on skis. One of the men skied off the run and is now dead, impaled on a sharp branch on a tree that he struck. He turned out to be named Roland P Dippman. I'm calling you because this happened in Placer County, your side of the basin."

"Where is this tree?"

"You know your local ski resorts, right?"

"I'm a skier," Santiago said. "So I'm familiar in general."

"Then you know the Majordomo ski run."

"Sure. Big sweeping cruiser. Grand views of Tahoe."

"Right. The dead guy is off the right edge of the Majordomo run, about halfway down the run. He's in the deep forest fifty yards off the edge of the trail. I'm currently going through his phone. I've established that he was the one who sent the threatening email."

"What about the weapon this Roland Dippman used to shoot at you?"

"I put it and his partner's gun and all their pocket stuff in the trunk of their Beamer. It's in the parking lot at the ski resort. His partner is named Hud Tenery Wallen. He also tried to shoot me while skiing. Hud is now zip tied off the other side of the ski run, skiless, bootless, hatless, gloveless. And one of his socks made a very nice gag, stuffed in his mouth. He's near tower number seventeen."

"Hold on while I make some notes." Santiago was silent a moment. "I'll get some men up that mountain and find them. One alive, one dead. You are creating too much excitement for our laid-back Placer County vibe."

"Sorry," I said. "You'll probably want to have the ski patrol go up with toboggans to retrieve both Dippman's body and, probably, to take Wallen down on a sled as well, because he's without ski boots and socks, and he may have a cracked rib. Although I took guns off both shooters, consider Wallen to be armed and dangerous until proven otherwise."

"Wallen's weapon?"

"Smith and Wesson MP Shield. I also put that in the BMW trunk. Next, the men were using a blue, stolen BMW. I'm sitting in it as we speak. They drove it to Geneviève's restaurant to hassle her and, probably, also when they returned to burn down the restaurant. That car, with its stolen license plate, is parked at the west end of the eighth row in the ski area's parking lot. The men's guns and personal effects are locked in the trunk. My gift to Placer County. The key fob is in the glove box. Considering the guns in the trunk, I'll lock the car when I leave. Which means you need to show up with your auto burglary tools.

"The only significant item that will be missing is Roland's phone, which I need to hang onto for another day. I'll get that phone to you when I'm done with it."

I went through my mental checklist.

I said, "Hud Wallen will be suffering from cold, so it would be important to get to him before the ski area closes for the day. Dippman's body can wait. Although, I suppose that some members of the animal kingdom would find him to be a good source of protein overnight. The pathologist would probably appreciate getting the body before much of that happens."

"Anything else?" Santiago asked.

"Lots. I'm about to use Roland's phone to set another trap for the men who took Roland and Hud at gunpoint from the Truckee police, and for that I need your help."

"Which is…"

"You probably know the Funnel."

"Of course. The steep bump run that drops down a canyon into a big hole. No way out except taking the chairlift back up the mountain."

"I'm thinking that I can use Roland's phone to summon the other men to a meeting in the Funnel. I'll tell them it's their chance to get their share of the money. They'll believe it because the summons will come from Roland's phone."

"That's a law enforcement action you don't have the authority to pursue."

"Right." I continued as if Santiago was giving me grief instead of a legal opinion. "I'm also thinking you could have a couple of deputies waiting at the bottom."

Santiago was silent long enough that I thought he was wondering if I was a help or a hazard to proper jurisprudence. "That's actually a great idea," he eventually said.

"You say that like you don't think all my ideas are great."

"Staking out the Korean restaurant without telling Lieutenant Oberman, was a bozo idea. Look where it got you."

"Yeah, I suppose you're right."

"Anyway, felons in the Funnel is a nice visual," Santiago said. "The men ski down to the bottom and see deputies in uniform. It spooks them. They wonder if the deputies are looking for them. But if they don't ride the lift out, they're screwed. And if we stop the chairlift, they're screwed either way. They can't climb up the Funnel canyon in downhill ski gear. It's too steep, and the snow is too deep. And if they try to ski out by going through the backcountry below the resort, they quickly get lost and maybe die of exposure."

I said, "So the question is whether you've got two deputies who are comfortable on Double Black Diamond ski runs and, if so, can you spare them tomorrow?"

"You're in a rush," Santiago said.

"Yeah. I think I'll get the best result if I make it seem like there's no time to think about it. Come and get the money or kiss it goodbye."

"What about these gunmen and skiing? Are they going to be willing to go into a Double Black Diamond funnel? I've known many gunmen who are skillful riders on their Harleys, but couldn't ride a pair of skis if they were in their own garage with their skis on the floor and a buddy on each side to hold them up."

"They'll absolutely be willing to try the Funnel to get the money. And if they don't have the skiing chops, they probably won't admit it. Macho attitude and all. If we get some ski newbie gunmen trapped in the Funnel, so much the better."

"Do you expect my deputies to face threats of violence?"

"It's possible."

Santiago paused. "I'm guessing you'll hang back above the bottom of the Funnel, look for anyone who fits the description of the shooters, and then squeeze them."

"The thought occurred to me. But I wouldn't confess that to an officer of the law. And speaking of descriptions, they were wearing Harry Potter ski masks."

I heard Santiago breathing over the phone. He said. "Hold on while I check our schedule." He was back in less than a minute. "I can spare Damon and Angela tomorrow. Would that work?"

"Perfect. Are they pretty good on the slopes?"

"Damon, not so much, although he's got basic chops. In a pinch, he can traverse at an angle across the mountain, do a one-eighty kick turn, and then ski back at the opposite angle."

"Zigzagging down the slope."

"Right. Whereas Angela went to the Junior Olympics six years in a row as a slalom racer when she was a teenager. She sometimes gets a little rough with suspects, but she can out-ski anyone."

"Great. Let's plan on them being in place late morning tomorrow until two in the afternoon. I'll use Roland's phone to request a meeting of the gunmen at noon."

"Let me know if anything changes your plan," Santiago said.

"One more thing. It might be good for me to be down at the chairlift, too, in case we have to take one or more of these guys in. Although I don't imagine how we could find probable cause with skiers."

"Me neither," I said. "Maybe something unexpected will develop."

It sounded like Santiago took a deep breath.

"Let's just consider a hypothetical," he added. "What if one of these guys feels squeezed? It might be best if I don't witness the details of how that came to be. So take that into account when you plan your position."

"You think I would do something illegal? What a shocking idea."

"Put it this way, I could imagine you and Diamond being unhappy at the way these lowlifes held you up at gunpoint in Truckee and then stole your prisoners from Truckee PD custody."

"Yeah, I am unhappy about that," I said. "See you tomorrow morning in the Funnel. Three sheriff's officers will make a nice impression. Oh, one more thing. I have no idea if anyone shows up to this meeting. You and your deputies could be waiting there for nothing."

"Understood. But the last two guys you contacted showed up on the Majordomo, so your track record is currently working."

"Thanks."

I used Roland's phone to text the three names I thought were most likely to be the three gunmen who showed up in the pickup behind the Korean restaurant and took Roland and Hud from the police at gunpoint.

I wrote with my best imitation of Roland's verbal skill.

'good news turns out tall guy we beet up was on the take with the truckee pd  tall guy musta had a inside guy he split with  now tall guy wants to work with me so I dont spill the beans on him and hurt his girl so i got a big chunk of the money and i will divvy it up tomarro  ever one gets a piece  we cant be seen on the street  so best place to meet on north shore is the funnel run  you all know the ski areas right?  cops dont go to ski areas so we can meet in private ski down at botom of chairlift at funnel  we split $  no one will no  be there noon'

I hit send and heard a beep. I got out of the BMW, locked it, and walked to my Jeep.

# FORTY-FOUR

Although Roland Dippman was dead, the other gunmen were still out there and possibly willing to make good on Dippman's threat to Street. So I wanted them to stay in the safe house another night.

That night, alone in my cabin, I spoke to Street on her cell, grateful that the safe house was high enough in the mountains to get a cell signal. I asked if she and Camille and Geneviève were okay.

She said that Geneviève was, of course, distraught but coping.

I explained that I'd caught the two men who had likely burned down her restaurant and sent the threatening email. They were no longer a concern.

She wanted to know how I'd caught them, so I explained what happened but left out the details.

I also explained that the threatening man was part of a small gang, and I hoped she and Camille and Geneviève would be okay staying another night so that I could assess whether the other men in the group would be a concern or not.

She was fine with another night.

"Which means you get stuck with dog duty," I said.

"No better protection than multiple dogs watching, listening, smelling," she said.

"True."

We talked for an hour, catching up, exchanging pleasantries. She told me about Camille discovering the bookcases in the den and how she was going through every book, looking at them, reading a page or two, then reshelving them.

"The kid is a natural autodidact," Street said.

"What's that mean?"

"Think da Vinci or Ben Franklin or Hedy Lamarr. A self-motivated learner interested in all subjects. Never settling for play or entertainment when she could, instead, add some knowledge to her world."

"And Geneviève?"

Street lowered her voice. "I worry for her. Her life is filled with darkness right now. It's a hard place for her to be. She really needs some light in her life."

"I'll do my best. In the meantime, I've got a meeting first thing tomorrow, so I better try to sleep."

"Good luck."

We said our love yous and goodnights and hung up.

Although it was late, I realized I should call Diamond to tell him the latest about the two men who got the better of us at the Korean restaurant.

"You're awake," I said when he answered. "Thought I'd be leaving a message."

"I'm still steamed about being played by those robber sleazebags," he said.

"Me too, which is why I'm calling." I told him about my day on the slopes.

"One down, one jailed?" he said. He didn't say it with glee, but I could sense that Diamond felt satisfaction when a robber arsonist enforcer hits a big tree branch while trying to murder me.

"Three more guys to go," I said.

"The guys who took back the men from us and the Truckee cops."

"Right. I used Roland Dippman's phone to send an invitation to those other guys to come and collect their share of the money."

"Good BS to lay on these guys," Diamond said. "What's your goal with them?"

"The usual."

"And if that's not likely?" Diamond's tone radiated skepticism over the phone.

"Then maybe I can use my powers of persuasion to convince them to take their business somewhere outside of Tahoe."

"This I want to see. An avenger with lofty goals."

I told Diamond my plan for the Funnel. "I've got Santiago showing up with two deputies."

"I'm off tomorrow. How about I join you?"

"That would be great. Santiago and I would both appreciate the extra manpower."

I was up at 7:00, coffeed, fed, and dressed by 8:00. I was bringing my skis out to my Jeep when Diamond pulled up in front of my cabin, his rattle-trap truck backfiring when he turned off the engine.

Diamond switched his skis from his pickup to my Jeep.

I said, "Last time we went into California, you left your weapons in your truck, and we got in trouble."

"Trouble would've been worse if I'd been carrying. I already put my guns in my secret cubby."

I nodded. "I made each of us two peanut butter sandwiches and a bag of chips, and I filled two thermoses with coffee." I handed him a flexible insulated bag Street had given me.

"Thanks." Diamond took the bag and put it into his backpack.

We were taking our first ride up the chairlift by 9:30. It was cold enough that our breath was like cloud puffs from a steam engine. The December sun seemed very low in the sky. Not low like in Seattle or Minneapolis or Montreal, but low for sunny California. It would be another hour before the sun's rays would reach down into the trees and begin softening the frozen snow. Only then would the skiing sensation move from harsh toward comfortable.

As the chair swung when it went by the first tower, Diamond said, "The meeting time you gave these guys is noon?"

"Right. That gives us enough time to work our way over to the Funnel, ride its chairlift, consider good observation points, and be in place before our targets get here."

"Santiago's men will be wearing their sheriff's uniforms," Diamond said, "which will unnerve the sleazebags."

"Actually, because it's cold, Santiago said they'll wear overcoats. If and when they want their uniforms to be seen, they'll drop their coats."

"What do you imagine for my role?"

"Sage, perspicacious wisdom," I said.

"My three middle names."

We skied three runs, gradually working our way across the

mountain, and then dropped into the Funnel. When I got near the bottom of the run, I paused 100 yards up from the chairlift loading ramp. Diamond did a hard, skidding stop nearby.

Without pointing and potentially providing information to an observer, I looked over to the right. "That group of trees would be a good spot for one of us," I said.

Diamond looked around. Nodded. Turned to look up the slope above us.

He studied the other side of the Funnel. "The trees over by that rock outcropping is another place that would be a good observation point. It's higher than we are now, but it has good sightlines." He looked at me. "How much in advance do you think we should be in position?"

I said, "If I were these guys, I'd be on my way already. So we should be ready as soon as possible."

"Be faster to go back up the chair and then ski back down to those points rather than hike up to the higher points from here," he said.

We skied down to the chairlift. I was ahead of Diamond. It appeared that one of Santiago's deputies was already near the lift, the man Santiago called Damon. Damon had on a tan coat like what someone would wear in the city. The coat was unzipped, hanging closed but providing easy access to his duty belt underneath. His dark green uniform pants were bunched up above his ski boots, but were easily visible beneath his coat. He had on black gloves and a dark green knit cap.

I made a slight nod as I skied by him. He might have thought I was the PI Santiago had prepped him about. But he might have also thought I was just another skier.

I coasted over to the chairlift loading ramp. Because it was a cold, weekday morning, there were few other skiers. I got on a chair by myself. Only hard-core skiers brave the Funnel early in the morning when it is still icy.

As I sat down on the approaching chair, I saw Diamond ski by in my peripheral vision. He came into the loading ramp.

When my chair swung by the first tower on its ride up the mountain, I shifted a little to see behind me. Diamond was two chairs back. The chair between us was empty. All was calm, nothing to concern anyone who might be watching.

Once at the top, I turned left off the off-load ramp. Diamond turned right. We skied down opposite sides of the Funnel, and went at different rates. Diamond took a little more time. He was an amazing skier for a man who grew up in Mexico City and spent a good part of his young adulthood as a migrant farm worker picking lettuce and cauliflower in the southern Central Valley.

Once I was in my fir-tree cover, I used my skis to pack an easy exit in three directions. Then I found the horizontal trunk of a fallen tree. I cleared some snow so I could sit for a time without melting snow soaking up into my black ski suit. Then I settled down to wait. I assumed that Diamond, 50 yards away, was doing something similar in his group of trees.

Few skiers came into view. A man and a woman, periodically stopping and talking to each other. Three kids of high school age. Two women who looked like college ski racers. They wore serious ski gear including helmets, and they skied like they were not out for fun but were working on technique. A lone man skied by. Then another lone man, this one wearing an overcoat over bunched-up dark green pants. I watched carefully as he went by at a distance. He was thick in the manner of someone very strong but not a steroid show-muscle body builder.

Santiago.

From my position, I could see all of the skiers except the two men in overcoats get on the chairlift to ride back up the mountain.

A woman skied by me, 25 yards to the side. She also had on an overcoat. Unlike the previous men, she wore stretch pants. They were green but a different brighter green than the other cops. She skied down, made a skidding stop near the two men. By her movements—athletic, carved turns with little hip movement—she telegraphed ski racer.

Although covered up with the overcoat, I could tell she was fit and tough.

Angela. The deputy that Santiago had said sometimes got rough with suspects.

Although I couldn't hear anything, the three cops seemed to talk and move around a little. Otherwise, the mountain remained quiet.

After a long wait, the three high school kids came back down. Then came the two women in helmets. Despite the Funnel's steep slopes and ungroomed icy snow, it was popular with those skiers who wanted challenge more than they wanted fun.

They all got on the lift and went back up the mountain.

Because there was no breeze and because the Funnel was vaguely shaped like a steep amphitheater, sounds carried well. I heard someone laughing. A raven cawed and then made its wooden castanets speech. A guy trying to attract a girl? Something chunked on the snow a good distance away. A falling pine cone? An old branch that finally gave way?

There came the soft whoosh of skis going through powder and then the crackle of skis cutting through refrozen crud. There was the scraping of metal ski edges on ice. Then more whoosh. A skier must have been navigating through shade-protected powder, then moving out onto skied-out bumps, then re-entering a wooded section where the sun didn't probe.

The sound stopped. I heard someone cough. I stood up off my hard log couch and leaned this way and that, trying to see the skier's location.

There. I could see through a tiny opening in the trees. Someone moved his arm. He was wiping snow off the bronze lenses of his goggles, snow that must have fallen off a branch he'd bumped.

I shifted more and then took a single side-step up the slope to get a better view through the trees.

The man was wearing a black ski mask. It had a red Harry Potter lightning bolt on the forehead section above the eye opening. The corner of the mask's mouth opening was torn, making it seem as if the man was sneering.

It was one of the men I'd seen at the Korean restaurant. The man who'd pointed the shotgun at Officer Chamberlain and held him motionless while the other men had grabbed Roland and Hud out of the patrol car.

# FORTY-FIVE

After a minute, the man pushed off and skied down toward the chairlift.

I did the same. I angled toward the man, trying to stay behind him. When the man made a turn to slow his speed, I did not.

I kept my speed up as I stayed on an intersecting course.

Like the events the day before, I approached him from behind and hit his shoulder with my shoulder.

The man pitched forward as he fell. I sat as I went down. I maintained control and slid on my butt as I came to a stop. The other man's right ski binding released, and the ski arced through the air. The man's goggles came off and skittered down the slope like a strangely shaped orange rodent.

He came to a stop with his head pointing downhill. As I watched from ten yards up the slope, he used his free boot to push down on the release lever of his other. Once free of both skis, he stood up in the snow and looked at me, rage on his face.

"You lousy piece of crap!" he shouted. "You hit me from behind!"

I stood and slowly slid down the slope until I was directly above him. I spoke in a raised voice equal to his.

"We were side-by-side. There would be no problem if you hadn't turned into me."

"I didn't see you, so I must have been below you. That makes it so I had the right of way!" he shouted. Although he was angry, he didn't seem to recognize me from our interaction behind the Korean restaurant.

Behind him, I saw two of Santiago's deputies moving our way, Damon walking in his boots, his skis left behind. Angela was doing a ski-skate toward us, pushing hard with her poles. Both had dropped their overcoats, so their uniforms were obvious.

The man in the Harry Potter mask was substantially shorter than me, and I leaned over him, trying to provoke him.

I said, "You don't have the right of way when you make a sudden turn into my path. You obviously don't know mountain etiquette. You are a scofflaw, a hazard to us law-abiding skiers."

Another skier approached, moving fast. He slowed as if interested, then sped down toward the chairlift. The man in the mask looked at the other skier and then turned to me.

"What's this scofflaw crap." he shouted. "Are you calling me names?"

"Yeah, maybe I am. If you don't acknowledge that you contributed to this situation, then you are a low-rent sleazebag dirtball."

He seemed to be too calm for the situation. I needed him to be outraged. I wanted him to take a swing at me.

I tried to summon a school-boy insult. "They wouldn't let you on this mountain if there were any old ladies here for you to prey on."

The man was red-faced. Instead of hitting me, the man pulled off his right glove, reached inside his jacket, and pulled out a pistol and pointed it at me, its big barrel opening staring me in the face.

I immediately realized I'd made the critical mistake of underestimating the man's predatory instincts. I was an idiot. I should have known that a man who'd pulled a gun in the past would be inclined to do it again.

Angela, the cop, anticipating a physical conflict, had ski-skated to within five yards of us. She was behind the man.

"Drop your weapon!" she shouted. "THIS IS THE SHERIFF! DROP IT NOW!"

The man started to turn toward her voice. He hesitated. Then turned farther. Saw Angela on her skis. Behind her, Damon was running in his ski boots.

I was worried the man in the mask would fire at her. I was tempted to leap onto him when he looked toward her. But that might cause him to shoot.

Angela shouted again. "THIS IS A SHERIFF'S ORDER. DROP YOUR WEAPON!"

He slowly reached down and set his gun on the snow.

He straightened up as the deputy reached him.

She shouted, "PUT YOUR HANDS ON YOUR HEAD!"

While her gun gave her a weapon advantage, he had a movement advantage of being out of his skis, while she was still in hers.

I eased up on my edges and slid a few inches toward them, ready to lunge and grab him.

The man slowly put his hands on his head.

"KNEEL ON THE SNOW!" she shouted.

He hesitated. Another skier came by slowly. He also wore a Harry Potter ski mask.

Our masked man saw him. "Jason, get out of here! These are cops!"

The skier turned his skis toward the chairlift and pushed forward with his poles.

Angela kicked out of her skis and dug her ski boots into the snow. With her new traction, she stepped up behind the first man and then slapped a cuff on one of the man's wrists. She jerked his hand off his head and pulled it around his back. She kneed him in the back, forcing him face down onto the snow, and, while still holding her gun in her other hand, cuffed his hands together.

"You're under arrest for brandishing a weapon."

Angela holstered her weapon, then looked around at the other skiers on the slope. Apparently judging risks, she stood one of her ski boots on the gun the man had set down, pushing the gun into the snow. She pulled a plastic evidence bag out of her waist pack as she Mirandized the man on the snow.

She turned to me. "You're McKenna?" she asked.

"Yes. Thanks for your good work. I see the man this guy called Jason down by Santiago. I'll go see if I can help."

I pushed off and skied toward the chairlift.

Seeing that Angela had control of her suspect, Damon had turned and was running toward the chairlift. I saw Santiago beyond Damon. He was pointing up the mountain. I stopped and turned to look.

Another skier appeared over a rise. He came fast and then stopped fast. He looked at Damon, then turned and saw Angela with her suspect face down on the snow, his hands cuffed behind his back.

The skier had a black knit cap bunched up at the top of his head. After a moment of cognition, he pulled the cap down over his face so that only his eyes were visible through the face opening. His cap also had the red Harry Potter lightning bolt.

He started forward and skied laterally across the slope toward heavy tree cover. As his path went horizontal and then slightly up, he came to a stop and started stepping sideways and up into the forest as if trying to climb out of the Funnel and escape into the trees.

An additional skier came down at an angle from the side and used his momentum to come up to the masked skier's side.

I realized the additional skier was Diamond.

Diamond appeared to talk to the masked skier. After a few moments, the man in the mask reached into his jacket just as the previous suspect had with me. Diamond made a sudden move that I couldn't see well because of the distance and because they were in the shade of the trees.

A few seconds later, it appeared that the skier was on the ground and Diamond had the man's hands cuffed behind his back.

Jack Santiago's voice came from behind me.

"On the ground!" He shouted at someone.

"You got no probable cause," came another voice. Then came a grunt.

"Fleeing from an officer," Santiago said. "And what's this? Carrying a concealed weapon. If we discover you've got no concealed-carry permit, you'll be cooked. If we find the gun is stolen, you'll be baked and broiled and facing a much longer stay at the state country club. And there's always the possibility you've already got two strikes. If so, you'll be an old man before you get out."

I turned and skied the rest of the way down to Santiago.

He looked up at Diamond and then at me.

"Looks like Diamond got his man. A citizen's arrest. That makes three men, all with weapons."

"A good haul," I said, nodding. "Thanks for your help. I went too far and almost made the man shoot. Your crew does good work."

I looked at the gunmen. All three were cuffed behind their backs.

Their weapons were in Santiago's backpack. Angela and Damon had taken off the suspects' Harry Potter ski masks. One of the gunmen was shaved bald so that people could see the devil tattoos across the sides of his head. Another man, who was naturally balding, had long, thin scraggly hair and a very long, very sparse beard and mustache, the thin strings of hair hanging down and partially caught in his mouth. Because his hands were cuffed behind his back, he couldn't pull them out. So, he repeatedly tried to spit the hair strands out. The third man had a black flattop that looked like it had been prepped with axle grease. He had a Hitler mustache and a patch of hair on his lower lip.

The cops also removed two goggles and one sunglasses and three pair of gloves and stuffed the gear into Damon's back pack. The unarmed, degloved and deglassed men blinked in the bright sun.

Santiago looked at them. He said to me, "What do you think?"

"I think you should remove their socks and boot insoles."

"Great idea. Escaping by skiing in hard plastic ski boots without socks would not be easy. And we don't want easy."

While Angela watched, Damon put each man on his stomach. Santiago sat on their backs while Damon took off their boots and socks. He pulled out the molded insoles of the boots and then replaced the now-empty ski boot shells on each man. They lifted each man up and had them step back into their ski bindings.

"I can't ski in ice-cold boots like this!" the tattooed man said. "One of my boots has, like, a screw or something sticking up into my foot! This is cruel and unusual punishment!"

"Yep, it's gonna be hard," Santiago said. "Be sure and tell the judge all about it."

They were substantially hobbled. They could, of course, attempt to escape by skiing into the back country, but they wouldn't get far before they fell in the junk snow. And without the use of their arms, they wouldn't be able to get up.

I spoke to Santiago. "Will you need help getting these lovely examples of humanity out of the Funnel and down to some transport?"

"Nope. Three of us armed and smart. Three of them, cuffed and stupid. Piece of cake."

# FORTY-SIX

As Diamond and I drove back to my cabin, we ate the sandwiches we'd hauled up and down the ski mountain.

I said, "I'm thinking it might be safe to let the women out of the safe house. Do you have an opinion?"

"Most of the dirtballs are in the clink. The guy who issued the threat choked on a branch. Anyone left is probably going to lay low. So, yeah, I think they could walk free. But, I could be wrong."

"Maybe I'll ask their opinion."

We got to my cabin, and Diamond transferred to his rattle box and left.

I went inside, called Street, and gave her an update.

"How is Geneviève doing?"

Street spoke in a very low voice. "She is a wreck, of course. But I've gotten her to eat a little. We're talking things through. My sense is that it's going to take a very long time for her to come through this."

"No doubt," I said. "I really wish I could bring her good news."

"You are. You've caught most of the men connected to these crimes." Street paused. "Maybe there's something that can be done on the insurance question?"

"I'm glad you mentioned that. I've been so focused on these immediate threats, I haven't had time to pursue the insurance. In the meantime, I'll stop by the safe house. Maybe you could talk to Geneviève and Camille and see how you all feel about going home. If you have any questions, we can talk about it when I get there."

"Okay. See you then."

I knew nothing about the life insurance business and nothing about Colin's policy except that Geneviève had said the company was Franklin Assurance Holdings International. She'd also said that

the phone call she'd gotten about the policy was from an attorney in
Reno named Madison Rappaport. And I'd seen the insurance card
on Jackson Trane's desk.

I Googled the name, got a phone number, and dialed.

"Rappaport and Sezner, Attorneys at Law," a woman's voice said.
"Please leave a message, name, time, date, and the nature of your
business. Thank you."

As she spoke I was thinking about what approach would be most
likely to motivate a return phone call.

"Hello, my name is Owen McKenna. I'm a private investigator
in Tahoe, and I've been hired by Geneviève Laurent, who is
connected to Colin Burns, a client of Madison Rappaport's. Among
other things, Geneviève wants me to look into the refusal of Franklin
Assurance Holdings International to pay on a life insurance policy
that was taken out by Colin Burns, a policy that named her as the
beneficiary. I don't expect my questions to take more than a few
minutes of your time. Thanks in advance for calling me back." I left
my contact info and hung up.

I thought to look up Huntington's Disease. It was an inherited
disease, caused by some kind of gene mutation. It was detected by a
simple test. People who get the disease often find out because one or
both of their parents have the disease. However, if their parents die
from some other cause and no one has reason to look for evidence of
Huntington's Disease, a person might not know they have it.

Madison Rappaport called back just as I was about to head to
the safe house.

I thanked her for calling.

"Could you come to my office for a short talk?" she said. "I'm in
downtown Reno, near the river walk. Say, four o'clock today?" She
gave me her office address.

I understood the purpose. You can't judge someone who calls
on the phone, which is a big concern if you're talking about private
matters. But if they come into your office, you can get a read on their
motivation, their sincerity, their earnestness, their honesty.

"Perfect," I said. "See you then."

First I drove south to Stateline, turned up Kingsbury Grade,
drove past my office and on up to the safe house above Daggett

Summit.

I remembered the gate code and let myself in.

I knocked on the door. The dogs didn't bark, probably because they could tell it was me by the sound of my Jeep.

Street came to the door. Camille was standing behind her. The mood was somber as I walked in. Spot and Blondie came over to greet me, but they showed no enthusiasm, an example of how dogs are emotionally locked to the people around them.

Geneviève was sitting by a sunny window holding a mug of tea.

We acknowledged each other but didn't speak more than a few words.

I reiterated what I'd told Street on the phone. We all made some small talk about how there probably wasn't any immediate threat. But we avoided the subject of Jimmy Baker.

I said to Street, "I'm thinking it would be smart to leave Spot and Lazlo at your condo for the next day or so. Both as a security issue and also as a… you know, dogs and people are kind of a nice distraction."

Street understood my meaning. "Yes. I think it's worth it to have the condo a bit crowded."

"Are we agreed, then? All in favor of going back home?"

Camille said, "Yes, all my books and games are at home."

I was pleased to hear Camille refer to her new living quarters as home. Her adjustment to being Street's daughter was continuing.

Geneviève made the slightest of nods.

I said, "Street, you might want to do as before, take Geneviève and Camille and Blondie, and I'll follow with Spot and Lazlo."

"Okay. Do I need to do anything to close up the safe house?"

"I don't think so. And Diamond drives the grade every day, so he can stop by and check on things if he wants."

We got everything loaded up and left.

We were in Street's condo lot a half hour later.

The dogs ran around as if they hadn't been there for days instead of just 24 hours.

I made an automatic check of the place, windows and doors and such. Everything looked fine, so I said goodbye.

# FORTY-SEVEN

I drove north and east on 50, over Spooner Summit, and down to Carson City. From there I got on the new 580 freeway and was in Reno thirty minutes before my appointment with the lawyer.

Madison Rappaport's office was in a smallish three-story office building just off the Truckee River, which was flowing with winter gusto from the recent storm snowmelt.

I went into an elegant foyer with polished marble floor, black mirrored walls with little gold flecks in the glass, and gold wall sconces. The lobby had an enclosed board with the names of tenants. Half were attorneys. There were two business names listed, both with Ph.Ds. Probably psychologists in private practice. The Rappaport and Selzner office was down a short hall on the main floor. I made a light knock, then pulled open the door. There was a small elegant reception room with the same polished marble floor and an unoccupied reception desk.

Behind the desk were two open doorways, one to the left, one to the right. Rappaport and Selzner, no doubt.

On the reception desk was a gold bell with a button in the center. I tapped the button.

"Be there in a moment," said a female voice.

A minute later, a woman walked out of the door on the left.

"Owen McKenna?" she said, reaching out her hand. "I'm Madison Rappaport. Good to meet you."

We shook.

She was wearing an olive-green pantsuit over low, delicate olive-colored shoes. She wore no apparent makeup. Her gray hair was pulled back and up into a bun, and she had on small gold hoop earrings with small olive gemstones hanging from the loops. They were similar in style to Geneviève's earrings. The olive clothing and earrings didn't match her green eyes, but it harmonized with and emphasized them. It was an upscale business look that communicated professionalism but not vanity.

"We can talk in my office." She turned and walked toward the door from which she'd come. I followed. I paused at the door. "Would you like me to close the door?"

"You can leave it open. We'll probably have the place to ourselves."

She sat at her desk, and I sat in one of her chairs. We chatted for just a brief moment before I asked my first question. "Geneviève Laurent called me and asked me to look into her insurance situation. This is not my strong suit, so I'm seeking help. She told me that Colin Burns's insurance policy had a three-year contestability period and that the policy had passed that milestone at the time of his death. My understanding is that insurance companies have to pay in that situation."

"Yes, the policy had passed the contestability period, and it is correct that insurance companies have to pay, unless the application was fraudulent. Franklin Assurance Holdings International alleges fraud. They say Colin Burns had Huntington's Disease and he didn't disclose it when he applied for insurance." She paused. "But before we get into that, let me first say that I'm glad you called me, because Colin left me with some instructions that tie my hands regarding Geneviève. He specified that I was not to speak of certain things until after Geneviève received the insurance payout. Because that hasn't happened, I'm actually eager to get your advice on the subject, as you probably know Geneviève better than I do. But let's table that for now and first answer your questions."

"As I understand," I said, "a person can have the mutated gene that causes Huntington's Disease and not know it."

"True. In fact, people with no symptoms and no obvious family history don't usually get tested until they develop symptoms. And sometimes not even then."

"So there is a reasonable possibility that Colin Burns might not have known about his Huntington's Disease."

"Yes," she said. "I agree with you. Perhaps I should point out that I am not an apologist for this insurance company or any insurance company. I am a family lawyer, helping ordinary people navigate ordinary legal issues. With regard to Franklin Assurance Holdings

International, I was merely the messenger bringing unfortunate news to the beneficiary of Colin Burns's insurance policy."

"Understood. Can you recommend an attorney who specializes in insurance company malfeasance?"

"No. That is far outside of my sphere of work. But I'm sure an experienced investigator would be able to find someone to fit the bill."

I realized that she was making a pointed comment about me and my job.

"Do you have the notice the insurance company sent about their refusal to make payment?"

"Yes, but without written authorization from Geneviève Laurent, I can't send you out with a copy."

I was thinking of an appropriate response when she said, "I could, however, let you see the letter. And, at this moment, I can't think of a compelling reason why you couldn't take a picture of it with your phone."

Another reason, I reluctantly thought, why it was probably smart that I finally gave in and bought the device that I disliked and blamed for feeling like I had a leash permanently tied around my neck.

Despite Street's and Camille's constant examples and phone-operation lessons, I had never taken a photo with my phone.

While Ms Rappaport opened a file drawer and flipped through some folders, I pulled out my phone and pushed several buttons until I found one called settings. I scrolled down looking for the camera menu.

Rappaport set the one-page letter on her desk with the letter facing me.

After a wait, she said, "I recognize a Luddite."

"How so?" I was still exploring.

"Awkward moves, puzzled frown, squinted eyes."

"Sorry, I'm trying to figure out how to turn on the camera."

"There is a camera icon."

"What does it look like?"

"A camera."

"Of course, there it is," I said.

"Tap it."

I did as she said. "Ah, that was easy."

She was nodding

I stood up, leaned over, and took a picture of the letter. I put the phone back in my pocket.

Rappaport put the letter back in the filing cabinet.

"Was there anything else you needed?"

"Just a quick question. How did you come to know Colin Burns?"

"I used to live in Incline Village. He went to the same athletic club that I belonged to."

"Can you think of any way to get an insider's view into the workings of this particular insurance company?"

"No. I should restate that I specialize in family law. I know nothing of insurance law. Unless we have cause to bring a civil lawsuit against the company, there is no discovery process, which means there is no way to find out about wrongdoing. If there were lots of evidence to suggest that the insurance company is denying lots of legitimate policies, then perhaps a class action lawsuit might be appropriate. Again, out of my arena."

She continued, "If you can find enough evidence of a crime to convince a DA to bring charges, then the DA is in control of discovery. Good luck learning about internal company decisions that way."

"Meaning you can't pry open a company's internal decision-making process."

"Correct."

I thought about it.

I said, "Then let's move onto your question for me."

"Colin Burns dealt with his estate in a very simple way. He left everything to Geneviève Laurent and made her executor. Because he didn't own a house or any other significant assets beyond his life insurance, he didn't even list them. His only possessions were a few personal items."

I asked, "Did Colin mention any other names in case Geneviève should predecease him?"

"No. He was quite certain he would live for some time. Barring that, he was even more certain that Ms. Laurent would outlive him."

"Did he list any alternative beneficiary on his insurance policy?"

"To my knowledge, no. But he arranged for the insurance himself. I was not part of that except that he put my contact information on the policy as Ms. Laurent's representative."

That puzzled me. "Why do you suppose he mentioned you at all?"

"Because he knew I'd been in business in this location for decades. He thought my address was less likely to change than hers. If Ms. Laurent were to move, it would be easier for me to find her whereabouts than it would be for the insurance company to track her down."

"Considering Colin Burns had few or no assets, how did he pay you for your services?"

"As I understand it, he researched how much the premium would be to get a high-risk term life policy, and he diligently saved until he could afford it. It is my understanding, the premium was very high. Because he worked as a waiter, I wouldn't be surprised if he had to borrow some of the money for the premium. Perhaps from his mother. He took the same approach with me. He asked me what it would cost for my services. I gave him a range. He saved for some time and then came in with a check for the high amount of the range I had told him."

I nodded.

She paused.

"My question for you is this," she said. "Colin wrote a letter. Some aspect of it apparently hinged on Ms. Laurent getting the insurance payout. So he sealed the letter and a few items in a large envelope. On the outside he wrote some words. I'll show it to you."

Madison Rappaport opened a file drawer, flipped through some folders, and pulled out a padded, manila envelope. It was sealed shut, yet I could tell it had one or two thick items in it.

Written in a rough, masculine scrawl, using a black pen, were the words:

'My Dearest Red, Red Rose Geneviève,

I've asked that this envelope be given to you only after you've received the payout on my life insurance policy. I'm hopeful that will happen within a few weeks of my death. Until then, I love you always. You'll forever be my Bonny Lass, and I'll be your Bonny Lad.

Q/Colin'

On either side of his name, he'd drawn hearts in a red pen.

I set the envelope on Rappaport's desk.

"His sentiment is so earnest, it's heart breaking," I said.

"Yes. So now you can understand my question. Colin asked me to wait until Ms. Laurent got the insurance before I gave this to her. Yet it's been nine or ten months, and it looks like she may never get the insurance. That puts me in a difficult place."

"What does the law say?"

"To my knowledge, this is outside of the law. The will required me to inform Ms. Laurent. But this envelope was a kind of side agreement as if between two friends. Colin had what I assume were strong sentimental reasons for me holding onto this until the insurance payout. It would be easy for me to ignore that, to simply tell Ms. Laurent that it's been too long, give her the envelope, and hope there isn't too much emotional fallout. So my question… Do you have advice? Should I continue to hold the envelope or give it to her?"

"I have only just started to think about insurance. So without much hope that I'll learn anything, I think you should hold onto the envelope for another few weeks. If I start to sense that I'm getting nowhere, I'll contact you, and you can give it to her then."

"Okay. Thank you for your advice."

She stood up.

I was being dismissed.

"Okay. Thank you very much. I'd like to pay you for your time."

"Not necessary. We'll call it professional courtesy."

"Thank you very much."

"You're welcome."

# FORTY-EIGHT

When I got back to my office, I opened my laptop to look up the insurance company.

Madison Rappaport had shown me the letter from the insurance company that said they were not paying on Colin Burns's life insurance policy because they claimed the application was fraudulent. The letter had Colin's policy number. I'd taken a picture of the letter. I found the photo in my phone and wrote down the information.

I searched on Franklin Assurance Holdings International. They were based in Miami and had offices in New York, Chicago, Seattle, San Francisco, Las Vegas, and Los Angeles. They also had four offices overseas, London, Paris, Berlin, and Rome. Like most companies, their website was carefully designed to not reveal any phone number or email address. All companies want to sell you something and take your money. Only a few are willing to have any contact with you.

Franklin Assurance's website showed no phone number, but they had a so-called live chat option that claimed to be a man named Kevin. After I wrote that I wanted information about their refusal to pay on a life insurance policy, the live chat Kevin asked what my problem was. Clearly he was a robot. When I explained further, the Kevin chat robot said he didn't understand my problem. Obviously he was a dumb robot.

I made one more attempt and got the same response.

Glory be Artificial Intelligence and the other wonderful tech innovations that have brought so much human communication to a screeching standstill.

I Googled the words 'phone number' and the company's name. I got two toll-free numbers and a third toll number. I used my landline, which didn't provide caller ID, and I dialed the numbers in the order they were listed. The first two made me sit through a slick audio advertising commercial that extolled the safety and reliability of Franklin Assurance Holdings International and then gave me a menu of choices. I could pick from wanting to purchase insurance, wanting to speak to an AI operator that could interpret my desires and connect me with a broker who could sell me insurance, wanting to switch language from English to any of four other languages, or wanting to log in to make a phone payment for my premium. There were no options for problem solving.

I said the words 'I want to speak to a customer service representative' several times, and the robot operator said he didn't understand. I tried again. Same result.

I said that I was trying to resolve a problem with a policy.

The operator said, "Could you please repeat your request."

I pressed one of the menu options, and the robot operator said I should enter my login and my password and then my policy number. I hung up.

Time to switch from bouncy beach ball fun to hardball. I conjured up a plan that would involve some time and might require some travel. But if successful, it would put a little fear into one or more of the higher ups at the company.

I searched on the company's name and found the stock market abbreviation. Typing that in got me Franklin Assurance's stock price and articles on their management, one of which went on at length about the new CEO, Phineas T. Edgerton the Third, and how his cost cutting and stock buy backs were responsible for a 30% jump in the stock price, which sent Franklin's Market Capitalization into a territory that no one had dreamed possible just six months before.

I called one of the big national brokerage houses and was forced to sit through a long voice menu. Eventually I was connected to an actual person. I explained that I was interested in investing in Franklin Assurance. That person thanked me and forwarded my call to a salesman.

"Hello, this is Maynard Stotts, how can I help you?"

I spoke with my best imitation good ol' boy Takes-Us accent. "Hello, sir, thanks for taking my call. My name is Auburn Moore, and I'm an investment influencer. The other night, I took my client to a performance of The Racy Blue Bonnies, and after the show my client and I were in the Green Room searching out fun and games. My client is the nineteenth largest stockholder in Oracle, which, as you can imagine, puts him on those lists the financial media scour for investors to write about. But Oracle is just his meat and potatoes. It's his desserts that get him up in the morning. And lately, those desserts have been insurance companies, ha ha.

"Anyway, my client got to chatting up a man next to us in the Green Room. And the big surprise is that man turns out to be some kind of relation to Mr. Phineas T. Edgerton the Third, who, as you know, is CEO of Franklin Assurance Holdings, which is the buzz of the Financial Tech world. Anyway, my client has been on an acquisitions roll, and, as I said, his darlings have been insurance companies.

"But when he asked the man about meeting his CEO relation, the man said not even he could get Mr. Edgerton on the phone. However, my client is persistent."

"So what can I help you with, Mr. Moore?" Stotts said, his impatience obvious.

"As you know, it's no secret that the insurance world has profit-enhancing techniques that get little if any oversight from state and federal agencies. And there are a dearth of laws that allow the little guys any recourse when insurance companies drop the hammer on payouts, if you know what I mean. The result of that is huge profits. Anyway, this is all background, and I appreciate your patience in waiting for me to get to the point.

"Which is this. My client has this thing where he wants to meet the big cheese of any company that he's going to invest in. Call it a quirk or call it a smart research impulse. If he likes the boss, he likes investing in the company. So I'm calling with a question about access. Like a lot of companies, Franklin Assurance has a closed-door policy regarding public access. If you were to know of a way to contact Mr. Edgerton, I would be very grateful. And if we succeed in arranging a meeting with the 'big cheese,' that would likely move us a long way down the road toward an investment.

"I don't know how to contact Phineas T. Edgerton," the salesman said. "Most companies these days have strict rules about executive privacy."

I continued as if he hadn't spoken, "The thing is, my client is one of those men who doesn't pursue trivial investments. His last four investments are practically up there in Berkshire Hathaway territory, averaging fifty or sixty million each. And if you were able to help me out on giving me contact info for Mr. Edgerton, I'd push my client toward working with you on his investment. As you know, commission on fifty mill is no small thing, Mr. Stotts. If you get your standard one percent, why that would be five hundred thousand for what? Fifteen minute's work?"

"Like I said, I don't know how to contact Edgerton." Stotts was sounding weary. "But tell you what, maybe if you and your client went to Vegas, you could show up at one of the Twelve Pack Insurance Group meetings and catch him there. Good luck and thanks for calling." He hung up.

I'd scored, having worn the man down enough that he gave me what might be useful information before he shut the door on me.

It turned out to be a good lead. With just five more minutes of searching, I found out that the Twelve Pack Insurance Group was an informal collection of twelve of the largest insurance companies, and they put on social/business gatherings for the bigshots. The financial press had the equivalent of gossip columns, and some mentioned Twelve Pack gatherings that were happening over the next several days in Las Vegas. One column in particular, Underwriters Undertakings, mentioned a big cocktail party with entertainment by a Bobby Darin tribute performer, three golf outings at nearby desert courses, and tickets to the Broadway musical Wicked performed at one of Vegas's biggest showrooms.

Of the various events, the cocktail party, which was scheduled for tomorrow evening, seemed like it would be the most fruitful.

I switched over to an airline ticket site and booked a ticket for the next morning. Next, I got a room at the hotel where the event was taking place. Then I texted Street.

'Sweetheart, can you please call me from a private location?'

My phone rang two minutes later.

"Thanks, hon. I just wanted to talk without your guest hearing me."

"I'm outside. What's up?"

"I'm looking into something regarding Colin Burns's insurance. I don't expect results, so I didn't want Geneviève to overhear and get hopeful."

"Understood."

"My plan involves a trip to Vegas tomorrow. I'll stay over one night for sure. Maybe more, but probably not."

"You want us to keep His Largeness and Lazlo for tonight and tomorrow night, too?"

"Yes, please. If that causes a problem, then I'll call Diamond."

"No, it will be fine. Do you have a plan of attack?"

"No. I'm just looking for possible access points into the insurance company."

"You must have an idea. I know how much you like hordes of people."

"Right. There's an insurance group that's having a getaway of some type. I'm probably going to be like a computer hacker, searching for flaws in their security, unlocked doors."

"Metaphorical doors," she said.

"Maybe literal doors. I don't know. Anyway, I won't be able to get out of there fast enough, so I can't imagine being there more than one night."

"Got it. Good luck. Call if you need to stay longer."

"Thank you. You are a dear."

Before I went to bed, I studied my destination hotel online, paying particular attention to images of the service workers. There were two primary uniforms, housekeeping and wait staff. The wait staff men all wore white shirts and black ties and pants. In case I wanted to impersonate a waiter, I grabbed the only white shirt and black pants I owned. The pants were Carhartt work jeans with the cargo pockets and hammer loop, but one works with what one has. I didn't have a black tie, but I had a dark maroon one that looked kind of black in yellow lights. My only black shoes were a pair of work boots. They'd have to do.

I also looked up Phineas T. Edgerton the Third, hoping to find out what he looked like so that I could identify him should he show up at the Bobby Darin cocktail party. In keeping with the company's policy of executive privacy, I spent some time searching out info on Phineas but had a hard time making any progress.

There was very little to learn looking at the standard business journals. But I was patient and scrolled down through pages of websites and blogs. I finally came to a Facebook page where someone had posted photos of a picnic to which several Franklin Assurance executives had been invited. The photos had cute captions. 'Here's Phineas at the barbecue pretending he knows how to cook. If you look closely, you can see his wife Charlotte rolling her eyes.'

The Facebook page also had a short bit of prose lauding Charlotte's upcoming charity work, a months-long engagement organizing a series of benefit events and fundraisers that would have her occupied in New York City.

Phineas was a pale, balding, paunchy man in his 60s, with curly white hair protruding from the open neck of his blue Polo shirt. He wore a blue visor that matched the shirt. His wife Charlotte upstaged him by being quite handsome with a significant mane of red hair.

Another photo was captioned 'Volleyball played the way the pros do it.' It featured several people laughing, three of whom were sprawled on the grass underneath a volleyball net. One of them was clearly Phineas T. Edgerton.

I printed the photos, thinking that no matter how much you try to protect your privacy, it is all undone by people who post photos on Facebook. If it's not 'Hey, look at me' selfies, it's 'Hey, look at my bigshot friends.'

The next morning I headed to Reno Tahoe International.

It was only one hour from wheels up to wheels down at Harry Reid International Airport. The shuttle dropped a busload of us on the Vegas Strip, and I began walking toward the address I had for the hotel. As befits the industry chiefs in one of the biggest financial industries, the hotel where the Bobby Darin Twelve Pack party was to take place was one of the glossy new glass towers.

I checked in and found my economy room on the third floor near the back of the thirty-floor tower. I spent some time exploring the hotel's layout and learned that the Bobby Darin party was going to be in the Cool Desert Grotto on the twenty-eighth floor. I took the elevator up to look around.

The Grotto doors were open. Next to the doors was an easel with a whiteboard sign that said,

'Private Party 8:00 p.m.
Twelve Pack Insurance Group'

The Cool Desert Grotto was a standard convention room that had sliding walls that could adjust the size of the space to the size of the crowd. If the point of the party was to talk insurance, I couldn't imagine that the Twelve Pack insurance companies could produce enough attendees to fill any space much larger than a dental office. But if the point of the party was to drink and groove with Bobby Darin's ghost, then the space they'd laid out made sense. There was a slightly-elevated bandstand dais. A lighting technician was inserting cables in vinyl floor channels. Two men and one woman were arranging enough chairs and tables for maybe 200 people. Two other women were setting up a rolling bar.

The space had dim hanging lights that looked like they were made of brown stalactite mineral, something you might see in a Disneyland Grotto ride. On the one permanent wall was a long mural of a desert with cactus in the foreground and mountains in the background. The artist had painted a winding path that led down into a large grotto.

To one side of the room was a moveable wall that had multiple doors in it. Three of the doors were open. I wandered through and found myself in a hallway that led to more doors that provided access to the room next to the Grotto. That one was being decorated in a Hawaiian theme. Palm trees and sea murals.

At the end of the hallway were two closed doors. I walked down and pulled on one of the handles and found it unlocked. The door led to catering facilities. Coming toward me were two men rolling a long metal buffet table that had openings for food trays. Underneath the table were what looked like heating elements.

I reversed direction and walked to the other end of the passage where two more doors opened onto the public access for the convention rooms. On the public side of those doors were signs that said 'Service Entrance.'

I thought I could use the hallway to bypass any security people who might be assigned to monitor the Twelve Pack revelers. I decided I'd wear my white shirt and maroon tie and my tweed professor sport jacket. The jacket would help me look like an insurance guy. If it turned out I'd misjudged, I could scrap the jacket and attempt to blend in with the wait staff.

I checked the time. I had three hours before party time. I could find a meal and take a nap.

I was fashionably late to the party. The Bobby Darin impersonator hadn't yet started singing, but there was a canned mix track playing songs by other singers from the 50s and 60s.

A hotel security man stood behind the table at the door. On the table were spread out many name badges. I bent over them as if searching for my name, reached out, and picked one up. It said George Freeley. I attempted to insert the pin through my jacket lapel and bent over to look at it as I shambled past the guard and through the door.

Once inside, I mingled with the crowd. If someone saw my name tag and knew I wasn't George Freeley, I could claim I must have grabbed the wrong one by mistake.

A hundred or more people were in the room, drinking, telling stories, being awkwardly loud. People lined up at the buffet and at the bar.

It didn't take long to spy Phineas T. Edgerton the Third. He was sitting at a table near the stage. He was slouched back and had his arms spread out and resting on the chairs adjacent to his. There were eight men at his table, one of the few tables in the room completely occupied. Some of the other tables in the room had women at them, but it appeared that it was mostly men who were attracted to the Bobby Darin party. Near the stage was a group of eight young women, all scantily clad. They were dancing like rock 'n roll showgirls. The showgirls, who were largely shapely and beautiful, formed a circle facing each other as they danced, and the circle rotated as a unit. As they turned, they glanced toward the small crowd, paying special attention to the men at Phineas T. Edgerton's table.

If any of the insurance people in the audience were particularly naive, they might have thought the young women were simply decorative, dancing as a group to make the party seem more festive.

But I realized it was choreographed. The women in provocative dress were prostitutes, and they'd been instructed to make their rotations so they could be observed from all angles, "shopped" by the men at Phineas's table.

After ten minutes, Phineas caught the eye of one of them who wore thigh-high boots and very little else. Without lifting his hand from the back of the chair next to him, he raised his index finger.

The observant young woman made the slightest of nods and

separated herself from the group. She made her way over to his table.

The man next to Phineas got up, and the woman sat down in the vacated chair. Phineas made a few comments to the woman, and she gave him her glamorous smile. After that, they didn't speak. Phineas hadn't arranged this affair so he could make conversation.

Phineas was of course one of the leaders of the Twelve Pack group and probably the boss of the men at the table. He'd likely agreed to—or even planned—the occasion as a Franklin Assurance business expense. Building morale among the troops.

Now that Phineas had chosen his favorite, the other men at the table were quick to make their choices. Once each of them paired up with one of the hookers, they sat down at other tables.

The canned music faded out, and an MC came onto the stage. He made a couple of jokes, tried to build some hype for Bobby Darin, then announced the impersonator. It was a goofy game no doubt repeated every night in Vegas at dozens of venues.

The impersonator came out, did a few intro tunes that most people, including me, wouldn't know. The songs built in style and volume. Probably they were the Bobby Darin standards that lots would know, even though I was still ignorant.

There were occasional whoops and hollers from the crowd, most of whom were quite drunk. By the time we got to Bobby Darin's biggest hit, Mack The Knife—a song everybody including me knew—people were signing along, some yelling the lyrics.

Before the party could wind down, Phineas and his courtesan got up and headed for a side door behind the rolling bar. I followed at a distance. Once in the catering passage, they walked at a good clip to the public lobby. The woman looked unstable in her very tall boots with the spike heels. She briefly looked behind and glanced in my direction. I pulled out my phone and was looking at it as I followed them through the door.

In the outdoor world, a clipboard, hardhat, and orange highway cone gets you free passage almost anywhere. In an upscale indoor world, an iPhone is the closest pass. You're not loitering, you're getting necessary information about your next business meeting.

I studied my phone as I followed them. When we approached the nearest elevators, I hustled around some columns, a fountain, and a sitting area and popped out on the other side, approaching the same elevators but from the other side. That made it seem as if I had come from a different party. To add to the illusion, I pulled out my black-rimmed eyeglasses with the plain lenses and put them on.

Phineas and his girl got in an elevator, followed by a single woman and then me. I stepped over to the front corner and still looked at my phone, appearing to concentrate on my email.

The lone woman got off on floor 29. Phineas and his lady friend got off on 30. I stayed entranced by my phone as the elevator door shut. At the last moment, I put my hand between the shutting doors. They reopened. I stepped out and stayed close to the wall as the doors once again began to close.

I carefully looked to the side. The hallway layout had angles so I couldn't see far in either direction. I stepped out and looked to the right. Empty hallway.

I stepped toward the other direction and, with phone still plastered to my face, looked to the left. Phineas and his infatuation were just walking through a door twenty-five yards down.

Because hotel room doors all look the same, I kept my eyes focused on that door as I walked toward it. As I got close, I made a mental note of the number. 3033.

# FORTY-NINE

Back in my room, I turned on my laptop, reviewed my research on Franklin Assurance's CEO and wrote.

'Dear Mr. Edgerton,

I enjoyed seeing you tonight at the party. The Bobby Darin impersonator was quite good, wasn't he! A good time was had by all.

You may not remember me because it's been some time. I had intended to re-introduce myself to you. But, frankly, I got distracted and forgot to come over and chat. I was heading to my suite very late when a young woman came out of your door (#3033). I wasn't paying attention to the time. But I knew it was your door because I'd seen you come from your room earlier. Seeing your door reminded me that I wanted to talk to you.

I write this in my room. Because it is late, I'll just jot down my thoughts on my laptop and slip them under your door.

My main concern was that a friend of a friend was made aware of one of your policy holders at Franklin Assurance. The policyholder's name was Colin Burns. My friend passed along the policy number, so I may as well share it here. CB-796353-SXY-647.

Apparently, Mr. Burns died after his policy's three-year contestability period had passed. But the payout was denied because your company decided that Mr. Burns hadn't been truthful on his application regarding having inherited the gene for Huntington's Disease. (For what it's worth, he died in an accident, not from Huntington's.)

I should point out that I know nothing about this situation. However, I'm contacting you because we insurance people have to watch each other's backs!

Anyway, my friend said that Roger Minkhaven (you've probably heard him called Roger "The Shark" Minkhaven) is preparing a suit that claims that Franklin Assurance has no way to establish that Colin Burns knew of his Huntington's Disease and that it's entirely likely that Mr. Burns did not know he had the genetic defect. Furthermore, Minkhaven claims to have evidence that the person who alerted your company to Burns's supposed Huntington's Disease is willing to testify that he knew that Burns was unaware that he carried the chromosomal defect and that the informant discovered the defect through surreptitious means and passed the information on to your company as part of a plan to cause trouble for Burns's beneficiary.

Because the beneficiary of Mr. Burns's policy has endured financial hardship and—especially—severe emotional hardship in the wake of losing a loved one and then having the insurance payment denied, Roger Minkhaven is apparently throwing a lot of preparation into this suit.

I probably don't need to remind you that Minkhaven's last lawsuit pursuing life insurance malfeasance resulted in a civil verdict awarding $73 million to the plaintiff. That, plus the legal fees related to the suit, make the original insurance payout insignificant.

Of course, you will have to follow your heart regarding whether you should intervene in this situation. But I wanted you to have the opportunity to review the case before it goes to court and you lose control of both the case and the public opinion on which you rely for the future success of Franklin Assurance Holdings International.

Sorry to bring you depressing news, and best of luck in resolving this looming lawsuit.

Sincerely,

Your friend and colleague Robert W. R. Jameson'

I decided that my lawsuit story was insufficient motivation for Phineas Edgerton. It was too easy for him to check, and too easy for him to ignore.

But the implied threat of exposing his sleazy personal habits would be much more potent blackmail. So I added an addendum.

'P.S. The woman I saw leaving your room was a real cutie, that's for sure. In case you had several visitors, she was the one in black leather thigh-high, spiked-heel boots, the strapless, lace-up corset, and the very tight, very short mini-skirt. She was probably 25 or 26 even though she looked 16.

I can't help thinking about how many men have been envious of you over the years because your wife Charlotte is quite attractive. And it was a shame Charlotte couldn't join you at the Twelve Pack festivities. Somebody told me she had to stay in New York to chair a children's cancer charity event. But when I saw that little hottie come out of your room, I realized how hard it would be for you to resist such charms, especially from a woman who looks like that and is less than half Charlotte's age. Whatever the price.

P.P.S.

(I'm sure you've taken precautions to keep your activities private!)'

I saved the letter to a memory stick and rode the elevator down to Ground level where there were many services. One of them was a 24/7 self-service office with copy machine and other facilities.

I put my room key card against the "tap-to-authorize" pad on the copier. The copier whirred and came to life. I plugged in my memory stick, arrowed down to the letter file and printed two copies so I'd have one for my own reference. I turned off the copier, took my copies and memory stick, and left.

I had a drink at a bar to kill some time. At 5:00 a.m., when Edgerton's hooker had almost certainly left, I rode the elevator back up to the 30th floor where the suites were, walked down to door 3033, and slipped the paper under Phineas T. Edgerton's door. Because I signed the letter Robert W. R. Jameson, it occurred to me that there might actually have been a Robert W. R. Jameson at the party, making him possibly exposed to blow back. But I thought it highly unlikely.

I went back down to my room.

I got four hours of sleep before checkout time and caught the shuttle back to the airport.

# FIFTY

Back home, I stopped at Street's and chatted with her and Geneviève and Camille, picked up the dogs, and drove up the mountain to my cabin.

Attached to the wall in my cabin's kitchen nook is a 30-inch-square fold-down vinyl table, which serves as a grand dining table, executive desk, workshop bench, banquet hall buffet, and conference room meeting surface.

I swung out the leg prop and lowered the table.

I set the box that Jackson Trane's roommate Bob had given me on the floor nearby, reached in and lifted out the stacks of paper notes and other miscellany that Colin's roommates had saved after he died.

There was no organization to the stuff. They had just needed to empty out Colin's side of one of the bedrooms so they could find another roommate to help pay the rent. They had taken everything they'd found in Colin's room and tossed it into the box.

I riffled through the papers and notes that I had set on the table and saw nothing noteworthy. Among a jumble of odd envelopes, photos, ski magazines, and three paperback novels and four collections of poetry with well-worn, frayed pages, were many handwritten notes on envelopes, sheets of paper, and torn pieces of yellow-lined paper. The notes were about countless subjects. I could understand why Geneviève didn't want Colin's stuff. Personal notes might be too painful for any person to face so soon after her fiancé's death. And living in a small apartment, where she probably stored paperwork from her restaurant, would have been another reason to hold off on taking a box of Colin's stuff. Although, after she eventually found new living quarters, she might be interested.

As I looked at each item, if I decided it was of no account, I tossed it back into the box on the floor. I thought the handwritten notes might have some continuity or theme that would reveal itself if

I looked at all of them together. So they went into a separate pile.

I had no idea of what I was looking for. Something unexpected, perhaps. Something unusual.

There were postcards from a friend who traveled in Japan. There was a dental floss container. A partial sheet of commemorative stamps that showed an image of Emily Dickinson. There were several Post-it Notes with writing in ballpoint pen. The writing said, Rossignol, Dynamic, Dynastar. French ski brands if I remembered correctly. Some scraps of white copy paper, hand-torn into small pieces and on them ballpoint pen sketches of ski racers in tuck positions. The most detailed portions of the sketches were the fairings at the back of a speed skier's calves. And on the skier's elbows were little fairings that looked like the curved wingtips on airline jets. As a pilot, I had paid attention when they started appearing on jets. I recalled that they were called winglets, and they reduced turbulence and thus reduced drag on planes. Colin had probably wondered if they would do the same thing for speed skiers. The various drawings were vaguely similar to drawings I'd seen done by clothing designers. But these were what an aeronautical engineer might draw. Technical illustrations that communicate a design concept.

I set the Post-it Notes aside and picked up a yellow pad of lined paper. The pad was the long type, like what lawyers use. On the top sheet of paper were what looked like appointment times.

*11:00 on the 3rd: Mike from Nordica (Which I knew was a ski boot company.)

*2:00 on the 4th: Pierre from Salomon (Which I knew was a ski binding company.)

*Cancel all clothing appointments

*Focus on connecting with helmet designers

There was some desk stuff, a scissors, stapler, bag of paper clips, calculator, a mug that held a variety of pens, markers, and mechanical pencils.

There was an old Chromebook computer. I opened the lid. It turned on and gave me a password log-in screen. No possibilities there unless I came upon a password list.

Eventually, I put everything back in the box except for the pile of handwritten notes. I spread them out and shuffled them around looking for any theme. There was none that I could see. Some notes were undelivered love notes to Geneviève. Some were comments on what looked like lines from poems. I didn't know the poet. But then I found a note about Robert Burns.

It said, 'Burns was no Yeats, but he understood meter and form and alliteration. He also showed a bit of brilliance. Most poets would and could write about a red rose. But only Burns had the genius to repeat the word red. You can't get punchier and more evocative than a red, red rose.'

There were many notes I didn't understand. Some were single words.

Breath. Fury. Anger. Devotion. Airfare. Focus.

Some were very short sentences. Some were questions with no question mark.

Check car insurance. What about taxes. Is life insurance taxable. Garbage bill paid. Call János. Every group has its Frollo. List the things you can't bring to France. Poetry is hardest to write. Where's the money going to come from. Geneviève will understand. Short term carbohydrate energy beats protein before a race. The doctor will be able to tell. High mileage is worth it. No car is better. The threat about Stockholm might not have been a joke. Poetry is like prose only written in verse. No one can teach speed skiing beyond the basics. Esmeralda makes it worth it.

I separated all the notes into two piles, those on yellow paper and those that weren't yellow.

I looked at the yellow paper notes and wondered if they could be assembled like jigsaw pieces so the lines all came together.

I ignored the words, and tried to fit them together. Nothing fit. After a few minutes of trying, I gave up.

My phone rang.

"Owen McKenna."

"Cruising the East Shore in my civvies," Diamond said. "Your vacancy sign on?"

"Shining like a red, red rose," I said.

"You got any burger?"

"Sí," I said. "But frozen."

"I've got a six pack of Sierra Nevada Pale Ale. In the bottles. Sounds like we're most of the way to a grilled cheeseburger lunch with a view."

"I'll put the burger on defrost and…"

I heard the crackle of gravel from out on my driveway.

"Oh, look," Diamond said in my ear. "I'm already here."

"You drove up the mountain and then called. Presumptuous."

"That's how you know I'm your best bud."

"Gonna cost you," I said.

"I just said I brought beer."

I hung up and stood up.

Spot had already jumped to his feet, and he stood, nose to doorknob. Lazlo stood as well but didn't move from his place.

I opened the door. Diamond walked in holding a Sierra Nevada Pale Ale sixpack.

I took the beer, Diamond bent down, put Spot in a headlock, and gave him a knuckle rub. Spot wagged like a windshield wiper turned to Thunderstorm.

Diamond looked over at Lazlo. "Good afternoon, sir," he said.

Lazlo made a slow, cautious wag.

Diamond's glance turned to my executive desk.

"Working on a jigsaw puzzle?" he said.

"These are notes from Colin Burns, the speed skier who died. I'm trying see if there's any meaning."

Diamond walked over, sat on my rickety chair, and stared at the notes.

Spot followed him, stood next to him, and set his jaw bone on Diamond's shoulder. Diamond reached up and caressed the giant head while he continued to stare at the notes.

I put the burger in the microwave, punched defrost, and went out onto the deck. I poured a pile of charcoal, added lighter fluid, and lit it.

I came back inside.

"Ain't no jigsaw puzzle," Diamond said. "The only thing I can tell is the dude was focused on Victor Hugo."

"The name you mentioned before. The guy who wrote Les Misérables."

"Sí. Hugo was maybe France's greatest novelist. Back in the nineteenth century. I haven't read Les Misérables because it's almost three thousand pages. But I have read The Hunchback of Notre-

Dame because it's merely pushing seven hundred. That's why I recognize some of these scraps."

"Which ones?"

Diamond picked up one of the bits of yellow paper. "This one says, 'Esmeralda makes it worth it.'"

"That's from the Hunchback? I saw the movie with—who was it, Anthony Quinn—but it doesn't ring a bell. I don't even remember what the story is about."

Diamond frowned. "Hard to say. It's a complicated novel that, first, sings a hymn to architecture and then to the printing press."

"Is that all." I meant the comment to be sarcastic. I think Diamond thought I was being sincere and earnest.

He gestured with the scrap of paper. "Pretty sure no one says Esmeralda is worth it in the book. It's just a general statement of Esmeralda's attractiveness. She was the focus of the novel."

"What is Esmeralda's allure? Personality? Charisma? Physical?"

"All of the above," he said. "All the men in the story are drawn to her. Some want to marry her. Especially a psycho priest. He's so fixated that he vows that if he can't have her, no one can."

"That statement is kind of scary," I said. "Good to look out for the priest."

"The priest's name was Frollo." Diamond reached for another scrap of yellow paper. He picked it up and handed it to me.

The paper he handed me said, 'Every group has its Frollo.'

"What do you think it means?"

"Well," Diamond said slowly. "I think it's about how in any large group you can find someone who demonstrates the greatest depth of depravity. In the book, Frollo arranges to have Esmeralda die by hanging."

"The girl he loved."

"Sí. Really sick. Frollo and the cathedral bellringer watch the hanging from the top of the Notre-Dame Cathedral. After that, the hunchback bellringer pushes Frollo off the Notre-Dame tower to his death."

"Are you thinking what I'm thinking?"

Diamond turned and looked at me. "The greatest French novelist wrote a story about a young woman named Esmeralda, who captivates all men. Maybe someone sees your French client

Geneviève as Esmeralda. Geneviève isn't a beauty queen, but she's attractive." Diamond frowned. "Is there a likely Frollo in the mix of people who know Geneviève?"

"I don't know. But someone—almost certainly a man—has been stalking her, calling, and breathing over the phone. I've wondered if that man may have hired the men who ran the extortion scheme and burned down her restaurant and apartment."

"One of whom is dead, and the others we caught, and they are now in custody."

"Right."

"Tell me this," Diamond said. "You didn't know Colin before he died. But have you by any chance seen a photo of him?"

"I don't remember, why?"

"I'm wondering if he was attractive. Or, is it possible he had some physical flaw?"

"Yes. I did see a picture somewhere, and I saw that he wasn't a real handsome guy. Then Geneviève told me he had a port-wine-stain birthmark on his face that went from his right cheekbone up and around his right eye. Why are you wondering?"

"Because in The Hunchback of Notre-Dame, the main character, the hunchback, who was the bellringer in the Notre-Dame Cathedral, is a very unattractive man, and he's also physically deformed. That man is also in love with Esmeralda, and he tries to save her from the evil Frollo."

"What's the hunchback's name? Or is he just called the hunchback?"

"No, his name is Quasimodo."

It hit me like a gut punch.

# FIFTY-ONE

"What's wrong?" Diamond said.

"Geneviève told me that Colin's nickname was Q. She said he chose it because he felt he was Quasi normal. He explained that his interests were not like those of other men. Poetry and books and such. But after what you've said, I now wonder if Colin, who told her he called himself Q for Quasi, actually was calling himself Q for Quasimodo, the hunchback."

"Because the birthmark made him look disfigured?"

"Right," I said. "In addition to trying to save Esmeralda, what else did Quasimodo do in the Hunchback story?"

"I think that's his main goal, to save the woman he loves."

"But he fails, and the woman dies at the hand of Frollo."

Diamond nodded.

I picked up the phone and dialed Geneviève's number. I got her voicemail. "Geneviève, it's Owen. Please give me a call back. I have an important question."

I hung up and dialed Street.

When she answered, I said, "Hi, sweetheart. Is Geneviève there?"

"No. She went out to run errands."

"Do you mean errands like one would normally do with a car?"

"Right."

I asked, "Did she borrow your car?"

"No. Someone picked her up."

"Do you know who?"

"No. Don't tell me..." Street suddenly sounded worried.

"Do you know what kind of errands she was doing? Or where she went?"

"No idea. I just assumed she needed to do some shopping or something. I didn't want to pry. Maybe an Uber ride picked her up. She has tried hard to be independent. She doesn't want to be a shut-in in someone else's house."

"Did Geneviève make a phone call before she left?"

"Like calling an Uber ride?" Street said. "She didn't make a call that I was aware of. But she received a call earlier this morning. She told her caller that the connection was breaking up, so she walked outside to talk. Maybe someone called her about meeting for lunch or something."

"Can you guess where she might go? Maybe in the past when she's gone out, she's mentioned places? Up to Truckee? Or down to Carson City?"

"I really don't know. I remember a couple of days ago that she mentioned something about South Lake Tahoe. But that probably wouldn't connect to someone calling her and picking her up today."

"Probably not," I said.

"One thing that does come to mind," Street said, now sounding very worried. "When Geneviève came back inside after taking her phone call, she seemed nervous."

"How so?" I said. "Like she was frightened?"

"No, I wouldn't describe it as being frightened. More like worried. Like she was going to have to do something distasteful."

"When she left, did she say anything about who might be coming to pick her up?"

"No. She just put on her winter jacket, said she'd be gone a couple of hours, then left. At the time, I also thought that she was maybe just going for a long walk."

"Okay, thanks. If you hear from her, please get her location and ask her to call me. Also, you could call me with the info in case I don't hear from her."

"How else can I help?" Street asked.

"I can't think of a way. But if she comes back, don't let her leave until she's called me."

"Can you tell me what this is about?"

"I don't know myself. But Diamond has come up with a cryptic idea that might lead to the identity of the man who has been stalking Geneviève."

"So his identity is still a mystery."

"Right. But Geneviève might know something that could reveal her stalker's identity even though she's not aware of it." I was about to say goodbye and hang up when I had another question. "Has Geneviève ever mentioned The Hunchback of Notre-Dame?"

"No, why? That's a subject out of left field."

"Diamond said there's an evil character in the novel who pursues a beautiful woman."

"I remember that," Street said. "The archdeacon Frollo is after Esmeralda, the beautiful dancer."

I shouldn't have been startled by Street knowing that. But I was still impressed.

"Maybe I got it wrong. Diamond said Frollo was a priest."

"A priest who was appointed archdeacon," Street said.

"Oh. Anyway, Colin Burns made a note about Frollo," I said. "Any chance Geneviève ever mentioned Frollo or Esmeralda?"

"Not that I ever heard. Let me ask Camille."

The phone went silent. Street came back a minute later.

"No, Camille doesn't think Geneviève ever mentioned the book or those names."

"Okay. Thanks."

"Wait, Owen. Are you remembering that you were going to take Camille to the library today? She's excited about it."

"Yes. I'll be there soonish."

We said goodbye and hung up.

Diamond had made burgers while I was on the phone, two large burgers that used the entire pound. "So Geneviève went off with an unknown person," he said as he carried the burgers outside and put them on the grill. They made an impressive sizzle.

He looked at me. "Now you have the additional task of trying to figure out who picked up Geneviève and where they drove her. Possibly, the driver is someone who, according to Colin's notes, represents Frollo." Diamond was holding the spatula as he studied the burgers. He looked up at me. "You have the woman's phone number?"

I nodded.

"We might be able to trace its location. I have new tracing software in my phone." He pulled it out.

"Let me get the number." I went inside to get my phone.

Back outside, I read off the number.

Diamond typed it into his phone. He waited. Nothing appeared to happen.

He flipped the burgers. This time there was flame with the sizzle. The aroma was so delicious that no vegetarians like Street and Camille could smell it without questioning their nutritional faith, environment be damned.

Diamond's phone made a small beep.

"Here we are," he said. "Forty-five minutes ago, the woman's phone pinged off a tower near Glenbrook."

"That's the closest tower to this part of the East Shore."

"So it could have come from when she was still at Street's."

I nodded. "Yeah."

Diamond put his phone back in his pocket.

I said, "In lieu of a trace revealing Geneviève's whereabouts, the other approach is to continue with your intellectual analysis."

"My analysis? She's your client."

"Marx said 'from each according to his abilities.' It's your brain power that got us this far."

"Okay. We have to discern Frollo's identity." Diamond paused. He put cheese on the burgers, set buns on the grill, put the plate on the warming side of the grill. He opened a beer for each of us, handed one to me.

I said, "Let's revisit. Colin wrote notes mentioning Frollo and Esmeralda. Your thought was that Frollo and Esmeralda were characters in the hunchback novel and, further, that Colin may have picked his nickname based on the hunchback. Colin was smitten with Geneviève the way Quasimodo was smitten with Esmeralda, right? It's possible that somebody else in Colin's world reminded him of Frollo. What else can you remember about Frollo?"

Diamond shrugged. He drank a sip of beer, then put the bottom buns on the hot plate, used the spatula to put the burgers on the buns, then set the top buns on the burgers. He picked up one of the burgers and took a large bite.

He spoke through a full mouth. "Frollo was an evil, duplicitous, mendacious, untrustworthy, Machiavellian sex predator."

"In other words, a bad guy," I said.

He nodded, chewing.

I grabbed a burger and took a bite. Spot watched me. I walked over to the edge of the deck. Spot followed me. Lazlo followed Spot.

I broke off two pieces. Tossed one to each dog. They both inhaled the burger bits and then stared at me with laser eyes.

"Nope," I said. "That's it until your next meal."

I wolfed down the burger.

"I better have another talk with Colin's friends," I said. I grabbed my keys off the coat rack. Spot trotted inside my cabin and across to the door, followed by Lazlo.

"I'm going to pick up Camille and take her to the library," I said. "You can stay here and enjoy a leisurely lunch." I drank a third of my beer and set the bottle next to Diamond. "The rest is yours. Good cheffing on that burger." I gestured at the scraps of paper. "Maybe you can find another Frollo clue in those notes."

"Yet another of these notes makes me nervous," Diamond said.

"Which one?"

We went inside, and Diamond picked up one of the torn pieces of yellow paper.

It said, 'The threat about Stockholm might not have been a joke.'

"What are you thinking?" I asked.

"It might refer to Stockholm Syndrome."

It took me a moment to remember. "When hostages come to sympathize with and care about their kidnappers."

"Right."

"Suggesting what?" I said. "That someone was threatening Colin or someone Colin knew? What would the threat be? Oh, crap. Geneviève."

Diamond shrugged.

"Why do you think Geneviève would be a focus?" I asked.

"Esmeralda was desired by many men. What if Colin knew someone who loved Geneviève and thought of kidnapping her."

I said, "You think she's been kidnapped?"

Diamond gestured toward all the notes that Colin had made.

I moved toward the door.

Diamond nodded as he chewed. "The best playground for kids," Diamond mumbled.

"How's that?"

"Libraries."

"Right." I left with the dogs.

# FIFTY-TWO

Before I got down to lake level from my cabin on the mountain, it started snowing. Tiny flakes, tentative little hints of a coming weather system.

Camille came out as I pulled into Street's lot. Street waved from a window. Camille got in the Jeep, forcing Lazlo into the back seat.

Camille looked like a Disney depiction of happy childhood with her orange jacket, red hat, and red mittens. Her golden hair had been pulled back into a ponytail, and it was tied with some kind of red elastic fabric that I had heard Street call a scrunchie.

She seemed excited to go on a library trip with just me.

I turned south on the highway. We were halfway to the Zephyr Cove Library when Franki Valli started singing Can't Take My Eyes Off Of You. I was focused on my driving because the snow had suddenly gotten serious. The sky filled with millions of flakes the size of quarters, floating gently down. I was grateful there was no wind to make conditions more hazardous. But the sky was so full of snow that I couldn't see much more than twenty-five yards down the road. Vehicle tires had turned that soft carpet into a slick, icy coating. We cruised slowly past looping tire tracks that marked where cars had lost control, skidding and swerving out of their lane, the tire tracks like giant cursive writing that spelled out warnings to other motorists, many of whom, judging by their speed, apparently couldn't read the messages.

I pulled off to the side of the road, pulled my phone out of my pocket and held it up so Camille could see it. It showed an old album cover of Franki Valli and the Four Seasons. Superimposed on the image was Geneviève's number and her name.

Camille took the phone and held it, feeling the vibrations.

She grinned, then handed the phone back.

Spot stuck his nose forward over her shoulder as if he wanted to see the phone as well.

"Hello, Geneviève," I answered. "I've been looking for you."

"Owen, I haven't been able to call." The tension in her voice was so dramatic, it was as if she were staring at a hand grenade with the pin pulled out and the handle about to be released. "Something is very wrong. I was…"

Her voice was cut off. There was a muffled grunt. The line went dead.

Camille tensed beside me as if she could hear the words.

I hit callback. It rang six times, then went to voicemail.

"Geneviève, got your message. If there is any way you can text your location… If not, I'll find you somehow. Don't be afraid to act! Run away. Or hide. I'll see you as soon as I can."

I clicked off, and dialed Diamond.

"Hola," he said.

"Can you run another trace on Geneviève's phone?"

"Sure. Have things changed?"

"Yes, she just called me, said she was in trouble. Then her phone went dead."

"What's her number again?"

I gave it to him.

I waited while we were still pulled off the road. He presumably was loading the app, typing in the number. There was no point in driving anywhere if I didn't have a clue which way to go.

Diamond spoke again. "Five minutes ago, her phone pinged off a cell tower in Incline Village."

"Does it show a location?"

"Sí, but very vague. The dot is to the north of the town. On the mountainside. If a phone has only been picked up by one tower, there is no triangulation from multiple towers to provide a more accurate location for the phone."

"Got it. Thanks."

"Any idea where she might be or what is happening?" he asked.

"Colin Burns lived in Incline when he died. Some of his old roommates are still there. That's the only location near Incline I can think of that has any connection to Geneviève."

"You want me to come to Incline and help look?"

"I think that would be premature. She took a ride from someone else, earlier today. But Street has no clue who that was. I'll first try the townhouse where Colin lived. That might give me a hint about Geneviève's location. If I learn anything that suggests you can help, I'll call."

I said goodbye and turned to Camille.

"I'm very sorry, but something has come up, and we can't go to the library right now."

She made a serious nod.

I set my phone on the dash, then did a U-turn as I pulled out on the highway, now heading north.

As I drove off, Camille lifted my phone off the dash. I saw her look at my calls. She inhaled and turned the phone to face me. On the screen was the new transcription service that was part of the phone system. I could see Geneviève's words printed out. 'Owen, this is Geneviève. Something is very wrong. I was…'

Camille shook the phone with insistence. It had probably been hard for her to understand all of my words by reading my lips from the side. Now she'd read Geneviève's words. I glanced at Camille. She looked horrified.

I nodded and turned a little toward her so she could read my lips. "Yes, she's frightened. We're going to look for her."

Because I was very worried about trying to find Geneviève, I couldn't waste the minutes it would take to drive back to Street's.

I drove as fast as I dared. It still took us twenty-five minutes to get to Incline Village and park in the townhouse lot where I'd previously visited Colin's roommates.

I said, "I'll be five minutes," and pointed to my blank wrist then held up my five fingers, an ignorant attempt at sign language.

I got out of the Jeep, ran up to the door, hit the doorbell and pounded my closed fist on the door simultaneously. I was thinking about when I was last there and saw the card and address from the life insurance company. It was on the desk in the room where Jackson Trane bunked.

The door opened thirty seconds later.

It was Jackson, his long locks wet as if he'd gotten out of the shower just minutes ago.

"Hey, man, what's happening in the—what would you call it— the world of Colin Burns's insurance?"

"You've met Colin's girlfriend Geneviève Laurent, right?"

"Right. A serious honey, that lady. Old for guys like Colin and me. But still a honey."

I wondered if he knew the woman was an intellectual with a doctorate. Or did honey only apply to her looks?

"Have you seen her or heard from her recently?"

He shook his head. "No, this is a honey desert. We don't even have women visiting, never mind actual girlfriends and such."

"Can you think of where she might be?"

He frowned as if wondering how I could ask such a stupid question after what he'd just said. "I have no idea. Try her house or something. I think she lives in Truckee." The way he said it, it seemed he didn't know her apartment had burned down.

I said, "I just got a message from her that said she was in trouble. Does that give you any kind of idea about where she might be?"

"Trouble, how? Like she got pulled over on a DUI or something?"

I wasn't sure how to phrase it. "I think it's more like she's worried about someone hurting her. Are any of your friends or roommates likely to cause trouble for her?"

Trane shook his head. "'Likely? No way. Could they possibly? I s'pose, but I still think no way."

"What about your former roommates? The ones who have moved out since Colin died?"

Another head shake. "I haven't even heard from Mo and Nate. And someone said that Bill and his partner just moved to Florida. But maybe that's just a rumor. You could ask Danny, but he went to Kauai on vacation. Talk about the best job. He can go and hang out on a beach someplace, take photos, and write it off as a business trip. How lucky is that? Of course, I don't even know what that means, writing off a trip. I suppose it means his business pays for it. Be like trading photos for a beach vacation."

I handed Trane one of my cards. "Please call if you hear anything that might help."

I looked past Trane and saw into the living room and kitchen. There were no lights on. The TV was dark.

He looked at my card. "Pretty sure I already got one of these. But okay, yeah, I'll call. Don't want anyone to get in trouble."

"Are you here alone?"

He frowned. "Yeah, why? Oh, you're wondering if one of us is seeing Geneviève on the side? Wow, you've got an active imagination."

"When I was here before, I saw a business card from Franklin Assurance Company, the company that had Colin's policy. I'm curious about why you have it?"

"Where'd you see that?"

"In that first bedroom. Let's go check it."

Trane looked puzzled as he turned, as if he was thinking I was nuts. He walked toward the bedroom. I pushed in behind him. He turned through the bedroom door. I walked past the door just enough to see that there were no lights on in the bathroom or either of the bedrooms. There was no other sign of anyone.

Jackson Trane came back out of the bedroom. He held the Franklin Assurance card. "Now I remember. Tamir pulled this out of the box of Colin's things. He's been taking a class in graphic design, and he thought this card was pretty cool."

I nodded. "Thanks."

I left and was walking back out to my Jeep where Camille and the dogs waited when my phone rang.

It was Diamond's number.

"Yeah."

"I learned something that might help," he said. "I'm still at your cabin. I was looking at the paper scraps like you suggested. I saw something I wanted to look up. You left your computer here. I realized I could use it. But before I started a new search, I saw you had a tab open. It was a Wikipedia page about Eadweard Muybridge."

"Right. The guy who invented stop-motion photography, which ultimately led to the invention of movies. But I haven't read the article yet. Does this have something to do with Geneviève?"

Diamond's response was to say, "You didn't see the part about the scandal that involved Governor Stanford?"

"I just started to read the page when I was interrupted. Stanford was connected to Muybridge?"

"Yeah. I'll be quick. After Stanford served as California's governor and before he became a senator, he hired Muybridge to do stop-motion photos of Stanford's race horses. Stanford wanted to know if a horse ever had all its hooves in the air at once. It turns out horses do that. But that's not the point. The point is they had a close working relationship. So when Muybridge was charged with murder in eighteen seventy-five, Stanford hired a lawyer to defend him. The lawyer must have been good because, even though Muybridge admitted the murder, he was acquitted."

My head was filled with confusion. While my original task was to get Camille to the library, I had been thinking about Victor Hugo's characters Esmeralda, Frollo, and Quasimodo. Now Geneviève was in trouble, and I was adding Eadweard Muybridge to the mix.

"Who did Muybridge kill?" I asked.

"His wife's lover. Shot him point blank."

It took a moment to sink in.

I got in the Jeep and started it to get some heat flowing to Camille and the dogs.

I said, "Muybridge killed his rival and got away with it."

"Sí."

"You said that, in The Hunchback of Notre-Dame, Frollo thought that if he couldn't have Esmeralda, no one could."

"Yeah," Diamond said again.

"And Colin maybe felt like Quasimodo, not especially handsome but madly in love with Geneviève."

"Yeah, again." Diamond spoke slowly, "And while Colin possibly felt like he shared something with Quasimodo, he might have felt that Geneviève was like Esmeralda. Now we have a new angle that Colin probably never thought of. In the same way that Muybridge got away with murdering his rival, maybe there is a person in the mix who was Colin's rival, a person who figured out a way to murder Colin during the speed race. Of course, what's the likelihood that anyone who knew Colin also knew enough about Muybridge to use him as a model?"

"Right," I said. "And that person would also have to be in love with Geneviève. But as I say it, I think I know who that person could be. A person who might identify with both Muybridge and Frollo."

Diamond said, "An acquitted murderer and a fictional character who was evil incarnate."

I shifted the Jeep into Drive and drove through Incline Village.

"And it is?" Diamond asked.

"Colin's boyhood friend—I think his best friend for years—was

Daniel Moretti. A former member of the Tahoe Terminals, a super fast skier."

"So he would have been a speed-skiing rival of Colin Burns," Diamond said. "But his main rivalry wouldn't be about speed skiing, it would be about who would get the girl. He might have known Geneviève as early as Colin did. He may even have met her before Colin did. But she fell for Colin."

"Right." I pulled out on the highway that went through the center of town. "Daniel Moretti quit skiing to focus on photography. I met him and found out that one of his main role models was Eadweard Muybridge. He studied how Muybridge took photos."

"If Moretti was in love with Geneviève all along," Diamond said, "when Colin wrote the note about Frollo that's sitting here on your table, he might have been thinking of Moretti as a Frollo. A rival in his pursuit of Esmeralda."

"And Moretti could have killed Colin just as Muybridge shot his rival," I said.

"Shooting him with a Pykrete bullet?" Diamond said. "Thus leaving traces of cellulose? But how could he manage to shoot Colin while he was skiing? You saw pictures of Colin on the speed course. No one was nearby, right?"

"True. I haven't figured that part out. Muybridge had something like a dozen cameras with shutters that were all activated as Stanford's race horse ran by. It could be that Moretti adapted the concept for a type of gun that fired ice bullets." I was going around curves on the highway, driving one-handed so I could hold my phone. "If the gun was white in color, perhaps there was a way to have it buried in the snow. Colin skis by, triggering the gun, and no one would be aware. Even if there was some puff of gunpowder, a skier at a hundred sixty miles per hour would create enough air movement to obscure any gunpowder smoke."

"Do you know where Moretti lives?" Diamond asked.

"In Kings Beach. I think I remember how to drive there, but I don't remember the address. A big, modern box house. A cube mostly made of glass."

"On my way," Diamond said. "I'll find the address. Don't do anything stupid."

# FIFTY-THREE

I drove too fast for my concern about the snow and ice and too slow for my concern about Geneviève. The huge gentle flakes that earlier had looked like a shake-up toy were getting smaller as a wind began. By the time I came around the curves in Crystal Bay and drove into Kings Beach, the conditions were no longer suggestive of a beautiful ski holiday in Tahoe. A storm was coming in, and the weather alchemy that could change a flower-garden morning into an afternoon blizzard was underway.

I slowed around the roundabouts, found my turnoff, and was at Daniel Moretti's glass-box house soon after.

There were no tire tracks in the snow-covered driveway. Either Moretti wasn't the person who picked up Geneviève from Street's house, or he hadn't brought her to his house. Then again, the snow had been vigorous. It might have covered all previous marks.

I pulled into his drive. Instead of parking in the pull-off for guests, I parked at an angle in the middle of the drive so that I blocked anyone trying to leave. I turned to Camille so she could clearly read my lips, and I put my hand on her knee for emphasis.

"Please stay in the Jeep. I'm going to go check this house. I'll take Spot with me. It may take several minutes. It's important that you stay here with Lazlo. Do you understand?"

She nodded.

"Thank you." I gave her knee a pat and got out.

I opened the back door to let Spot out, then shut it. I hit the key fob to lock the doors.

Normally, Spot would run into the woods, exploring and sniffing out the fresh scents that seemed, for dogs, to be more obvious after the air had been cleaned by a fresh snowfall. But Spot didn't run and didn't put his nose to the ground. Instead, he stood next to me, head held high, and looked into the forest. His eyes seemed to penetrate the woods, his ears turned this way and that picking up sounds that

I couldn't hear, and his nostrils flexed.

I took Spot's collar and walked toward the house.

When we got to the garage windows, I raised up on my toes and peered in. The black Range Rover was inside. I couldn't tell if it had recently been out in the snow. If so, any snow on the vehicle had melted. Were those water drops creating glints of light on the hood? I couldn't tell.

Just like when I'd been at Colin's friends' townhouse, I rang the doorbell and pounded my fist on the door at the same time.

There was no response. After thirty seconds, I did it again. I watched Spot. His ears would reveal any noise from inside.

He didn't react.

Still holding Spot's collar, I walked back down the walkway and looked up at the house windows. The house was designed so that people could see out, but the window reflections were such that no one could see in except to see the ceilings high above, and only then if one stood in the right place and if the outdoor light wasn't too bright while the indoor light was quite bright.

"Daniel Moretti!" I called out. "Are you here?"

There was no response.

"Time to explore, Largeness."

We went around to the side of the garage.

At the corner of the house was a wooden archway like one would buy at a Home Depot store. The archway led to a path. Although the falling snow had covered everything, the path of unbroken white was clear. We followed it along the side of the house toward what might be a backyard. The landscape undulated. There were many Aspen trees in the low spots, conifers on the higher ground.

There was another path that came from the back door of the house. It, too, had a smooth coating of new snow. Although as I changed position, I sensed faint marks on the path from the back door. I squatted down thinking the angle might help my perception.

There were slight undulations in the new snow. They followed a pattern. Footprints that were being quickly covered by the new snow. Not just one set. Two people had walked along the path long enough ago that the most recent snow had nearly erased most traces of them.

In the distance, the ground rose up gently to an escarpment

that was a hundred feet high. In some places the escarpment was comprised of a tree-covered slope that was too steep to scramble up. In other places it was a vertical wall of rock that probably attracted rock climbers. The low ground in front of the escarpment was mostly treed with Aspen, their light bark blending in with the snowy landscape. The high, drier ground above the cliffs was treed with conifers, California Red Firs and Ponderosa Pine, some of which were old growth, as evidenced from below by their singular huge trunks rising sixty or seventy feet before their impressive look-at-me vertical essence was interrupted by their lowest branches.

The walkway we followed narrowed from a broad path to a single-track trail that wound through the Aspens and headed back toward the escarpment.

We came to another archway, which seemed to mark the rear of the backyard, a boundary between the human-shaped landscape and the natural forest. I paused and looked around. Spot's sentience was pronounced. His ears turned back and forth. His nostrils flexed. He was focused on the land ahead. He didn't pull forward with eagerness but with caution. He was preoccupied with assessing the landscape.

Getting no response from knocking at the house and seeing the faint footprints under the snow made me want to follow the footprints. But the main reason to head toward the escarpment was Spot's pull. He had an unerring ability to sense the presence of people, especially people under stress.

Who had been through the area? Daniel Moretti? Geneviève Laurent? Were they still nearby? I thought the escarpment and the surrounding woods were Forest Service land. Much of the public land in Tahoe was laced with trails. One could follow Tahoe trails for endless miles, connect up with countless back roads and parking areas. A person could carry backcountry skis on a backpack. When you went up in elevation and encountered deep snow, you could put on your skis and go anywhere. From Kings Beach were trails that led all the way to Truckee and beyond.

I didn't want Spot to run ahead and alert anyone. So I kept hold of his collar.

A hundred yards past the second archway was a young Aspen tree. Two of its small branches had been recently broken. The exposed wood was light in color and seemed moist.

Spot pulled forward.

Still holding his collar, I said, "Easy boy. Be patient."

The escarpment was a quarter mile back. The trail wound in gentle S curves, following the easiest way through the landscape.

As we got closer to the cliffs, I sensed movement of some kind up on the cliff. I looked up and saw a trail of sorts that crossed the face of the escarpment, a geologic anomaly where, millions of years back and possibly miles underground, one type of rock had created an intrusion into another. Now, thrust up into the sky, glacial processes had eroded softer rock and left harder rock. The result was a cliff ledge that was sixty or eighty feet above the Aspen forest but still a good distance below the top of the escarpment.

It looked from below as if someone could walk along the ledge, as long as one could find access. From up on that cliff edge, one would have a comprehensive view of the forest below, and they could see any interlopers.

I squinted and focused on the rocky uplift, wondering if the movement I'd sensed came from there or if my sense of movement was faulty.

In one place, the escarpment had an unusual feature. At the top, above the ledge, was a curved slope like a small amphitheater. Large versions were called cirques, bowl-shaped depressions carved out by glaciers. The snow in this miniature cirque collected and slid down as if from a bowl tipped on edge. At the bottom lip of the bowl, the snow appeared to periodically pour off like a snow version of a waterfall. The momentum of the snowfall carried it out past the ledge below it and down to the steep slope below the ledge, where it built up in a thick, white snow slope.

Spot and I approached the escarpment, following a path that probably originated as a game trail, a logical way that deer and other wildlife would transect the forest.

I heard a bird call off to the right. I turned toward it just as there was a pneumatic-sounding snap from the trail in front of me. At the same moment, it seemed an invisible assailant slugged my left shoulder hard.

I don't know if it was the impact or the surprise that knocked me off my feet. But I went down sideways, landing on my hip, realizing that I'd been shot.

# FIFTY-FOUR

I was on my back in the snow. Spot was standing over me, lowering his head, sniffing and making a crying sound. With my right hand I reached up to my left shoulder. There was a hole in my jacket fabric. As I palpated the area, pain mixed with numbness. I put my finger in the jacket hole and felt around. There was nothing dramatic. No shards of bone, no gushing blood. It seemed the bullet had hit the outside of my shoulder, penetrating my deltoid muscle. Although the pain was confusing, I thought the bullet had gone all the way through the deltoid and exited out the back of the muscle. The wound felt cold to the touch. And it felt wet.

A Pykrete bullet like Diamond had referred to? Ice mixed with sawdust for strength? And remnants melting as soon as it entered my body.

I'd never been more than grazed by a lead bullet. I was confident this wasn't as bad. But it had enough power to rip through my jacket and penetrate through my flesh. Which meant the weapon could kill if it hit in the wrong place.

I struggled to sit up. As the wound warmed, the pain started to sear. Sitting in the snow, I looked around. There was no shooter that I could see.

A sniper? That wouldn't fit with a Pykrete bullet. Snipers shot from a distance, and I was quite sure they would need high-powered, regular bullets.

I saw motion to the side. Lazlo appeared and ran to Spot. Then Camille came running.

No!

She stood next to me. "I saw you fall," she said. She kneeled next to me. "Are you okay? I know you told me to stay in the Jeep. But Lazlo started to claw the seat. I thought he had to go to the bathroom. But when I let him out, he ran away. I'm so sorry."

Her face showed worry and fear. She saw my shoulder. "You're bleeding!" Her eyes brimmed with tears.

"I got…" I stopped to consider the impact of my words. "I fell and hit something. But it's okay. I'm okay. But you are in the wrong place. There's a bad man out here."

Her face turned to fear. She looked around, her eyes frantically searching.

I tapped her to get her to look at my face.

"Take Spot and go into those trees." I pointed. "Those trees will give you protection."

She took hold of Spot's collar and pulled him. The tug of a 50-pound girl was nothing to a 170-pound dog. But he knew her. He understood that he should go with her. As they moved, he sniffed at a notch in a large Aspen.

They headed into the thicker tree cover. Lazlo followed them, ever the good student. I crawled through the snow on hands and knees. My left shoulder was on fire. But it didn't seem broken. I palpated it again. My fingers came away bloody. An ice bullet was still a bullet.

As I crawled past the Aspen that caught Spot's attention, I paused. Partly because my left shoulder felt on fire. Partly so I could look at the tree. It was a medium-sized Aspen, about forty feet tall. The tree was robust, with a vigorous crown. However, the trunk had just a few lower branches. All were covered with snow. I looked at the notch where Spot had sniffed. It was a snow-covered branch that was bare of twigs and had probably lost its leaves years before, but it still looked strong. I turned to crawl past it, then stopped. Once again I looked at the notch. Nothing but snow, except…

I realized an area I thought was a narrow stripe of snow on a branch was actually a piece of white PVC pipe like what is used for backyard irrigation systems. The pipe was about an inch in diameter and ten inches long. It was fitted into the branch notch so that it pointed out toward the trail where I'd been walking.

I touched the pipe. It was rigid, firmly jammed into the notch of the tree. I pulled myself to my feet, grabbed the pipe, and rocked it back and forth. It came free.

The back end of the pipe had a cap glued onto the pipe with blue PVC glue. I didn't dare look in the open end of the pipe in case it was still loaded. I held it near my nose and sniffed it. Nothing but a vague sense of plastic and electronics, like the smell that came out of my computer.

It appeared I'd found a remote controlled weapon. Could that fire a Pykrete bullet? Is that what hit Colin Burns and caused the accident that killed him?

I glanced over at Camille and Spot and Lazlo. They seemed well-ensconced in the group of trees. I took a moment to sit in the snow and think through what had just happened.

I ran my fingertip around the open end. It seemed I was feeling the edge of a smaller pipe that had been inserted into the PVC pipe. I gave the pipe a shake. Was there a slight movement?

I pounded the open end of the pipe against the tree. More movement? I did it again and again. Each time the movement seemed a little more pronounced. On the tenth or twelfth stab, the inner pipe fell out. It was black metal, maybe aluminum like a section of ski pole, but made of a heavier gauge than a ski pole.

At the rear of the metal pipe was a metal fitting that looked like the quick-change connector for tools that used different attachments. It made no sense. Then it did.

The quick-change connector had a hole in its center and looked like it was designed to attach a high-pressure hose like what one would use for pressurizing a pellet gun, the modern version of which was called a Pre-Charged Pneumatic air gun. I didn't know the details of how it worked, but I could imagine. Take the guts out of a PCP pistol and fit them into a metal pipe. Make the appropriate adjustments so the device fired Pykrete ice bullets instead of metal pellets. Charge your homemade PCP gun with a high pressure pump, just as you would a normal PCP gun.

Replace the physical trigger with an electronic actuator that could be triggered with a radio signal sent by a remote device. An automobile key fob might work. When you press the button, you fire your remote Pykrete ice bullet gun.

But how could you aim your gun from a distance? You couldn't. But you could pre-aim your gun to fire where people would walk down a well-worn trail. If I hadn't turned when I heard the bird, I would have been hit square in the chest. Depending on whether the ice bullet had hit one of my ribs or gone through to my lungs, I might have been lying on the ground, slowly dying.

The downside from the shooter's point of view was that the pipe guns would need to be kept cold enough to prevent the ice bullets from melting. In the case of the pipe gun that fired at me, it was in a low-lying area, and such depressions often get very cold at night and hold their cold temperature throughout the day, even when the temps are supposed to rise above freezing. The area where we took cover was also heavily shaded from the south, preventing the sun's heat from getting into that part of the forest. A Pykrete pipe gun could be loaded with an ice bullet, charged with compressed air, and possibly left for days during a cold spell such as what we were currently having. And even if heat began to degrade the ice bullet, it might still cause major injury.

Was this what happened to Colin Burns as he set a new world speed record? Was he shot by a white PVC pipe containing a Pykrete ice-bullet gun, buried in the snow next to the speed course?

Daniel Moretti had shown me a photo of the course as Colin flew through the timing zone. There were no people nearby.

What are the chances of such a gun hitting a skier going by at 160 miles per hour?

Probably miniscule.

But what if there were a dozen or two dozen pipe guns, all buried in the snow, ready to fire at the same moment or in close succession, like Muybridge's cameras that captured the movements of Governor Stanford's race horses.

The person who planned the attack could have gotten to the course before dawn and buried many pipes so that they all pointed toward the timing zone with only the very ends of the pipes pointing out of the snow. Maybe they were completely buried, with the last of the snow covering being just a thin amount, something an ice bullet could fly through without any impediment. All of the pipe guns could be set to go off on the same signal, making it easy to trigger.

In designing Pykrete ice bullet pipe guns, there would be many aspects to solve, such as the question of how the devices would be brought into France. But if the components were disassembled, they might not look threatening. And if the perpetrator was thorough in his research, he could have designed his Pykrete guns with components that could be purchased in France. The perpetrator could have come into the country with nothing but a plan and purchased PVC pipe, a compressor, and other components once he was in the country. Even electronic actuators like key fobs could probably be acquired through the automobile manufacturing industry. Once a person had found a match between metal tubing size and a container in which to freeze a water-sawdust mix, the bullets could be homemade.

I resumed my crawl back toward Camille and Spot.

Camille was shivering, more from fear, I thought, than from cold.

I wanted to scoop her up and run back to the Jeep. But I probably couldn't ignore the pain in my arm enough to carry her. And where would we run in a snowy forest that might have many hidden, white-colored, pneumatic guns?

My first priority was to prevent Camille from coming to harm. I was about to tell her to follow me back to the Jeep, when I heard a high-pitched squeal. It sounded like the cry of a Bald Eagle.

I looked up. No soaring eagles were visible. The snow was coming down too heavily to see far.

I scanned the escarpment. Bald Eagle nests were huge conglomerations of sticks, as much as eight feet across. Even in a snowstorm, I would likely see a huge nest. But I saw nothing.

The noise came again. This time the sound was less like the piercing call of an eagle and more like a plaintive keening. A woman crying out in misery.

I leaned left and right, trying to see around the tree trunks and through the foliage. I sensed movement in my peripheral vision. Not up on the cliff, but down on the ground, maybe twenty-five yards off to my right. Like the flash of an animal running to escape people. I turned to see, but saw nothing except Aspen trees and falling snow.

The piercing cry came again. I looked up at the cliff edge.

Movement.

I leaned left, then right, trying to see through the trees.

There were two people up on the cliff edge, mostly hidden from view. I wondered why they weren't hiding?

I bent down and spoke very quietly to Camille, knowing that she could read my lips whether I shouted or whispered. "I'm going to move so I can see better. Please stay here in the trees with Spot. Keep hold of his collar. Hug him. He will keep you warm."

She nodded.

I touched Spot on the head to get his attention, then held my hand out, my palm to his nose. I put my finger across his nose, the sign to be quiet.

Lazlo was near but stayed still.

Still hunched to minimize how much of a target I presented, I moved through the trees, stepping carefully to stay silent. After several steps, I saw an open area where I would have a better view of the people on the cliff ledge.

I came to an area that was somewhat open. I now had a view window up toward the ledge. I straightened up to see better.

There was another pneumatic spit of air. This time the blow was to the left side of my waist. As before, the impact knocked me down. In a moment, the impact morphed from a physical smack to a red-hot torch through the flesh of my side.

As I collapsed to the ground, I realized too late how stupid I'd been. The people weren't exposed on the ledge because of their ignorance. They were there to lure me to a place where I could see them. Having done that, they could see me and fire another PVC pipe gun. I had fallen for one of the oldest tricks of hunters. I had been lured by the very predator who was hunting me.

There was a PVC pipe positioned on a tree in front of me. It had a big ugly opening. Above it were the people on the ledge. Now they were moving out of my field of view. A big man and a small woman. Daniel Moretti and Geneviève Laurent?

The man carried a camera and tripod over one shoulder. The tripod was collapsed, the sections of tubing slid into each other to make the tripod short. With his free hand, he pulled the woman along behind him. She moved awkwardly, her hands held together in front of her.

Handcuffs.

The camera was puzzling. Although the camera suggested that the man was the photographer Daniel Moretti, I couldn't imagine why he had brought it with him.

Was he a freak who wanted to photograph bondage scenes, a woman in handcuffs in the forest? Or did he want to photograph her hanging like Esmeralda in the Hunchback book?

I looked at the area at the base of the escarpment. It seemed clear that if I could get against the slope under the ledge, I would be out of sight from Moretti. Same for Camille.

Both ice bullets had struck me on my left side. With my left side and shoulder nearly paralyzed with pain, I did my fastest crawl back to where Camille and the dogs waited in the group of trees.

Making certain Camille could read my lips, I whispered, "We should run to the base of the cliff where we'll be out of sight from the shooter. Ready?"

Camille nodded.

I forced myself to my feet. I was wobbly and light-headed, but I didn't think it was from loss of blood. There were no major arteries in the deltoid muscle or the side of the waist. But there was major pain.

I took a few deep breaths. Camille still held Spot. Lazlo was still next to them.

I looked at her. "Okay, let's run."

I did my best stumbling wobble run, zigzagging through the trees, staying away from any area that looked like a good place to position a pipe gun. My left side burned with shooting pain.

As we approached the escarpment, I saw the people above us. Now that they were closer, I recognized both Daniel Moretti and Geneviève Laurent. Moretti moved with confidence, like an imperial king in charge of his countryside. He carried the tripod and camera over his shoulder as if showing it off like a king's sceptre or a weapon like a lance. Maybe he was trying to intimidate me. Or, if sufficiently twisted, impress Geneviève.

In contrast, Geneviève moved like a meek subject being led to prison.

She seemed to give an intense look down over the edge of the ledge as if she were considering jumping off. Then it appeared that she looked directly at Camille. I was preoccupied with pain that felt like the left side of my body had been set afire.

Camille made a shake of her head. Maybe she was distressed at seeing Geneviève in such trouble. Or maybe she was trying to tell Geneviève not to jump. I couldn't tell.

I herded Camille and the dogs into another thicket of trees, under the ledge and away from the easy view of Moretti.

We crouched among some conifers, nowhere near as hidden as I'd hoped. We could peer through the foliage. I leaned out to look up at the ledge.

Geneviève was now behind trees and shrubbery. But, as Moretti moved along the ledge, pulling Geneviève behind him, her look continued to be focused on Camille's location. Was Geneviève communicating misery? I wanted to shout up to Moretti and say something that might convince him to let Geneviève go. But, because of my pain or perhaps my mental numbness, I didn't know what was best.

Moretti continued along the ledge. I had no idea of his purpose. He probably wanted to lure me into the open once again. Get me to a place where an invisible pipe gun could give me a kill shot.

He still pulled Geneviève. They were coming close to where the pouring snowfall dropped from the cirque above, past the ledge, and down to the slope below the ledge. From my perspective, it seemed they probably couldn't see the accumulation of snow below them.

As the two of them progressed to a point directly above the steep snow slope, Camille pulled away from Spot and me and ran out into full view.

Moretti swung his collapsed tripod and camera off of his shoulder. In a sudden moment, I realized he wasn't carrying them for photographs. It was a weapon in disguise. He put what looked like the camera against his shoulder and pointed the three shortened tripod legs toward Camille.

I shouted. "Camille! Run back here."

But, of course, she couldn't hear me.

Camille held out her hand, palm up. She took her other hand, made a V with her fingers and set her fingertips on her outstretched palm. Then she quickly lifted her hand up and curled her fingertips.

I realized it was the sign language I'd seen when Camille taught Geneviève and Street the sign for 'Jump.'

Geneviève didn't hesitate.

Although it appeared she couldn't see the steep snow-covered slope below the ledge, she immediately followed Camille's American Sign Language command to jump. She jerked free of Daniel Moretti's hold, took a running step, and leaped off into space.

As if anticipating her leap, Daniel Moretti swung his camera and tripod up in a blur of motion.

# FIFTY-FIVE

I've learned that in situations of stress, our brains seem to process in slow motion. We see details that are normally beyond our ability to notice.

As I looked up in fear, I saw Daniel Moretti swing his tripod weapon up and point it at Geneviève as she leaped.

I heard the pneumatic snap of a pipe gun firing as she fell through the air. His tripod was a three-barrel pipe gun. The spit of compressed air sent another ice bullet as Geneviève dropped out of his view.

She hit the steep slope of snow with her feet. Her feet slid out from under her, and she went down on her back and careened down the snow. At the bottom, she jumped to her feet, apparently uninjured, and ran, still handcuffed, over to the protected cover next to the cliff.

I leaned out and looked up at Moretti, worried about his actions. Geneviève huddled against the base of the cliff, out of sight from Moretti above. She scrambled through the snow to the group of trees at the base of the cliff and dropped to her knees in front of Camille.

Geneviève spread her handcuffed arms and put them over Camille to hug her.

Her words were a whispered burst of emotion, barely audible but still a communication that Camille would be able to read on Geneviève's lips. "Merci beaucoup," the hushed voice said. "Vous m'avez sauvé la vie You saved my life."

I shifted into the trees as well, away from Moretti's view. Time for my own misdirection. I feigned a howl of agony.

I shouted up toward the trees above. My words sounded a natural rage, which I tried to amplify.

"You killed her, Moretti! You shot her and now she's broken her neck. You are a twisted, sick, nightmare. This is the end for you."

Moretti's voice was a muffled boom through the snowy forest. "It's not my fault the stupid woman jumped off a cliff. You should have kept out of my world, McKenna. What is gained by probing into Colin's death? His death was fair. He got his speed record and his place in history. I got retribution for him stealing my girl. I knew Geneviève first. I introduced the two of them! I thought I was being nice, letting the ugly poet have his moment with the French woman."

"You admit you murdered him."

"He deserved it. It was easy, ordering synthetic test tubes that won't break from freezing water. They come in all sizes. You just match the size to the aluminum tubing. My tripods had telescoping tubes, each one bigger than the next. Once you take the trigger mechanism out of a pneumatic pistol, it looks harmless. Like a car part. Then you stir sawdust into the water in the test tubes, and presto, you've got your pipe gun. I went out before dawn at the Vars speed run and buried twenty-five of them in a line next to the course. I watched the racers before Colin to get a sense of the timing. It worked great! Eadweard Muybridge would have been very proud to see how I developed the technique he used with Stanford's race horses.

"But then, even after Colin was dead, Geneviève was still in love with his words! What is the attraction to poets? Colin kept repeating the same lament to her. 'I'm just a disfigured Quasimodo, but you're my Esmeralda. You're my red, red rose.' He said it to her face! It was so transparent the way he manipulated Geneviève. But instead of seeing his ugliness, she thought he was wonderful. It was insane! So I took him away from her. I got rid of the homely Quasimodo and saved Esmeralda for myself. Then I sabotaged his insurance. I could tell something was wrong with his mother BB. But she got nosy, so I had to silence her. It was easy to get Colin's DNA off his toothbrush and get it tested. He didn't deserve to take my girl and then give her insurance money, too.

"Geneviève's life was a constant struggle to prove herself to her father. But she failed at that, and she failed at teaching at Stanford. The dean had to force her out. And she was failing at her restaurant, unable to pay the bills, unable to pay the security guard.

"I was there to rescue her. I had the money. I offered to give her anything she wanted. I had the charm, the looks, the confidence. I had the education. I had the social stature. I would have won her back in the end. I told Colin what I would do. I told him I would use the Stockholm Syndrome to win her. Her need of my support and money would eventually lead her to love me. Just like what happens with hostages who come to believe in the good intentions of their captors. But Colin didn't believe I could win over Geneviève. He lived in his stupid world of words. Calling her his red, red rose. It was disgusting."

Moretti moved sideways, trying to get a glimpse of me.

I was hidden below him, just out of his sight. It was easy to hear him.

"The alpha male always gets the girl, right McKenna? I was the alpha male. That's the way nature evolved. Look at women all over the world. For that matter, look at the females of all species. They give themselves to the biggest, strongest, richest, best-looking, and most powerful males. Colin was a fantastic skier. I'm the first to admit that. But he really was a Quasimodo, just as he claimed. A marked, deformed, poor man who had no larger vision. He might have been a champion skier. But I was the champion in life. I was going to rebuild Geneviève's restaurant. I would have given her everything she could ever want. I would have been the handsome father to her beautiful children. I am the rightful patriarch of Geneviève's world."

"Such stupid claims, Moretti. You wanted to use your pet psychology to make her a victim so you could play rescuer. Kidnapping Geneviève to attempt to win her love makes you the lowest scum. You took Muybridge as your role model in murdering Colin Burns. You thought you could get away with killing your rival just as he did with his. And then you hired Roland Dippman to extort Geneviève. You are pathetic."

"I didn't hire him. I didn't tell him to blackmail her. I merely pointed him toward a business opportunity, selling guard services to business owners. I didn't know he would turn it into a scam and burn down Geneviève's restaurant. But when he did, I stepped forward to save her! To rebuild. But she turned me down! Anyway, the extortionist got himself killed in some kind of skiing accident, so there's your justice. Meanwhile, I was Geneviève's backup plan even if she didn't know it. Even if she didn't initially accept my help. She would have come around. She would have submitted to the alpha male."

I moved out from the base of the cliff just enough to glimpse Moretti through the trees. He was still holding up his weapon. He leaned over the edge of the ledge, looking down, seeing for the first time the slope of snow that Camille had directed Geneviève to slide down. There was movement above Moretti. I couldn't see details. Then I saw it was Diamond, wearing a camo jacket, moving toward a point directly above Moretti on the ledge.

"I'm coming for you, McKenna," Moretti shouted, unaware of Diamond above him. "I will take you down. Death by ice bullet is no different than death by lead bullet. All bullets rip apart your insides."

I didn't respond. We were just out of sight below him. Best to keep him guessing about whether we were still there. We huddled against the escarpment while Moretti railed. I leaned out to take another look up.

I watched Moretti step back and then take two running steps toward the dropoff.

But he never got a controlled leap, because Diamond dropped down from above him like a mountain lion dropping out of a tree onto its unsuspecting prey.

# FIFTY-SIX

Diamond landed on the back of Moretti's shoulders. Though Moretti was a much bigger man, he nevertheless collapsed to one knee at the edge of the dropoff. Like a cougar with a deer, Diamond had one arm locked around Moretti's neck. He pressed Moretti forward, pushing with his feet, and drove the two of them off the icy ledge.

They dropped ten feet through space and landed on the snowfall slope below. They rolled, rotating and tumbling, to the base of the escarpment, and came to a stop lying on their sides. Diamond still held Moretti's neck in a choke hold.

Had I not been injured, I would have jumped on them and helped subdue Moretti. As it was, I could offer almost no help.

Moretti dropped his tripod gun and stood up as if Diamond weighed nothing. Moretti backed up forcefully, striking a tree behind him, smashing Diamond against it. The blow was hard enough to break ribs.

I heard Diamond grunt, then gasp.

Moretti turned and saw Geneviève.

"You're not dead?! I didn't succeed in shooting you? And you didn't break your neck. Now you will experience real torture."

I had limped over and picked up the tripod gun out of the snow. I was swinging it around in a weak effort to point it toward Moretti.

I had one strong hand that was rendered helpless by fatigue and one nearly useless hand that was hobbled by the bullet wound in my shoulder. Moretti grabbed me hard, his right hand to my wounded left shoulder. I stifled a yell as I dropped the tripod. Moretti reached to pick it up.

Diamond leaped back onto Moretti's back, still trying to choke him. Moretti had one hand up on Diamond's arm, trying to protect his neck from Diamond's hold. Other than that, Moretti acted as if he didn't notice Diamond. With his other hand, Moretti fumbled at the tripod as if to get hold of the center of the pipes. Maybe he simply wanted a rifle grip, one of his hands on the barrel, his other hand on the center of the tripod.

It was easy for Moretti to grab the tripod from me and turn it. But, as he gripped the center of the tripod, Spot leaped up from the side and put a serious bite on Moretti's shoulder, damaging Moretti's arm and pulling himS down.

Moretti screamed. He let go of Diamond's arm and reached to hang onto a projection on the tripod that looked, to my obscured vision, like a key fob. The tripod, hanging from the key fob, swung around so that the open ends of the three legs were pointing at Moretti's abdomen. Moretti tried to let go of the key fob projection, but it seemed to be hooked on the fabric of his jacket. Moretti shook his hand as if shaking off a threatening wasp. But his movement pushed the key fob buttons, first one, then another.

There were two pneumatic snaps, high-pressure air being released as ice bullets penetrated Moretti's abdomen. Moretti bent forward at the waist. The tripod fell to the ground first, and Moretti fell second. Except, he was partially held up by Spot.

"Let go, Spot."

Spot was always reluctant to let go of a bad guy.

"Let go, Largeness. It's okay. You done good."

Spot released his bite, and Moretti, clutching at his stomach, fell to the snowy ground. His knees hit the snow first, and then he dropped forward onto his face.

Diamond already had his phone out, dialing 911, identifying himself, explaining to the dispatcher the who, what, and where of our location, the parties involved, and the various injuries, both Moretti's and mine.

"Send two boxes," Diamond said. "Do you copy that? Two injured men, so we need two rescue units."

Diamond paused. "Yes, both men were shot. No, they weren't shot by a firearm. They were shot by PCP pipe guns. Pneumatic, pressure-charged guns." Pause. "I'm out of my jurisdiction, so I'm just a civilian in this case. I'll explain to the first responders. Can you patch me through to Sergeant Jack Santiago, please? Okay, I'll wait for a call back."

Diamond hung up, then patted Moretti down, finding no more

weapons. I hobbled over to Geneviève and Camille.

They both stared toward Moretti, horrified looks on their faces.

"Are you okay?" Geneviève asked.

"I think so."

"You have a lot of blood on you!"

I nodded. "Even just a cup of blood looks like a great deal when it's on the outside of a body."

Geneviève looked toward Daniel Moretti. "Is he dead?" she asked.

"I don't know. Probably not. But he's probably seriously wounded. He could die from shooting himself in the gut."

"I hope so. He was a monster. Killing Colin. Kidnapping me. Then handcuffing me." She held her hands up. "Pulling me around like a dog on a handcuff leash. That was… Torture." The word in French sounded somewhat like the word in English.

"I'm very sorry you had to go through this."

"You did what you could. You were…" She stopped and looked at Diamond. "You two men both tried to help me. I haven't had a lot of that experience. Colin gave me purpose and love. You two saved my life. Merci, merci." She reached out, very shaky, and took my good hand in both of hers, shaking as she cried.

# EPILOGUE

They found János Szabó, alive if not well. He'd been hit over the head by Roland Dippman, angry that János wouldn't pay for his restaurant guarding scam. Dippman dumped the dying János in the Truckee River. A local man with dementia had seen it and fished János out of the ice water and nursed him back to physical health, although not to sustained consciousness. The local man, Mordant Johnsrud, had been a medic in the Viet Nam War. He was too confused to think of calling 911. But his medic experience kicked in, and he knew exactly how to treat János. Later, Mordant's neighbor Millie Hamm had stopped by to bring Mordant a pie she'd baked, and she saw János who was recovering on Mordant's couch. Millie arranged for János to be transferred to the hospital.

When I got the news, I found out János's room number and drove to the hospital. I left Spot in the Jeep, and I hobbled in with Lazlo. When the nurses at the reception counter tried to stop me from bringing in a dog, I used a technique I'd adapted from Camille. I pretended I couldn't hear them.

Lazlo and I walked directly to János's room. It was slow going with the left side of my body on fire, but no one stopped me.

János appeared to be unconscious.

Lazlo nevertheless jumped up on the bed and had what might be called a happiness fit. He jumped on János, and leaped into the air, and licked and pawed and whined and wagged and spun around. János's IV tube came undone. Lazlo jumped down to the floor, then made a second leap, this time running at some speed. He landed on János's chest and slid into János's face.

János woke up. He managed to get a feeble arm around Lazlo and held him down. He started grinning. His smile grew to major excitement.

Nurses came in and started exclaiming.

I said, "I apologize for our intrusion. Lazlo is making a mess of

János's bed."

"No, don't apologize!" One nurse said. "János has been mostly unresponsive. We've been so worried that he was going to slip into a permanent coma. Now he's responding for the first time. It wouldn't be too much to say that this dog..." The nurse paused because he was choked up. "This dog is saving his life."

Three days later, we all met at János's Hungarian Restaurant. János arrived in a wheel chair. Lazlo pranced by his side, with his leash coiled in his mouth. It was clear that János, under Lazlo's influence, was making a fast recovery.

Geneviève spent some time chatting with János. Spot and I stayed back. I didn't want Spot to use his charm to turn the gathering into a love fest for him.

My bullet wounds had been repaired and closed, stitched up and bandaged. But they were so sore that I almost couldn't feel the remaining bruises from being beaten up.

We were near enough to Geneviève and János to hear them talk.

"You were Colin Burns's girl?" János said.

"Yes."

János nodded. "I'm sorry he died."

Geneviève was still depressed as I imagined she would be for a very long time. But it seemed good for her to talk to an old man who knew Colin and who was also in rough shape.

"I've always wondered why you fired Colin," Geneviève said.

János took a deep breath. "To save his life. A big man came into my restaurant. He wanted to sell me a burglar protection service. It sounded suspicious. When I asked him his name, he started to say Dippman, but then changed it to Stoppard. So I walked Dippman/Stoppard over to the Brew Pub and talked to him there. I asked him many questions. In the process, he mentioned a friend who was a sports photographer. I realized that the man's photographer friend was Daniel Moretti, whom I'd met through Colin.

"Colin was afraid of Moretti. He thought Moretti was amoral at best, truly evil at worst. He worried that Moretti might kill him in an attempt to steal his girl.

"So when the big man came in my restaurant, I said, 'Let's take a walk' to the big man. We went out of the pub. I turned away from where I'd tied up Lazlo and enticed the big man to the parking lot. Then I pretended I had a phone call. I was going to call nine, one, one. But the man got suspicious of me. He hit me on the head. I don't remember anything after that. But I was told he drove me to the river and dumped me in. He assumed I'd die. But of course, he didn't realize that old man Mordant Johnsrud, who had a house on the river, saw us. Johnsrud was well down the dementia road. But he hauled me out, got me into a wheeled lawn cart, and took me to his cabin near the river.

"I thought Colin was probably right about Daniel Moretti. So I fired Colin, hoping he would move far away from Moretti and hopefully take you with him."

Diamond came in with Jack Santiago and Hattie Foster, the Truckee cop. The three of them walked over to Geneviève, said hi, then left her to continue talking to János.

Hattie and Jack came over near me, and Hattie stood next to Spot. When she pet him, he leaned against her and started panting.

Diamond walked over to Street and Camille. They exchanged some words. Then Diamond pointed toward Geneviève. Camille nodded and then approached Geneviève.

In a minute, Jànos stopped talking and nodded at Camille.

Camille handed Geneviève a little package wrapped in kraft paper. On it she'd drawn a ribbon and bow in red ink.

"What's this?"

"Open it!" Camille was bouncing on her toes.

Geneviève carefully opened it, flattening the paper to avoid damaging Camille's drawing.

Inside was a little white box. Geneviève lifted the lid and pulled out a golden pendent in the shape of a Bald Eagle flying.

"You gave me a Gallic Rooster," Camille said, "the symbol of France. So I'm giving you the Bald Eagle, the symbol of America."

"Merci beaucoup. Thank you so much. You also saved my life by teaching me to sign 'Jump!'"

Both Geneviève and Camille suddenly held out their left hands, palm up, and used their right hands to make the sign, first and second fingers in an inverted V, touching down on the left palm, then raising their right hands into the air while bending the fingers.

Synchronized jumping, American Sign Language-style.

Several people laughed, including Geneviève, which was a great pleasure to see and hear.

János rolled his wheel chair so that he could face Geneviève more directly. Lazlo shifted with him, staying precisely by his side.

"Geneviève, I've been thinking. I learned that your restaurant and your apartment burned down. That must be a very hard thing. I was also told that you are staying with this young girl and her mother." János gestured toward Camille and Street.

"I'm sure that is a good situation for you," he said. "However, it occurred to me that you might like more room. So I thought I would mention to you that I have a house in Tahoe City. It is four bedrooms, two upstairs and two down. Since my wife Dolores died many years ago, much of the house is unused. You would be welcome to take over those upstairs bedrooms as your own space for sleeping and for an office. There is a bathroom upstairs as well."

János continued, "I have no need for money, so there would be no need to pay rent. And I like to be alone, so I wouldn't pressure you for social engagement. But it would make me happy to provide you with shelter."

Geneviève was wide-eyed and speechless.

János paused, thinking. "The doctor says I'll be out of this wheel chair in another week, so I don't think I would cause you much trouble."

Geneviève stammered, "That is an amazing offer. And I... Well, I'd love to take you up on it! But I would insist on helping you in some way. What could I do to make your life easier?"

János frowned, thinking. He looked down at Lazlo. "My pal, here, has lots of energy. You could help walk him now and then. And of course Lazlo could use practice with his French." He thought some more. "And I suppose I should confess that I am quite tired of eating the food from my home country. Hungarian food is great, of course, but an occasional bit of French delight would add some excitement to my diet. The smell of French pastries turns a house into a home, don't you think?"

"Oui, oui! I accept your offer! And I'm sure I'll find lots of ways to make myself useful!"

As Geneviève said that, she seemed to undergo a transformation.

The depressed woman who'd lost so much, was suddenly glowing. The door to the restaurant opened and in walked the lawyer, Madison Rappaport.

Geneviève turned away from János in his wheel chair and saw her.

Rappaport approached Geneviève.

"I don't understand," Geneviève said to the attorney. "I don't mean to be rude, but I'm curious why you are here? Is everything okay?"

"Yes, everything is fine," Rappaport said.

"Geneviève," I said, interrupting her and Madison Rappaport. "I spoke to Ms. Rappaport yesterday, and she said she'd just received a package for you. So I asked her to come today."

Geneviève suddenly looked very worried. "You're scaring me. Am I in trouble with immigration?"

Ms. Rappaport put her hand on Geneviève's forearm. "No, you're not in trouble, dear," Rappaport said. "There's nothing to be concerned about. I got an express delivery yesterday. I signed the form for the courier and didn't even think to look at the address before I unzipped the pull ribbon. I had read half of it before I realized it was a letter to you, not me. I called you, but I got a message that your voicemail was full. So, I called Owen McKenna and asked him if he knew where you were. He said he'd check and call me back. He called an hour later and asked if I could come to a meeting today."

Rappaport handed the express envelope to Geneviève. "Here's the envelope." Under her arm was another thick envelope, but Rappaport held onto that.

The Express Delivery package was a 9 X 12 Post Office envelope with Express Mail printed on the outside.

Geneviève took it gingerly as if it were hot.

She frowned as she looked at it and then looked back at Rappaport. Geneviève turned to me and held out the envelope. Her hand shook.

"Can you read this, please? I... I don't do well with sudden news."

I took the envelope and pulled out the letter.

"It's from Franklin Assurance, the life insurance company," I said.

I read,

"'Dear Ms. Laurent,

Colin Burns authorized his attorney Madison Rappaport to receive communications from our company. We are sending this to Ms. Rappaport in trust that she will personally deliver it to you.

You, Geneviève Laurent, were named as the sole beneficiary on Colin Burns's life insurance policy with our company. As you may recall, we had some questions about Mr. Burns's original application for that policy.

We have recently undertaken a review of the policy and the application and have found that it meets our standards for payment.

We are, therefore, including a certified check for two million, eighty-one thousand, four hundred and fifteen dollars, which covers the two-million-dollar face amount of the policy plus interest accrued since the date of what would have been our standard payout date. Please deposit the check promptly as it expires in 90 days.

Thank you for your patience in this matter.'"

I looked at Geneviève. "It's signed Franklin Assurance Holdings International."

Geneviève looked stunned as if she'd just had an electric shock. Her eyes flooded with tears. She wiped them away roughly with her sleeve, which left her eyes red and swollen. She found a chair and sat down.

She turned to look at me.

"You must have made this happen. You are like Colin, the opposite of all the bad men who've made my life difficult. How did you do it?"

I shrugged. "I didn't really do much. I just appealed to one of the executives of the company. He came to understand there was no fraud on Colin's application."

Geneviève stood up and wrapped her arms around me. I held the envelope and letter out to my side.

Eventually, she pushed away from me and took the envelope out of my hands. She reread the letter and then pulled out the check and studied it. She put the letter and check back in the envelope and tucked it deep in a front pocket of pants that I recognized as belonging to Street.

"I have another item for you," Rappaport said. "When Colin had me write his will, he told me that I was to give you another package but only after you had received the insurance payout. As you can imagine, I wasn't certain how to proceed when the insurance company initially refused to pay on the policy. But now that you've gotten the check, I can give you this other envelope without worrying that I'm not following Colin's wishes."

Rappaport pulled the second padded envelope from under her arm and handed it to Geneviève.

Geneviève took it, studied the handwritten address.

She once again handed it to me.

"It might be too personal to read aloud," I said.

"Please look it over first. If it's too personal, then you can just hold onto to it and tell me another day. If it won't embarrass me too much, and you think it's okay to read, then please read it."

"Okay."

I pulled the strip to open the package. I flexed the envelope and looked inside. I saw what looked like some jewelry and a letter. I pulled out the letter. It took me a minute or two to scan it.

"I think this would be good to read," I said.

Geneviève swallowed hard. "Okay," she said.

Before I started reading, I pulled out a dried poppy and a gold chain with a piece of pale blue mineral attached. I handed them to Geneviève.

Then I read.

"'My Dearest Geneviève,

If you get this letter, it means I have died, probably in a skiing accident. I am very sorry about that.

I'm writing this letter to tell you several things. First, I want to say that I've loved you from the moment I first saw you on that paddle board four years ago.

We were both at Sand Harbor. We hadn't yet met. I was walking the paths, casting about for a life plan, and I saw you and your friend

Lita on paddle boards, exploring around the big boulders off the north beach. Lita is of course an eye-catching woman. But I only noticed you, your charisma and charm, your effervescence.

.

It made me think about one time when I was at a flower garden where there were many beautiful flowers. But there was one that drew the attention of a hummingbird. When the bird flew away, another came and took its place, and then came another. I realized there was something indescribable about that flower that upstaged all the other beautiful flowers.

I hadn't even gotten near enough to you to speak, but I felt my life starting to take on a focus the way a hummingbird, suffering from grandiose thinking but eager to drink sweet nectar, might decide to focus his life on a single, magnificent flower. I know that sounds overwrought, but it's true.

When I waited for you to come ashore at Sand Harbor and then asked you to coffee, I assumed that you would see me as an unattractive Quasimodo, a character I read about in a famous novel. My only hope was that you would give me just enough attention to learn that, while a Quasimodo I might be, I had an appreciation for your beauty. And by that I mean not just your physical beauty but your interior beauty. You shimmered with radiance. You were scintillating.

After several morning coffees at the coffee house in Truckee, we progressed to evening dates. A month later, when you asked me to come to your restaurant after hours, and you cooked me your Quiche Lorraine and served it with a Beaujolais, and then you quoted Maya Angelou on love jumping hurdles and leaping fences, I was hopelessly smitten. Ever since that night, I have been fueled by your passion, your focus and drive and energy.

As we got to know each other better, we learned that our ambitions (your restaurant and my speed skiing) came with struggles. Your struggles with running a restaurant were largely financial. Who could have known about the thousand expenses that restaurants have? If I were with you now, I could help, if only by washing dishes or pouring wine.

My struggles trying to be the world's best in an athletic field weren't far behind yours. In addition to my never-ending fitness routine, I had a constant focus on practicing, developing technique in a sport where there was no agreement yet about what was the ideal form and process.

I think that is similar to a relationship. In the early stages, we don't know what are the ideal ways for people to mesh their individual selves into a couple.

But I realized that if I could ease your financial stress, that would be great.

Which made me think about life insurance. It was a tedious pursuit, like trying to find the best way to fertilize a flower.

My research mission eventually resulted in an insurance policy.

The premium was excessive. But I had started a savings account when I was 16 years old. I was never able to put much money into it. But it slowly added up. I also prevailed on my mother to help with the premium. She came through with a big chunk of what I needed. She likes you and wanted to contribute. I also got a loan from my boss János at the Hungarian Restaurant.

The money this policy pays doesn't seem so much considering the cost of Truckee real estate. But maybe you will be able to buy a townhouse or condo. Mostly, the money should help with your restaurant. But what will help get you through this life isn't money. Your greatest asset is that you are tough as rocks, and you have the heart of a rose.

I have almost nothing else to give you but my love. I've long had a piece of uncut Benitoite. I bought it at a rare gemstones dealer because it's the same pale blue as your eyes. I had a jeweler put it on a gold chain so that you could remember me.

I'm also putting a dried poppy in this envelope. You'll remember that we picked it when we had that lunch picnic one spring day on a sunny hillside near the coast. I saved it as a memory of you.

It always makes me think of one of my favorite lines from Robert Burns.

Pleasures are like poppies spread
You seize the flower, its bloom is shed

You are the flower I seized, Geneviève. I'm so glad I did.

And I am graced by the time you have gifted me with your presence and affection.

I love you forever.
Your "Q"

About The Author

Todd Borg and his wife live in Tahoe, where they write and paint. To contact Todd or learn more about the Owen McKenna mysteries, please visit toddborg.com.

A message from the author:

Dear Reader,

If you enjoyed this novel, please consider posting a short review on any book website you like to use. Reviews help authors a great deal, and that in turn allows us to write more stories for you.

Thank you very much for your interest and support!

Todd